I0607181

Michael W. Sherer

BLIND TRUST

MICHAEL W. SHERER

Blind Rage
"Tremendous book. Flat out loved it." —Ken Bruen, Shamus, Macavity and Barry Award-winning author of *Green Hell*

Blind Instinct
"Amazing thriller very well written!!! Highly recommend!" —Cathy Fleming, Amazon review

"Gripping and intense—bring on #3!" —Brenda Telford, Goodreads review

Mistaken Identity
"Sherer keeps the live wires of his complex plot sparking and distinct. Jenny is a ticked-off but highly capable heroine, whose family of cops adds depth and texture so that motivation and revelation keep coming to the very end. This is a sharp and satisfying thriller." —*Publishers Weekly starred review*

"*Mistaken Identity* revs up as characters are introduced and then goes all out in a high stakes Indy race of a novel. You come to know the characters. You know who you're rooting for, but the plot turns fast. It's fingers crossed until the last turn and the redemptive end."
—Kirk Russell, author of *No Hesitation* and *Gone Dark*

"Sherer is a master at creating unforgettable characters. Take Jenny Roberts. She's smart, complex, a little bit broken and totally kick-ass. *Mistaken Identity* starts your adrenaline flowing and ramps to a frenzy. A thriller that's impossible to put down." —Chris Goff, author of *Red Sky*

Stolen Identity
"...high-octane, compulsively readable thriller from Thriller Award finalist Sherer...is a first-rate hijacking of any thriller reader's attention." – *Publisher's Weekly*

"This book is terrific. Well plotted, all the elements of a classic thriller with a fresh take on the characters, especially the hero. It paid off every promise and more." —S.G. Redling, bestselling author of *Flowertown* and *Trigger*

"Love it!" —Timothy Hallinan, author of *Street Music*

Night Drop
"Looking for an adrenaline rush? You'll find that and more in *Night Drop.* Blake Sanders is back, and that means the action is nonstop!" —Alan Russell, author of *Multiple Wounds* and *Burning Man*

"I LOVED this story. *Night Drop* is a fast-paced, tension-filled thriller that will grab you by the throat until the very last page. Blake Sanders is one of the most intriguing characters I've read in years. This is definitely Sherer at his best."
—KT Bryan, author of *Team EDGE*

Night Tide
"A great, great read! Even better than *Night Blind*, and that's not easy." —Timothy Hallinan, author of *The Fame Thief*

"A cracking good story and a first-rate thriller."
—J. Carson Black, *New York Times* and *USA Today* bestselling author of *The Survivors Club*

"A tight, well-constructed story and characters that leap from the page. I'll definitely be back for more."
—Robert Gregory Browne, author of *Trial Junkies 2: Negligence*

Night Blind
"An appealing, empathetic lead."
—*Publisher's Weekly*

"This is an exciting, well-crafted thriller and most certainly a satisfying one."
—*Mysterious Reviews*

"Thriller writer Sherer renders a sympathetic lead character and an engaging . . . story line in his latest."
—Allison Block, *Booklist*

"Loved every page of it."
—Brett Battles

"A tightly paced page-turner that's impossible to put down. Terrific!"
—Allison Brennan

"Pay attention. You won't want to miss a word."
—J.T. Ellison

"Rich, complex, and deeply satisfying."
—Bill Cameron

Also by Michael W. Sherer

Tess Barrett Thrillers

Blind Instinct
Blind Rage

Identity Series

Mistaken Identity
Stolen Identity

Blake Sanders Series

Night Strike
Night Drop
Night Tide
Night Blind

Emerson Ward Mysteries

Death on a Budget
Death Is No Bargain
A Forever Death
Death Came Dressed in White
Little Use for Death
An Option on Death

Suspense

Island Life

BLIND TRUST

by

Michael W. Sherer

Cover Design: Anne Kaye-Jewett

Guys drool. Girls rule.

BLIND TRUST

BLIND TRUST

1

The soldier crouched motionless in the dark, blackened face and woodland camo uniform making him virtually invisible. Rainwater dripped from the bill of his cap onto his nose, but he ignored it as it rolled to the tip and dropped soundlessly onto the forest floor. The small wooded area, a narrow strip of trees and dense brush between the parking lot in front of him and houses behind, was practically the only area of concealment on the whole block that surrounded the target. It had been enough to hide his approach, and enough, he hoped, to mask his intent until it was too late to stop him.

Who would suspect him anyway? He wasn't one of those sad, messed up kids who would be remembered after the fact as a loner, an oddball, someone whose social media account they'd find out later, was filled with angry rants and screeds about being misunderstood, bullied as a kid. Boo-hoo. No, he didn't even belong here, wasn't from here. No one would suspect because no one knew him here.

Soldier. He still thought of himself that way, even though it had been years since he'd served his country both at home and on foreign soil. He called himself that because he'd never been anything else. He'd joined the army right out of high school, had gone through boot camp and specialist training to qualify for every job in both the mounted and dismounted elements of a Stryker Brigade Combat Team (SBCT), from radio telecommunications operator (RTO) to operation of the remote weapons system (RWS) mounted on top of the eight-wheeled, armored infantry carrier vehicle (ICV). He knew how to drive it, too. The army had been interested in cross-training him on only a few positions, but he'd been a quick study. And his wide-ranging skills set had earned him two tours in Kandahar Province, Afghanistan.

The second tour had ended abruptly with his dishonorable discharge for striking a superior officer. The facts and the truth were entirely different.

Fact: yes, he had cold-cocked his platoon leader, a lieutenant whose name he'd rather forget.

Truth: Some bad HUMINT—human intelligence—had resulted in a disastrous mission. While out on patrol and despite the best efforts of their forward observer that day, one of the ICVs in the platoon hit an IED powerful enough to roll it over, taking out its weapons systems and most of the crew. The other ICVs had pulled into a defensive formation, and the men had dismounted from the vehicles and walked right into an ambush.

With both the rifle squad and weapons squad under heavy fire from terrorists, both the fire team leader and the platoon sergeant had taken direct hits and had been dragged back to an ICV by a couple of combat medics, putting the platoon leader directly, rather than indirectly, in charge of the firefight. Pinned down by the hail of bullets and watching men all around get hit, the lieutenant had suddenly lost his nerve and had started blubbering like a baby.

As the weapons squad leader, the soldier had been next in command after the platoon sergeant, So, he'd smacked the lieutenant. Hard. While the lieutenant lay in the dust in a daze, rubbing his sore chin, the soldier had shouted orders to the other men, gotten most of them behind cover, and rallied the weapons squad. Both the automatic rifleman on the ground and the RWS operator in one of the ICVs had laid down some withering return fire, giving the rest of them a chance to take up better positions and knock out the terrorist fighters one by one.

The platoon had lost more than a dozen men that day to horrendous injuries, but not one had died. But he and his squad and the rifle squad had dispatched nine enemy fighters. The squad's fire team leader had recommended the soldier for a medal for his actions, but the lieutenant he'd clocked had filed a formal complaint. Rather than press for a full court martial, the dickwad had settled for the soldier's dishonorable discharge.

The soldier's name was Sam. But he carried nothing on his person that gave any indication of who he was. When he'd returned home after his discharge he'd realized that the only thing the army had really taught him was how to kill. There were no Stryker M1126 ICVs driving around on the streets of Seattle, so he couldn't open up a repair shop. And there was little call for guys who were experts at handling an M289 SAW, a Javelin close-combat missile or shoulder-launched rocket munitions. He'd tried his hand as an Uber driver for a while, but mostly had hung out with the mostly Latino group of day laborers outside big home improvement warehouse stores to get odd jobs.

So when he'd gotten an anonymous call from someone willing to pay him to be a soldier again, he'd leaped at the chance. The caller had promised him half a million dollars. Sam had scoffed, of course, sure it was a prank call. Sam asked why he'd been picked. The caller had described Sam's army training and service in detail and said that Sam's experience was exactly what the job called for. Sam had still hesitated. The man on the other end of the line had been insistent, telling him he'd wire half the money into an offshore account as a show of good faith, and pay the other quarter million upon completion of the job. When Sam had asked what the job was, the man had simply said, "Kill someone." Sam had received an account number via e-mail, and when he'd checked the account, someone had deposited $250,000.

Now, here he was, not in the mountains of Afghanistan or Iraq, but the suburbs of Seattle, hiding in a grove of trees with only a parking lot separating him from his target. The misty rain had stopped for the moment, which was both good and bad. His visibility was much better, and he would stay a little drier, not that it mattered. But the rain would have helped camouflage his approach. He had some time still. The weather could easily change.

The large, sprawling building on the other side of the parking lot stood ablaze with lights. Muffled rhythmic thumping came from inside the building. For the past half hour, a steady procession of stretch limousines had pulled up in front and spilled their occupants—men and women dressed in black-tie formal wear—onto the wet sidewalk. Those with the foresight to bring umbrellas had gathered close together on the sidewalk under their cover and walked to the building, a procession of giant mushrooms bobbing up and down to the front door. The few who had forgotten scrambled out of the cars to madly dash for the door, the ladies hiking up their skirts or dresses and tottering as fast as they could on high heels. Now, he stiffened like a hound on point as a limo pulled up to let its occupants out.

After the money had been deposited, he'd been briefed on the target and what to expect. The limo arriving that night, he'd learned, wouldn't be a standard issue or stretch, but would look like an off-the-shelf black Range Rover. This particular vehicle, though, was a supercharged model on a long wheelbase tricked out with armor plating, bulletproof glass, and puncture-resistant run-flat tires. He'd been told that a detail of at least two bodyguards and a chaperone would accompany his target. Armed with that knowledge, he'd spent nearly two weeks observing the target's movements, schedule, and bodyguard contingents to discern patterns, assess both strengths and weaknesses in security, and figure out the best way to accomplish his mission.

The same Range Rover he'd observed and followed now disgorged two large men, one from each side, who scanned the parking lot before one of them opened the rear door closest to the building. A shorter, slender man in semi-formal attire emerged, followed by his target, a young woman in a simple but elegant black silk cocktail dress with spaghetti straps. Her long black hair, normally worn straight or in a ponytail, was swept up into a loosely braided bun, a few strands framing her face. Her escort snapped open an umbrella to hold over her head, and they walked slowly to the door with the bodyguards a few steps behind, heads in constant motion as they surveilled the surroundings. Behind them, the Range Rover pulled away from the curb. The driver would park and come back to stand watch outside. The soldier had to make his move now.

Party time.

He reached for the satchel on the ground behind him, unzipped a pocket, took out a pack of wet naps and used them to wipe the black greasepaint off his face. Slowly and carefully, so as not to get mud or dirt on himself, he stripped off the camo gear, revealing semi-formal attire beneath it. He traded his boots for a pair of black dress shoes, and finally pulled a suit jacket from the satchel and donned it over the special shoulder holster he wore. Under one arm a short-barrel, pump-action shotgun nestled in the holster. It had one shell in the chamber. He had a 10-shell magazine in his pocket. The holster under his other arm held a modified H&K MP7A1 personal defense weapon that could fire its entire 20-shot magazine in about one-and-a-quarter seconds. He also carried several small M84 flash-bang stun grenades modified to detonate via RF signal.

Patting down his pockets to make sure everything he needed was in place, he nodded to himself and stepped out of the woods onto the asphalt parking lot. His heart hammered in his chest, and he took deep breaths and rolled his head on his shoulders to relax and get his pulse under control. The guns and ammunition he carried weighed him down, but he barely felt it with all the adrenaline coursing through his system. He ran his fingers through his hair again, hoping he looked presentable enough. The suit was custom-tailored to hold everything without bulging or sagging.

As he approached the brightly lit front door of the building across the lot, he slipped two fingers into the breast pocket and drew out a fake plastic student ID and the slim piece of card stock waiting there. His ticket. The thumping sound became a visceral blast of hip-hop dance music that reverberated in his gut as he opened the door. The dull roar of hundreds of voices trying to talk over the music assaulted his ears. He blinked against the bright light. Red velvet ropes on brass stanchions guided him to a reception table. He handed his ticket to a fresh-faced girl of around seventeen sitting behind it, and flashed the student ID. His facial features, though hardened and more chiseled by both age and what he'd seen and done, were still youthful. He had one of those faces that still made store clerks and bartenders check his ID when he bought an occasional beer. The girl mouthed some words that he couldn't hear over the din. He turned and cocked an ear, and she leaned over the table toward him.

"I need to stamp you," she shouted.

He nodded and held out a hand, palm down. She inked the back with the stamp, and he moved aside as a group of half a dozen formally attired teenagers crowded through the door behind him, laughing and talking loudly. Round tables covered in white linen with seating for ten or twelve dotted the large room. Candles on the tables lit flower centerpieces with a gold "Oscar" statuette standing in the center. Spotlights hung from lighting bars high on the walls highlighted special areas around the room—a photo booth, a palm reader, and others he couldn't quite see. A red carpet led from the reception table to another room, the source of the throbbing music.

He took in the scene carefully but casually. Other than the detail assigned to the target, security was practically nonexistent. People thought they were safe here in the suburbs. There were no metal detectors at the entrance. Civilians manned the other exit doors to prevent unauthorized entry by uninvited guests. He spotted only a handful of facility employees, only two of whom were actively making rounds with watchful eyes. He didn't see the target, but wouldn't go searching until he was ready. When the layout and the key players were imprinted in his memory, he nodded and moved, his plan in place.

His first task: plant some diversions. He walked purposefully to the nearest men's restroom, and entered to find it empty. He locked himself in the nearest stall, and hiked up his trousers legs. He'd secured all four flash-bangs to his legs with gaffer's tape over fabric so they could be removed easily and still leave enough adhesive on the tape to mount them. He taped one charge low on the wall behind the toilet and leaned back against the stall door to look at the toilet from different angles. Satisfied that it wouldn't be seen, he removed another flash-bang from his leg and put it in his jacket pocket. He left the two others in place above each ankle and shook his pants legs

23

down over them. As he unlocked the stall door, he heard the men's room door open. He froze.

Soundlessly, he turned the lock the other way, and backed up until his legs straddled the toilet, then opened his mouth to breathe silently. He didn't want people to remember him. A chance encounter in a men's room minutes before the place exploded might prompt someone's memory later. The sound of liquid hissing down a smooth surface slowly turned to the plashing of water on water as the newcomer relived himself at a urinal. Sam tipped his head back and stifled a yawn. Not enough sleep in the past two weeks. He shook his head. He had to stay sharp. He hoped this guy would hurry.

The lights flickered, and suddenly he was as alert as if he'd downed four double espressos. He heard muttering on the other side of the stall door, but it quickly faded away, and once again he found himself wishing this guy would just finish his business and get out. Impatiently, he reached for the lock, and the room went pitch dark. He froze again.

"What the actual fuck!" The shout echoed off the walls. "Dylan, if that's you, it's not funny! Turn on the damn lights!" The voice quieted to muttering again. "Jesus, I'm gonna pee all over my pants if someone doesn't turn on the lights."

Just as suddenly, the lights came back on, and the soldier breathed a silent sigh of relief. He listened to the urinal flush, then a soft zip, and footsteps to the door. Shaking his head in disgust that the kid hadn't even washed his hands, Sam changed his mind and pulled his hand away from the stall door, leaving it locked. He didn't want to take a chance on someone finding the explosive he'd left behind the toilet. Quickly lowering himself to the floor, he lay on his back and shoved himself into the next stall over, jumped up and pushed the lever on the toilet before exiting.

The soldier washed his hands thoroughly at the sink, staring at the worried face in the mirror. He needed to finish this tonight. A power outage would send everyone home, and he would have to start over. But the longer he stayed and watched for another opportunity, the greater the chance that the target's security force would detect and neutralize him. He needed to do it now. He quickly dried his hands and left.

He sauntered over to a vacant banquet table, avoiding the scattered few where couples already sat and talked, and eased into a chair. Leaning forward as if to tie a shoe, he reached down and removed another flash-bang from around his ankle and taped it to the underside of the table. His eyes scanned the room all the while, checking to see if he had attracted anyone's notice. When he'd pressed the tape in place, he leaned back in the chair and casually gazed around the room. His pulse raced, but he felt an inward calm that came from intense focus on his work. Moving quickly, he rose and placed another charge on the wall behind him, a corner dim enough it wouldn't be spotted.

Through the doors, the room with music and dancing was dimmer, and swirled with couples and colored spotlights that moved in time to the music. The volume of both music and shouted conversations might have deafened him, but he had already pressed foam earplugs into his ear canals, muffling the noise.

He found another dark corner and taped a charge to the wall. The first two would get everyone's attention, but the last two would have maximum effect of an extremely loud bang and intensely bright flash that should disorient at least some people in each room within twenty-five feet. People any farther away in these big rooms would be little more than startled, but the combination of explosions would likely cause people to panic. He counted on it. Hundreds of people screaming and running for the exits would give him cover to get away when he finished the job. That was the plan, anyway.

Without pause, he walked the perimeter of the cavernous space, gaze directed toward the couples in the middle of the floor, eyes searching out his target. A low set of telescoping bleachers folded into a wall presented a natural shelf for another stun grenade. A glance over his shoulder several paces later confirmed his supposition that it would go unnoticed. He'd gone nearly halfway around the room when he spotted the target, her escort, and two of the bodyguards. Concern set in when he didn't spot the third bodyguard. He searched the crowded room, breathing growing shallower as concern almost turned to panic until he remembered the driver had probably stayed outside. He shook his head slightly at his own folly, and breathed deeply, relaxing his shoulders. This was no time to screw up.

Like all plans, though, his looked like it was going to change yet again when the few lights burning around the perimeter of the gymnasium flickered once more, went out for a second that felt like an hour, and blinked back on. He held his breath, but they burned steadily now. He glanced toward his target. Her two bodyguards had their eyes directed toward the crowd as he did, and didn't notice him. He ambled closer to the target, putting his hand in his pocket. His fingers found the remote RF detonator, and he thumbed the switch on its side to turn it on. He mentally accounted for each weapon he had and the muscle memory it would take to retrieve it.

Steeling his resolve, he touched the button on top of the detonator in his pocket. The remote was designed to change radio frequencies each time he pressed the button, so each flash-bang would detonate in turn. He watched the target as her escort leaned in close, as if to say something, their lips nearly brushing, and he pressed the button once.

After a half-second delay, the boom from the men's room stall, even at this distance, sounded like a cannon, jerking people's heads up. The bodyguards scanned the room warily but didn't move. He waited nearly ten seconds until the fear that had frozen the crowd started to dissipate like a slowly thinning fog. Couples began milling around on the floor, and the murmur of voices grew louder. He pushed the button again.

The second explosion was louder, followed immediately by screams from the other room. The music stopped, leaving the room in silence. The crowd in front of him froze again, then undulated as fear once again took hold. The target stood unmoving, but had covered her ears and was talking excitedly to her escort, brows creased with concern. He saw the two guards exchange a look, and one headed toward the other room. He pushed the button once more, and another explosion ripped through the other room, followed by more screaming and the sounds of obvious panic. The noise rippled through the clusters of couples on the dance floor, spreading fear like an airborne plague. Shrill voices urged everyone to run, to get out, and dozens broke for the exits, jamming doorways in their haste to get out.

He squeezed his eyes shut tight and pressed the button twice in quick succession, and the flash-bangs in the corner and on the bleachers concussed the air and threw off bursts of light so intense they seared his retinas even with his eyes closed. When he opened them, one of the bodyguards had disappeared into the other room, and the other swiped at his eyes as he looked toward the target and her escort.

"Get her out of here." the bodyguard shouted. He turned and staggered half-blindly in the direction of the bleachers, the source of the last explosion.

The diversions had worked. The soldier slowly approached the target, reaching inside his jacket to withdraw the personal defense weapon. He'd done it. He'd figured out a way to get through her phalanx of security and get close enough to complete his mission. He could have killed her on any of a dozen occasions in the time he'd scouted her security. He could have easily put her down with a sniper's rifle and a good scope. But whoever had hired him wanted him to get up close and personal, to send a message.

As he drew closer, though, he realized that the only thing he hadn't counted on was the girl. She appeared younger than he'd originally thought. She was beautiful despite the long, jagged scar that ran the length of her face, though he knew that already from photos and the long-range surveillance he'd done. But there was one piece of information whoever hired him had left out.

He stared at her now in the dim light, from not more than six feet away, noting the way she looked intently in his direction but not quite at him. She didn't paw at her eyes the way those affected by the flash did.

"You're blind," he said.

"Who's that?" her escort said, screwing his knuckles into his eyes. "Who's there? What the hell is going on? Tess, are you okay?"

The soldier ignored him, still mesmerized by the girl. No one had told him he would be killing a blind girl. His surprise, and the ethical debate that suddenly raged in his brain, caused him to hesitate. It couldn't have been more than a second or two, but that was enough.

"Tess!" someone shouted behind him. "Gun!"

Before the soldier could react, the girl moved. Not away, as he expected, but toward him, hiking her dress up as she dropped into a crouch and spun. Before he could bring the machine gun to bear on the blurred figure, her leg sweep caught his ankle and started to up-end him. And as he thought once more that he hadn't counted on the girl, he felt bullets rip into his chest with the force of sledgehammers before he heard the loud, sharp reports of gunfire. The world tilted on its axis and rotated as he fell. He didn't feel the hard floor crash against his cheek, but he saw the girl's face turned sideways as she crouched next to him, hands up, ready to fight.

He knew he was already dead, but the neurons in his brain kept firing, giving him an instant of regret, a feeling that he should have done it all differently. He felt ashamed that he'd taken money to assassinate a blind girl, and that his life had gotten so screwed up that he couldn't even accomplish that. And finally, he felt relief that at least his failure meant he hadn't killed her. With brilliant clarity, he suddenly knew what he had to do, to make it right, to redeem his entire fucked-up life.

He coughed, his mouth filling with blood, and with a last desperate gasp before everything went dark, he said, "S...Sam. Tell...them...Sam sent you."

2

"She has to go."

"No," Travis says. "She's worked too hard for this."

"I'm sorry, Mr. Barrett, but I have to think of the safety of the other students."

"It's only another month or so until the end of the semester. You can't do this to her now."

I sit stiffly in the hard chair and shove my hands into the folds of the black silk evening gown between my knees to keep them from trembling. I can't stop the rest of my body from shaking, a natural reaction to the adrenaline that flooded my system when a presence I sensed in front of me expressed his surprise in just two words. But something else contributes to the tremors—anger. The two men—Uncle Travis and a voice I recognize as belonging to Peter Jenkins, the school principal—speak about *me* as if I don't exist, as if I'm deaf as well as blind. My name is Tess Barrett, not Helen Keller.

"I'm already getting calls from parents," Jenkins says. "By tomorrow they'll be calling by the dozens, asking me what the hell we're doing about security. This is the third shooting inside the school in almost as many weeks. I should have put a stop to it after the first incident."

"We'll put metal detectors up at all the entrances, add staff to beef up security. I'll pay for it all."

"Really, Mr. Barrett, I'm truly sorry, but as long as Tess remains in classes here, I don't think there's anything you can do to guarantee students' safety. These incidents are traumatizing the staff, too, not just the students. We've had to add five more counselors just to handle the additional load."

"You can't expect me to find another school for her to attend in the middle of a semester."

"I can give you some names to call. That's the best I can do."

"I can't accept that. There must be something—"

"I'm telling you there's nothing. The school board already wants to fire me, and after this, the parents will probably take matters into their own hands and run me out of town."

"Excuse me." I've heard enough. I push myself to my feet. "I can hear, you know. Does anyone care at all how I feel about it?"

"Tess," Travis says, "this probably isn't the—"

"Principal Jenkins," I interrupt. It takes effort not to let my voice crack in a hysterical shriek, but I forge ahead. "Do you have any idea what it's like to have someone threaten your life? To actually try to kill you? These people, whoever they are, want to kill me. *Me*. Not other students. Not teachers. Not you. And you're worried about your *job*? Despite the fact that I can't see, that I lost my parents, that people keep fucking shooting at me, I come here every day. To school. I didn't want to. My uncle made me, to learn how to deal with the world in my condition. I hated the idea, but I came. So I could feel like a normal person. And you want to take that away from me?"

"But you're not normal," Jenkins says. "And watch your mouth, young lady."

"Here's the thing," I say, ignoring him, "these incidents aren't just about me. Whoever is behind these attacks has bigger concerns than some teenage girl. This has something to do with my father's company, something so big, that goes so high up, they'll stop at nothing to get what they want."

Jenkins actually snorts. "Don't be melodramatic. You think that you're part of some grand conspiracy? Grow up."

My face grows hot, and I tremble even harder trying to contain my anger. "What do you call an attempted assassination of the vice president?"

"I call it a sad case of mental illness," Jenkins snapped. "The vice president's son—"

"Austin," I shout. "His name is Austin. And he's not a nut case anymore than you are."

"Watch yourself!" he says sharply.

"He was brainwashed! By a mobile app."

"One that MondoHard—your father's company—developed. Maybe that's the problem. Maybe your uncle should look into making sure the company's products are safer."

"Someone sabotaged it, changed the software," I say hotly, tears stinging my eyes.

"It's okay, Tess," Travis says quietly. "He's right. I need to look after security at the company."

"Why are you defending him?" I cry. "You were there. You know what happened."

I take a deep breath. I'll never get what I want if I act like a princess, something my former BFF Adrienne would resort to in a heartbeat.

"A month," I say more calmly. "A measly four weeks, that's all I ask. By then it'll be the holidays, and after that, mostly review before finals. I can take those at home. Please, just give me the chance to feel normal. You can't tell me that everyone in this place doesn't face risks every single day. You know we do. Life is thrown at us in high school. We have to deal with drinking, drugs, sex, cyber-bullying and a hundred other decisions every damn day. Let my uncle set up the security the way he wanted to in the first place. Four weeks, and I'll be gone, out of your hair for good."

"You want me to sacrifice the safety of everyone here so you can pretend to be something you're not," Jenkins says. "I'm sorry if that sounds insensitive, but it's not going to happen."

"So, that's it?" I'm so frustrated I want to punch something. Or someone.

Suddenly, a hand rests gently on my shoulder, and my uncle's voice whispers in my ear, "Give me a minute, Tess. I think I can make all this go away. Trust me."

3

I saw red as I went looking for Tess. Literally. My ears still rang, too, like church bells on Sunday. The explosions in the commons had jerked my attention away from Tess just when I'd thought we were about to have a moment. It wasn't something I'd really considered except in fleeting, passing moments, since I'm seven or eight years older than her and her employee, not to mention the fact that we haven't always been on the best of terms. She resented the fact that I'd been hired to be her assistant, her "seeing-eye" guy. I don't think it was me as much as the principle of the thing. She hated relying on other people, hated the fact that she'd lost her former, "normal" life, if you can call being popular, smart, beautiful, graceful, athletically gifted and exceedingly rich normal.

Then again, I guess I wasn't what most people would consider normal, either. I'm a memorist—a person blessed, or cursed, with good memory, nearly perfect, eidetic memory in my case—and until a few weeks earlier, I'd been a professional student. I'd procrastinated so long on finishing a PhD. dissertation on comparative 21st Century American literature (tweets vs. texts) that I'd run out of money and had been forced to look for a job. Lacking any particular skills like auto mechanics or carpentry, I'd interviewed for a position as a personal assistant and was hired before I even met my "client," Tess.

We'd gotten off to a rocky start, made more difficult by a series of events unfortunate enough to make Lemony Snicket jealous. Having been chased, shot at and beat up multiple times in those few weeks, I couldn't say the job was boring.

Despite everything that had happened in that time, Tess had managed to talk her uncle into letting her go to homecoming. The problem was no one had asked her. So I volunteered. Travis liked it because it meant an extra employee to watch out for Tess instead of worrying about where a date might be putting his hands. To my surprise, Tess accepted. Then I thought about it—homecoming, Tess's senior year... My high school experience was brief; I skipped a couple of grades. But I remember homecoming had been a big deal to many.

So, I did some research to learn what's proper homecoming etiquette. Fortunately, I did own a nicely tailored, dark suit, which I'd purchased for special occasions when times were more flush. Since homecoming was semi-formal, not formal, I didn't need to rent a tux. I checked with Yoshi, the Barrett family's gardener, to find out what flower—or scent, at least—was Tess's favorite. He told me she liked lilies because their fragrance reminded her of root beer floats. But he warned me that what variety to get would depend on what color Tess decided to wear.

I checked in with Alice, the housekeeper—more like estate manager—to see if she could clue me in to what Tess would be wearing. I also asked her about Tess's favorite foods, so I could figure out where to take her for dinner. Most kids, I found out, attended parties at someone's house early where they took pictures while clothing, hair and makeup were still perfect. Then they'd take limos in smaller social groups to different restaurants for dinner before finally attending the dance later. No way Travis was going to let her risk that kind of exposure, and Tess was on the outs with most social groups anyway after being gone for a year. But Travis had okayed dinner as long as the security detail went along with us, so I made reservations.

The corsage Yoshi had made up for me with a bloom from his greenhouse had been a hit with Tess, and the early evening had been successful enough that when we'd arrived at school for the dance, Tess had seemed as relaxed and happy as I'd seen her in our short acquaintance. I'd escorted her inside under an umbrella to keep the rain from messing up her hair, and I had to admit that she looked radiant, stunning, really. Alice had hired a cosmetologist from one of the big department stores in town to do Tess's makeup so even the wicked scar running from hairline to chin that Tess had gotten in the accident that killed her parents was mostly hidden.

Inside, we'd both gotten caught up in the atmosphere, the excitement generated by the hundreds of talking, laughing students ready to party. A couple of girls I didn't know—casual acquaintances, not former BFFs, apparently—had come up and told Tess how cute she looked, which had elevated her mood even further. When we'd entered the gym, I'd walked her around the dance floor with the music beating in our ears, and leaned close to describe the decorations and the dais where the coronation of the homecoming royalty would occur. She'd taken it all in with a smile and expression of wonderment.

As we'd stood there, I'd gotten caught up in her happiness, had seen her visibly melt in a relaxed pose, face tilted up with a dreamy expression, full lips parted slightly. Impulsively, I'd leaned closer to tell her how great she looked—hot, even—when all hell had broken loose. A muffled boom followed by another, and another, had sounded like a giant bass drum marching toward us. But the screaming and shouting from the commons had suggested the sounds weren't part of any band.

The next explosion had lit up the dark gym like a miniature sun going nova. The flash had pretty much killed my night vision when a second blast had gone off. I'd been looking in the general direction of the detonation, so the second flash had blinded me completely. After that...well, I wasn't sure. I was still trying to sort out what had happened next, and the center of my vision was still a blob of red from the flashes when I finally spotted Tess sitting at a table not far from where Travis stood talking to another man.

I hurried over and sat down, putting a hand on her shoulder. "Tess, are you okay?"

She whirled toward me. "Where have you been?"

"Me? I've been looking for you."

"No, I'm *not* okay. Someone just tried to kill me, in case you didn't notice. And the principal is trying to get me thrown out of school. Why didn't you help me?"

"The explosions...I couldn't see anything. By the time I could, you were gone."

"You didn't see the guy? What the hell, Oliver? He was right in front of us. I'm *blind*, and I knew where he was."

"Don't get all high-and-mighty on me. Those were flash-bangs. Lots of noise and an incredibly bright burst of light. The flashes made me blind, too."

"Yeah, well, while you were standing around, I took the guy down with a leg sweep, and I think somebody shot him."

"Luis," I said somberly. "I'm pretty sure he saved your life."

"What happened to the man? Did they arrest him?"

My eyebrows lifted. "You don't know?"

"How could I? Someone grabbed me—Barney, I think—practically dragged me away, sat me down here, and told me to stay put. I haven't moved since."

"The guy's dead, Tess. Fred made me help him carry the body out to the SUV."

Her sightless eyes widened, and her hand went to her mouth.

"He didn't look much older than me," I said. "But the guy was armed to the teeth. Like some kind of Rambo."

"Sam," she said softly.

I frowned. "Who?"

"He said, 'Tell them Sam sent you.'"

"What does that mean?"

"I don't know!" Her voice rose.

"Hey, hey, it's okay. We'll figure it out." I patted her hand reassuringly, despite the fact that my heart rate was much too high. "I just feel bad that the evening was ruined. You looked so happy. I guess that's a moment we'll never get back."

"What? What moment?" She frowned at me, and pulled her hand away. "Wait. Don't tell me. You were about to go in for a kiss, weren't you? Oh, my God, Oliver. What the fuck were you thinking? That is just so wrong on so many levels."

I deflated like a punctured tire. For once, I was glad she was blind and couldn't see my face turning what I was sure was a brilliant shade of red. I did what any self-respecting guy would do— I changed the subject.

"Who's that with Travis?"

"That's Jenkins, the principal. You know, the one who wants me out of here?"

"Never met him," I said. I'd already had run-ins with Greg Olton, the assistant principal, but hadn't seen this man before. "I thought you'd jump at a chance to stop coming here. You hate this place."

"I do not. Sure, some people can be mean, but I worked too hard to come back to give up now. And don't tell me what I hate. You don't know me that well."

"I guess this is one evening that's shot to hell," I muttered.

She groaned. "That's so not funny."

I wondered if there was way to get my foot out of my mouth when Travis walked over.

4

Travis looked around the commons. Students in formal wear huddled at tables, speaking in hushed tones, concern written on their faces. Fear, too, he noted. They wouldn't be able to contain it much longer. Even the parent chaperones had clustered in small knots, heads leaning in toward one another as they talked in low tones, looking perplexed.

Motion drew his attention to one of the doors to the gym as it opened. Barney, a member of the security team assigned to Tess, stepped partway through and scanned the room until his eyes found Travis. He flashed a thumbs-up and disappeared back into the gym when Travis acknowledged him with a nod.

Jenkins shifted his weight with a look of irritation. Travis stepped up to him and stared at him stonily, watching his impatience turn to discomfort.

"Why isn't this place crawling with cops?" Travis said quietly.

The blood drained from Jenkins's face. "I...I tried to call earlier, but the lines are down and cell service doesn't seem to work."

Travis nodded. "You really don't want to lose your job over this, do you? The fact is, you didn't try calling out until I walked through the door, nearly four-and-a-half minutes after the first detonation, and three minutes after the man who tried to kill my niece was dead."

"I didn't know what was going on," Jenkins protested. "I didn't know if there was an active shooter in the building or not."

"You heard explosions then gunshots, but didn't call for three minutes?"

"I told you, I tried earlier."

Travis reached for the phone in Jenkins's hand. "Shall we check your phone log?"

Jenkins snatched his hand away. "No need for that."

"I think you're so worried about losing your job that you didn't call until you made sure no one else was hurt."

"What do you want?"

"I told you, I want Tess to remain in school here. If she stays I'll make all this go away. You've got ten seconds to make up your mind."

"Impossible. You can't undo this. A man was killed."

"Where? What man? Did you see this person?"

Jenkins threw an arm out and pointed toward the gym. "In there. A man was shot."

Travis smiled. "If you go take a look in there, I assure you, there's no dead body on the floor, no sign of anyone being shot. But there will be rumors and a lot of talk. A lot of these kids will say they saw what happened, though I doubt any of them actually did. My security team says the flash-bangs did a good job of temporarily blinding most of them."

Jenkins looked bewildered. "Then what will I tell all these people? They all think the school was under attack."

Travis smiled again. "All an unfortunate accident. As a surprise, a small pyrotechnics display was planned for the dance tonight, but someone stole some of the fireworks, and set them off as a prank, without warning."

"They'll never buy that."

"Sure they will," Travis said cheerfully. "You just have to sell it. No one's been able to call out since the attack ended. My team has been jamming cell service to keep this contained."

"But the land lines..."

Travis shrugged. "Must have been cut. Not by us. But if you don't get out there and start explaining your version of what happened, the rumors will start flying as soon as cell service is restored, and then you'll have local, state and federal cops crawling down your throat. I don't need that. I'm sure you don't, either."

"Okay, okay. I'll do it."

"And Tess stays?"

"Yes, yes. But only if you provide additional security. Which you pay for, of course."

"Of course. But you'd better make an announcement quick. The natives are getting restless. And if I were you, I'd get an e-mail out to all the parents, whether their kids were here or not, to squash any rumors being spread by kids who got out before my team locked the school down."

"Fine. But if this ever happens again, they'll have both our heads." Jenkins walked away, muttering under his breath.

Travis turned and saw that Oliver had finally found Tess, though neither of them looked very happy. He sighed. He guessed from their perspective the evening hadn't been all that successful. He was used to the kind of violence that had occurred in the gym minutes earlier. They'd prepared for it, though it troubled him that they hadn't done a better job of anticipating it. That was partly Jenkins's and the school's fault. If Travis had had full control over school security, the assassin never would have gotten inside. Travis would have checked every kid who came through the door for school ID as well as a ticket to the dance. Water under the bridge.

He made his way over to the unhappy couple. "Oliver, glad to see you found us. I want you to escort Tess home in a few minutes, as soon as I can spare someone to drive you both."

"Yes, sir," Oliver nodded.

"What did you tell Jenkins?" Tess demanded.

Straight to the point. Travis saw her father James's stubborn streak in her, and his practicality. He marveled that she was still alive, through her own quick thinking and instinctive reaction, no less. When Luis had filled him on how Tess had taken the assassin down with a perfectly executed spinning leg sweep, Travis's chest had swelled with pride. But it had been a close call. Too close.

"I told him none of this ever happened," Travis said, keeping his voice low. "He agreed."

Tess's mouth opened in astonishment. "You can't hide this, Uncle Travis. There are too many people here."

"Maybe so, but we might slow it down. We can't risk having the police and the FBI sticking their noses into this. They'll put my team in a straightjacket, and the company under a microscope. If we're ever going to get to the bottom of what's been happening since your accident, Tess, I need freedom to operate. And if you think it's been bad with the guys protecting you, you can't begin to imagine what it would be like if the FBI or Homeland Security came in and took over."

"So, we act like nothing happened?" Oliver said.

"Jenkins will explain it. I think he went back to the main office to make the announcement over the school P.A. system. Wait for it. I have to go check in with Barney, Fred and the rest of the team."

Tess's face scrunched with a sour expression. "Marcus isn't with you, is he?"

"No. I told him to stay and make sure the house and grounds are locked down tight."

"Good."

Travis hesitated. "Look, I know you two don't get along. But he's good at what he does."

She shook her head. "Too good, maybe. He's got you fooled. I just hope he doesn't come after me in my sleep some night."

Travis let a smile play across his lips since she couldn't see it. "Not going to happen, princess. Not on my watch. Anyway, sit tight. I'll be back in a few. Or I'll send Luis to drive you home."

He turned away, but Tess stopped him with a quiet question. "Who was he?"

"Don't know yet. That's what I want to find out. Hang tight."

Leaving them, Travis quickly made his way through the doors to the gym. The dim lights obscured a lot of detail, but Travis could clearly see that the assassin's body had been removed, along with any traces of blood. Nothing looked out of place—decorations transforming the cavernous room from a basketball court to a homecoming court, DJ station set up on a platform along a side wall, colored spotlights casting multi-hued glows onto the dance floor, a mirror ball reflecting a slowly revolving galaxy of stars on every surface—except the emptiness, the lack of music and laughter and buzz of excited teen voices. The only sign Travis saw that something had been amiss was a throne on the dais for the homecoming court that had been knocked on its side.

Across the floor, Barney stood talking to Luis, but he hurried over when he spotted Travis.

"What's your take?" Travis said as Barney approached.

"I think we're in pretty good shape," Barney said. "As soon as Luis made sure the shooter was down, Fred, Luis and I rounded up the chaperones in here, started calming everyone down, and herded them all out into the commons. Fred made the school's security guys stay in the commons with the chaperones and kids to keep a lid on things while Luis and I cleaned up in here. As soon as we hustled the body out, I sent Luis out to double-check the perimeter just to make sure we hadn't missed any other threats." Barney tipped his head over his shoulder. "He just got back."

"Good work." Travis motioned for Luis to join them.

As Luis hustled over, Jenkins's voice came out of the loudspeakers above their heads. The three men all tipped an ear up to listen for a moment as Jenkins laid out a story pretty much as Travis had suggested. As Jenkins droned on, reassuring students and parent chaperones that all was well, Travis looked at his men.

"Okay, you get the gist of what we're going to say happened here tonight. Luis, anything on your recon rounds?"

The young former marine nodded. "I found a blind in some woods across from the parking lot where the guy set up. Backpack with night vision gear, camo suit, boots. Probably wore the camo over his dress clothes until it was time."

"It's my fault, Trav," Barney said. "We did a thorough sweep of the building before the dance started, but I didn't think to check outside the perimeter other than a check for surveillance. It's mostly houses. I never thought a team could find a hiding place in the neighborhood."

Travis shook his head. "No one's blaming you. We do the best we can and learn. Sounds like this was just one guy, not a team, so it's not surprising you didn't spot him earlier. You would have seen a team."

Barney looked doubtful for a moment then gave a small nod. Travis knew it would eat at him anyway, but that meant he'd do better next time. What roiled Travis's guts was that he was supposed to figure out how to prevent a "next time." He pushed the feeling aside and concentrated on the intel that would help him.

He turned to Luis. "Any clues in what you found to tell us who this guy was?"

Luis shook his head. "No ID, no labels in his clothing, nothing I saw that could help. But definitely a pro, someone with military experience. Everything he had was military spec."

"If so, his prints should be on file," Travis mused. "The bigger question is who sent him?"

"Above our pay grade, boss," Barney said.

Travis heaved a sigh. "Maybe mine, too. Okay, Barney, are you good with getting the shooter's prints and transporting the body out of here?"

"Yeah, no problem. But where?"

"Head south toward Lewis-McChord. I'll get hold of General Turnbull and find out where we can keep the body on ice until we find out more about what the hell's going on. Luis, I want you to take Tess and Oliver home. Take my vehicle. Fred and I will get a ride back with Red."

Travis tossed a key fob to Luis, and stood a moment watching the two men hoof it for a side door leading to the parking lot. They were still short a man since Kenny had been killed a few weeks earlier. And Travis knew that sooner or later he'd have to do something about Tess's suspicions regarding Marcus, the head of his personal security team.

The on-duty contingent had been lucky tonight—lucky no one had been hurt or killed. Tess had saved her own life, somehow. But if the attacks kept coming, he'd need more than a replacement for

Kenny. The whole team was running a little ragged, trying to do too much with too few men on too little sleep.

He squared his shoulders. Right now, he had to see how well the story he'd come up with for Jenkins kept things contained.

5

I sit and fume. I want to cry, but I won't give anyone the satisfaction. The entire night has been a complete and utter failure. I'm so far on the outs with my former crowd of royals that I didn't get an invitation to any of the pre-dance parties. Not that Travis would have let me go. And though dinner was nice—sort of—not even Oliver noticed that Travis had bought out an entire seating at the restaurant to make sure he could control security. Instead of the usual loud buzz of conversation, music, clatter of dishes and silverware, clink of glasses, the silence in the restaurant was nearly deafening.

When we finally got to the dance I thought that the evening might be looking up. I loved the energy as soon as we walked in the door. The music, the excited voices, the vibration of the floor beneath my feet. I swear I could even feel the spotlights as they moved across my face. I pictured the scene as Oliver described the decorations in the gym and the stage on which the homecoming royalty would be presented.

And it all went to shit when some asshole tried to kill me. Even *that* failed. I suppose I should be grateful I'm alive, but I don't feel gratitude. Just anger, resentment, and self-pity. Can't something go right, just once?

I feel numb as we sit and wait.

"Can I get you anything?" Oliver says. "A glass of water?"

"Yeah, right, like a glass of water is going to fix all this?"

"I'm trying to help."

I fold my arms across my chest and turn away from his voice. Now I *am* Helen Keller, mute and deaf as well as blind.

Finally, Luis comes to get us, and Oliver takes me by the arm to lead me out to the car. I don't want any part of it, but I do want to go home. I remove his hand from my arm, and put my hand on his shoulder instead. I let him lead me, but I don't want him to get any more ideas about "escorting" me or being my date. I was beginning to trust him a little, but apparently he's getting some romantic notion in his head that I might actually like him. Now I have to worry about his feelings? That won't do. He'll be no good as my assistant if he's mooning around like some love-struck puppy.

Or am I worried about *my* feelings?

I roughly push that thought aside. Must be the shock.

In the car, I scrunch up against the door, as far away from Oliver as possible. The two men are thankfully silent, letting me stew. But the thoughts in my head grow so loud I have to voice them.

I sit up. "Does it bother you?"

No one answers at first then Luis replies so softly I have to strain to hear it.

"Sure. Taking a life always weighs on you. It steals a little of your humanity." He pauses.

"How can you live with yourself?" I blurt.

"I don't think about taking a life; I think about saving a life. It's my job to protect you."

That shuts me up again. Until I remember my manners.

"Um, thank you." A couple of words seem inadequate for what he did, but he quickly makes them irrelevant.

"No thanks necessary. Like I said, just doing my job."

I vow not to say another word. I'm a job to these people. Luis, the security team, Oliver... Hell, technically Alice and Yoshi work for me, too. Even Travis, who's actually a family member—the only one left, as far as I know—considers me a task he has to check off his to-do list. Since I'm his legal ward, I'm a thing he has to guard and take care of, not someone he treasures and cares for. Screw them all. If that's the way it is, I'll make them earn their keep.

At the house, Luis lets us know he's parking in one of the empty bays in the garage attached to the main house. For direct entry into the house, he says, so I'm not out in the open. Letting me know, I suppose, that he takes his job seriously. I know my way, so I don't wait for Oliver. He catches up as I'm opening the door to the mudroom leading into the kitchen. He sounds out of breath as he comes in right behind me.

Alice and Yoshi meet us in the kitchen, worried voices greeting us. Alice is her usual take-charge self.

"Thank goodness you're both all right," she says. "Oliver, Travis thinks it's best if you spend the night until he has a better sense of the danger to Tess. You can stay in the guest house. I'd offer you the plaid room but it's not made up."

"Thank you, Alice," Oliver says.

"Tess, I'll make you some tea to calm you down," Alice goes on as if Oliver hasn't spoken. "You must have had a terrible fright."

I shake my head. "No, thank you. Yoshi, I'll meet you in the fitness room in five minutes."

Ignoring Alice's protests, I head for my room, change out of my dress, and put on my *gi*. It's late, and probably unfair to ask Yoshi to help me, but I need to punch something, throw something. I hurry down to the fitness room next to the basketball court.

"*Kobanwa*," Yoshi says quietly as I enter the room. "Good evening, Tess."

I bow, and wrinkle my nose. I detect a faint odor of rotten eggs—sulfur. I ignore it.

"*Onegai shimasu, sensei.*"

"You defended yourself tonight. Show me."

I'm not surprised that Travis passed on details of what happened at school. I focus and take a step forward based on where I imagine he stands, then whirl into the crouching spin, extending my leg to sweep his out from under him. Only his legs aren't there. As I plant the sweeping foot and come into a ready stance, Yoshi is already on me, grasping the lapels of my *gi*, placing a foot behind my back leg and not-so-gently putting me on my back on the mat. He sits astride me just to let me know that he can effectively pin me, and once again I'm struck by the strange odor. He quickly gets off and lifts me onto my feet by my lapels. Blood rushing to my face, I adjust my *gi* and bow.

"*Futatabi*," he says. "Again."

I listen to his voice carefully, and move more quickly into the spin this time, not taking any time to adjust my position. If I thought I surprised him, I was badly mistaken. Again, my sweep misses him entirely. He grabs my arm and tosses me over his hip. I land hard, and even though the mat is padded, my breath leaves me in a whoosh. Yoshi leaves me there for a moment while I gasp like a fish out of water until my lungs finally take in air. Then he grasps my forearm and pulls me upright.

"*Imaichido!*" he barks. "Once more."

Frustrated almost to the point of tears, I know he's trying to rattle me. And I suddenly realize why I'd managed to defeat my attacker. He hadn't expected it. I take a deep breath and compose myself, focusing on the spot not where Yoshi's voice came from but where his breathing sounds. I drop into a crouch and feint with my right shoulder, then drop my left hand to the mat and spin the opposite direction of my last two attempts.

My heel hooks the back of his ankle, and I put more effort, more strength into my leg and upend him. I hear his body crash to the mat, and from my crouch I leap on top of him, finding the lapels of his *gi* with opposite hands. I pull, squeezing the backs of my wrists against the carotid arteries in his neck, cutting off the blood to his brain. He arches his body, trying to throw me off, but I feel his strength quickly waning. He goes limp and slaps the mat, tapping out. I stand and bow, holding my pose.

"*Yoi*," he says. "Good. What you do tonight, very foolish. But very brave, and *unavoidable*. You understand? Not your fault."

"*Domo arigatō gozaimasu, sensei.*"

"What did you learn?"

"Surprise is my best defense."

"*Hai!* Yes, missy."

I hear the smile in his voice, and for the first time tonight, I feel proud. The feeling startles me. There's no reason I shouldn't have felt it earlier when the evening started. Going to homecoming was an accomplishment. Looking as good as people said I did was an accomplishment. It's a little strange that what gave me the most satisfaction, the greatest sense of achievement was kicking some dude's ass before he could shoot me. Eighteen months earlier I would have downplayed saving my own life and put my stock in how fabulous my hair and makeup were.

"*Oss*," Yoshi says. "Now, surprise me."

We spar for another thirty minutes until I'm drenched in sweat and my muscles are sore.

"Enough," Yoshi says. "*Gokurosan rei.*"

"*Doitashimaste*," I reply, and bow deeply.

He takes my arm to lead me to the door. The sulfur smell is stronger now.

"Yoshi, I hate to ask, but what is that smell?"

"I so sorry, missy. I work in greenhouse while you dance. Maybe I can show you?"

"Certainly. Lead the way." He can't show me, of course, but judging from his excited tone, he wants to take me to the greenhouse to explain his latest project.

"Actually," he says as we walk, "is not so much *in* greenhouse as *under* it."

Now I'm curious, and I try to picture what's under the greenhouse, finding it strange that I still have visual memory even though I'm blind. Like a lot of houses in this part of the world, mine is built on a slope, so half of the lower level is below ground and half is ground level. When my parents built it, they put the nontraditional rooms down here. In addition to the fitness center with workout room, dojo, spa, and gym, there's a wine cellar, home theater, game room, and indoor/outdoor entertainment space. But I don't figure it out until we're there.

Yoshi stops me and says, "You go."

With gentle prodding, he positions me inside a tight space that is as claustrophobic as a tiny closet. The wall curves, instantly telling me it's the revolving door to the darkroom. I push the flat surface and take baby steps as the outer cylinder turns, and I'm in. Under the almost overpowering odor of sulfur here, the faint scent of film developer and acid bath still lingers. The smells trigger an onslaught of memories, a time when I actually still liked my parents. Well, my father, at least.

When I expressed an interest in photography in elementary school, my father said if I was ever going to have a true appreciation for it I'd have to learn the old-fashioned way, with film. He had the darkroom put in, and we spent hours down here while he taught me to thread exposed film onto stainless steel spools by feel so it wouldn't get ruined before it went into developing canisters. He taught me how to measure and mix film developer, paper developer, stop bath and fixer chemicals at the proper temperatures. He showed me printing tricks with diffusers and filters for the enlarger, and even a rapidly moving hand to shade a "hot" spot in a photo.

I haven't been down here in years, not since I started shooting with digital cameras, and those days are gone, too. Most of the memories are happy ones, but I curse them anyway for reminding me that my parents are gone. Fortunately, Yoshi comes in right behind me, his presence dispelling the ghosts.

"What's this all about, Yoshi?"

"You not use this room for long time, yes? So, is perfect for Yoshi—very dark, running water, sinks and space for working."

"What work?"

"Just doing things I do best."

"Growing things? What are you growing? It stinks."

"Green sulfur bacteria."

"Bacteria? Why would you want to grow something that smells so vile? All your flowers smell so beautiful." My stomach feels queasy.

"I so accustomed to it, I not notice smell."

His voice moves as he talks, and a whirring noise abruptly reaches my ears. Immediately, the odor dissipates as the darkroom ventilation system draws air from the room and replaces it with filtered air from outside.

"So," he says, his voice close to me again, "only place on Earth this grow is deep in ocean, near thermal vents in sea floor."

"I don't understand. You grow plants. This is bacteria. What's the point?"

"Is *like* a plant. But plants make oxygen. This use 'anoxygenic photosynthesis,' which mean it make something besides oxygen—sulfur."

"Photosynthesis requires light, if I recall. This is a darkroom." I'm unable to keep a trace of sarcasm out of my voice. I think Yoshi's gone over the deep end.

"Yes! Very good. This bacteria need only tiny bit of light to grow. That how it grow so deep in the ocean."

"I still don't get the point, Yoshi. Why? And why are you telling me this?"

"Scientists at university in Tennessee make bio-hybrid solar cell to make electricity with spinach protein and blackberry juice."

The significance astounds me. "This is real? You can do this?"

"I read about super-efficient solar cell that work even in starlight. I learn about bio-hybrid cell, and wonder why not make cell that generate electricity from light of stars, even darker sky, so I build my own."

My jaw nearly drops. "You built a solar cell that works with this awful smelling stuff?"

"*Hai.* I work on putting two kinds—spinach and bacteria—back-to-back in one cell. Makes electricity day and night."

I still can't believe what I'm hearing. "When did you have time to do all this work?"

"You sick in bed a long time, missy. Parents gone. Not so much to do, so I look for something to do so I feel useful."

"Oh, my god, Yoshi, you do so much around here. How could you ever feel useless?" He doesn't answer, but I think I know how he feels. Sometimes it doesn't matter how much you do, you still don't feel like you're pulling your weight. I took so much for granted before the accident—my family's money, my looks, my physical abilities—that having to ask other people for help after I got hurt was torture. It still is.

"I still can't believe you know all this, Yoshi," I say. "Don't you need an advance degree in bio-chemistry or something to even understand this stuff?"

"I learn many things before I am gardener," he says quietly.

I suddenly realize that I know nothing of Yoshi's past life. He's been a fixture in our family for so long that I never thought about what he did before he came to work for us.

"How did you meet my parents?" I say, curious now.

"At university."

"Not as a student, though, right?" I say. "You mean you were a groundskeeper or something?"

I take his silence as agreement. "But...I don't understand. Why would you come work for my parents if you had a job at the university?"

"They needed me," he says simply. "And then *you* needed me."

We walk in silence while I consider that. Before I react, he speaks again.

"Even long before accident, missy. Since you were baby girl, we take care of you, watch out for you, teach you."

"We?" I'm puzzled. "You and Alice?"

"*Hai*. Yes. And your parents."

My mouth twists in a grimace. Before the accident, my parents had become all but useless. My father still thought of me as his little girl, and my mother was on my case almost every waking moment about something. For a couple of years, things at home had gone from bad to worse, the fights with both of them over everything from clothes to curfew grew louder and more frequent. Now that they're gone, I can't help but wonder if some of that was my fault.

And as much as Yoshi and Alice have always been part of the family, they're not family. Not really. I think about how only a few weeks ago they—the gardener and housekeeper of all people—fended off a crazy woman with a kitchen knife and two men armed with assault rifles. I'm beginning to realize I've taken my whole life at face value and maybe it's time to reevaluate. Nothing is as it seems anymore. It's a lot to take in.

I feel my way back into the revolving door and step out into the hallway. I sense Yoshi join me a moment later, and he helps guide me up the corridor with the barest touch of his fingers on my elbow.

Another thought pops into my head. "Who knows about this?"

"You first person I show, but Alice know what I working on."

"Why me?" I ask. "Why tell me?"

49

He doesn't answer, and for a moment I think he's gone on ahead. But I hear him breathing close by.

"I know your parents long time," he says finally. "They good people."

"You could have fooled me," I say, the taste in my mouth even more bitter than my morning coffee.

He stops me. "In time," he says softly, "you see. They sacrifice everything for you."

"Yeah, well, look where that got them."

He doesn't respond for a moment. "Long ago, I make promise to protect them, and to carry on their work."

"What work?" I'm confused. My father made video games. He got government contracts because he was brilliant at game theory and AI. And my mom...my mom was a rich, pampered housewife with too much time on her hands. Sure, she dabbled in philanthropy, probably to make a good impression on the other rich bitches in the PTA.

"They work very hard to bring peace and understanding to all people," Yoshi says. "Your father hate all war, so he work to make military better at game theory and negotiating peace, not fighting. Your mother help poor people all over the world learn to feed themselves, and start schools where there are none."

I shift my weight, unsure if I like hearing my parents painted in glowing terms. They're not here, so what good are they now? "What's your point?"

"I do not know your uncle so well. He is warrior, an honorable man, I think. But yin to your father's yang."

"You haven't told Travis about your work?"

"No. I do this for James, your father. I carry on his work. Not sure if uncle will put to same use your father intended. Besides, is not ready."

"Why? What's wrong with it?"

"Still don't know how to keep bacteria alive and reproducing. Cell only last short time before organic material used up or rot."

I debate internally. MondoHard's R&D lab can probably solve whatever problems Yoshi encounters faster than he can by himself. But too many things have gone wrong in my father's company since the accident. I trust only one person there, and it isn't my uncle. Now I see that Yoshi doesn't quite trust Travis, either. No, it's better to keep this under wraps. I might be able to use it as leverage somehow.

There's something he isn't telling me. I press him. "But I still don't understand why you told me, Yoshi. I'm not a scientist."

'Ah-so, but you are. How much you know about chemistry just from learning to smell?"

He has a point. What he's taught me about the chemical composition of scent has helped me in AP Chem.

"You are curious about the world around you, missy, as much as you think you only interested in yourself."

Anger bubbles up inside me. Yoshi's never spoken to me that way. And I realize that maybe he's right. I'm not that girl anymore. He's giving me a lot to think about.

"I'm not my father," I say.

"No, but you are his daughter. And you will someday own company. You must run it, guide it the way he would have."

For a moment, shock prevents me from speaking. It's one thing to go into a board meeting like I had recently and try to stop the company from launching a badly flawed game app. But run the company? I don't even know if I'll survive high school.

"I don't know the first thing about running a company."

"Is like anything else in life. You learn by doing. Soon, you must. You will have no choice."

No choice? I sense there are things he hasn't told me, but I think about what he did say. The idea of running a multi-billion-dollar company terrifies me. But Yoshi's right—it's *my* company. Or it will be someday. I know what I want MondoHard to stand for, and it isn't the image the company has now.

I say, "Maybe you better not tell anyone else what you're working on."

"Yes, missy. I, too, think this. For now, it is our secret."

6

Once he saw Luis escort Tess and Oliver safely out to his SUV, Travis met Jenkins in the center of the cafeteria. The principal's shoulders sagged, and the weariness and worry on his face had aged him ten years in the past hour.

"Are you sure this will work?" Jenkins murmured as Travis approached.

Travis shrugged. "We'll find out."

He used a chair to step onto a table, stuck two fingers in his mouth and let out a shrill whistle that brought the hum of conversation to an abrupt halt.

Speaking loudly but calmly, Travis said, "Thank you all for your patience while the school's been under lockdown. For those of you who don't know me, I'm Travis Barrett. My niece, Tess, has been under extra security recently, which is why you've seen members of that team in addition to regular school security guards. Working with Principal Jenkins and his team, we've determined that there is no threat to anyone here, and we'll soon be lifting the lockdown and letting you all go home. As Principal Jenkins already announced, we discovered that some of the fireworks that were going to be used for a surprise pyrotechnics show later this evening were taken as a prank, mishandled, and accidentally went off. No one was hurt. The remaining fireworks have been removed and safely stored, and the school secured. We're confident we'll find out who was responsible. Now, I'll be happy to answer any questions."

"Someone said they saw a gun," a student shouted.

"I saw someone with a gun," another boy said on the other side of the room.

Travis shook his head. "Members of my security team did draw their weapons when the fireworks went off, but no one else had a gun."

"I heard shots," a girl insisted.

"Again," Travis said calmly, "what you heard were fireworks. I realize that once you're free to go, there will be a lot of talk and rumors outside these walls. Please don't perpetuate false rumors. Despite how frightening this experience has been for many, I repeat: *no one was hurt,* and at no time did anyone other than the security team have a weapon."

He was surprised at how easily the lie left his lips. But then, that had been the nature of his work all those years in Afghanistan—tell both allies and enemies what they wanted to hear, whether it was the truth or not.

"What about the guy on the dance floor?" a boy shouted. "He sure didn't look too good lying there. Some girl went down, too."

Travis thought quickly. The gym had been dark, lit only by the disco ball and swirling spotlights. Details would have been hard to spot. And most people had been blinded by the flash-bangs, even the DJ. Travis had interviewed him briefly, and offered him a large cash bonus if he was willing to stay and crank up the tunes again after everything was straightened out.

"Actually," he said, smiling, "the person you're talking about passed out, likely from fright. The girl you saw was my niece, who was trying to help him."

"How the hell could she do that?" someone said. "She's blind as a bat."

Travis's smile disappeared, and he scanned the crowd looking for the speaker. He wanted to take whoever it was by the scruff of the neck and shake him, or at least give him a quick retort. But he took a deep breath and let it out slowly. He knew he couldn't afford to fuck up, and picking a fight with some insensitive kid wouldn't look good.

A thin version of his smile reappeared. "You'd be surprised at what disabled people can do if you give them half a chance."

A lot of students suddenly looked at their feet or off into space instead of at him.

After a long moment of silence, someone yelled, "When can we get out of here? This dance is a bust."

Travis glanced toward Jenkins and saw a slight nod.

"You're free to go whenever you wish," Travis said. "But the DJ has assured Principal Jenkins that he'll stay. The dance is still on for those who want to party."

As if on cue, the rhythmic beat of drums and heavy bass guitar reverberated through the wall separating the cafeteria from the gym. The crowded cafeteria slowly emptied as students either gave the dance one more shot or exited outside to get their cars or call for rides.

Travis turned to Jenkins to gauge his reaction.

Jenkins scratched his head. "I don't like it, Barrett, but I don't see that I have a choice. We'll see if the ruse works. But if you can't keep the students and staff safe, I'll make sure you spend the rest of your life in a jail cell."

"If I don't keep everyone safe, then what happens to me won't matter." He lowered his voice and glanced around quickly. "That wasn't just some stalker who tried to kill Tess."

Jenkins looked at him quizzically, but Travis didn't volunteer any more information. Jenkins's eyebrows slowly unknitted and rose.

"All these attacks are related. This all has to do with whatever's going on at your brother's company. You really can't keep everyone here safe, can you?"

"There's only one person these people seem to want, whoever they are."

"But she puts everyone else around her in jeopardy," Jenkins protested. "She has to leave."

"New security measures will be in place by Monday, I promise." Travis almost pleaded. "She stays. Please. At least give her the rest of the semester, and we can talk about it then."

Jenkins held his gaze for a moment. "We'll see."

He strode off, leaving Travis standing by himself. Travis waited there for several minutes to see if anyone would approach him with more questions, but now that the excitement had died down, people seemed disinterested in him. Some students eagerly headed to the gym, drawn by the pulse of the music. More slowly filed out into the night air, shuffling their feet and hanging their heads as if they'd been delivered the worst news of their lives. Movement at the corner of his eye caught his attention. He turned to watch Red, the former Navy SEAL on his security team, stroll up, hands in his pockets.

Red gave him a shrug. "Could've been worse."

Travis sighed. "Yeah, could've been a *lot* worse. We good here?"

"Can't see how there's much more you can do, boss. There'll be rumors, and they'll get worse after you tighten security here. But the story's plausible. And without pictures or a body, nobody can say otherwise."

A shudder ran through Travis now, and he groaned. "Please tell me none of these spoiled, snot-nosed brats had a phone out taking video of this fiasco. That's all we need—the shooting on social media."

"Good point. I'll text Luis and have him start checking after he drops the kids at home."

"We good otherwise?"

"Yeah, I think so." Red gave another shrug.

"Let's go home."

By the time they got back to the Barrett family compound, Travis was so wound up with unspent adrenaline he wanted to punch a wall. Actually, he wanted to hit James for putting him in this situation. His brother's absence had caused all this trouble. The Barrett family was down to two people—Travis and Tess—and one of them stood to inherit majority ownership of a huge international high tech company. And Travis's job was to make sure that person stayed alive long enough to take over the company, as well as keep the company running so there was something to actually inherit.

As he went upstairs to the guest suite that was now his he realized that he was almost as angry with Sally as he was with James. Travis had never had any kind of long-term relationship let alone a marriage and kids. As a soldier, he'd never had the time for a relationship, or the inclination to put people he loved in the position of worrying about losing him every day. The nature of his job in the Strategic Intelligence Collection & Containment unit, a secret branch of the Army Special Forces, meant hunting terrorist cells in some of the most rugged and remote countries in the world. He knew how to wage war, not how to parent a teenage girl.

In his room, he stripped off his work clothes and changed into shorts, T-shirt and athletic shoes and jogged down the stairs to the glass-fronted exercise room on the lower level. He hit the treadmill first to loosen up and get warm, then switched to weight machines, and ran through a routine that worked most of his muscles groups, not just his upper body. From time to time, he could hear a loud *kiai* and a slap on the mat from the room next door. He guessed that Tess must have felt the same way when she got home, and now she was taking out her frustration on Yoshi. Their voices alternated as first one then the other attacked.

Ignoring their yells, he settled into a rhythm, working through the reps for each exercise, channeling his anger into his movements. Soon, he was drenched in sweat. When his muscles burned and ached to the point that he couldn't push one more rep, he swung himself off the equipment onto his feet. Breathing heavily, he walked on rubbery legs to a wall shelf and grabbed a clean towel to mop his face. He slung the towel over one shoulder, got a bottle of water out of a mini-fridge, and drank half of it down in greedy swallows. He walked in slow circles until his heart rate and breathing settled, then flipped the lights off and reached for the doorknob. Voices in the hallway froze his hand in mid-motion, and he paused to listen.

Tess and Yoshi were leaving, but instead of turning for the stairs, Yoshi led Tess down the hallway the other direction. Curious, Travis cracked the door open, and peered down the hallway. The pair disappeared into the darkroom. Now Travis was doubly curious. He didn't think the darkroom had been used in years, and why would Yoshi take Tess there when she could no longer see? When Tess had finally gained enough mobility through rehab to get around the house, she'd begged Alice to remove the photos she'd taken from the spots where they hung on the walls. Travis remembered all too well the sheer despair in her voice that came with the recognition she'd never use a camera again.

He stepped away from the door and glass wall next to it, and edged farther back into the darkness. Sitting on a weight bench, he nursed his water bottle and waited. Before long, he heard their voices again, and quickly crept up to the door, putting his ear to the crack to listen. He caught bits and pieces of their conversation until they drew closer.

"You haven't told Travis about your work?"

"No. I do this for James, your father. I carry on his work. Not sure if uncle will put to same use your father intended. Besides, is not ready."

"Why? What's wrong with it?"

Travis pressed himself against the back of the door and held his breath, heart racing. *What was Yoshi up to?* He focused on their words as they passed by.

"But I still don't understand why you told me, Yoshi. I'm not a scientist."

Yoshi's response was too soft to hear.

"I'm not my father."

"No, but you are his daughter. And you will someday own company. You must run it, guide it the way he would have."

"I don't know the first thing about running a company."

"Is like anything else in life. You learn by doing…"

Their words became unintelligible and their voices faded as they reached the stairs and headed up. Travis stood unmoving for a long moment, thoughts tumbling through his brain, still in shock at the revelation. Yoshi had been holding out on him, on the company.

He tossed his empty water bottle in a receptacle, wrapped the towel around his neck and left, closing the door behind him. *Time to see what was in the darkroom.*

He padded quietly down the hallway, dimly lit by soft uplighting in the dropped soffets lining the walls. As he slipped inside the darkroom through the revolving door, a rotten-egg smell smacked him in the face, and he wrinkled his nose. He flipped on the red darkroom lights and slowly toured the circumference of the room. Rows of Petrie dishes sat in the rectangular developing pans on the counter near the sink.

"What are you up to, Yoshi?" Travis murmured.

He picked up one of the little round containers and read the label attached to its side, "*C. ferrooxidans*" then another labeled "*C. bathyomarinum.*" He moved on to a countertop. Electric and electronic lab and test equipment littered the workspace. He stared at it, trying to make sense of the experiments. Images of other equipment he'd worked with or seen during his time in the military flashed through his mind. Finally, he nodded to himself and turned away. Shutting off the lights, he slowly eased into the revolving door and stepped out into the corridor. *Empty.*

Still mulling over what Yoshi's secretiveness might mean, he headed upstairs for a shower and some sleep.

7

Jeremy Latham loved the view from his office in the Russell Senate Office Building, no matter the weather or the time of day. Through some trees on the mall he could see the white dome of the capitol building lit up against the dark night sky, where he and men like him made laws that the country lived by. Right outside the window, traffic on Constitution Avenue was light at this time of night, contributing to the relative peace and quiet of a city at slumber. Latham felt more comfortable walking the halls of power during the day, negotiating and cutting deals, keeping his eyes, ears and fingers on the pulse of conversations, listening for tidbits of useful information, watching people on the go and in meetings like a hawk, checking for tells—sweating brows, nervous tics, fearful expressions—indicating they had something to hide.

The real seat of power lay here, in this spacious and comfortable office. As chairman of the Senate Appropriations Committee, Senate Armed Services Committee, and the Senate Judiciary Committee, he controlled the military's purse strings and oversaw appointments to judgeships for both federal courts and the U.S. Supreme Court. Deals were made here. More than that, however, the office served as the central hub of the network of informants and contractors who got things done behind the scenes.

But even Latham needed to decompress, let the stresses of the day roll off him. Though he sometimes spent the night in the office on a comfortable pull-out couch, he normally wasn't here this late. He'd attended a concert at the Kennedy Center earlier in the evening, and had come back to the office for a nightcap and to check that nothing had happened in his absence that required his attention. Between the smoky amber liquid on ice in the cut crystal tumbler he held and the quiet street outside the window, the tension in his neck and shoulders eased. He still had problems to solve, but nothing that couldn't wait until morning, and none that would require much effort to put right.

He idly scanned the bank of television monitors normally hidden behind a drop-down wall that matched the wood-paneled walls, taking in the information without really focusing on it. The buzz of a phone from his desk startled him. No one should be calling at this hour. He checked the monitors once more as he made his way to the desk and fished a burner cell phone from a drawer.

He put the phone to his ear. "Yes?"

"Someone tried to kill the girl," the caller said.

Latham's gaze went to the monitors again. "When? There's nothing on the news channels."

"They locked it down."

"Damn it. I need her alive."

"Why? I thought that's what you wanted. Get her out of the way and be done with it."

"No," Latham said sharply. "I changed my mind. That would put too much focus on the company. I'd rather try to control it from the inside. She's key. How could you let this happen?"

"I wasn't there. I wouldn't have known if I hadn't heard it from the security team on duty."

"Who the hell was it?"

"Info is sketchy. We don't know. A single hitter. Trained, but something threw him off."

Latham's mind raced. "We've got a bad situation here. Some third party angling for something. Who? Why? Why would someone else want her dead? I need answers."

"I'll find out what I can."

"And you'll be more vigilant?"

"Of course, but it won't be easy. She doesn't trust me."

"I don't care what it takes. I have other plans for her."

"Despite what I think of him personally, Barrett put together a good team. She's safe."

"You better hope she stays that way."

Latham disconnected and tossed the phone back in the drawer in irritation. He wondered how Barrett had managed to contain something as newsworthy as the attempted murder of the daughter of one of the richest men in America, the founder of MondoHard, who'd been killed in the car accident that had left his daughter an orphan.

He'd underestimated Travis Barrett. Barrett's dead brother James had been remarkably astute despite humble beginnings and naiveté. Travis Barrett was nothing more than a soldier, a person who took orders, but apparently he could think on his feet and improvise. This was the second time in as many weeks that Barrett had managed to interfere in Latham's business. His last plan had been so audacious—a plot to have VPOTUS assassinated by his own son—that Latham had been disappointed but not surprised it failed. What had surprised him was Barrett's resourcefulness, somehow managing to escape from imprisonment in an abandoned mine in Montana and getting to D.C. in time to stop the assassination attempt. Latham realized he'd have to be more careful in his dealings with the man. He'd see if Barrett was clever enough to find out who tried to kill his niece.

Another phone rang. Again, it wasn't his office line, and for a moment he frowned in confusion. At this hour, no one should be calling. Then he realized that the sound came from the computer on his desk. He rounded the corner, sat in the leather swivel chair and jiggled the mouse, bringing the monitor to life. An alert for an encrypted video conferencing app blinked on the screen. He moved the cursor over the symbol and clicked.

The screen instantly revealed the image of a dark conference room surrounded by eight high-backed chairs. The chairs were backlit by recessed pin spotlights in the ceiling. A figure sat in each chair, their faces obscured in shadow by the discreet lighting. Even though the conference was encrypted, trust among these nine men only went so far. They had common interests, but none was so foolish to believe that any of them might succumb to greed or impulse and try to use leverage against the others. So they fiercely protected their identities.

Latham, however, knew the identities of most, but not all of them, since bringing them together to form the world's most powerful cabal had been his idea. One was a Russian oligarch with close ties but no allegiance to the Russian president. Another was a Texas oilman who'd helped put three U.S. presidents and half a dozen congressmen in office. Latham suspected the soft-spoken Chinese in the group was a general and high-ranking member of the Communist Party's powerful inner circle, the Central Committee, but the Russian had brought him into the group, so Latham couldn't be sure.

Latham knew that the conference room was only an illusion, that in reality each of those chairs was located in a different part of the world, cameras positioned in such a way to make them all feel as if they were sitting at the same table. They were equals in their own right, some richer, some in positions of more power, and though they all operated independently, they pursued no policy or strategy without at least the two-thirds majority vote of all. Unlike the better known Nine, the U.S. Supreme Court, which only required a majority. Here, the gravest circumstances required a unanimous vote. He let his face settle into an unreadable mask to hide his surprise. These nine weren't scheduled to meet via video-conference for another month. Latham remained silent and waited to see who had called the meeting and why.

A silhouette leaned forward and spoke. "You failed. For the third time."

Latham recognized the voice. A sheik from a small Middle Eastern country, one of the richest men in the world. His mind raced, wondering how they had heard the news to assemble so quickly. More importantly, who had informed them?

"No," Latham said firmly. "I did not."

"Do you deny the target survived a third assassination attempt?"

"Not at all." Latham shrugged. The key to power with these men was to never give them an opening or advantage. "There's another party in play. I—*we* had nothing to do with what happened. I remind you, gentlemen, you all agreed to this project, both its aims and importance. I also remind you that you gave me free rein to run the operation as I see fit."

"Perhaps we need to consider adding some performance clauses. So far, we haven't seen any return on your efforts. And what's this about another entity in play?"

"I don't know who yet, but I promise you I will find out."

"Nonetheless, you have failed twice. Just because someone else was as unlucky as you doesn't mean the target isn't still a threat. And security now will be tighter than ever."

"She's no longer a target," Latham said calmly. He heard another man sputter, and a third cough into his hand. "I have other plans for her. Better plans than simply removing her from the field. She's of more use to us as a pawn on the board, one we can use to block our opponent's bishop."

Silence hung in the air for a moment before the sheik spoke again. "You'll need to convince us this new strategy is working, and quickly."

Latham waved a hand in front of what he knew was his pixilated face on the others' screens. "Fine. I'll give you proof of performance within a week. Will that do?"

Murmuring came from several of the men at once.

"A vote, then," the sheik said. "In favor?"

Latham saw seven hands rise above the black outline of the chairs. He had no way of telling who the holdout was, but he'd convince whoever it was of the value of his plan before long.

"You have a week," the sheik said. "Use your time well."

Latham's monitor went blank. He leaned back in his chair and took a large swallow from his glass, relishing the whiskey's burn as it went down his throat. He held the glass up to the light and swirled the contents, noting the changing patterns refracted through the ice cubes and cut crystal. He also noted with some surprise that his shirt was damp under his arms.

8

The monitors of six of the other screens in the conference call went dark as the men who sat behind them signed off and went about their normal lives wherever they resided. Two screens continued to glow until all the others had left the videoconference. The two figures remained motionless and quiet for several moments.

Finally, one of the black silhouettes spoke. "We failed."

"No, the assassin failed." The other man's Slavic-accented voice was confident. "We knew it was a risky gambit from the start. 'Sled-Dog' was unproven, tested only under standard rules of engagement. He showed promise. We saw an opportunity and moved on it."

"I'm worried about potential blowback."

"Why? There is nothing to tie us to what happened. We moved the funds through the shell corporation that owns the ranch in Montana. The only person who can possibly be linked to that is Latham. And half the funds came from the other kid."

"I admit, coming across the fool in that chat room who led us to Sled-Dog was a fortuitous bit of luck. But the fact remains the girl is still alive. And Latham becomes more dangerous and unpredictable by the day."

"You don't think much of his plan?"

"To use the girl? I don't think he knows how much danger she actually poses. We're better off rid of her altogether."

"Your source is reliable?" said the Russian.

"Very. You know we wouldn't have attempted this otherwise. The document just came to light. It hasn't been made public yet. Latham doesn't know it exists."

"Barrett's game theory at work again," the Russian mused. "I would have liked to have played chess with him. A worthy opponent. Not many men would have conceived of the idea, let alone implemented such a plan. It's genius."

"Clever, maybe. But we'll never get our hands on the technology we want unless we have a more pliable board of directors and control more voting stock. And we can ill-afford to have a teenage girl running that company."

"We already have insiders on the board."

"Yes, yes," the other man said impatiently. "We hold sway over their opinions and board votes, but they don't control enough stock. Don't forget, Barrett's brother owns a small percentage, as do loyal household employees."

"Are you sure the document exists?"

"The rumors are too far-fetched not to have some basis in truth."

"But you don't know where it is?"

"No, and we can't destroy it if we can't find it. That's why—"

"Another attempt so soon would be foolish," the Russian interrupted. "Security will be tighter than ever, and Latham's inside man has been given strict instructions."

A sigh came over the speaker, and the Russian saw the other man's shoulders rise and fall.

"Don't be so morose," the Russian said. "We'll give Latham's plan a chance. One week. If he doesn't perform, we get rid of the girl another way."

The other man gave a short laugh that held no humor. "Who knows? Maybe the fool who led us to Sled-Dog is angry enough to do the job himself. I'm sure losing the money he put up hurt him far more than it hurts us."

The Russian waved. "Pocket change to us. The fool helped defray our costs, though. No refunds."

The other man laughed again, a real one this time. "'No refunds...' Good one, Yuri."

9

Over time, the guesthouse where the security team bunked had transformed into a typical man-cave. The huge flat screen television in the living room, tuned to a sports network, was on constantly, beaming images of men running into each other, tackling each other, hitting each other, racing each other, always trying to outperform each other. Self-disciplined and focused, the team didn't sit around drinking beer and eating pizza while watching, and from time to time I'd actually seen a couple of them reading quietly rather than numbing out in front of the TV. But someone watched at almost all times, almost as if the cable hook-up offered only one channel. I like sports, but a break from the fun and games would have been nice once in a while.

The house wasn't messy or dirty, though. Trust former military men to keep things neat and tidy. But with all the coming and going, it definitely felt lived in, and while I couldn't quite smell the testosterone in the atmosphere, a lingering undertone of manly sweat was easy to detect. These were guys of out-sized proportions, big men who took up space, sucked up oxygen, and made me feel small even at my six-foot height.

I flopped into a chair and tried to watch whatever was on-screen, but couldn't focus and soon got up and prowled the rooms on the ground floor, looking for the source of my irritability and restlessness. I ended up in the kitchen where Luis stood in front of the open refrigerator drinking orange juice straight from the container. His throat worked as he gulped down the juice in big swallows. He emptied it, and turned around while swinging the fridge door shut. Crumpling the carton, he moved to throw it in the trash but something in my expression must have stopped him.

He pulled up and looked at me hard. "You okay?"

I shrugged. "Any milk in there?"

Luis threw a glance at the fridge over his shoulder. "Yeah, I think so. You look like you need something stronger than that."

I shouldered past him, opened the fridge and pulled out a carton of milk. Setting it on the counter, I opened cupboards looking for a glass.

"It got to you, huh?" Luis said. "What happened at the school."

I remember with perfect clarity everything that happened up until the time the second flash-bang exploded in the gym. I remember, of course, because I am blessed—and cursed—with eidetic memory. Anything that makes an emotional impact will imprint itself in my memory banks in such a way that I have virtually perfect recall. And what happened at the school stirred up a lot of emotions. I was still trying to sort them out.

"Here's the thing," I said. "Sure, explosions and guns going off nearby tend to get my adrenaline pumping. I'm not shaken by what I saw, though, because I didn't see squat. That flash-bang or whatever, totally blinded me. I still see a big red spot in the center of my vision."

"Happens to the best of us," he said.

"It didn't happen to you." I can't keep the irritation out of my voice.

"I'm trained for that sort of thing. Soon as I heard the first explosion I was prepared for more. Especially near the girl."

"Tess," I said. "I stood right next to her and I couldn't do a damn thing to help her."

"Like I said, that's our job, not yours."

"I'm supposed to be her assistant. That means I'm supposed to *assist* her. What good am I if I can't fucking help her?"

Luis stared at me, unblinking, and I reined myself in, dropping my gaze.

"Don't be so hard on yourself," he said. "At least you didn't wet your pants."

I looked up in surprise. "You did that?"

He nodded. "First firefight I was in. Scared the piss out of me. But I didn't turn tail and run. I fought back."

The memory plays against the movie screen in my head.

"You like this girl," he said.

"What? No. I mean, sure, I find her interesting. But I don't *like*, like her." My face grows hot as I think back to what I almost did before a crazed gunman so rudely interrupted us. "I'm too old for her. Besides, I work for her. Getting involved with her would be a disaster."

"Ri-ight," he said, apparently not convinced.

"Anyway, right now she seems pissed at the world." I couldn't bring myself to admit that she was pissed at me mostly for acting like a lovesick puppy. Luis would probably think me an ass for trying something so eighth-grade, and then he'd tell the other guys, and I would have zero cred with these guys. It wasn't like I was trying to compete—they'd all been military and had more life experience than I—but I didn't want to come off like some kid still wet behind the ears.

"I don't even know why I'm hanging around. You shot the bad guy. Why should I waste the rest of the weekend here?"

"When you could be hitting on a pretty co-ed in some bar off campus, you mean?" His sarcasm wasn't lost on me.

"Maybe so I can get ahead of Tess on her schoolwork. How about driving me home?"

Luis glanced at the heavy military spec watch on his wrist. "Sorry, man. I go on shift in less than twenty minutes."

"Screw it," I muttered. "I'm not staying in here in the bunkhouse with you guys. The couch is hard as a rock, and every one of you snores. No offense."

Luis shrugged. "None taken. Doesn't bother me."

"Fine. See you later."

I let myself out the front door and walked across the courtyard to the six-bay garage attached to the main house. Alice had given me keys to one of the family cars—Tess's mom's—to get Tess to school and wherever else she needed to go. And frankly, I didn't care that Alice and Yoshi thought I'd be safer staying. Alice said she would have offered me the "plaid room" across the hall from Tess. It was a mirror image of Tess's suite, with large, spa-like bathroom and a huge walk-in closet/dressing room. I'm glad it wasn't available. I actually thought, given all that had happened, I'd be safer somewhere Tess couldn't take out her moods on me.

Punching the code into the keypad next to one of the doors worked its electronic magic, and in a matter of moments I had that sweet ride purring up the winding driveway and onto the main road. No doubt Alice would be angry, but what could she do to me? Fire me? I needed a job, but they sure as hell didn't pay me enough to dodge flying bullets, let alone deal with a rich, spoiled, blind, high school senior.

10

Exhausted, I sleep like the dead, deep and dreamless. I saw nothing, so have no visions to haunt me. When I wake, though, memories rush back in—the ear-splitting explosions marching closer; the screams of panicked students rushing away from me; the sudden shout warning me; my body's instinctive physical reaction to the presence in front of me and his soft utterance of surprise; the scent of blood; and the man's dying words.

Tell them Sam sent you.

So many questions. Sam who? Who are "they?" What does Sam want me to do if I find whoever sent him? Why did he try to kill me? And why didn't he?

Even though I don't want to, I know the answer to that question. I heard the surprise in his voice when he realized I'm blind. He didn't finish the job for the worst reason of all—pity. That moment of weakness cost him his life, and saved mine.

Now I'm pissed. "I'm no one's charity case," I murmur. "Not yours, Sam. Not anyone's."

I know he can't hear me. I'm not *woo-woo* or stupid, but saying it aloud makes me feel better. He was right about one thing. Whoever sent him picked the wrong person to mess with. The accident that killed my parents and blinded me put me in an untenable position—alone, handicapped, targeted by people who want to destroy my father's company, and ill-equipped to find my way to school let alone solve the problems facing me. It's ruining my life, and I'm sick of it. I'm supposed to be in my prime, a royal in senior year, top of the heap for once, with only one worry— getting into college. Instead, some asshole crashes homecoming with a gun.

Screw them all. As much as part of me wants to, crying about it won't help. If Sam wants me to give a message to whoever sent him, I'll be more than happy to oblige. Who am I not to grant him his dying wish? I'm through being other people's punching bag. Just one problem—how do I find out who Sam is, or was?

I know where to start.

I swing my legs out of bed and rush through my morning routine. It's Sunday, a day for lounging, but that's not on my schedule today. I wash my face and brush my teeth, then make my way to the big walk-in closet and dressing room. I pick out a pair of soft, comfortable jeans by feel after counting hangers, then a tee and a hoodie, and get dressed. At the vanity, I throw on enough makeup to look presentable and brush my hair. I'm still self-conscious about the scar that runs the length of my face, so I don't pull my hair back into a ponytail. I sigh at the mirror that I can't see. Whatever I've done is good enough. If it isn't, Alice never shies away from voicing her opinion on how I look. In some ways she's worse than my mother was.

On the way downstairs, the smell of bacon makes me rethink what's on my diet. By the time I reach the bottom, I've convinced myself that it's always been on the list of foods I can eat. The kitchen bustles with activity, filled with the sounds of silverware clattering on dishes, water running in the sink, food cooking and men's voices. The chatter quiets as soon as I enter, and I wonder if I screwed up my eyeliner or something.

"Good morning, Tess," Alice says, her voice ringing out in the sudden silence.

"Morning, Alice."

I hear a murmured chorus of "Good morning" from the men, then the scrape of chairs on the floor and shuffle of feet as some get up to go.

"Don't everybody leave on my account," I say. "I just came to get some bacon before it's all gone. It's not gone, is it, Alice?"

"No, there's plenty," she says, surprised. "Pancakes, too."

"Pancakes?"

The instant the word leaves my mouth I smell the browned butter, the toasted flour, the maple syrup. I've been so focused on bacon that the smell of pancakes didn't register until now. I *love* pancakes. I shouldn't eat those, either, but I'm tired of playing Glinda. Once in a while it should be okay to be bad.

"Can I fix you a plate?" Alice asks hesitantly, as if she can't believe I want something as normal as pancakes and bacon. But she knows when I put my mind to something, I set higher expectations for myself. Recently, I set a goal of losing some of the chunk I gained during my long rehab after the accident.

"Yes, please." I try not to sound too eager. I'll go back on my diet tomorrow.

There's more shuffling and scraping at both the big island in the center of the kitchen and the table in the nook off to one side.

"Thanks, Alice," says Fred, I think. "Great breakfast."

Others echo his thanks as they take dishes to the sink and file out. I find my way to the island and sit on a vacated stool. I've barely gotten comfortable when I hear Alice set a plate in front of me and place a napkin and silverware to its left.

"Juice?" she says. "Coffee?"

"Um, coffee, please, black." Pancakes and bacon are one thing, but no sense in taking my self-indulgence any further than that.

I reach for the napkin and my fingertips find a fork and knife. Once I place the napkin in my lap, I find the edges of the plate with my fingers, then lift silverware in each hand and cut the pancake into what I hope are bite-size pieces, stab one with the fork and raise it to my lips. Warm, sweet, fluffy, buttery...heaven. I take another bite, chew slowly and swallow.

"Is Uncle Travis up yet?" I say.

"I'm up," he calls from the hallway. I hear his footsteps as he enters the kitchen. "Good morning. Smells awfully good, Alice. No, don't trouble yourself. I'll get it. Be right there, Tess."

"Just leave your dishes in the sink," Alice says. "I'll tidy up later. I have other work to do."

Travis pours coffee, then walks to the stove to get a plate of food. He sets both on the island.

"How are you feeling?" he says, sitting next to me.

I want to snap off a sarcastic reply, but I hear real concern in his voice and I bite my tongue.

"Tired." I yawn. I really am tired after the late-night workout with Yoshi.

"No, really, are you okay?"

"No, I'm not fucking okay," I say in a low voice so Alice won't hear me swear and yell at me. Even though she's gone, she has ears like a bat. "All I wanted to do was go to homecoming and have a good time. Instead, all hell breaks loose, someone tries to kill me, gets shot and dies right in front of me. Would you be okay?"

"If I were you, no, I wouldn't. But I've been through it. It can help to talk about it with someone who knows what it's like. That's why I asked how you're feeling."

"I don't know," I tell him truthfully. I'm not sure what to feel, so I ask the question that's been on my mind since I woke. "Did you find out who he was?"

"Yes," he says softly, his tone serious. "We did. His name was Samuel Palmer. We don't know much more about him. We know he grew up in Alaska, and that he served in the army for several years, but retired after his last tour. Since then, it seems he hasn't held a steady job or residence. He bounced around a lot."

I don't tell him I already knew the dead man's name. Hi first name, anyway. "Did he do anything crazy in the army?"

"Not as far as I can tell. His record was pretty good. Good enough that he trained other soldiers. My guess is that he left because he was getting passed over for promotions. It happens."

I take another bite of the pancakes and chew slowly.

"Some guys come back from active duty traumatized by what they've seen and done. They can't cope when they get back, can't fit in, and feel like there's no place for them here anymore."

"PTSD," I say.

"That's right. Post-traumatic stress syndrome. And I'm a little worried about you after what you've been through in the past few weeks."

"The last year and a half, you mean."

"Good point. I forget how long it's been, how hard you've worked."

Reminding him that losing parents and going blind is traumatic doesn't mean I want to revisit the past. "You never had it, though, right?"

"No, but I think a lot about what I had to do in Afghanistan and other places." He pauses. "I had different training and a different mind-set than most grunts—guys who enlist. I was prepared for the work I did over there. I signed up for it, and I was good at it. This guy Palmer may have just cracked. Often, PTSD makes people depressed and suicidal. Angry, too, and they try to take out as many people as they can before they kill themselves."

I shake my head. "You know this wasn't a school shooter. He came for me."

"We don't know that until we find out more about him, Tess."

"He stood right in front of me. There was no one else out there on the dance floor except Oliver. And you can't tell me that *he* did something so bad that this guy wanted revenge. Oliver wouldn't know how to make someone that mad."

"Fine, it looks like an assassination attempt, but I still don't want you freaking out until we figure out who the gunman is and what his motives were."

"Seems pretty obvious to me—money."

"Probably. But he may have had other reasons. He could have been a stalker for all you know. You don't go from being a soldier to an assassin just because someone offers to pay you."

A shiver runs up my spine. The way he says it makes me think he's talking about himself.

"Well, I think someone hired him, and I want to know who. I certainly didn't know him. If he was stalking me then I imagine he'd *want* me to know who he was."

He doesn't say anything.

"So, what now?" I say.

"I'm putting the best people I can find on this, Tess. We'll get to the bottom of it."

"And in the meantime there's still a target on my back? Great."

"I'm hiring more security."

I pound a fist on the counter. "No! We have enough men with guns around here."

"These guys are exhausted, Tess. They work long shifts, and despite how good they are, someone almost killed you last night."

"In case you haven't noticed, I'm still here. They stopped that guy. *I* stopped that guy. I can't live in a prison."

"This doesn't look like any prison I've ever seen. Pretty cushy, if you ask me."

"You're not the one under a microscope! I'm surprised they don't follow me into the bathroom. I don't want more guards. I want this all to stop."

"It's my job to protect you."

"Then find out who's behind all this! Who wants me dead? Why? If you don't figure it out, then I will."

Suddenly, I don't feel like eating pancakes. I push away from the counter and walk out.

"Tess," Travis calls. "Stay and finish your breakfast. C'mon, let's talk about this."

His words grow fainter as I head down the hall toward the library. Even more than my bedroom, this room is my sanctuary, a quiet place filled with so many thoughts it inspires my own thinking. Before I even get settled, though, I hear the door open.

I whirl toward the sound. "No, I'm not coming back. I'm finished with breakfast."

"Well, I assumed as much," Alice says. "I just wanted to know if you've seen Oliver."

My face flushes. "No, I haven't. Sorry. Maybe he's sleeping in. It's Sunday."

"I'll check with Marcus or someone in the guest house. Thank you, Tess."

"Sure." I don't know why she's thanking me. I didn't help her.

It's just as well Oliver is asleep. He's turned out to be pretty useless at most things. Except prepping me for tests. His memory turns him into a human deck of flash cards, and he's pretty adept at figuring out from classes what each of my teachers is likely to ask. As for the rest of it, sometimes it seems like he's never been around other people. Anyway, I have someone else in mind for what I need.

I pull my phone from my pocket and speed dial Derek.

11

A grizzled, battle-scarred marine leaped from the parapet, pulled an automatic assault rifle from the sheath slung on his back as he somersaulted in mid-air, and started firing at the alien invader before his boots hit the ground.

Derek Hamblin thumbed the game controller furiously until the alien's head exploded in a shower of red and green gore. He frowned. The effect wasn't quite what he wanted, so he wheeled closer to the desk and traded the controller for a keyboard. As he typed commands, his phone rang. Not taking his eyes off the monitor, his fingers groped until they found the phone and he answered.

"It's your dime."

"What?" a woman's voice said. "What do you mean?"

"You called me. Speak."

"But why a dime?"

The questions messed up Derek's focus on writing code for the video game. He shoved the keyboard away.

"Pay phones. You probably never heard of them, whoever you are."

"I thought pay phones cost a quarter."

"Yeah, well before that they cost a dime. And I bet they cost a nickel once upon a time. It's still money, and your wasting mine. I've got work to do, so get to the point."

"Derek? This is Derek, right? It's Tess."

Derek sat up so quickly the pizza slice resting in his lap flew onto the floor.

"Shit," he mumbled, brushing pepperoni and sauce off his jeans, then remembered he still held the phone. "No, not you. Did you say Tess? Tess Barrett?"

"Do you know any other girls named Tess?" She paused long enough to make him feel dumb, but not long enough for him to answer. "Are you busy right now?"

"Well, yeah," he said slowly, "but I could probably take a break from what I'm doing. What do you need?"

"Your help. Can you come over?"

Derek's thoughts kicked into overdrive. This was potentially dangerous territory. He'd only known Tess for a week or two, and what a wild ride it had been. First, the girl was exotically beautiful in spite of the disfiguring scar on her face from the car accident that killed her parents. Second, she was as rich as a Kardashian—hell, she probably had more money than all of them put together. Third, her dad had been a game theory and AI genius and one of Derek's idols growing up. As a kid, Derek had played one of James Barrett's earliest video games, *Street vs. Vert*, for hours, and in one of life's strange coincidences Barrett had hired Derek to work at Mondohard, potentially saving him from a life of cybercrime. Fourth, Travis Barrett had recruited Derek on the sly for some spy stuff that he and his niece were involved in, and people were getting killed. Not to mention that Travis was Derek's boss's, boss's boss, the big cheese at MondoHard now that James Barrett was no longer around. All of these were reasons to tread lightly.

"Where's Oliver?" Derek said, thinking of Reason #5.

"Not here," she said. "And he can't help with this anyway. This is more up your alley. So, can you come?"

Derek knew that somehow he'd regret it, but he wasn't so stupid he'd turn down a personal appeal from Tess Barrett.

"Sure. Why not?"

"When you get here, text me, and I'll give you the code for the gate."

"Give me thirty minutes."

Derek disconnected, scrubbed his front teeth with a finger and wiped it on his jeans, ran his fingers through his hair, and grabbed his leather jacket. Not bothering with the elevator, he took the stairs down to the garage level where he'd parked, and retrieved his motorcycle. It roared up the ramps two levels and out onto the relative brightness of the street, where he weaved through light Sunday traffic to the freeway. There, he let the bike have a little more throttle.

Derek couldn't think of anyone his age who relished going to the office on a Sunday, but he loved his job. He'd lucked into it. Or maybe he'd been recruited from the start. He wasn't sure. He only knew that James Barrett had found him in an obscure chat room for hackers. Derek had barely made it through high school, not because he wasn't smart, but because he was bored. Two years of part-time community college and working a crappy job as a grocery store bagger to pay for it had convinced him that school wasn't his thing; computers were. And Derek had found he was good at hacking. Barrett had let Derek know that he'd figured out Derek's best hacks and found tracks leading back to him.

Derek hadn't believed him at first, but Barrett had dropped enough clues to convince him. That could have meant jail time. Derek hadn't hacked just any sites; he'd gone for the big trophies, the secure sites that would cement his rep. But instead of threatening Derek, Barrett had offered him a job, letting him know that Derek's skills were worth far more to a company like MondoHard than a reputation in the hacker world. Barrett had not only given him a chance to turn his "gray hat" hacking to white, he'd put him on one of the company's video game teams and had given him free rein. Yeah, it was a cushy job for someone like Derek—all the free pizza he could eat, and the chance to work with the most sophisticated computer equipment in the world.

His thoughts took him right to the tall iron gate of the address his GPS app projected onto the heads-up display on his helmet visor. He turned into the drive, pulled up next to a keypad mounted on a post and sent Tess a text letting her know he'd arrived. Seconds later, a six-digit code appeared on his heads-up screen. He entered it on the keypad, and the heavy gate trundled off to one side behind a stone wall. Derek gave the bike some throttle and eased through slowly before the gate had cleared the drive.

The drive sloped downhill through dense woods toward a sharp switchback. Using the brakes instead of the accelerator, Derek let gravity take over, but he hadn't gone more than a hundred yards before a large, black SUV roared up around the curve from below. Though narrow, the drive was wide enough for the big vehicle to get past, so Derek let the bike drift toward the right shoulder. Instead of passing, the SUV swung in a tight arc with a screech of brakes so it angled across the road, completely blocking Derek's path.

He braked to a stop and watched two men get out either side of the SUV and move to opposite shoulders of the drive as they approached him. Dressed in casual but nice slacks and sport shirts topped with windbreakers, they appeared friendly but alert. Both were solidly built, but the man on Derek's left was a head shorter than his partner. They moved with confidence and projected an aura of authority like a strong aftershave. They reminded Derek of cops or military.

"Can we help you?" the smaller man said.

"Just here visiting a friend," Derek said.

"Sure you're not lost? This is a private lane, and no one here is expecting visitors."

They drew closer until they were ninety degrees apart and equidistant from where he sat.

"Look, man, I was invited, okay?" He raised one of his hands off the handlebars to reach for his wallet.

The smaller man barked a command. "Don't move! Leave your hands where they were."

Derek froze then realized they couldn't see who he was behind his visor. He lifted his hand.

"I said, "Don't move!'" the man yelled.

Before Derek could blink, they both had semiautomatic pistols aimed at his head.

12

Travis fumed in frustration, immobilized by indecision. He was used to a chain of commands, a world in which some men gave orders and others obeyed, a hierarchy that was both rational and logical. Tess didn't listen to reason. She let her instincts and emotions rule her actions, and that was dangerous. He didn't know how to relate to that world, the microcosm of a teenage girl, one that held its own dangers as she and her peers struggled to find their place as young adults. And Tess had been pushed harder, further than many of her friends and classmates, forced to face the hardships of losing her parents, dealing with a disability, and taking on adult responsibilities in the outside world.

He shook his head. That didn't excuse her walking out like that. At least he was trying to communicate, trying to find a way to connect with her and keep her safe at the same time. She needed to meet him halfway. Determined now, he swung away from the island, and looked up as Alice strode into the kitchen with her usual purposefulness. She stopped abruptly as their eyes locked, and he froze in place.

"Better not," Alice said. "If you were thinking of going after her, that is. Sometimes, you just have to give her space."

"I don't know how to reach her," Travis said. "She needs to know how much danger she's in. Why it's important to beef up security."

"She knows. You must have heard her practicing with Yoshi last night."

Travis wondered how Alice knew he'd worked out the night before. Not much got by her.

"Then she needs to let me protect her."

"You can't guarantee her safety, Travis. No one can. You could assign a dozen men to guard her at all times, and you know there would still be a chance someone could get through those defenses."

"I wish I could get through her defenses." Travis grumbled. "Where was she, anyway?"

"In the library, where else? I was looking for Oliver. Have you seen him this morning?"

Travis shook his head. "He's probably sleeping in."

"I asked earlier when the men were here for breakfast. No one's seen him."

Alice crossed the kitchen as she spoke and disappeared into the mudroom. Travis heard the sound of the door to the garage being opened then shut. A moment later, Alice stepped back into the kitchen, her mouth a grim line.

"One of the cars is gone," she said. "I distinctly told him last night that it was too dangerous for him to go home until you find out more about this attempt on Tess's life."

Travis shrugged. "He's a big boy. And I guess you can't expect him to give up a personal life unless you offer to pay him to stay."

She folded her arms. "You sang a different tune a minute ago when it came to Tess."

"Because she *is* different." Travis ticked off his fingers. "She's not even eighteen yet; she's my responsibility; and someone just tried to kill her. And, she's family."

"Well, since he's an employee," Alice said, "I expect him to honor our requests, if nothing else." She looked up at the sound of the door to the garage closing, and waited expectantly.

Luis walked into the kitchen, his gaze panning from Alice to Travis and back. "Are you talking about Oliver? I couldn't help overhearing."

Alice nodded. "We are. Have you seen him?"

"He left last night," Luis said, heading for the stove. "Are those pancakes? Pretty sure he went home."

Alice's eyebrows rose. "And you didn't think to say anything?"

Luis turned to glance at her then grabbed a plate and spatula. He spoke as he filled the plate with a stack of pancakes and several strips of bacon. "No, why? Was he not supposed to leave?"

"What with the potential danger..."

"Beg pardon, ma'am," Luis said as he turned and made for a stool next to Travis, "but Miss Barrett's attacker is deader than a dinosaur, no thanks to me. And Oliver's a grown-up. Weird, but an adult."

"So I've been told," Alice said, icicles dripping from the words. "Well, since I'm not needed here, I have other tasks to attend to, like getting Oliver back here to help Tess with homework. Unless one of you wants to fill in? I didn't think so. Excuse me."

She stalked out.

"I'd watch your back around here from now on," Travis murmured.

Luis stopped chewing and stared at him. "What was I supposed to do? Put the kid under house arrest?"

Travis grinned. "You thought last night was tough? Alice is tougher."

"Shit," Luis groaned. "Just what I need."

Travis stood. "Enjoy your breakfast. I have to go make new security arrangements at the high school."

13

Startled and a little unnerved by the sight of two large semiautomatics pointing at him, Derek slowly lowered his hand back to the handlebar. "Shit, man, no reason to get your undies in a bunch."

"Who are you?" the shorter man said.

"If you'd have let me, I was reaching for my ID. Derek Hamblin. I work for MondoHard."

With a nod from the short guy, Derek raised the visor on his helmet, and slowly dug in a pocket of his leather jacket for his wallet. He flipped the wallet open and held it up. Neither man moved or relaxed their aim.

"What are you doing here?" the big guy asked.

"Barrett's niece called me and asked me to come over and help with some project."

The men exchanged glances. The taller one spoke again. "You the one who's been helping Travis on the inside?"

"Yeah, that's me. Do you mind?"

The men exchanged glances again and nodded toward Derek.

"Sorry, kid," the smaller one said. "I'm Barney. That's Fred. We've heard you've been a real asset."

Fred gave Barney a narrow-eyed glance. "Maybe thank you, even, for helping find our boss in that abandoned mine a couple weeks ago. We kind of like the guy."

"Right," Barney said. "Didn't mean to scare you, but we're being extra cautious around here right now."

"No one told us Miss Barrett was expecting you," Fred said. He raised his gaze up the hill behind Derek. "She give you the code?"

Neither of the men had lowered their guard or their weapons.

Derek nodded and swallowed. "What's going on?"

"If you don't mind, I'm gonna double-check your invite," Barney said, ignoring Derek's question.

Fred kept a watchful eye on Derek as Barney turned and spoke into a cell phone. When he faced Derek again, his expression was more relaxed.

"She confirms you're okay to come on down to the house. She'll meet you at the front door. You can park in the circle as long as you don't block anyone."

Barney spun around and walked back to the SUV. Fred gave Derek another long look before he turned, headed for the open driver's side door and climbed in.

He started the engine, backed up in a semi-circle and leaned out the window. "Nice bike."

Derek let out the breath he didn't know he'd been holding.

14

I hear the rumble of an engine that sounds nothing like the half-dozen vehicles kept on the property, so I open the front door just wide enough to slip through, and wait. The engine dies with a sputter, and footsteps approach me up the stone steps, Derek's scent reaching me long before he does. I drink it in, getting notes of orange blossom and floral tea, rose wood and water lily, musk and cedar. I know this because Yoshi spent hours drilling it into my head when I was trapped in bed after the accident. Together, they add up to the clean scent of a cologne that is sufficiently woodsy and musky to be masculine, but citrusy enough to be fresh, not cloying.

My mind processes all this unconsciously in a blink while the rest of me tingles and goes a little weak at the knees.

"Tess?" he says. "You okay?"

I'd forgotten how much I like the timber of his voice, calm and soothing, a half-octave lower than Oliver's. He touches my shoulder lightly, unexpectedly, and I feel the warmth of his body close to me. I try to hide the shiver that runs through me then realize he must be asking about last night and won't think the tremor odd.

"Yeah, I'm fine. Did Barney say something? Those guys weren't even supposed to see you coming. I should have known better."

"It's okay, Tess. They're doing their job. Protecting you. I'm glad, actually."

"Thanks." I shrug, suddenly embarrassed, and turn to the door. "Come on in."

He follows me in, and I lead him to the library. Now I notice the smell of pizza and a distinctly masculine odor, not the guy's gym locker or funky sneaker kind, just clean sweat.

"Wow," he says. "You actually live here?"

"Well, yeah." I can't keep a bite out of my voice. I'm sick of defending my circumstances. My family's rich—get over it. "Something wrong with that?"

"Nothing wrong with it," he says matter-of-factly. "Just seeing what my stock options are going to buy me some day."

"You get stock options?" It's my turn to sound surprised.

"Sure. Based on performance. I perform."

He sounds pleased with himself. Maybe it's time to bring him down a notch.

"Okay, big shot, I have a problem. Let's see if you can solve it."

"What is it?"

"Someone tried to kill me last night. I want to know why."

"Wait. You're kidding, right?"

So, Mr. Cool can be shocked after all. "Do I look like I'm kidding? You think I asked you here to hang out?"

"Sure, why not?" His tone is cocky, but after a pause it turns serious. "So what happened?"

"Okay, but first you have to pinky-swear not to breathe a word to anyone outside this house." I hold out my hand, pinky extended.

"I won't ask why," he says. "After seeing what I've seen the past couple of weeks..."

He hooks my little finger with his and gives my hand a shake. His touch is electric. I force myself to ignore it and catch him up on the events at the dance. Just talking about it makes my heart race and my stomach clench.

"You took the guy down," he says when I finish.

He doesn't believe me, I can tell. A flash of anger burns through me like lightning.

"Yeah, well I'm here, and he's dead. Shot, right in front of me."

"It's not like you *saw* him get killed, right?"

"I have four other senses, Derek. I didn't ask you over to be an asshole. I get enough of that around here."

Derek doesn't have a snappy comeback this time. "Sorry. I don't get it. Why isn't this news? You're rich—I mean important. This should be all over social media, if not TV."

"Travis hushed it up. Got the school principal to make up a story. And they did a good job of crowd control while they cleaned it up. That's why I made you pinky-swear."

He's quiet for a moment. "You know this guy?"

"No, of course not! But Travis checked his fingerprints and found him in the military database. His name's Samuel Palmer."

"What, exactly, is it you want me to do?"

"Find out where he lived, who he knew. Find out why he tried to kill me."

I hear the exasperation in my voice and take a deep breath. Derek's already moving. I know where he's heading.

"Not that computer," I say. "We can use my father's office. It's more private."

"How did...?"

The question dies on his lips. I hear him follow me as I feel my way to the right bookshelf, reach back, place my hand on the biometric scanner and lean in so another scanner can read my irises—they're still good for something. The panel beeps, and I key in a code on the keypad. The lock clicks, and the entire section swings open when I push on the shelf. He sucks in a breath as he follows me inside.

"I assume you've got a good Internet connection," he says as he brushes past me.

"Fiber optic cable in the house, and a T-1 connection, I think, to the outside world. All encrypted."

"Yeah, that'll do." The desk chair creaks and the keyboard clicks busily.

I find the couch where I used to curl up and watch my father work, and sit down.

"So, what else do you know about this guy?" he says as he types.

I tell him the few details I was able to get from Travis earlier. For a long time, there's no sound except the occasional click of the mouse or random patterns of keystrokes.

"What are you doing?" I ask finally.

"Reading." It comes out more of a grunt, as if that's a painful undertaking.

I let a little more time pass then say, "Mind telling me what you're reading?"

The clicking goes on for a bit before he speaks. "Everybody's got an online presence, right? Social media, subscription services, bank accounts, that sort of thing. Mostly social media. You said your guy was from Alaska originally. So I've been looking for a social media profile and handle that fits."

I'm so frustrated I want to pound an answer out of him. "And...?"

"Oh, I found him. Sam Palmer. Calls himself 'Sled Dog.'"

This is better. I feel a flicker of excitement, but don't want to get my hopes up.

"Have you figured out where he lives? I mean where he stayed last before...before..."

Like a punch to the gut, the realization hits me that the man who came to kill me was a living, breathing person just like me. No, not just like me. Nothing like me.

"I know what you mean," Derek says. "Later. That could take time, if it's even possible."

"Okay. So what are you doing now?"

"From what you told me, Sam had a lot of gear with him, military-grade gear. He got it from somewhere, and if he was smart, he bought it in a way that it couldn't be traced back to him."

The keys clack furiously for a moment then he goes on. "It also makes sense that he acted for someone else, either as a hired gun or an employee. Mercenary sounds more like it, especially judging from his online posts. To find a job like that, he probably trolled the Dark Web. That's where I am now, trying to follow him. And...there he is. Gotcha."

"Wait. How do you know it's him?"

"How often do you change your password online? How often do you change your user name? As much as people say they want to protect their privacy and security online, they're a little lazy and self-absorbed. Think up a user name that you like and you'll keep it. Come up with a strong password you can remember, and you probably won't change it. I found '$led D0g2'—same name spelled with special characters—in a chat room on ordnance. No buying and selling, of course, just chat. But if you give me some time, I'll figure out who he spent time chatting with. Eventually, I'm pretty sure I can figure out where he got the supplies for the job, and who hired him."

"Wouldn't it be easier if you had his computer?"

"Well, yeah, but unless this guy is a total moron he should have been using a VPN which would make it very tough."

I frown. I know a VPN is a virtual private network, but what bothers me is Derek's seeming reluctance.

"I thought you were good at this stuff," I say. "What's the problem?"

"The problem?" He sounds surprised, defensive. "This isn't like following a trail of bread crumbs or a stream back to its source. But for your information I'm not just good, I'm the best. Your father wouldn't have hired me otherwise."

"What? My father hired you?" Now his comment about stock options makes sense. "So, if you're the best, why can't you trace Sam's computer?"

Derek starts muttering. I can't tell if he's talking to me or himself, but I hear phrases like, "…maybe tap into his social media account…," "…thinks this is a walk in the park…," "find who hired him? Hmm, or find his computer?" The muttering stops as his keystrokes gain speed, the sound punctuated with brief pauses as he switches to a new web page or strategy of attack, I imagine.

After several minutes he says, "So, coffee would be nice."

"I'm sorry. Did you just ask me to fetch you coffee?"

"It would help. Unless you can make me a twenty-ounce triple mocha, no whip."

"Fine. I'll see what I can scrounge up. But this better be worth it."

15

I'm usually a cheerful guy. But nothing about the past few weeks had been close to usual. I don't think I'd be alone in describing life in the Barrett household as very *un*usual, which is one of those words that may or may not have been first used ("invented" isn't quite right) by Shakespeare, though he would have been somewhere around fifteen at the time. Some people don't know it, but about 1,700 words in the English language are ascribed to Shakespeare. He *usually* (clever, right?) created adverbs from adjectives, verbs from nouns, or put the German *un*, meaning "not," in front of some other word, like real or dress, to create "unreal" and "undress."

I like Shakespeare. His comedies, especially, put me in a good mood. The unusual circumstances, however, made me grumpy and paranoid. I'm not what you'd call a Type A personality, but I like a little excitement now and then, a little spice in life. This job, though, had me dodging fists and bullets. The bullets had missed, but several fists had not, and they were a lot slower. I wondered if it was only a matter of time before... No, that was not a thought I wanted to dwell on.

My place in the U-District is a first-floor studio that looked small and sad compared to Tess's house, or even the guesthouse where I could have slept if I hadn't bolted the night before. I felt badly about leaving the way I did, but there hadn't been any point in staying. Now, however, I felt guilty, as if Tess might have needed me for something. Not likely. She'd been proving over and over that she needed me for very little. So I was surprised to get a call not from Alice berating me for taking off against her orders, but from Tess.

"Where are you?" she said without preamble.

"At home. Why?"

"You need to get here quick."

Annoyance chased my guilt away. "Again, why?"

"Uh, because you work for me. That good enough for you?"

Irritation morphed into something bordering on anger, but she had a point. I sighed. "Where's 'here?'"

She rattled off an unfamiliar address that my weird memory automatically catalogued. Before I could ask any more questions, she ended the call.

I got the car and headed for the freeway, exiting just south of downtown toward the bridge to West Seattle. I turned off before I reached it, down into an area mixed with small industrial plants, material wholesalers, junkyards and warehouses. Ten minutes later I found myself cruising through a neighborhood that looked way more iffy than mine.

Homelessness in the city had gotten so bad that crime was rampant in neighborhoods where vagrants panhandled during the day. The area around the university was one. They stayed and committed crimes at night. Crime in some neighborhoods, though, was just plain bad regardless. The neighborhood rolling past the car windows looked like the grin of a gap-toothed meth addict, some houses solid but worn and in need of maintenance, others derelict, with cardboard taped over broken windows, yellowed peeling paint, blue tarps covering leaky roofs, or simply absent. Weedy, overgrown yards, rusted cars up on blocks, trash on the sidewalk and broken windows gave the area its character, and gave me the shivers.

I spotted the address Tess had given me and pulled over to the curb. Some of the numbers tacked to the side of the house dangled precariously from rotted siding, but they matched. A shiny, new-looking motorcycle parked at the curb looked as out of place as the expensive car I drove. It was a safe bet that Tess hadn't ridden the bike here on her own, which made me wonder who'd usurped my position and given her the ride. I also wondered who the hell lets a blind girl ride a motorcycle, even as a passenger, and especially to a neighborhood like this. Indignant as well as curious, I parked and walked up to the front door. The screen door hung askew on one hinge. I opened it far enough to knock, and waited. No one answered.

Male and female voices arguing inside the house next door strengthened to a shouting match. A man stepped onto the stoop just as a shriek erupted from inside and something crashed against the doorjamb.

The man ducked reflexively. "Fucking bitch! Who's gonna pay for that? Huh?"

"Not you," the invisible woman screamed. "You're a low-life loser with no fucking job!"

"You ever hit me with something, I'll mess you up good," he shouted. "You hear me?"

Despite the chill of a gray day, he wore a T-shirt. He raised a can of beer to his lips, and his Adam's apple bobbed as he took several swallows. He lowered his arm and belched, then turned my direction and saw me watching.

"What the fuck you looking at?" he said, eyes narrowing.

The woman inside shouted something.

"I ain't talking to you, bitch," he said loudly, never taking his eyes off me. "Nothing to see here, asshole. Go on about your business."

"Someone should teach you some manners," I said under my breath.

"What did you say?" He took a menacing step toward the edge of the stoop. Apparently, his hearing was better than I'd estimated.

"Nothing," I mumbled.

Finding Tess was more important than giving this cretin lessons in etiquette. I skipped down the steps and cut onto the grass to circle the house. In the backyard, I heard low voices coming from what looked like little more than a storage shed. Since I was trespassing, I approached it cautiously in case the homeowner was anything like the neighbor. The closer I got, though, the clearer it became that one of the voices belonged to Tess.

I peered through the cracked doorway into the dim interior. Inside the tiny space, a cot ran nearly the length of one side. A long table took up most of the other side, covered with a camp stove, canned and boxed foods, a couple of books and some magazines. Tess stood halfway down the aisle in the middle, her hand on the shoulder of someone I couldn't see seated at the table, a piece of plywood set on two sets of stacked milk crates. A laptop screen glowed on the table, lighting the seated figure's leather jacket. The motorcyclist, I presumed.

"Tess," I said. "What's going on?"

She started at the sound of her name and whirled to face me, hand rising to her heart. "Oliver, don't sneak up on people like that. You scared me."

The figure in front of the laptop turned. "Hey, man, what's up?"

"Derek," I said. "I wondered whose bike Tess rode in on. It's yours, right?"

He nodded.

"What the hell are you doing here, Tess? This neighborhood isn't safe."

"Derek wouldn't let anything happen to me."

Oh, so Derek was her protector now. "So, why am I here? Whose house is this? And who lives here in the shed?"

I took another quick look around and noticed that there wasn't even a bathroom. I wondered if whoever lived here had to go into the house to use the facilities.

"Duh," Tess said. "This is where Sam lived. You know, the guy who almost killed me?"

"Derek found this place?" I said, stepping inside. There was barely room. "How?"

"Digital wizardry." He lifted his hands off the keyboard and did a lame version of spirit fingers. "Get it?"

"Seriously?"

"I'm always dead serious when it comes to this stuff. You think it's easy finding someone who doesn't want to be found? Lucky for me this guy wasn't as good with computers as he was at blowing up school bathrooms."

"They were flash-bangs, FYI, and they almost accomplished what he intended. My ears are still ringing."

"Yeah, yeah, I know all about it." His gaze had already gone back to the laptop screen. "Tess told me."

I turned to her reflexively, forgetting she couldn't see. "So, what am I here for? You found the place, and you're mining his computer. What do you need me for?"

"Someone's a little cranky today," she said.

"Yeah, well, how'd *you* sleep?"

"How do you think, Oliver? Quit whining. You're here because we need a lookout. You saw how easy it was to sneak up on us. Derek needs another five or ten minutes, then you can take the laptop back to the house."

I frown. "Wait. What do you mean? What are you going to do?"

"Finish searching this place. Well, Derek will search; I'll decide if we should keep whatever he finds."

"Doesn't sound like much to do," I grumbled.

"Are you going to help us or not?"

"You're coming back to the house when you're done?"

"No, I thought I'd move in here."

From the amount of sarcasm dripping off her tongue, even I could tell that it was time to shut up.

"Okay, I'm going," I grumbled.

I turned and retraced my steps out into the backyard. But I hadn't gone ten yards when the sound of sirens stopped me. I cocked my head to listen. Still some distance away, they grew steadily louder.

"Uh, guys?" I said loudly. "Hurry it up in there. I don't think you have much time."

Without waiting for a response, I hurried around the side of the house to the street. Next door, the porch was empty, and loud, angry voices reverberated from inside. Apparently the man who'd confronted me had taken the argument back inside. The sirens sounded a lot closer now, and I nervously glanced toward the back yard and down the street toward the wailing sound now so loud it hurt my ears.

Two cop cars roared around the corner and raced down the block, screeching to a stop in the street. Still no sign of Tess and Derek, and too late for me. My stomach twisted into a knot, and my hands started to rise in surrender as an officer bounded out of each patrol car and headed straight for me.

16

Already weary, and flustered from his attempts to smooth things over with Principal Jenkins, Travis parked outside the front of the house and stalked up the steps. Jenkins had hovered the whole time Travis oversaw the crew installing metal detectors at each entrance to the high school, and had taken whining to a whole new level. Travis's black mood wouldn't do anyone any good, least of all himself, so he tried to summon the calm rationale he'd used to stay alive on his missions overseas.

He suddenly understood how so many soldiers had come back from seemingly endless tours in Afghanistan or the Middle East with PTSD. As much as he hated seeing Tess in the line of fire, he felt most alive when confronting the enemy. "Normal" life seemed so tame, so uneventful, so unimportant compared to the life-or-death experiences of a combat soldier. Some guys couldn't rationalize killing another human being, couldn't deal with the way it changed them, stained their souls. Others were so shocked by the horrors of war that they actually lost their minds, or at least a piece of them.

What Travis realized he found most difficult was the balancing act between civilized man of peace and savage soldier of war. The attack on Tess had been a reminder that he needed to maintain his soldier's psyche even while he presented a facade of civility to all those around him. Only vigilance would keep Tess safe.

He'd barely hung up his coat in the large closet in the foyer when Alice hurried across the floor, flat heels clacking on the marble tile floor, a grim expression on her face.

"What's wrong?" he asked.

"She's gone." Alice stopped a few feet away and peered up at him. "I feel terrible."

Surprise sapped his reasoning. He couldn't make sense of her statement. "Tess? What do you mean, 'gone?'"

"I'm so sorry, Travis, it's all my fault. You'll have my letter of resignation before the end of the day."

Reminding himself of his promise of a few moments ago, he took a deep breath, and waved a hand in the air. "Nonsense. Whatever happened, you know I won't accept it."

He started for the hallway. "Tell me about it while I get coffee."

Alice fell in step beside him, taking two for every one of his long strides. "I thought she was in the library studying, so I turned my attention to some maintenance issues I've been neglecting. A short time later, I remembered something I wanted to ask her, but she wasn't in the library or her room. I checked everywhere. She's not here. And she's not answering texts or her phone. I should have paid more attention."

"You can't watch her every second, Alice. No one can. This isn't your fault. If it's anyone's, it's mine. I don't know how to get through to her. I'm not cut out for parenting."

"You just haven't had enough practice yet," she said, following him into the kitchen. "Even then, no one gets it right all the time."

"Why didn't you call me?"

"You have enough on your plate, Travis. We can't go running to you every time there's a problem."

"If you didn't want to bother me, why isn't Marcus handling this? He's supposed to be heading up the team."

Alice nodded. "When I couldn't find Tess anywhere in the house, I called the guest house and asked for him. He wasn't there."

"Marcus has gone AWOL, too?" Travis nearly exploded.

"Apparently, it's his day off."

Travis poured himself a cup of coffee, and gathered himself. More calmly, he said, "I don't like it when my people go off the reservation without telling me."

"Tess doesn't like him," Alice said after a moment.

"Tess doesn't like anyone."

"That's not true. I'll admit, she's not the easiest person to get along with, but besides the usual teen angst over the right group of kids to be friends with, Tess is a pretty good judge of character. I don't mean to tell you your business, Travis, but I don't like him, either."

He sighed. "Fine. Marcus is no teddy bear. But he's the only man on the team besides Red with a spotless military record, and he was decorated twice in Iraq. All the others have questionable backgrounds, yet I trust them all. You like them more?"

"Whether I do or don't is beside the point. Frankly, I do like them all better, and I trust them more, too. Don't ask me why. It's just a feeling."

Uneasiness settled in his stomach like a lead ball. He took another deep breath.

"Your concerns are noted. And I'm well aware of how Tess feels about him."

Travis had his own uneasy feelings about Marcus, but he'd never actually caught Marcus doing something he shouldn't.

Then again, Marcus *had* killed Kenny, and Travis had only Marcus's word that Kenny had been a mole and was about to kill Tess and Marcus if Marcus hadn't acted quickly and shot him. Travis hadn't been there, so he couldn't dispute it, but he still couldn't believe that Kenny had turned on them. For all his faults, Kenny had seemed the most loyal, the most eager to learn, and the least interested in money of all the members of the team. Travis still missed him, still mourned the loss of a good soldier.

He shook off the memories and vowed to keep a closer eye on Marcus. The sound of the door to the garage opening and closing made him turn in anticipation. Maybe Tess was back. His face fell as heavy footsteps headed through the mudroom toward the kitchen.

Barney poked his head through the doorway, looked at them both, then stepped into the room and addressed Alice. "Yoshi said you're looking for Tess. She bugged out of here, oh, close to an hour ago."

"How?" Travis said sharply.

Barney glanced up in surprise. "That kid Derek showed up on a bike. Said he was invited. Came in, stayed ten, fifteen minutes, and they left. I assumed you told them it was okay." Barney's face flushed and he shifted his weight as he realized his mistake. "You know, him being Derek and all. I guess that wasn't the case."

Travis tamped down his anger. "You didn't know. But don't assume. You should have checked with me. Any idea where they were headed?"

Barney shook his head. "No clue. But I got the impression they didn't plan on being gone for long."

Travis pondered a moment until he was struck by a thought. "A bike? How'd she...?"

"Not just any bike, boss. A Ducati. You must be paying the kid too much."

"Ah, right... Motorcycle. Thanks, Barney."

"Sure. Sorry about not clearing it with you. Won't happen again."

Travis nodded as Barney left, his mind already churning with his next thoughts.

"I'll kill her," he muttered with a glance at Alice. "Well, you know what I mean."

"You have no idea," Alice said.

"She needs to get her ass back here." Travis pulled out his phone. "I'll text Derek. Maybe that'll work."

He quickly typed out a message. Almost as soon as he sent it, his phone chimed with an incoming text.

If you're wondering where your niece is, I've got tabs on her.

Travis frowned and checked the incoming phone number. He quickly texted back: WTF?!

Can't talk now. I'll explain later. Gotta go.

Travis glanced up and saw Alice raise her eyebrows.

"Derek?" she said.

No, Marcus."

Alice's eyes widened in surprise.

17

The only sound for several moments is the clacking of keys on a laptop. Then, from a distance, the whoop of a siren intrudes.

I feel a thrill run up my spine. Part of it is adrenaline, the rush that began the instant I sat on the soft leather seat of Derek's motorcycle and heard the deep-throated burble from the exhaust when he started it up. The other part, though, is a tingling reaction to the light, citrusy scent of cologne mixed with a guy smell that is uniquely Derek. It's so unlike Oliver's clean, just-out-of-the-shower smell, and something about it excites me.

Not that I like Derek or anything. I barely know him. I mean I just met him a couple of weeks ago when someone infected a game app he'd developed with an AI virus that brainwashed kids. Like my sometime friend Matt Tsang. And Austin Dunn, the vice president's son, who was brainwashed into killing his own father. Almost.

I stand right behind Derek, leaning over his shoulder as if I'm peering at the laptop screen, but of course I can't see a thing. I gently rest my hand on his shoulder. The keystrokes don't hesitate. Heat rises off him, adding to my own rising body temperature, making my palms as moist as some other parts of me are getting. Maybe this is just a reaction to coming as close to death as I did yesterday, but I don't care. I feel more alive than I have since the accident.

"Uh, guys?" Oliver's voice drifts in from outside. "Hurry it up in there. I don't think you have much time."

His voice breaks the spell, and I straighten. Oliver is such a Boy Scout compared to Derek.

"Finding anything?" I ask Derek.

"Oh, there's plenty of stuff here to work with. But I don't have time to hack into all his files or track his movements online. We'll have to take this with us."

The chair creaks on the floor, and I move aside a half-step to let him up. The shed is tiny, with barely enough room for the two of us. I kind of like it, but I doubt he thinks of me the way I was just thinking about him, so I stand still, careful not to bump into him.

"Did you look around to see if there's anything else here that could tell us more about him?"

"I rifled through his stuff. I'd like to go through it more thoroughly, but we don't have time, babe. We need to head out."

He's right. The sirens sound closer now. While I don't think they're coming for us—no one knows we're here, and I doubt anyone would care—I don't need anyone else snooping around my life. It's bad enough that I'm practically a prisoner in my own home.

He called me "babe," I just realize. Normally, that would peg my #MeToo meter coming from someone who is *not* my significant other. But from Derek it sounded natural, and my internal temperature rises even more.

"Yeah," I say, "let's get out of here."

He places the laptop in my hands, then puts one hand on my shoulder and the other in the small of my back, fingertips barely making contact. Gently, he turns me and guides me out the door onto the grass. It's much cooler out here, which I need before I combust spontaneously.

"Hang on," he murmurs.

The door shuts and the padlock that secured it snaps back into place. His arm wraps around my shoulder, and I fall into step with him, feet swishing through the grass as he guides me to the street. The sirens echo all around us now, and are so loud my ears hurt. Abruptly, they stop.

"Whoops," he murmurs, and steers me in a slightly different direction.

"What?" I say, nervous now.

"Cops are headed straight for Oliver," he says in low tones. "He looks like a scarecrow, arms up—no, a signaler doing semaphore."

He suddenly tickles me, and I giggle loudly, nearly dropping the laptop. I wriggle away, but he pulls me in tighter, laughing along with me.

"Hey!" I say when he pokes me in the ribs again, prompting another giggle. "What's that for? Stop it."

"You're doing great," he murmurs. "Almost there. And..."

I hear a conversation not far away as he keeps walking me, but I can't make out what they're saying. One of the voices sounds like Oliver's. They both go silent.

Derek pulls me to a stop. "Made it," he says in a normal voice.

I feel my face go from smile to scowl. "What are you talking about?"

"The cops, babe. I wanted you to act normal so they wouldn't hassle us."

"Normal? Tickling someone you barely know is normal for you?"

"Worked, didn't it? They didn't give us a second look."

"Where did they go?"

"Oliver directed them next door, where we heard that couple fighting. Remember? Anyway, cops are inside dealing with the neighbors, so we can split."

I hear someone approaching.

"Whew," Oliver says. "That was close. I thought they were going to arrest me."

"Why?" Derek says. "For standing there?"

"More like standing there looking like a dweeb," I mutter. I thrust the laptop at Oliver. "Here, take this."

"Okay, okay. No reason to get nasty. See you back at the house?"

"Maybe," I say. "Or maybe Derek will take me for a ride."

Derek places a helmet in my hands. I put it on and fasten the strap under my chin. He takes my hand and places it on the seat. I swing a leg over and straddle it. Suddenly, everything feels all wrong, and I don't know why. Derek climbs on the bike in front of me, and I wrap my arms around his waist, thinking furiously, trying to figure out what's bugging me. Just as Derek kicks the bike into gear and pulls away from the curb, I figure it out.

I smell coconut.

18

The cops had nearly given me a heart attack, but when I realized someone had called them about the disturbance next door, not us, I'd pointed them in the right direction. Just in time, too, since Tess and Derek had chosen that moment to appear. Laughing and talking as if they didn't have a care in the world, they'd headed straight for Derek's pasta rocket. I'd joined them as soon as the cops had gone to check on the domestic disturbance, only to be abused by Tess and handed a laptop to take back to the house.

Errand boy. Flunky. Lapdog. Lapdog with a laptop. On the drive back, I thought of a dozen other labels I could stick to my forehead or pin on my back. But why berate myself any more than necessary? Tess was doing a fine job; she didn't need my help. I'd had this job for only a couple of weeks, and already it was getting old. Tess said, "Jump," and I was supposed to sweetly ask, "Would you like a double-twisting flip with that?" Maybe the close call the night before had something to do with my bad mood, but it wasn't about to get better.

I stopped at the gate blocking the drive, keyed in my new security code, and let the scanner read my facial features. The security feed had already sent an alert and video to anyone in the house who was paying attention before the big gate rumbled aside. I drove through, and snaked down the long drive to the six-bay garage attached to the main house. One of the doors automatically opened when it recognized the car I drove. I pulled in, and stuffed the laptop in my backpack before getting out.

Alice stood inside the door from the house, lips pressed together in a grim line.

She crooked a finger. "My office, Oliver."

She turned and marched through the mudroom into the hall outside the kitchen before I had a chance to protest. I followed as enthusiastically as a little kid who senses a spanking coming. By the time I entered her office she'd already turned to face me from behind her desk.

She crossed her arms. "Did you once stop to think of the repercussions of your actions last night?"

I opened my mouth, then stopped to do what she accused me of not doing. "What? No one needed me, so I went home."

"Did it not occur to you that by leaving you could put Tess in greater jeopardy?"

I frowned. "No. How?"

"Don't you think the people trying to kill Tess would do anything to get to her, including using you?" She waved a hand. Her eyes narrowed, and she went on, voice fierce. "For a bright young man, Oliver, you can be awfully obtuse sometimes. It's my job to protect that girl."

"I understand that," I said.

"What you don't seem to understand," she interjected quickly, "is that it's your job, too. Just as much as mine or Travis's or Fred's or Luis's. You're responsible for that girl's life while you're in her employ, Oliver, and I will *not* have you take that responsibility cavalierly in the least. Is that clear?"

My face flushed and I rocked back on my heels under the onslaught. When I could make my mouth do more than open and close like a fish, I said, "Perfectly."

She stared at me, then her jaw unclenched. "Good. In the future, when I make a suggestion, I advise you to take it. Now, as soon as we figure out where Tess is and get her home, I want you to make sure she's caught up on homework. And, if possible, get her started on her essays."

I caught myself before I let on that I knew where Tess was, and said, "Essays?"

"Yes, yes," she said impatiently. "For her college applications."

"Ah." I nodded. "They're due by...?"

"November, if she wants early admission. January, for anything else." She cocked her head. "Any other questions, Oliver?"

"No, ma'am."

"And no reservations about what we discussed?"

I shook my head, afraid that if I spoke my subconscious might voice the hundred reservations that ran around playing hide-and-seek in my head.

She nodded. "Fine, then—"

Before she could dismiss me we both turned toward the door at the sound of raised voices, loud enough to be heard from another part of the house.

19

"You just don't get it!" I yell. "I nearly *died*!"

"That's the point," Travis growls.

Anger radiates from him like a heat lamp. I know I've pushed him too far, but I don't care. He has no clue how pissed I am, and he doesn't want to find out.

"I can't protect you if I don't know where the hell you are," he says. "Which is why you are officially grounded."

The notion is so absurd, I laugh, but it comes out high and shrill. "You're grounding me? That's a joke, right? I can't go anywhere *now* without someone driving me or someone following me. And you can't protect me anyway."

"Sir, it's my fault," Derek says quietly. "I didn't know that—"

"I'll get to you in a minute," Travis interrupts with a growl. "Tess, you can't just—"

My turn. "No, you can't keep me in a bubble! You really don't get it." I turn toward Derek's voice, his scent. "And I don't need any help from you. Stay out of this."

Feet shuffle next to me, and I sense Derek chafing. Again, I don't care.

"I *do* get it," Travis says, his voice low now, but fierce and slowly rising. "I've seen things, done things, that would turn your stomach, watched friends as well as enemies blasted into unrecognizable chunks of bloody flesh and bone by bombs, seen heads explode in a mist of red from sniper rounds, or taken clean off with a swipe of a sharp blade. I can't tell you how many times I've been within inches, a hair's breadth, of dying. Every time, all I wanted afterward was to go somewhere, do something reckless— jump out of airplane, swim with sharks—just to prove I was still alive. But that kind of thinking is what gets you killed. Until you get that through that thick head of yours, you're grounded."

"What's going on here?"

Great. Alice apparently has joined the party.

"You heard him," I say. "Travis is grounding me. For taking a ride on Derek's bike."

"That's right," Travis chimes in. "For life."

"See?"

"Travis," Alice says in her voice that brooks no dissent, "we can talk about it later. And Tess, telling people where you're going when you leave the house and what time you'll be back is just common courtesy. Otherwise, we worry."

"Right," I snort. "If I'd told you I was taking off with Derek to tool around on his bike, would you have let me go? Either of you?"

"*Hell*, no," Travis blurted.

"Well, perhaps not, under the circumstances," Alice says in a more measured tone. "But you see my point."

I sigh wearily, knowing I'm not going to win this argument. I take a little comfort in the fact that I did manage to sneak out of the house for a bit and feel the wind in my hair.

"Don't I always—well, except this once—tell you my plans?" I say.

"Normally, you do," Alice concedes. "But nothing in this household has been normal since—well, for quite some time. Now, don't you still have some homework? Oliver's here, ready to help."

"But—" Travis says.

Alice tut-tuts. "No buts. She needs to get to work."

I can see her wagging her finger at Travis in my mind. It doesn't cheer me up much.

"Fine. I'll do homework." As if I can go back to school tomorrow and pretend everything's normal. Alice is right; nothing's been the same since the accident.

"Thanks for bringing her back in one piece, Derek," Travis says sternly. "I'll see you at the office tomorrow."

"No," I blurt. "I need him. I asked him over to take a look at my laptop."

"What's wrong with it?" Travis says, sounding peeved. "I can probably fix it."

"If it was something *simple*, I would have asked you," I tell him—after asking Oliver, Alice Yoshi, or anyone else is what I don't say. "It's complicated, so I thought Derek could help. You shouldn't be mad at him. He didn't do anything wrong."

"He took you off the property. On the back of a motorcycle!" His voice rises until he's nearly shouting.

"He didn't know!" I stamp my foot. "Fine! I won't leave without telling someone."

"You won't leave, period! You're grounded! Why don't you get that?"

My face is burning hot, and I clench my hands into fists. *Breathe.*

"I'm going to the library to do homework," I say as sweetly as I can manage. "Oliver?"

"Right here."

I take a step toward his voice. "Are you coming, Derek?"

"Sure. Right behind you."

"Tess, I'm warning you..." Travis says.

"Let her go, Travis," Alice says softly.

I never thought I'd hear Alice take my side, but I'm sure she'll use it against me later. I don't care. Right now, I want to figure out who's trying to kill me.

I lead the guys to the library and find my way to an oak study table under a hanging lamp with a green glass shade, I can feel the warmth of the light even though I can't see the golden glow on the table. Oliver plunks a book bag or backpack on the table and rummages through it.

"Come on, man," Derek says from across the table. "Where's the laptop?"

"I've got it," Oliver says. "Don't get your undies in a bunch. Here."

The laptop exchanges hands in front of my face, and Derek settles into a chair, the laptop already making sounds of booting up. Oliver rustles some papers and opens a book on the table before sitting and pulling his chair up closer.

"Oh, crap, don't tell me," I say, finally remembering what I left undone on Friday before the homecoming festivities began with the parade in town, and then prepping for the dance on Saturday. The dance that never was. The unfairness of it hits me, and for just a moment I want to cry. But not in front of these two.

"Yeah, sorry," Oliver says, mistaking my momentary sadness for dismay at what's in front of me. "Chemistry."

It's not just chemistry. It's AP chemistry, and I have to ace it if I'm going to get into the schools on my list of college applications. Shit, another task yet undone. My shoulders sag.

"It's not that bad," Oliver says. "Come on. Here's your first question: What's N_2O_3?"

"Di-nitrogen trioxide," I say automatically.

"What happens when you combine it with H_2O?"

"Acid rain," Derek says before I can open my mouth.

"Hey, *man*," Oliver says, "stick to your job and let me do mine."

"What's the big deal? Everybody knows that."

"Guys, guys, chill," I say sharply. I face Oliver. "When you combine N_2O_3 with H_2O, the result is two HNO_2. And everybody does *not* know that, Derek. How come you do?"

"The 'rents," he mumbles. "Always going on about how they couldn't go outside and play when they were little kids because of acid rain."

One more piece of useless trivia stuck in my head. But it does make him seem more human somehow.

Oliver sighs. "If we can continue, tell me how to draw a Lewis diagram of the HNO_2 molecule, including any lone pairs of electrons."

Okay, this is what Jessup warned me about, what she was sure I couldn't do without eyes that work properly, like, see. But what isn't supposed to work—my mind's eye—still does. My forehead wrinkles in concentration, and I visualize the letters H, O, N, O spread out on a blank sheet of paper, and then tell Oliver where to connect the dots, so to speak.

Derek mutters something to himself, which Oliver apparently finds as distracting as I do.

"Wait," Oliver says. "What did you say?"

"Sor-*ry*," Derek says. "Didn't mean to disturb you. Stick to your job and let me do mine, okay?"

I didn't miss the jibe, but Oliver did, or else decided to let it go.

"No, really, what are you doing? You said something. What was it?"

"*Fed Ent, AOC, B. Evans*, one of those?"

"Yeah, that last one. What are you reading that from?"

I frown. This back-and-forth between the boys is getting us off track. "Uh, what's going on?"

"B. Evans," Oliver says, getting excited. "Don't you remember, Tess? From the ranch in Montana. The manager—Buck Evans."

"So-o-o?" I don't get the point.

"Derek," Oliver says. "Does AOC stand for Amalgamated Operating Companies?"

"Uh, yeah." He sounds surprised.

"Where did you find that?" Oliver presses.

"It's complicated."

I'm curious now. I want to find out where Oliver is going with this. "Come on, Derek. Everything about my life is complicated. Tell us."

"Okay, so I'm going through the cache on the laptop. Sam was using Tor to browse the Dark Web, so I can't track his browsing history. Instead, I'm getting clues from the cache to see what else he was up to. I found e-mail drafts to "Fed Ent," and in his trash I found a file with what looks like bank routing numbers and funds transfer instructions, also from Fed Ent. So, I did some research and found a company named Federated Enterprises, incorporated in the Cayman Islands. You still with me?"

I nod impatiently. "It's not *that* complicated."

"I'm giving you the Cliff Notes, babe," he says. I hear the cockiness in his voice. "So, I ran a search in another engine that does deep background checks for companies and the government, and found out that Federated Enterprises is owned by a company called AOC, and the only officer of the company I can find is B. Evans. Not much other information listed."

"Because it's a shell corporation," Oliver says. "Remember, Tess, we checked into it when we looked up the ranch. Derek, you're the one who found it."

"Well, yeah. I did." Now he sounds peeved. "I hacked into the ranch's system, too. But I don't recognize any of these names. Are you sure?"

"Of course I'm sure. A little hard for me to forget, like, anything. Maybe you just weren't paying attention."

"Hey, I always pay attention when I'm hacking. It's the reason I've never been caught."

"Well, maybe it's because I'm more thorough and looked up the shell companies that own the shell companies."

"Stop! *Both* of you." I raise my hands in frustration. "What is *wrong* with you two? You're not helping."

"Sorry," Derek mumbled.

Oliver is silent.

"Why don't you both go get us something to eat?"

"What about chemistry?" Oliver says.

"I'll work on something else while you're gone. Just get out of here, will you?"

"Yeah, sure." Oliver stands. "Whatever you want. Come on, Derek."

Derek doesn't move. "Tess, are you—?"

"Go on." I sigh. "I'll be fine. Just give me a minute."

Derek's chair scrapes on the hardwood floor, and two sets of footsteps head away from me. I lower my face into my hands and shake my head. *Men.* I prop my chin on my palms and my elbows on the table and sigh. I know there's some French homework that

I could do, a lesson online I could listen to. But my thoughts are whirling with all that's happened.

I don't get a chance to sort them out. Something changes in the room. I'm not alone, and my senses go on alert. There's no sound at first, just the barest movement of air, as if someone is walking toward me. Before the soft tread of footsteps reaches my ears, I catch a scent and stiffen. *Coconut.* I swallow the fear that sends my heart racing, the pulse loud in my ears.

I'm safe here, in my own home. Right?

"Have a nice ride?" The deep voice is rich, but filled with menace.

I take in a sharp breath. "Marcus," I choke out.

20

"So, what's the deal with you and Tess?" Derek said.

"There's no deal." I let the words float over my shoulder as I led the way to the kitchen. "I'm her personal assistant. You know that."

"Yeah, the seeing-eye guy. So, what's your problem?"

"What are you talking about? You're the one acting like a jerk."

"Me? What did I do? Look, you work for her, right? *And,* you say there's nothing between you two. So, what's it to you if I'm interested."

I whirled and faced him in the middle of the kitchen, and he almost bumped into me.

"You need to lay off, okay? She's been through a lot. She doesn't need the head trip right now of some Lothario with a hot bike putting the moves on her."

"How do you know what's good for her?" he said, hands clenched. "Maybe that's exactly what she needs. Something to take her mind off all this shit. She's a prisoner in her own home, man. Don't you think that sucks?"

"Of course it does. The difference is that I actually care about her as a person, not just a score." The words that came out of my mouth surprised me.

Derek's eyes flashed, and for a moment I thought he was going to take a swing at me. But he shifted his weight onto one foot and let the tension drain away.

"Look, you're an okay guy. I could even see us being friends, despite our differences. But I don't take orders from you. And Tess can make up her own mind."

I tried appealing to his logic. "She's not even eighteen. She nearly got killed last night. She's vulnerable. Taking advantage of her now would be like shooting fish in a barrel. You really want that notch on your belt?"

He gazed away for a moment, thinking. "Okay, truce. We help her figure out who this Sam character is, and who hired him to kill her. When she's out of danger, all bets are off, and may the best man win."

"I told you, Derek, I'm not trying to beat you out here." I paused, wondering if I was telling either one of us the truth. But another thought jumped into my head. "You think Sam was hired."

"Duh. The routing numbers."

I nodded. "I thought so, too, but wasn't sure. It could have been personal."

"Still might be. Either way, Sam was just a hired gun. So, we follow the money."

Made sense to me. I turned and opened cupboards to get out plates, then opened the fridge to see what sort of snack we could put together. Derek pitched in, and we had sandwiches made in no time.

On our way back to the library, I heard voices at the front door and motioned to Derek to stop while I took a few more steps until I could make out what they were saying.

21

The small, bespectacled man fidgeted nervously, right hand smoothing the fabric of his suit trousers, eyes darting around the large foyer. He clutched a briefcase under his left arm. Light from the recessed floods overhead reflected off his high, damp forehead. A few strands of dark hair were combed over the large bald spot on his head.

Travis recognized him from work, but couldn't say he'd actually met the man. Corporate counsel tended to shy away from the operations side of the business, as if to maintain objectivity. He was sure he'd never heard the man speak, though the man had rendered plenty of opinions. In writing, of course.

"Are you sure you won't come in?" Travis said.

"No, thank you. Really, I'm sorry to be a bother, especially on a day of rest, but I felt this couldn't wait. And it will only take a moment."

"It's Blair, right?"

"Yes, of course." The man smacked his palm against his forehead, then wiped it on his trousers again before extending it. "Where are my manners. We've never formally met. Blair Wallace."

Travis gripped his hand, careful not to squeeze too hard. As he expected, Wallace's grip was soft, uncommitted. But James had known Wallace a long time and had trusted him, so Travis was willing to keep an open mind about him.

"What can I do for you?"

Again, Wallace's gaze darted around the large space before landing on Travis's face, somewhere below his eyes.

"How shall I put this? When your brother and sister-in-law, uh, passed away, your brother's will left his holdings in MondoHard in trust for your niece, as you know."

Travis nodded. "I'm aware of the terms."

"Yes, well, I received a call from Dan Steingart on Friday."

"Dan... Our family attorney..."

Wallace's head bobbed. "He drew up the will, of course. And apparently, at the time, he also received a signed, sealed and notarized envelope from James with instructions not to open it until the first anniversary of his, uh, death."

"That was several months ago."

Wallace swallowed hard before speaking again. "Six months, actually. Dan did as he was instructed and opened the envelope. It contained a letter from your brother, witnessed by his wife, Sally, and his executive assistant, Robyn Alia, stating that there is a codicil to his will and asking that it be followed explicitly."

Travis frowned. "Why didn't Dan call me?"

"He didn't have the codicil, so he asked me to handle it."

"You've known about this for six months? Wait, don't tell me. There is no codicil."

Wallace swallowed again and looked miserable. "Not that I can find. Dan called the other day to remind me. I've looked everywhere I can think of. Obviously, I can't ask Mrs. Barrett, and Miss Alia recalls that she was asked to witness the codicil, but has no idea what's in it or where it is."

"It can't take full force and effect if it doesn't exist."

"Yes, but it's my duty as corporate counsel to abide by James's wishes, and those were clear—execute the codicil. I should have told you months ago, but now I'm at my wit's end, and I need your help finding it."

Travis blinked. "How can I help?"

"By going through all his personal papers and belongings here in the house. Surely, there's someplace he might keep important documents."

"I haven't come across anything like that. I can look, but we've been through all his things. He kept important papers in a safe deposit box."

"And it wasn't there?" Wallace asked.

"Not that I recall. I can check again tomorrow when the bank is open."

Wallace clutched the briefcase to his chest with both hands now, as if afraid it might escape. "I appreciate any help you can give me. And I apologize again for not bringing this to your attention sooner."

"It's fine," Travis assured him, but he was puzzled. "What has you so concerned?"

Wallace drew himself up to his full height, still a head shorter than Travis. "Beyond not having done my job properly? The contents of the codicil, of course. Miss Alia didn't know the specifics, but said Mrs. Barrett let slip while speaking with her husband that James intended to put the entire company in a blind trust, or at least his voting share."

Travis felt his brows knit. "I don't understand. He already put his shares in trust for Tess. What does a blind trust accomplish?"

"There may be multiple benefits, at least for some. It depends on how it's set up, and who the trustees are. I can't really say until I see the document. We must find it."

Travis nodded. "I'll look for it. I promise. And I'll speak with Robyn in the morning. Maybe she'll remember more details."

"Thank you. I'll let you get back to your weekend now."

Wallace bowed his head and backed up until he nearly bumped into the door, then turned and let himself out quickly.

Travis rubbed his jaw. *One more thing to worry about.*

22

"What do you want?" I say, pressing my hands into my lap under the table to hide my trembling.

"I'm just checking up on you," Marcus says. I can picture his grin. "You shouldn't take off like that without telling people."

"So I've heard." I put as much sarcasm in my voice as I can so he won't think I'm afraid of him. But I am.

Of all the men on the security team, I trust Marcus the least, and he's the titular head of it. He killed Kenny—another man on the original team Travis put together. To save me, he says. Because Kenny was a traitor, he says. It's hard for me to know, since I couldn't *see* what happened at the time. But I could *feel* it. I wasn't sure if I trusted Kenny, either, as he led me away from a horrific gun battle at our—well, my—vacation home in the mountains. In Kenny's final moments, however, I really sensed something horribly wrong with the whole situation. Kenny had a gun; he could have used me as a shield and killed Marcus. Instead, he'd pulled away from me at the last second so I wouldn't get hit.

Unfortunately, despite the evidence, I haven't been able to convince Travis that Marcus is dirty. But I don't think Marcus is likely to try anything here in the house. Hire someone to kill me at school, maybe...

"I'll be keeping a closer eye on you now," he says. "I feel terrible about what happened last night. I should have been there to make sure your detail was doing what it was supposed to."

I can't tell if he's the one being sarcastic now, but somehow I don't believe him.

"My 'detail' as you put it, did just fine," I say "They kept me alive."

"That's not what I heard." Marcus's voice turns hard as ice. "I heard you put up an adequate defense just long enough for your detail to catch up to events, and put the shooter down. They got lucky. They should have checked the perimeter."

"It doesn't matter." I shrug. I push on with momentary bravado. "If someone wants to get at me badly enough, they'll get through somehow. You, for example. You've certainly gotten yourself into a good position."

I hold my breath, wondering if he can be baited into admitting what I suspect. Marcus chuckles, and I deflate like an untied balloon.

"You just make sure you're more careful from now on," he says.

His footsteps, not stealthy at all now, retreat.

As he opens the door to leave I call out, "Stop following me."

The room falls silent for a moment except for the rapid beating of my heart. Suddenly, footsteps start toward me again, launching my heart back into my throat. But the smell of food and the realization that there are two pairs of shoes clomping in makes me laugh with relief.

"About time," I say. "I'm starved. What did you bring?"

"Sandwiches," Derek says. "Well, wraps, really."

"And a plate of veggies with ranch dip," Oliver says. "I wasn't sure what's on your 'approved' list, diet-wise, these days. We cut up a couple of apples, too."

"What kind of wraps?"

"Looks like whole wheat tortillas, and we threw in some sliced turkey, avocado, jack cheese and salsa," Derek says.

"Sounds good if you have enough," I say.

"There's plenty," Oliver says.

I hear plates hit the table, and Oliver puts a napkin in my hand. He tells me where everything is, and I go for the wrap on the plate in front of me first. I take a big bite and chew contentedly. Breakfast doesn't seem that long ago, but I'm really hungry. Seems the guys are, too, since the only noise is the sound of munching.

"So, did you two kiss and make up?" I say with my mouth half full. "If so, after we eat maybe we can all get back to work."

I don't hear an answer.

23

"Time to put the book away, Ben," Robyn said. "We're almost there."

She didn't have to look to know how intently her brother studied the pages. The book had been his constant companion since he'd received it more than a year ago. A mash-up of a children's storybook, a graphic novel and a comic book, it never failed to hold his rapt attention.

"This book gives you s-s-superpowers," he said.

"What's your superpower, Ben?" Robyn asked absently, focused on the traffic as the wipers intermittently smeared the mizzle across the windshield.

"I'm strong! Strong, so I can guard this book. He said so."

"He did, huh? You're keeping your book safe?"

"Yes. Safe."

"Well, time to put it away so it stays safe until you can read it again."

Benjamin sighed. "I miss Uncle J...James."

The sentiment startled her, but she realized that talking about the book had stirred up thoughts about the person who'd given it to Ben.

"I do, too," she said, feeling a twinge of melancholy.

She shrugged it off as the daycare center came up on their right. Rustling and a protracted *z-z-z-zip* let Robyn know Ben had stowed the book in his backpack. She pulled into the semi-circular drive in front and stopped. She turned her head, and was met with a Cheshire-Cat grin.

Benjamin had a happy face. Not that he always was happy. Most of the time, though, he took life as it came, and greeted it with wide-eyed innocence and good cheer. And his smile was infectious. People he encountered were put off at first by the almond-shaped eyes, the flattened nose, short neck and stubby build. But that radiant smile of his—literally from ear to ear—drew people in, made them feel at ease. She thought he was handsome; the smile made him more so.

"Do you have everything?" she said.

"I have my lunch," he said in his nasal, sing-song voice, another feature of his syndrome.

She nodded, and he turned, opened the door and climbed out, lunch sack in one hand. She rolled down the passenger window and waited. They had a ritual. Benjamin liked routines; his lunch, for example—peanut butter and jelly. Every day.

Benjamin squatted down and peered in the window and put on his best expression of bewilderment. "Where's Nana?"

The name always brought back memories, most of them good. Holding back a smile, Robyn said, "On the big playground in heaven."

"And she'll push me on the swing when I get there?"

"Yes, and catch you on the slide when you come down."

His face split into a big smile. "And Um, too?"

Robyn nodded. "Um, too. I'm proud of you, Ben."

"Thanks. Bye, Robyn."

"Bye, Ben. See you later."

Without a backward glance, Benjamin marched into the center and disappeared. Robyn smiled and put the car in gear. She *was* proud of her brother. He'd overcome tremendous obstacles to get where he was. Goals he set for himself that she thought were far out of his reach toppled under his determination.

The job here at the daycare center had been his idea. Though not quite fully self-aware enough to know why, he was intellectually developed enough to handle the responsibilities, and emotionally immature enough that he had the same sense of wonder and playfulness as the kids he helped care for. At first, she'd been reluctant to give in to his pleas to apply for the job—though "apply" was too strong a word—his desire to help with the kids. But he was an adult now, and Robyn had to let him act as much like an adult as he could.

She'd vetted the center, without telling him, of course. The center really operated as both a nursery and pre-school. Children were grouped by age, with babies, from six months to a year old, in a nursery; toddlers in a play room; pre-kindergarten age kids in other class/play rooms; and kindergartners in yet more. The center was run as a co-op, with parents required to volunteer to work in the nursery or classrooms at least one week a semester, and each room had a teacher and an assistant. The center's director, Marni Reynolds, had agreed to hire Benjamin as a floater who would fill in for staff or parents who called in sick, or help out wherever needed. The center had a good reputation, and Robyn hadn't been able to find any complaints about it.

Still, she would never stop feeling protective. She and Ben had been a team for so long—first when Nana had slowly slipped away from them, the dementia gradually robbing more and more of her mind, and then even more so after Nana died—that Robyn couldn't imagine her life without him. And their mother had been gone so long that Robyn was a little surprised that Ben remembered her as well as he did. And that he still called her "Um," the Arabic word for mother.

So long ago... Robyn herself could barely remember the place they'd called home then, so different—so *foreign*—from here. A vibrant city of gleaming steel and glass skyscrapers mingling with the classic old stone buildings of the past, some dating to antiquity. The streets flowing with cars and busses, sidewalks teeming with people in colorful clothes, the air filled with the sounds of traffic and babble of conversation in Arabic, French, English and tongues she'd never heard before or since. The memories all an indistinct swirl of impressions, really, like bits and pieces of a dream. But, then, she'd blocked out so much of that time after...well, after Um was gone, and their American grandmother, Nana, had sent for them.

It had been just the two of them since they'd lost Nana, too, and it hadn't been easy. Now, Robyn was slowly learning to give Ben more rein, let him stand on his own two feet, or stumble and fall. But she would always be there to help him up if he needed it.

All the reminiscing turned her mood as gloomy as Seattle's winter. She put the thoughts out of her head and focused on the day ahead. Travis had been more preoccupied than usual recently, and she'd been fending off queries and complaints from multiple sources. Today would likely be no different, so she mentally juggled appointments and obligations just in case.

Within minutes, she pulled into the underground parking lot, wound down one level and parked in the reserved slot next to the one marked for Travis. It was the one perk James had bestowed upon her that she really appreciated. She sighed as she got out and locked up. She missed James something fierce, his kindness and thoughtfulness, his gentle manner. But that was a road best not travelled. She took another deep breath. Travis was so unlike his brother. She was slowly getting used to him. Sort of.

The elevator took her up to the executive suite, and she let herself in with her key card. As usual, she was the first person in.

She dropped her purse on her desk and went to make coffee. While it was brewing, she checked the calendar on her computer, and made sure she had copies of the agendas for every meeting Travis had that morning along with any documents pertinent to each. She slipped the contents for each meeting into manila folders, stacked them in order, and placed them neatly on Travis's desk.

After pouring herself coffee, she settled back in at her desk and had started on some correspondence when her cell phone rang. She looked at it and frowned. Few people had her number, which meant the call was either from Benjamin, the daycare center, or a robocall center. Her frown deepened when she realized that it was a text, not a phone call. That raised the odds on it being a telemarketer or scammer. She put her finger on it, ready to swipe and delete it when she noticed that a photo was attached. No, a video. The scene looked familiar. She paused and peered at it more closely.

The daycare center.

Reluctantly, with a sense of dread filling her stomach like molten lead, Robyn tapped the video and watched the street scene on her phone leap into life. Shot from across the street, the perspective took in the entire front of the building and several feet on either side of it. Cars zipped through the frame, and one turned into the semi-circular entrance to the center. A car door slammed and over the roof of the car, Robyn saw a little girl run toward the front entrance and pull the door open. Benjamin appeared in the opening from inside and leaned on the door's push bar to help, greeting the girl with his signature smile. The girl rushed past, and the door shut.

Robyn's gaze was glued to the small screen, her sense of foreboding growing. The street was quiet for a few moments, then she noticed movement on the right side of the frame. On the sidewalk, a woman moved into view. Dressed in a trench coat with the collar up and a wide-brimmed floppy hat to ward off the drizzle, she yanked on a leash impatiently. A small dog followed her into the frame. She turned and scolded it, and the little fellow cowered, shivering, until she straightened. She faced forward again and once more yanked on the leash, half-dragging the dog behind her.

The daycare center door opened. Benjamin stepped out and yelled, "Hey!"

Robyn felt torn. Part of her was proud of Ben for coming to the aid of an obviously abused little dog. But another part of her wanted to scream at him through the phone to go back inside and mind his own business.

The woman in the scene ignored Ben's shout and yanked on the leash a few more times. Then abruptly, she dropped the leash and hurried away. Looking as confused as Robyn felt, Ben called after her, "Hey, what about your dog? You forgot your dog!" He stood there a moment, and when the woman didn't return, Ben walked out to the sidewalk, bent down and scooped the dog up in his arms and took it inside. The video ended a few seconds later.

Robyn didn't know what to make of it. Other than the woman's odd and awful behavior, nothing terrible had happened. She wondered who had sent it to her and why. She put the phone down and resolved to get back to work. Before she made another move, another text came in.

She read it with growing terror.

If you don't want to see your brother get hurt, do exactly what we say. We'll be in touch.

24

I thought I liked Derek when I first met him a few weeks before. He seemed kind of cool in a slouchy, slacker way, and was a whiz with computers. But now this rebel without a cause was a pain in my ass. I couldn't help wondering if he'd become as big a jerk as I thought he was, or if my altered opinion of him was colored by my feelings for Tess. And that was an even bigger surprise.

Did I *have* feelings for Tess? I wasn't supposed to. I thought I was above all that. After all, she was way too young for me, and she was my employer. And after that almost disastrous attempt to kiss her at homecoming, her feelings for me were as clear as a spring-fed lake. All of which were good enough reasons not to have "feelings" for her. The truth was, I didn't know how I felt about her.

In any case, I managed to get her through the rest of her homework assignments, though not without difficulty. She was moody, remote, with the attention span of a minnow. I had to keep steering her back on track when her mind wandered, and that seemed to irritate her even more. I could chalk it up to the fact that A) someone tried to kill her the night before; B) she just had a fight with her uncle; C) despite some progress, we didn't know who hired Sam; D) she was pissed at me for even thinking about kissing her; E) she was pissed at me for sniping with Derek; F) she was pissed at me for something I didn't realize I'd done; or G) all of the above. Then again, like she'd reminded me several times a few weeks before, her period could make her a little cranky. I did some mental math and decided that was a low probability. I didn't rule it out, though. I'm no expert.

If she'd told me about her visit from Marcus just before we came back in with the food, that would have explained her mood. And I might have put some things together, maybe preventing a lot of what happened later. But she didn't say a word. I didn't know Marcus had been there.

Derek took off with the laptop saying he needed access to some programs on his computer to continue following the money and the leads in Sam's cache. Since my job was essentially finished for the day, I went looking for Alice to get "permission" to go home. I didn't believe I was in any danger, and though the "plaid" room upstairs was way more posh and comfortable than my apartment, sleeping across the hall from Tess just didn't sit well. Even the comfortable guest room a couple of doors down the hall felt too close. I couldn't put my finger on why, exactly, but it made me edgy, as if I couldn't trust myself—to do, or not do what, was the question. And that's what bugged me most. I didn't know. So, once I convinced Alice that Red had taught me how to spot a tail and check the perimeter of my apartment, I went home for the night.

In the morning, I came back fresh and early to take Tess to school. She and Travis stood nearly toe to toe in the kitchen arguing when I arrived. I gave them a wide berth and poured myself coffee while I waited for them to either cool down or combust in a fiery supernova.

"Nothing about this is normal," Tess said heatedly. "It's bad enough I have Oliver in classes with me, but my 'normal' high school life is over if any of your goon squad's there, too."

"Good morning to you, too," I said.

She had the good grace to blush. "Sorry, Oliver, I didn't know you were here. But you know what I mean. And I'm not trying to call the guys names—I like them, at least some of them—but I'm sure they look like what they are. Don't put them in class with me."

"We've gone through this, Tess," Travis said. "How am I supposed to protect you if I don't assign you a detail?"

"Go ahead, assign me a detail. I have all their phones on speed dial and voice dial. Oliver does, too. It worked before."

"Barely," Travis concedes. "You and Oliver almost didn't make it out alive. And Saturday night proved again that even with a detail you're in danger."

"You're not putting guys with guns in classrooms. I won't stand for it. The other kids won't stand for it. Principal Jenkins won't, either, and neither will parents."

"If I could make a suggestion?" I said.

Travis threw a glance of annoyance my way, then nodded.

"The detail *did* work before, as long as the guys were close enough they could get to us quickly. You said you were adding extra security personnel, right? They should be able to cover all the entrances and exits, so the team is free to respond if Tess needs them."

Travis stared out the window.

"If you want to protect me," Tess said, "find out who hired Sam. If you don't, I will."

A frown darkened Travis's face. "Don't even think about it. This is no joke."

"Do you see me laughing? I have to go, or I'll be late. Are you ready, Oliver?"

"Sure." I slurped some coffee and set the mug next to the sink. "Where are your books?"

"Already by the front door," she said.

"I still don't like it," Travis said.

"I don't care," Tess said, "as long as…"

"What?" Travis looked at her sharply. "As long as what?"

"Never mind. Do whatever you're going to do. Just make sure none of those guys sets foot in school unless someone's shooting at us. Me. Whatever. Come on, Oliver."

I gave Travis a "what-can-you-do" shrug and followed Tess down the long hall and out the front door where I'd parked the car. I held the book bag while she got in, then handed it to her and went around to the driver's side. One of the SUVs backed out of the guest house garage and drove up. I waved and got a nod from Red, the driver. Marcus sat shotgun, and didn't even acknowledge me. Red stopped at the circle and waited for me to pull out, then fell in behind us.

Less than fifteen minutes later, I'd parked and walked Tess toward the doors to the school commons, but saw a big, beefy man directing students away from there to the front doors. I changed direction and steered Tess toward the front where a large crowd had gathered. As we came up behind the group, I heard rumblings and mutterings about how messed up this was.

"What's going on?" Tess murmured.

"Not sure," I said. "Hang on."

I stepped forward to nudge a kid in front of us. "Do you know what's going on?"

More students had come up behind us, so now we were wedged into the crowd.

The kid turned around and said, "New security, I guess. Someone said we have to go through a metal detector now."

"Come on, let's go!" someone in the crowd yelled.

"Yeah, move it!" another voice shouted. "We're all going to be late."

Several yards in front of us, a guy a full head taller than others around him scanned the crowd with a bored expression. When his eyes met mine, his face hardened and scowled.

"You!" he said.

Several students looked up, and grumblings quieted. I felt my brow furrow in surprise as one hand came up involuntarily to rest on my chest. I'd never seen him before.

"*Yo, chonky*!" he called out. "This is all *your* fault. Your uncle set this up. What's the matter, princess? You scared someone's going to take you out?"

Tess paled, making the long, ridged scar stand out like a twisty road on a desert map. People in front of us parted, giving the guy's gaze a wide-open expressway in our direction.

"Oliver," she murmured, "is he talking to me?"

"I guess so. He's looking this way."

"Crap. I knew Travis would screw things up for me."

"I thought he locked down the story about what happened Saturday night," I murmured. "How would this guy know?"

"People talk, Oliver, spread rumors."

"Hey, bitch, I'm talking to you," the kid hollered.

Almost everyone paid attention now, and like spectators at Wimbledon their heads turned in unison from him to Tess.

"Say something," she hissed.

"Like what?"

The corners of her mouth turned down. "Oh, never mind." She turned and called, "Hey, asshole, I don't know who you are, but did you ever think maybe this is to protect *you*, not me?"

The guy laughed. "What are you talking about?"

"I'm still standing here," Tess said. "Carl Gant wasn't so lucky, was he? And what about Matt Tsang? Where's he now? Suspended? Expelled for bringing a gun to school and shooting up the commons?"

She was shaking now, but I couldn't tell if it she was afraid or nervous. The basketball player rocked back on his heels and blinked as if thinking it over.

Tess stayed on offense. "And oh, BTW, next time you call me names, be a man; introduce yourself and do it to my face, not from wherever the hell you are."

"Screw you, Barrett." The kid threw a one-finger salute, which obviously missed the point since Tess couldn't see it, and faced forward again as the line inched ahead.

Tess pawed air until her hand landed on my arm. She gripped it, then slugged my deltoids.

"Ow! What's that for?"

"Try sticking up for me next time."

"Why? You were doing fine on your own." I guided her forward a few feet as the line started to move.

"It's your job to protect me."

"My job is to assist you. And you didn't need protecting. Sticks and stones..."

"You're an even bigger jerk than you were yesterday."

"Yesterday? What did I do yesterday?"

She grouched something unintelligible about men, boys, and games. Figuring it had something to do with me and Derek, I didn't pursue it.

Whatever bottleneck had held up the line seemed to have cleared. We moved steadily toward the entrance, then through it and into the screening area. Similar to TSA checkpoints at the airport, conveyor belts pulled backpacks, coats and other items through x-ray machines, while students walked in single file through several scanners. The entry hall beyond still filled with students milling around instead of hurrying off to class. A hum of voices and anticipation suffused the air.

When Tess stepped through the scanner, thunderous applause erupted from the crowd. I hurried through the scanner behind her and took her elbow.

"What's going on?" she said.

"I don't know."

Close by, a small kid who must have been a freshman must have overheard her. He leaned in, grinning, and said, "You're a star."

"Who's a star?" Tess said. "What does he mean, Oliver?"

The boy held out his phone and tapped it. I bent and peered at the small screen, listening to hoots and laughter all around me.

"Uh-oh," I said. "You're not going to like this."

"What?" Tess said. "Tell me."

"Hang on." I told the boy to text me the video, and rattled off my number. Seconds later, my phone buzzed, and I pulled up the video. I stared at it in disbelief for several frames, not sure of what I was seeing. I thought I was pretty chill, but the video shocked me.

"What is it?" Tess said through clenched teeth.

"I...I..." I didn't know how to explain it.

There were still titters in the crowd, but the noise level had dropped, and I realized that people were staring at Tess and me, waiting for me to tell Tess about the video. Suddenly, a door banged shut, and footsteps reverberated off the tile floor in the silence.

"All right, everybody. What's going on here? It's time to get to class."

I shoved the phone in my pocket and looked up. Greg Olton, the vice principal, weaved his way into the middle of the crowd, smoothing his tie over a rounded belly. Students quickly turned away and broke off singly, in pairs and small groups, heading for hallways that led to their classrooms.

"That's exactly what I like to see, people," Olton called out. "Enthusiasm. Purpose. Determination."

I took Tess's arm and pulled her along to her first period class, looking at the video more closely as we walked. In the relative quiet of the 300 hallway, she slowed, resisting.

"What the hell, Oliver? What was that about back there?"

"Lower your voice, okay? That was your worst nightmare."

"Tell me, damn it!"

"There's a video circulating around school. Apparently, you're on it."

"What? Why...? How...?"

"It's not pretty. On the video it looks like you're giving some guy a, uh, hand job. Oops, fellatio, too." I frowned. Something didn't add up.

She stopped dead in her tracks, blood draining from her face. "A blowjob? Oh, god, I think I'm going to be sick. Me? How the hell could someone...?"

"Shoot video of you in such a private moment?" I said, backing the video up a bit and looking at it again.

She jerked away from me, staring with those sightless blue eyes. "No! I mean how could someone do this to me?"

"Welcome to high school." From the little time I'd spent as a secondary school student, I knew it was a dog-eat-dog world. In my time, though, mean kids would just shove you into a locker. This stepped over the bounds of the worst that I could imagine.

"I didn't do anything to deserve this," she whispered, her face now ghostly pale.

"Come on," I said. "Let's get to class. We'll figure this out later."

25

Travis was in a foul mood by the time he pulled to a stop on squealing tires in his parking slot. First, he'd had another fight with Tess. He couldn't get her to listen to reason. Then, when his worries had shifted to problems at work and from there to the muddle of his personal life, some jackass in a fancy sports car had swung across two lanes on the freeway and cut him off as he was getting on the exit to downtown. The jerk had nearly caused an accident. All that had caused him to be late, which he hated.

He sighed as he got out of the SUV, grabbed his briefcase and hustled for the elevator. Life had been so much simpler in the military. Well, not really, but it had seemed that way. A clear chain of command; a well-defined enemy; simple, straightforward goals... Now, everything seemed so complicated. Change one little thing—a word in a conversation, even—and a dozen other events fell like dominoes.

He knew he wasn't being rational. The same had been true of his assignments overseas. One little detail could affect the outcome of an entire operation. And the stakes had been as high as they get. Lives, his included, had hung in the balance. Maybe the difference was in emotional investment. He'd been emotionally vested in his career, of course—duty, honor, pride, and the elation of pulling off seemingly impossible sorties into enemy territory all were valid feelings for the job. But this business of dealing with Tess was emotional in an entirely different sense, and it made Travis uneasy. He was on shaky ground, and never seemed to be able to get a solid footing with Tess.

Sighing again as the elevator rose to the executive level, he put those thoughts aside and focused on the day ahead. By the time he reached the top floor, he thought he was ready.

The receptionist on the floor gave him a smile as he stepped off the elevator.

"Good morning, Mr. Barrett."

"Good morning, Janine."

He turned left and walked down the hall to another, smaller foyer—the antechamber of the "C Suite." Robyn, the guardian of all the executives in the suite, had her head down, poring over something on her desk. Hearing his approach, she tipped her face up and gave him a tentative smile.

"Good morning, M—Travis," she said.

She still had to catch herself to keep from calling him "Mr. Barrett." Travis found it both endearing—an intimation of her character—and vexing. They'd known each other long enough to be on a first-name basis, if not friends.

"Your schedule is on your desk," she said. "Would you like coffee?"

"Don't trouble yourself. I'll get it, Robyn." His irritation grew, and he couldn't tell if her selfless assistance or his discontent caused it. Maybe it was just his mood, but he didn't need to take it out on her. "Thanks for the offer," he said more brightly.

She lowered her voice. "Franklin Hayes is in your office. I told him you have a full calendar today, but he insisted on seeing you first thing. Should I reschedule your nine o'clock meeting?"

"No, that's all right. If I can't take care of it now, I'll work something out with Franklin."

She nodded and turned back to her desk without her usual smile.

Travis hesitated. "Are you okay? You seem—I don't know—troubled."

She shook her head and flashed him the smile, but it didn't reach her eyes and disappeared as fast as it formed.

"I'm fine. Just tired, is all."

"You should take some time off. Go somewhere. You work too hard."

"Maybe someday." She offered another weak smile.

Unsure of what else he could offer, Travis nodded and turned for his office.

Inside, Franklin Hayes, the company's chief financial officer, stood next to the large windows overlooking the water. He turned as Travis entered and stepped forward to meet him, hand outstretched. Travis gripped it, then quickly let go to put his briefcase down on the desk.

"Robyn said you have something that can't wait?" He gestured to an empty chair as he sat behind the desk. "Please, have a seat."

"Thanks, Travis, but this won't take long," Hayes said in his deep bass voice. "I just wanted to see where we are on the drone contract for the Army."

"Not where I'd like to be, but a lot further than we were a few weeks ago." Travis smiled.

"Is it even close to being delivered?"

Travis realized charm wasn't going to help him. "We're getting there, Franklin. We believe we've largely overcome the virus that kept infecting the software. And we're making progress on the battery and solar cell technology."

"The project is more than twenty million over budget already. What do you want me to say to shareholders in our next quarterly report?"

Travis threw up his hands. "I don't know what to say, Franklin. The problem is that James kept so much information in his head we're reinventing the wheel in many instances."

"The problem is that you blew up his only prototype."

"Well, I didn't know it at the time, or I wouldn't have blown it up, now would I? Maybe the 'problem' is that James didn't confide in his engineers, and then went and got himself killed in a car accident."

Travis looked him up and down, noting with little pleasure the effect his barb had on Franklin. "Why the concern, anyway? The family still owns the majority of the company, and with the new video game back on track, we're not losing money."

"I'm the CFO, Travis," Hayes said, chastened. "It's my job to worry about money. James would have, too. And without him here, activist investors could push for control of the board."

Travis felt a tingling of alarm. "Why? What have you heard?"

Hayes put a hand out. "Grumblings, that's all. But it only takes one or two disgruntled board members to sour everyone."

"Noted." Travis tried to read Hayes's expression. "I'll rein in the drone project. We'll get it finished and delivered."

"Seriously, what's it going to take? If it's not going to work, better to cut our losses now."

"I'm telling you, just those two pieces—the battery and the solar cell. We're close."

Hayes nodded. "Good. A win on the defense side of the business would really help."

"Franklin," Travis said as Hayes turned. "Let me know if there are people you think I should speak with personally. You know, to offer reassurances. I met with Latham a few weeks ago since he's on the Senate Appropriations Committee. Maybe someone else who can persuade him to stick with us?"

Hayes mused for a moment before giving a short nod. "I'll think about it."

When he closed the office door behind him, Travis let out a breath. Trying to put the conversation aside, he scanned the materials Robyn had prepared for him. As usual, she'd been meticulous and thorough. With a glance at his watch, he saw he still had twenty minutes before his first meeting. After that, the day looked to be pretty much non-stop. He wondered how James had done it—the endless meetings, navigating the office politics and the personalities to get what he wanted, all while keeping an eye on the big picture so the company continued to grow and thrive.

Travis's attention waned as the meeting with his chief financial officer kept bubbling up in his thoughts. And that jogged loose bits of his conversation with Robyn. As the image of her face fixed in his mind, his focus strayed completely off track.

Travis knew his military career most likely was over. And if he was going to be a civilian from now on, he might as well embrace civilian life. He'd never had any sort of long-term relationship, and had envied his brother's marriage. James and Sally had made a good team. But if he had to sum up the qualities he'd want in a partner, Robyn's seemed like a good fit. At least from what he knew about her, which he realized with chagrin wasn't much.

That he knew so little surprised Travis. After all, she'd interned when James had first started the company, and had practically been a part of the extended family that James and Sally had collected, Alice and Yoshi among them. But Travis had already joined the army by then, so he'd never known her except through letters and emails from his brother and sister-in-law.

Robyn also was easy on the eyes, Travis had to admit, and while he knew she'd had a platonic crush on James for years, Travis realized he'd secretly hoped she might find him interesting, too. Or at least see him as something other than a boss. But he'd suggested having coffee twice, and had gotten turned down twice. He didn't want to make an ass of himself a third time, or be labeled a stalker. Just knowing about the #MeToo movement should have waved him off altogether. He was now, after all, the head of a multibillion-dollar corporation, and even the whiff of impropriety could bring down everything James had worked for like the World Trade towers in New York. But a cup of coffee, for God's sake, wasn't sexual harassment. *Was it?*

Oh, well, no use worrying about something over which he had no control. The more he thought about her, though, what did worry him niggled at the edges of his consciousness until it jumped out of the shadows. She hadn't been herself this morning. Something bothered her. She'd run through the normal morning ritual—a smile and a greeting, a heads-up on what his day held, an offer to get coffee. But none of it held the usual artless sincerity. She'd been preoccupied before greeting him. The smile felt feigned, pasted on, and the offer to fix coffee, rote. He didn't want to pry, but he did want to help.

He remembered, suddenly, that he was supposed to ask Robyn about the codicil to James's will that Blair Wallace said she'd witnessed. That would give him an excuse to see if his intuition was correct, and perhaps assist her for once instead of the other way around.

He was about to call her in when a knock on the door signaled his first meeting. His questions would have to wait.

26

"All right, class, settle down," Mr. Prescott calls out. "Let's be seated and get started."

Prescott teaches my first period AP American Lit/Comp class, and after the shock I just got, I'm not ready. But Prescott waits for no girl.

"If you recall," he says, "before your homecoming weekend of debauchery, we were discussing literature as theater. Nineteenth century authors like James, Melville and many others, in fact, considered novels a better version of theater. So, let's see... Miss Barrett, what early twentieth century American literature classic featured an actress as its protagonist?"

My heart leaps into my throat. Of course he has to call on me. "Um, *Funny Girl*?"

Snickers ripple through the room.

"Not even close, Miss Barrett. The answer I was looking for is *Sister Carrie*. I understand you have ambitions of becoming a thespian. If so, you'll have to do better than that."

I have no such ambitions, and the way he says it is so smarmy that I know he's referring to the video. I don't know how he could have seen it unless... Of course; it was posted to social media, probably that new one, Clamor. Now, I'm mortified. Prescott, who gets off by teaching a yoga class for PE credit just so he can look at tits and asses in tight yoga pants and stretch halter tops thinks he's seen me naked, giving a hand job—*and* a blowjob, for fuck's sake—to some nerd. I will never live this down, even though I had no part in the video.

I try to sink into the seat, turn invisible against the beige plastic. But judging from the titters of laughter around me, I'm still on display, and have fallen even further from royalty. No longer an ace, or even homecoming queen, I'm the joker, the butt of bathroom humor. Worst of all, I'll now be known as a slut, a designation from which there is no recourse, redemption or cure. It will stick to me like toilet paper on my shoe for the rest of my senior year and beyond. I feel sick.

It's not like sexting doesn't happen all the time, or that some of those pics get leaked, somehow, to a wider audience, bringing temporary shame to the photo subjects. I've never done it. Not because I'm a prude—I'm aware I have a smoking hot body, or I did, before I chunked up after the accident. Back then I wasn't afraid to show it off in a cheer outfit or a bikini. Toby and I just never got that far when we were still an item. I didn't feel comfortable doing that shit. Maybe I was too young back then. Now I wouldn't be caught dead in the nude.

The remainder of the block period is an interminable blur as I fight to keep breakfast down and wrack my brain to figure out who hates me that much to make the video in the first place. And who wants to destroy me so badly they'd risk appearing in it.

27

Robyn felt sick to her stomach. She'd wanted to scream at Travis to get him to move, to leave. Instead, she'd calmly told him that Hayes was waiting to speak with him. Before he'd closed his office door, she'd snatched up the phone and dialed the daycare center's number.

"Marni, it's Robyn Alia." She could barely keep the panic out of her voice.

"Oh, hi. How are you? I keep missing you at both ends of the day. Hey, I've been meaning to call you. Benjamin brought a dog to the center this morning. Did you get him a dog? Because we really can't have dogs running around. I mean it's okay this once, but it's disruptive, you know?"

"No, I didn't get him a dog, Marni." Robyn tried to keep her voice light. "Is he there? Is he all right?"

"Sure, he's here. But what about the dog? If it's not your dog, where did he get it?"

"He found it outside," Robyn said, her jaw clenched.

"How do you know? I mean if you dropped him off and left... Come to think of it, he kept saying some woman left it. I thought he meant you."

"Marni!" Robyn said sharply. "The dog probably has a tag with the owner's phone number on it. Write it down and save it for me. I can't get away from work right now, so if you can't keep the dog, call its owner. But I need that number. Now, is Ben there? Can I talk to him?"

"He's down the hall," Marni said, her tone sulky.

"Are you sure? Can you see him?"

"Fine. Hold on just a second."

Before Robyn could protest, Marni put her on hold. Robyn gritted her teeth at the sound of the center's terrible music loop, and tapped her toe. "Just a second" became several, which turned into what seemed an eternity.

Finally, Marni came back on the line, her tone a bit frosty. "He says he's fine. He can't talk now because he's showing the dog to the kids."

"You're sure he's okay?"

"Benjamin is *fine.*"

"Thank you. I'll see you later, then."

Robyn hung up with relief, but she was frightened. She didn't understand who would want to hurt Ben, or what anyone could possibly want from her. Things *weren't* fine, as far as she was concerned, and her fears quickly turned relief into unease. Her thoughts raced, and the beat of butterfly wings in her stomach radiated outward until her knees bounced on her toes and her fingers tapped the edge of her desk. *So many questions.* She knew she wouldn't get any work done until she had some answers.

Grabbing her phone and purse in one hand and her jacket in the other, she rushed out of the C suite and down the hall toward the reception area. Janine looked up from her desk, startled, as Robyn approached.

"Are you okay?" Janine said, a worried frown on her face.

"Yes," she said, her nod turning to a shake. "No. I don't know. Look, just cover for me, will you, Janine? If Mr.—Travis, I mean— if he asks, tell him I had an emergency and should be back by lunch."

"Sure. No problem."

Robyn rushed past and got on an elevator down to the garage.

In less than twenty minutes, she strode up to the daycare center's front door, glaring at the camera mounted above it. The lock buzzed obligingly. She yanked the door open and stepped inside, intending to head straight for the classrooms to find Benjamin. But Marni was already in the hallway to intercept her.

"I told you, Ben's fine." Marni said, blocking Robyn's path.

"Have you called the dog's owner yet?" Robyn said.

Marni blinked. "I haven't had time yet. Why? What's so important?"

"Where is he?" Robyn tapped her foot.

Marni's head swiveled as if expecting to suddenly find Ben behind her. "I'm not sure. Probably in with the pre-K kids. I couldn't say which room."

"I'll find him myself."

Robyn tried push past her, but Marni quickly sidestepped in front of her.

"Robyn, stop. You can't just go wandering from room to room. If you insist on seeing Benjamin, I'll go find him and bring him back to the office. Please, just go wait there."

Every instinct screamed at Robyn to do anything she could to find out who was threatening her brother, but she recognized how impulsively she'd acted. She nodded and turned for the office. The wait, probably only a minute or two, seemed interminable. Her stomach twisted in knots. Finally, she heard footsteps echoing in the hall outside the open door, and Benjamin's infectious giggle.

"Robyn!" he said as he burst through the doorway. "Look what I found."

Cradled in his arms was a brown fluffy ball of fur that wriggled like a fish, and stretched its neck up until a little pink tongue darted out to lick Benjamin's cheek. Ben giggled again, and the dog scooted around in his arms until it faced Robyn. Intelligent brown eyes and a black button nose stood out from a mop of fur. A small cute terrier mix, maybe a Dorkie. Robyn gave Ben a wan smile, unable to match his enthusiasm, and nodded her thanks to Marni.

"That looks like a very nice dog," Robyn said.

"It's very friendly," Ben said. "All the kids like it, all but Annie. She's afraid of dogs. I tell them be careful when they pet it."

"I'm proud of you for taking such good care of him," Robyn said. Benjamin beamed. "What's his name?"

"It's a girl dog, duh."

"I'm sorry. What's her name?"

"Minnie." He groped in the fur around the dog's neck and pulled on a metal tag attached to the dog's collar. "See? She has a name tag."

"That's good. That means we can find out who she belongs to. You know we have to give her back to the person she belongs to, right?"

Benjamin hugged the dog tighter and turned his body away. "You can't give it back to that mean lady."

"We have to, Ben. But maybe we can talk to her about her behavior." Robyn turned to Marni. "Can he come along? Can you spare him for a little while?"

Marni heaved a sigh. "Yes, I can. Go. Just don't be long."

Robyn knelt on one knee and beckoned with one hand. "Can I see her?"

Ben stepped in front of her, his mouth drooping into a pout. "I don't want to take her back."

"I know," she said, fingers turning the pet ID tag to read it. She looked up at Ben "But don't you think her owner misses her?"

"That lady was mean."

Robyn stood. "Well, then, maybe we should go talk to her."

"Okay, I guess."

Robyn herded Ben out to the car and slid behind the wheel. Leaning over, she checked the dog's ID tag again, and keyed the owner's address into her phone. The map indicated it was only a few blocks away.

Benjamin was silent on the way. Robyn wanted to reassure him somehow, but she knew she shouldn't make promises she might not be able to keep. Her thoughts kept drifting back to the video, her brow knitting in concentration. None of it made any sense. She sighed as she spotted the address and pulled over to the curb in front of a small bungalow. A newer boxy townhouse development with lots of metal-framed windows stood to one side. A few more small houses filled lots on the other side, but Robyn knew the townhouses presaged more of the same. Progress seemed to mean more people packed into the same space.

"We're here," she said. "Let's go, Ben."

Robyn climbed out and closed the door. Hunching her shoulders against the sprinkles of rain, she rounded the front of the car and stood on the curb. She felt Ben's reluctance as he got out of the car and slowly followed her up the walk. Casting a glance over her shoulder, she saw him struggle to control the wriggling dog in his arms. Robyn set her mouth in a determined line and rang the doorbell. Behind her, Minnie let out tiny yips.

"Hold on to her, Ben," she said, turning to look.

"I'm trying."

The door opened, and Robyn swung back around as a diminutive woman in a housedress materialized behind the screen door. She had a halo of curly white hair circling a round face the color of mahogany.

"Yes?" Her voice creaked with age.

Robyn blinked, for a moment unable to form words. The woman in front of her looked nothing like the one in the video.

"Ms. Jackson? Mabel Jackson?"

"Yes, that's me," the elderly woman said.

The dog's earnest yips turned to barks, and it squirmed so hard in Ben's arms that he bent down to place it on the ground. Before he could, it jumped out and raced past Robyn's legs and pawed at the screen.

"Minnie!" Mabel cried. "Oh, my goodness, Minnie, there you are!"

Robyn stepped back as Mabel pushed the screen door open. Minnie raced inside and barked excitedly as she ran around

Mabel's feet. She stooped, caught the little bundle of fur up in her arms, and slowly straightened, wincing as she became upright.

"Where did you find her?" Mabel asked. "I thought I'd never see her again."

"I found her," Benjamin said loudly. "She was at school."

"I'm sorry," Robyn said, still confused. "I'm Robyn Alia. This is my brother Benjamin. He saw a woman walking your dog outside the daycare center where he works. But you look nothing like the woman he saw. Are you sure this is your dog?"

"Oh, I'm sure," Mabel said as Minnie licked her wizened face. "Had her since my husband died. My daughter thought she'd be good company, and she is."

"The lady was mean to her," Ben piped up. "And she left her on the sidewalk. She could have been hit by a car. So I took her."

"You took her?" Mabel's voice rose.

Robyn waved her hands. "No, what he means to say is that he was keeping Minnie safe."

Mabel calmed down immediately. "Well, in that case..."

"Was the woman Ben saw walking Minnie for you?" Robyn pressed.

"Oh, no. I can explain. Would you like to come in for some coffee?"

Roby's face fell. "I'm sorry. I have to get Ben back to his job at the school. But I would like to know what happened."

"Well, I don't really know," Mabel said. "I usually take Minnie out for a morning walk before breakfast, but I was feeling a little faint this morning, so I let her out by herself. She had her leash on and everything. I knew I shouldn't have, but she had to tinkle, and I felt so weak I had to sit down. So I did, and I watched her from the front window.

"Then, a car stopped in the street, and a tall person in a raincoat and floppy-brimmed hat jumped out and grabbed Minnie. In a flash, the person was back in the car, and just like that, my Minnie was gone."

"Had you ever see this person before?" Robyn searched the woman's face, desperate for answers.

"Goodness, no. I couldn't even tell you if the person was a man or woman. She would have been tall for a woman, maybe average for a man." She sighed. "Lordy, all this talk has tuckered me out. Are you sure you won't come in?"

"Please, Robyn?" Ben said. "I want to say goodbye to Minnie."

"No, I'm sorry," Robyn said reluctantly. She could see the woman just wanted some company, and now Ben looked so crestfallen she felt terrible. "We really do have to go. But thank you for telling us what happened."

"Oh, my, thank *you*, child, for rescuing my Minnie. I didn't think I'd ever see her again."

"Benjamin's the real hero," Robyn said.

"Well, thank you, young man. And God bless you."

Ben brightened a little. Robyn said her goodbyes and steered Ben to the car, then drove him back to the daycare center. All the way there, she wondered who would kidnap a dog in order to send her a message. She shuddered and felt sick to her stomach. Whatever these people wanted from her, it couldn't be good.

"Ben," she said, "you remember what to do when there's stranger danger, right?"

28

My day gets worse, not better. People attack me in the halls with snide comments like, "Nice security, bitch," and "You suck—get it?" Taunts and laughter echo through the halls, and now I can't tell what's aimed at me, and what's the general nattering that goes on every day. Oliver is no help, remaining strangely silent through all of this. At first I want to shrivel up and die, the verbal assault poured on me like salt on a slug.

But the more crap I take, the angrier I get. Until finally, I think *screw them*. I've done nothing wrong. None of this is my fault. I hold my head a little higher, determined to let the name-calling fall on deaf ears. If I don't let them see it get to me, they'll get tired of it, I tell myself. I'm not the kind of girl who lets herself be bullied into something stupid, like suicide. That works fine until lunch.

"You want to get a sandwich in the commons?" Oliver says in the hall.

They're the first words out of his mouth in two periods, and I wonder where the hell he's been all this time I've been taking abuse.

"What, and be a laughingstock in front of half the school at once? Uh, no."

"Then where?"

"In town."

"What about security?"

"They have to buy their own lunch." I tug on his arm. "I don't *care* about security. Come on, let's go!"

"All right, all right," he mumbles.

His steps seem tentative at first as he leads us on. I realize he's fumbling with his phone when I hear it dialing.

"Red?" he says. "We're headed for the car... Yeah, going to town for lunch... Okay."

"You're such a Magoo," I mutter.

Okay, fine, so it's probably good that he's a boy scout, but I am *not* having lunch with Marcus. Or Red.

When we're in the car on the way to town, I can't stand it anymore.

"What is the matter with you?" I say.

"Me? Nothing. Why?"

He sounds perplexed, which makes me even crazier. "You've hardly said two words since first period. You're not talking to me. You didn't say anything to all those people making fun of me in the halls, didn't once try to defend me. Don't you care how I feel?"

"Well, sure I care, Tess. I figure you feel humiliated, angry, scared, powerless, singled out, maybe worthless."

"Hey! You're supposed to make me feel better, not worse. And that's going a little too far. How would *you* like it if that was *your* dick out there for the whole world to see?"

"I wouldn't like it at all. What do you want from me?"

"A little understanding maybe? A little sympathy?"

After a pause, he says, "Look, there's one thing I know about bullies." His voice is fierce. "The best thing you can do is walk away. Run if you have to. Ignore them, and you take away their power."

He doesn't strike me as the type to be bullied. He's so harmless. So vanilla. But I'm not the type, either. I'm a royal, damn it! I'm the kind of girl people envy. My hand goes to my face, and my fingertips trace the ridge of scar tissue that bolts down my face and retreats under my hair. I'm not that girl anymore. Now I'm the kind that people pity or make fun of. The monster they chase with pitchforks.

Yes, I feel humiliated and scared. But my anger is stronger than those feelings.

"There's no running away from this. It's out there, Oliver. That fucking video is out there for all the world to see. I can't just ignore it. It's not going away. It'll live on the Internet forever. And every time it makes the rounds, I'll be known as '*that* girl.'"

"That's what they want," he growls. "They *want* to see you suffer. That's the only way they feel in control of their own lives. *Don't* give them that. Don't give them the satisfaction."

His forcefulness presses me into my seat. I hate this. I *hate* my life. I hate the accident for stealing away everything I had—friends, status, respect, influence. I hate how much it's changed me, made me an object of derision, not envy. But maybe he's right. Maybe I'm only powerless if I give my power to my tormentors.

"And you know this, because, what, you were bullied in school?"

He snorts. "Youngest, smallest kid in every grade, with the mutant power to remember what I had for breakfast on just about any date in the distant past? What do you think?"

I don't need to say anything.

"Where are we going, anyway?" he says.

I give him the name of a coffee shop in town, and we drive the rest of the way in silence.

After he parks, he comes around the car to open my door and give me a hand out. I get a very faint whiff of coconut, and know that Marcus is nearby, close enough to help if we need it, but not so close that it looks as if he's with us, I hope. Then again, I don't know if he'll jump in to save us if something happens. Maybe he's changed his tune. Maybe I'm wrong about him. I don't think so. And my distrust has forever put me off coconut anything. I shiver.

I follow Oliver with a hand on his shoulder, now almost used to his murmured instructions—"...curb in two...five steps to corner...right turn coming up in three, two, one..."

Then he says, "Uh-oh. Your former posse is hanging out in front of the shop. Smile."

I paste on my best cheerleader smile and straighten up. "Tell me who's there," I say out of the side of my mouth.

"Toby, Adrienne, Emily," he mutters. "What's-her-name, the skinny brunette...um, Jordan. A couple of guys... I don't know all their names."

"Why Tess, what a pleasant surprise," a girl says as we get closer. "You look adorbs."

I know the voice instantly. It's Adrienne, my former BFF, the new captain of the cheer squad, and the girl who stole my now ex-boyfriend Toby.

"Oh, hi, Adrienne," I say sweetly. Addie, the girl I once traded secrets with, is dead to me.

"Tess, your new boyfriend must be one lucky guy," she says, her voice as syrupy as mine. "You know, judging from the video."

Laughter erupts in front of me, along with hoots of appreciation, and my face suddenly feels like it's on fire. My mind races, searching for a good reply. I hear Oliver's words in there, too, about ignoring them, walking away. Well, fuck that.

"A whole lot luckier than yours," I say, with all the honey my voice can muster.

The laughs, if anything, are louder this time from the guys there, which I'm betting is because Toby is sitting next to Adrienne. Sure enough, his voice calls out over the din.

"Not funny. Guys, it's not funny!" Finally, the laughter dies down.

"You really should see the video, Tess," Adrienne says. "Oh, that's right. You can't."

Snickers erupt again from the table in front of us, and my scar burns. That one hits too close to home. I have to bite my lip to distract me from all *those* memories, the ones that remind me how far I've fallen.

I give Oliver's arm a gentle tug. "Come on. Let's let Addie and her friends get back to watching porn."

"Sure, let's get something to eat." He leads me to the door.

"Tess, wait," Toby calls. "Wait up!"

A chair scrapes, and Adrienne's voice pipes up shrilly, "Toby, come back here! Don't you dare. I mean it."

But as Oliver opens the door, Toby's suddenly close by, out of breath.

"Tess, why do you want to diss me like that?"

"You can't be that clueless." He doesn't say anything, so I educate him. "Because your new girlfriend—the one you dumped me for—insulted me first. Good enough for you?"

"Still..."

He leaves it hanging, and I shift my weight impatiently. "What do you want, Toby?"

"Um, well, there's a rumor going around that someone got shot at the dance the other night. I just wanted to make sure you're okay."

"You see me standing here. Do I look okay?"

"Hey, just because you and I aren't, you know, together, doesn't mean I don't care."

What he said finally hits me. "Wait, you didn't go to homecoming? But what about the coronation?" I'm so surprised by the realization that I don't call him on his bullshit.

"I'm surprised you didn't hear," Toby says, sounding sheepish. "Madison and Paul got the vote, but I guess coronation was a bust anyway because of whatever happened. Addie said she didn't feel like going to the dance if she wasn't going to be queen, so I hung out at her house."

This is a development I never considered. If it hadn't been for the accident that turned me into a freak, I assumed that Toby and I would end up being homecoming king and queen senior year. Once I decided to let Oliver take me to the dance, though, I never gave the coronation a second thought.

"Too bad," I say. "You and Addie were the perfect choice."

Toby actually thinks I mean it. "Nah, Maddie and Paul are better ambassadors for our class. They deserved it."

"So, lunch?" Oliver says. "Or are you guys going to relive your freshman and sophomore years, too? I'm hungry."

Rather than being annoyed with him, I laugh. I realize that maybe I'm getting over Toby. The fact that Toby's obviously not over me makes it easier to let him go.

"Yeah, well, I'm glad you're okay," Toby says.

"Toby!" Adrienne yells. "Get your ass back here."

"Ooh, someone's cranky." I try hard not to smile. "Guess you better go."

29

I went back to the video whenever I had a spare moment. Not out of prurient interest, of course. Don't get me wrong; I can appreciate a hot bod as well as the next guy, and it was hard not to watch the darn thing without my jeans feeling a little tight and uncomfortable in the crotch. And one pass is all it would have taken to imprint the film in my memory. I kept viewing it, though, because I wanted to take in all the details, the nuances. Something about it seemed off to me. I'm no forensic video expert, but something about it didn't sit right. It's easy enough to fake a video these days, especially with the AI software that's out there, but I didn't think this was a fake. It just wasn't right, somehow.

So as soon as I got Tess seated at lunch and put in our orders, I pulled out my phone and played it again on mute. Tess nattered on about homecoming, and how surprised she was that Toby and Adrienne hadn't been a shoo-in for king and queen, and how that meant that if they weren't legitimate royals maybe they wouldn't be able to sway popular opinion against her.

"Oh, who am I kidding?" she said. "If the accident didn't shut me out, the video will."

"Mm-hmm."

"Hey! Hello? Oliver?" She reached out and lightly touched my arm, then slugged me. "Have you heard a word I said?"

"Sure. If the royals aren't so royal, then your fall from royalty might not be as royally bad as your highness thought. Except for the video."

"Wait. That's it. You've been quiet all morning because you've been watching the video. Oh, my God! Oliver, how could you?"

"It's not you," I said. I scrubbed back several frames and let it play again.

"What do you mean?"

"I'm not sure, but I don't think it's you on the video."

"Well, of course it's not me," she said indignantly. "First of all, *eewww*. Two, I'm not that kind of girl. And C, I would never let someone shoot a video of me naked. Not that I'm a prude or anything." She paused. "But how do you know it's not me?"

"I don't know. There's just something off. Not quite right."

"Well, is it me or not?"

"It's your face. But the way the video's edited, your face and the—you know, hand job—are never in the same shot."

"Oka-ay," she said slowly.

"And this body...well, I've never seen you naked, but I think—I'm not sure, of course—but I think this girl's boobs are bigger than yours."

"Oliver!" She slugged my arm again for the umpteenth time.

"Ow! Shit, you have to stop doing that. And the—well, that other stuff is a close-up shot so you can't see your face, just lips and...well, you know, a woody, a hard-on."

"Erection, Oliver. Penis. You can even say that on TV, you know. Gross. What else?"

"The video is pretty high quality, but it was shot in black-and-white. That, or whoever posted it used a filter on it. So it's hard to tell if the skin tone matches yours, and I wonder if that was deliberate."

"Hardly conclusive evidence. I need irrefutable proof, Oliver. I am so screwed."

"Just wait, okay? Here's the kicker. Whoever the 'star' is has ink. Tattoos."

I took her hand, lifted her arm, then touched my finger to a spot on the outside of her wrist. "A tiny circle here, and a half-circle in the same spot on the other arm. You don't have tattoos...unless they're hidden somewhere under your clothes."

She heaved a sigh, but didn't look relieved. "No, I don't have any tattoos. Not that I didn't want one. It's one of many things my mother and I used to fight about."

"I'm sorry, Tess."

Her eyes brimmed, but she blinked back the tears. "Fuck! There goes whatever reputation I had left in this school."

"But it's not *you*, Tess."

She shook her head. "It doesn't matter. People will think it is. And besides, it's too late. The video's out there. I can't stop it from getting around."

"Anyone with half a brain should be able to tell the video's a cut-and-paste job."

"Well, that leaves about ninety percent of the school that still needs to be convinced," she said sarcastically.

She might have been right on that score, and I couldn't think of any more words of encouragement.

30

His mind reeling, Travis headed back to his office after what seemed like the hundredth meeting of the day. He wondered how James had done it day after day, year after year. Travis was used to the military way of doing things, a clear chain of command that issued specific orders which were carried out by those best trained to do so.

As soon as the thought had fully formed, he laughed out loud, drawing a look from Janine at the reception desk. When he'd been a grunt in the army, orders from superior officers had often seemed arbitrary and uninformed, half the time resulting in CATFU situations that could have gotten him and his fellow soldiers killed. The other half turned out to be goat-roping expeditions that went nowhere. By the time he became an officer, he knew that snafus were a part of life in the army, and knew that every command came with implicit FITFO instructions. Yeah, a bunch of acronyms that everyone knew because they happened that frequently.

He snorted again as he walked into his office. That's what he had to do now, he realized—figure it the fuck out. He'd always been good at that, improvising, changing his approach on the spot. He'd had to adapt to survive in Afghanistan, not only to the harsh conditions in which he often found himself, but to the shifting loyalties of the people he lived among. One day they might be honor-bound to the local tribal chief, and subservient to the patrolling band of Taliban fighters the next. He had to use the same skills now as then, figure out who was friend and who was foe, who he could count on and who needed persuading.

Travis never imagined when General Turnbull called him back from his assignment overseas that his new mission to protect his brother James's family would be even more fraught with danger than Afghanistan. He couldn't have conceived that a business designing and selling video games could have as many enemies as he'd faced as a soldier, could be inhabited by as many people with as many agendas. Now, after being thrust into the position of running the company for more than a year since the accident, he was only beginning to discover what he was up against. *Who* was another question.

He thought he could trust Alice and Yoshi because he'd known them since James and Sally hired them. Eons ago, it seemed. But now Yoshi was keeping secrets from him, and Travis wasn't sure whether or not Alice was hiding things, too. Tess had voiced her opinion about Marcus, the head of Travis's security team, on several occasions, but Travis had more concerns about MondoHard's security chief, Cyrus Cooper. The only person Travis thought he truly could trust was Robyn. And only because James had trusted her. Travis certainly didn't know her well enough, but she'd been indispensable since he'd moved into the executive suite. He, and the company, would not have survived without her.

Now that he thought of it, he wondered where she was. He didn't remember seeing her on his way into his office, but he'd been preoccupied. He poked his head out the door. She wasn't at her desk. The ladies room, perhaps. He glanced at his watch. Or maybe at lunch. Sighing, he turned back to his desk, then did a double-take and checked the watch again. He swore under his breath. In less than five minutes, his next meeting would walk in the door. He hurried to pull the appropriate file from the stack on the desk and sat down to review it.

The next two and a half hours were a steady succession of meetings punctuated by short stints online to answer email. When checking email again after his last meeting, he noted one from Robyn reminding him about some client callbacks he needed to make. Though not sure why she hadn't come in or called to tell him, Travis was relieved she was back in the office.

A late afternoon sky heavy with clouds stained the windows gray by the time Travis got off the phone. He felt tired—schmoozing and mollifying customers, or anyone for that matter, wasn't his forté—but he recognized the necessity of building relationships, both personal and professional. The calls had warmed one client's cold feet regarding a new cloud-based service app, preventing the loss of several million dollars in sales, and encouraged another customer to set up a meeting to discuss expanding into new service areas using MondoHard's AI software. Travis gathered all his notes and walked them out to have Robyn type them up into meeting and call summaries.

"Everything okay?" he said, handing her the stack of notes. "You weren't here when I got back this morning."

She nodded and looked down at her desk. "Sorry. I had to step out for a bit."

"Nothing to be sorry about." He waited, but she didn't meet his gaze. He shifted his weight. "Say, there's something I wanted to ask you. Blair Wallace stopped by yesterday."

Her face turned toward him, eyes wide in surprise. "At your house?"

"Yes. He said he was looking for a document. A codicil to James's will. Blair seemed to think that James had you sign it as a witness. Do you know anything about it?"

"Oh, my, that was some time ago. I remember it, of course. But I wasn't a witness. I notarized it electronically. I notarized the letter of instruction to Mr. Wallace as well. That was a hard copy, of course. Sally was here and witnessed both documents." Robyn's brow furrowed. "Let me think. A young man in development came up. Derek...Derek Hamblin, that's it. He also signed."

Startled, Travis tried to mask his surprise. "Do you know where it is? Apparently, Blair can't find a copy anywhere."

She stared into space as if an answer would appear in mid-air, and shook her head. "No idea. Since it's an e-document, it could be filed anywhere. I can check his—your—office computer if you like. But I have no clue what file name he might have used."

"Then you don't know what's in it." Travis hoped she'd hear a question in his statement.

Robyn's face twisted, a range of emotions playing out in fractions of a second before she regained her composure.

"James was always very straightforward with me. Honest. If he wanted me to know what was in that document, he would have told me. He just asked me to notarize it in front of witnesses." Her expression turned pensive. "Though I do recall hearing Sally ask James if he thought a blind trust would really work."

Travis rubbed the back of his neck. She confirmed Wallace's story, but he couldn't imagine what advantage a blind trust offered over the existing trust.

"James could have filed it anywhere," he said. "Laptop, thumb drive, server..."

Robyn nodded. "Even his phone, I suppose."

Travis rolled his eyes and sighed. "You wouldn't happen to want to help me look, would you? I mean, you knew James about as well as anyone."

Robyn hesitated. "Maybe. I suppose I could suggest places to look."

Travis pressed. "You could come to the house for dinner. Check James's office and stuff."

She leaned away from him. "I don't think that would be a good idea."

Feeling his ears get hot, Travis tried to erase what he'd said by wiping the air in front of him with both hands. "No, no, of course not. I didn't mean... I just thought..."

"No, I understand. It...I don't think it would be right, that's all."

Travis tipped his head toward the floor and scuffed a shoe on the carpet. "Sure. I get it."

The sound of Robyn's cell phone buzzing brought his gaze up just in time to see her face register fear as she looked at it.

31

My public humiliation on a grand scale—twice now since breakfast—puts me in a mood so foul that not even the memory of one-upping Addie can bring me out of it. I dread facing afternoon classes, or any classes for the rest of the semester. The silence in the car is the perfect antidote, a nothingness I crave right now. It doesn't last.

"It'll all blow over," Oliver mutters.

I sigh to remind him of how clueless he is. "No, it won't."

"What's the big deal? People make fun of you for a few days, get bored and move on."

"The big deal," I say, my voice rising as fast as the heat in my face, "is that my reputation is being ruined!"

"I thought your rep already was trashed because of...well, you know."

I squeeze my sightless eyes shut trying to figure out what he means. "What? The accident?"

"Well, yeah."

"You mean the way I look?"

"Hey, you said it, not me. Besides, I thought you didn't care what people think anymore."

"Oh, my God, Oliver! You can be so infuriating."

"Me? What?"

"Aren't you the one who...?" I remember him telling me about being bullied in school, and then realize it was no pep talk. "Oh, never mind. But this *isn't* going to blow over, I assure you."

Right on schedule, my phone chimes with an incoming text. I thumb the phone on.

"Play text," I say.

"You have one text from 'Unknown,'" the phone intones. "Slut!"

"See?" I yell, tears welling up. "It's not going to stop! It's *never* going to stop."

Thankfully, Oliver doesn't speak. Anything he might have said just would have been lame. For all of two minutes the car fills with blissful silence that gives me time to star as the guest of honor at my own pity party. I never should have agreed to go back to school, never should have allowed Alice to hire my jerk of an assistant who's about as empathetic and helpful as a Nurse Ratched, which is to say any guy for that matter. So when Oliver opens his mouth again, I almost lose it completely.

"What's the deal with you and Adrienne, anyway?" he says.

"I already told you!" I shout.

"Yeah, yeah, she stole your loser ex- Toby. She did you a favor." He pauses. "No, I mean what happened between you two?"

I clamp my jaw shut and turn my face away so he can't see my eyes leaking with anger, frustration and—I don't know. Regret? Addie and I were inseparable from third grade on. I had her back, and she had mine, flip sides of the same coin. She was the base to my flyer. I was her conscience, and she was my temptation. I brought the class, she brought the sass. Addie could walk into a room and feel instantly at home and comfortable talking to anyone. She could talk an alum into a donation for the computer lab or a parent into one for a new piece to our cheer outfits, and she could talk a teacher out of putting us in detention for vaping in the girls' bathroom or skipping last class so we could go up to the pass for night snowboarding with a couple of guys. And when a conversation turned to accomplishments, prospects, achievement and possibilities, she always deferred to me, made me look good.

Tess aced that AP exam; that'll clinch the valedictorian spot for her this year.

The stunts Tess came up with earned our squad the state cheerleading competition last year.

I told Oliver that the accident drove us apart, but I lied. And lies were what had driven a wedge between Addie and me long before I got my scar.

I'm still upset when we get back to school, and the titters and murmurs that float over the general din of students heading back to classes don't cheer me up any. We haven't even wound our way to the 400 block hallway when my fears are confirmed.

"Hey, Wuhan!" a voice calls out.

The background noise diminishes, and Oliver slows then stops.

"I'm sorry," he says, "were you speaking to me?"

"No, numb-nuts." The speaker is closer, but no quieter. "I'm talking to *her*. Maybe you oughta stop making videos, bitch. Bad enough you brought that kung flu back here. Nobody wants you spreading STDs, too."

"Hey, shut the hell up, man!" Oliver says. "Don't talk to her like that."

"Yeah?" the voice sneers. "Or what?"

"Come on, Tess," Oliver says. "Ignore this moron. Let's go."

I'm too shocked to do anything but stumble after him.

"Wear a mask!" the guy yells after us.

The other thing I missed during my eighteen-month rehab besides my junior year, apparently, was a global pandemic. It was only after vaccines became widely available, that people stopped wearing masks most places—except for COVIDiots who never wore them anyway. I hadn't had to worry about it because as messed up as I'd been from the accident, with rehab and everything I'd basically been in quarantine all that time.

Behind us, a bunch of guys chants, "Wu-han! Wu-han! Wu-han!" as if they're at a football game. I know that everyone is staring at me. I can feel their laser gazes boring holes in me, a hundred tiny suns burning my skin. I want to lash out at my tormentors, make them stop. But I know that this is just the beginning, that trying to inflict blows on all those who are being turned against me is like punching the tide—the water will rise inexorably higher until I drown.

32

Derek twirled a pen in his fingers and stared at the monitor. Suddenly, he clenched the pen in his teeth and typed furiously for several seconds, then sat back and fingered the pen again. *I'm the best, damn it, the best hacker this side of Ukraine. No, better.* The keyboard clacked again like machinegun fire, and he peered at the screen to see the result. With three clicks, he saved a screen grab to a thumb drive. Then he began the slow task of backing out of the site, careful not to leave any footprints. Finally, he jotted some notes on a pad next to the keyboard and logged off. He wasn't sure what it all meant yet, and he wasn't done trying to get more information. But he knew it was time to let Tess know what he'd found out so far.

Pushing back from the desk, he grabbed his phone and checked messages, email and his calendar. He didn't have much on his plate at the moment. He and his team had burned through a lot of energy drinks in the past few weeks repairing a video game the company had been about to launch. *His* video game—*Never Bitten.* Someone had sabotaged it, screwed with the code to incorporate an AI program that brainwashed users. The son of VPOTUS had gotten an infected beta copy—from Travis, no less—and had almost assassinated his own father. Derek and his team had put in hundreds of hours poring, line by line, through a copy of the source code that he'd stashed to make sure it was clean. As a result, the launch had gone off without a hitch, and the app was a smash hit.

Derek had his suspicions about who was responsible for the hack, but he'd remained silent. Without proof, incontrovertible evidence, he'd never convince anyone of the perpetrator's guilt. The guy was too high up the food chain, and Derek knew in a case of "he said/he said," Derek would lose. So now, he trusted phones and email even less than before. He wouldn't send important texts or email unless he was on a VPN, and they were encrypted. And he wouldn't use the phone for anything other than chit-chat—too easy to eavesdrop or hack into, again unless he was on a burner phone or a VPN.

That all meant the best mode of communication was meeting face to face. Not tough duty when it came to Tess Barrett. He grinned at the thought. All in all, a pretty decent looking chick. Exotic, with baby blues that could melt cold steel in addition to hearts. That scar made her look dangerous, and Derek felt sure she was. A rebel, like him. He just knew they were *sympatico*. Besides, if it came down to a choice between him and Oliver there was no contest. Nothing against the seeing-eye dog. Derek actually liked Oliver, sort of. The guy's fail-safe memory made him wicked smart, and he was decent enough. But boring. And too old for Tess.

Derek slipped the thumb drive in his pocket and lifted his rain gear off a peg on the wall. The jumpsuit was clumsy but necessary when the Northwest rainy season began. A sudden thought made him stop. He threw the rain gear over the back of his chair, opened the bottom drawer of his desk and rummaged around in the back before finding what he wanted. Holding the glass bottle up to the light, he nodded and spritzed cologne on his T-shirt under each arm. After wriggling the suit on over his jeans, he pulled on his leather motorcycle boots. Then he stuffed "Sam's" laptop in his backpack, shrugged the backpack on over the bulky rain suit, grabbed his helmet, and headed for the elevator.

Once he weaved his way through downtown traffic, he leaned his bike onto the ramp to the floating bridge across the lake. His helmet's heads-up display told him he could still catch Tess at school if he hurried. He twisted the throttle. A thrill ran up his spine as the engine's growl changed pitch and the acceleration made him grip the handlebars tighter to keep from being thrown back. With the HOV lane all to himself, he blew past the other traffic, feeling the envy of the mere mortals in the other lanes.

The bike ate up the miles so quickly that the school looked deserted when he arrived, so he lounged against the seat, ankles and arms crossed until the last bell rang. Doors in the building erupted and spewed a colorful, cross-cultural flow of teen-aged humans, laughing, yelling, name-calling. Derek watched with bemusement and thought of his own high school years—already ancient history—without a shred of fondness. His gaze roved over the throngs that clumped near the doors and dissipated in all directions in small streams like water from a shower head.

Suddenly, he spotted Tess, looking much like any other girl emerging from the building except for the way she kept her head tilted just so, to keep the side of her face hidden behind a cascade of black hair, and the hand she kept on the shoulder of the guy in front of her. *Oliver*. Derek sighed. He could do that, lead a girl around. Would do it, too, except that his job was way cooler, and way more important. And definitely paid more.

He summoned the energy to raise an arm and shout to attract Oliver's attention, but saw it wasn't necessary as the pair headed in his direction. They crossed the plaza in front of the cafeteria—neon food station signs still lit behind the glass-fronted section of the building—and mounted the stairs leading up to where Derek stood. They weren't talking, and Tess looked unhappy. Downright miserable, in fact. Derek thought he might look unhappy, too, if he had to hang out with Oliver all day.

A big-ass black SUV in his periphery slowly pulled up behind his bike. He didn't give it a second thought, keeping his eyes on the pair below as they rose toward him. When they reached the top of the steps, Derek pushed away from the seat toward them.

"Yo, Tess," he called.

Tess stiffened, sniffing the air, and Oliver's head snapped up, eyes searching for the source of the greeting. Derek raised a hand, but before he took another step, someone grabbed his wrist out of the air, swung it around behind his back and painfully thrust it up between his shoulder blades against his backpack. At the same time, a hand clamped down onto his opposite shoulder and pulled him back into the wrist lock behind his back.

"Holy crap, man!" he cried. "What the fuck?"

"He's okay, Red," Oliver said. "We know him."

"Know who?" Tess said crossly. "The slacker you're hanging onto?"

"Jeez, Tess, it's me, Derek. Call off the dog."

"I know it's you, Derek," she said. "I'm blind, not deaf. And I'd know that cologne anywhere. What are you doing here?"

A deep voice behind him said, "So you're the infamous Derek. Why didn't you say so? Should I let him go, Ms. Barrett?"

"Yeah, I guess."

"You guess?" Derek mumbled. "Nice welcome."

Hands released him, and Derek glanced back to see a red-bearded grin towering over him.

"Much obliged to you for all the intel you provided a few weeks back," the giant said. "Might've had a higher body count up at Ms. Barrett's place in the mountains if you hadn't helped out."

Derek flushed and dropped his gaze to the sidewalk. "Yeah, no problem."

"We haven't met. You met Fred and Barney, though," the man said. "Got them into some hot water, too, I hear. Call me Red."

Derek looked up sharply, but instead of anger, he saw a bigger grin on the bearded man's face than before. It faded though as another man got out of the SUV and strolled over. Tall and powerfully built, but smaller than the giant, he reminded Derek of a film actor, maybe one of the Wayans, or one of those rappers turned action-movie star.

"Everything copacetic here, Red?" the man said.

"All good, sir," Red replied.

"We're fine, Marcus," Tess said. She looked as if she'd found anchovies on her pizza.

"Glad to hear it" Marcus said. "I'll wait in the car then."

Despite his movie-star looks, Marcus left Derek with the feeling of having worked on his bike all day—slick and oily. He shrugged it off. Not his problem.

"Hey, sorry I ruffled your feathers, kid," Red said. He turned and walked back to the SUV.

"Why are you here, Derek?" Oliver echoed Tess.

Swiveling his gaze to face him, Derek found Oliver and Tess just a few feet away.

"What, I can't check out where Tess goes to school and say hi?"

"Travis told you to keep your distance," Oliver said.

Derek's eyes narrowed. "No, he didn't. He just said he didn't want me giving her rides."

"Hey, you two!" Tess said. "I'm right here. Don't talk about me like I'm not."

"I learned some stuff." Derek lowered his voice and glanced over his shoulder to make sure Red and Marcus weren't listening. "From Sam's laptop."

"Oh, yeah, that," Oliver said, looking a little deflated.

"I needed to show you in person," Derek said, "but didn't want to take the chance of running into Travis at your house."

Tess frowned. "He's at work."

"Well, yeah, but he could leave anytime."

"Okay, but we can't do it here. Follow us to the house, and if Travis comes home, so what?"

Derek shrugged. "Okay, babe, if that's the way you want to play it."

"That's right, '*babe*,' that's the way she wants to play it," Oliver said.

"Oh, just stop it, you two," Tess said, peeved. "Come on, Oliver, let's go."

"See you at the house," Derek said. "Last one there buys coffee."

Five minutes later, Derek sat patiently astride his bike on the apron outside the gate to the Barrett compound. Oliver and Tess pulled up in a sweet ride a minute later, followed by the black SUV with the security guys. A moment later, the gate trundled open and the two vehicles drove through. Derek swung in behind them before the gate began to close, and paraded down the curvy lane in the rear. He turned into the circle at the front entrance while Oliver parked in one of the garage bays and the SUV peeled off and drove into a garage attached to the guest house.

Derek killed the engine, kicked the stand down, and took off his helmet. By the time he walked up the steps onto the portico and peeled off the rain suit, Oliver and Tess had joined him, and Tess opened the front door by placing a hand on a biometric scanner. Once inside, she led the way to the library.

"So what's this all about?" she said when she sat at the big study table. "Have you figured out who Sam is yet?"

Derek put the backpack on the table and pulled out Sam's laptop. "Are you sure this room isn't bugged?"

Tess looked startled.

"Why would the library be bugged?" Oliver said.

"I don't know," Derek said "But like you said, Travis seems to want to keep close tabs on Tess. Close enough, maybe, to listen in on your conversations."

"He better not be," Tess said. She looked pissed. "I never thought about it before, but if he is I'll kill him."

"Well, if you're sure it's not bugged... I could bring a scanner next time."

"That'd be good." She sighed. "By the way, fair's fair. You beat us here, so I'll buy coffee. What do you want?"

"A triple *venti*, since you're buying."

"Okay, sure. Oliver, I'll have a skinny mocha, no whip."

Oliver stared at her.

"I don't hear you leaving." She glowered.

"Wait, why do I have to go get coffee?" Oliver said.

"Hmm... How about because I'm blind? Or because you're my assistant, and I need assistance. Because I don't want to bother Alice, and we don't have a cook-slash-snack-lady since Rosa was...well, you know."

"Slashed? Okay, fine." Oliver practically stomped off in a huff.

Derek pulled out the chair in front of the laptop, spun it around backward on one leg and straddled it. He leaned forward, folding his arms on the back of the chair.

"Was he mad?" she said.

"Pretty much," Derek said.

"Good. I swear sometimes I think he forgets he works for me."

"He's not so bad, is he?" Derek couldn't believe he felt sorry for the guy.

"I guess not." She looked as if she was about to say more but thought better of it.

"Something the matter, babe?"

Her nose wrinkled. "More like what isn't the matter?"

"No, seriously."

"Promise you won't laugh? Or worse?"

"Sure. Cross my heart."

"Oh, what the hell. The whole world knows by now. I'm surprised you don't. There's a porno making the rounds on social media."

"And you're in it?" Derek's pulse quickened. This chick was even cooler than he thought.

"Oh, my God, no!"

The look of shock and horror on her face was like a bucket of cold water down his shorts.

"Apparently, I'm the star," she went on.

"'Apparently,'" Derek said hesitantly. "Meaning you're not, natch. What's the big whoop?"

"Well, at least you didn't laugh." She paused. "Don't tell me you're as clueless as Oliver."

"No, I get it, babe. The 'star' looks like you but isn't, and you're concerned about your rep."

"Well, yeah. I'd never do anything like that."

"Fuck 'em. It's your senior year, right? You're outta there in six months. This will blow over long before then anyway."

"Funny," she murmured. "That's what Oliver said."

"You want me to see if I can trace who posted it?"

"You can do that? I mean, you'd do that for me?"

"That'd be yes to both."

"I might take you up on that. Let me think about it."

She tapped a finger against her lips. Derek didn't want to think too hard about those lips.

"Say," she said after a moment, "how are app sales?"

"*Never Bitten*? Through the roof. From what I hear, best initial sales of a MondoHard game since your dad's original. Thanks for asking."

"Wow, that's great. I'm happy for you."

Derek heard the bittersweet tone in her voice.

"Hey, well, I had a lot of help. Not like back in the day when it was just your dad and mom designing games. I mean that had to be pretty insane, doing all the work themselves—the art, the design, the coding..." Derek let his voice trail off.

"You miss him—them—don't you?" he said after a moment.

She shrugged. "No. Yeah. Not really. It's complicated."

"Sure. I get that."

"What about you? Do you get along with your parents?"

"Nah. My dad took off when I was in middle school because he didn't like my mom's drinking. The guy who took his place was a real asshole. I managed to stick it out until senior year, and was lucky enough to bunk with a buddy and his family until graduation. Then I left town. Came here. Kicked around until James—your dad—tracked me down."

"Maybe I don't have it so bad," she murmured.

Before Derek thought of a reply the library door opened.

"Got your coffee," Oliver called. "I found some biscotti in the kitchen, too, in case you're hungry."

Oliver placed a tray on the table, passed out the espresso drinks, and put a plate of biscotti in front of Tess where she could reach it easily.

"Anything else I can get you, princess?" he said.

Her nostrils flared, but Derek couldn't stifle a laugh. "Sorry, couldn't help it."

"Jerks," she mumbled. Then in as haughty a voice a she could muster, she said, "No, thanks anyway, Oliver."

"So, what did I miss?" Oliver said. "Did you cover everything? If so, we might as well start on your homework, Tess."

"No, Mr. Smarty-Pants," she said. "We were just talking."

"Oh," Oliver said, his mouth staying open in surprise. "So, Derek, what did you find out?"

"Well, I learned Tess is a porno star."

"Derek!" Tess shrieked.

Oliver looked surprised, and Derek laughed again. "You're not going to like it," he said as he booted up the laptop.

"Why not?" Tess said.

"Let me just show you," Derek said, "well, show Oliver and tell you, and you can make up your own minds. Okay, so I went at this a whole bunch of ways. First, I dug into that ranch in Montana a little deeper. A lot deeper. I hacked in and did a data sort of all the guests for the past five years. Most of the ranch's business looks legitimate—conferences, weddings, that sort of thing. Guest names and billing information all match. But like we learned before, the place focuses mostly on government retreats. Even then, room charges and banquets all get billed back to the department or agency that hosted the event.

"But I came across something unusual. In a lot of instances, rooms were booked and used by people listed not by name, but by code. Seems these guests wanted to remain anonymous, and the ranch obliged. Most showed up in the reservations database only once or twice. But one showed up a lot, and whoever was assigned that particular code always stayed in the same suite."

"But you can't tell who it is because the ranch used a code, not a name," Tess said.

"Yeah, except for one thing," Derek said. "I got curious, so I looked at how often that particular suite was reserved and found out only one other person was ever booked in that room. I mean ever."

"Well, come on," Oliver said. "Tell us who."

"Senator Jeremy Latham."

Tess frowned. "Who's that?"

"Probably the most powerful man in Washington, D.C."

Tess laughed. "Oh, come on, Derek. The president is the most powerful person. Even a 'dumb' girl like me knows that." She hooked her fingers in the air to make her point.

"Sure, that's what everybody thinks."

"I see where Derek's coming from," Oliver said quietly. "Latham is chairman of the Senate Appropriations Committee, chairman of the subcommittee on defense spending, and he's on half a dozen other influential committees, too. There probably isn't a dime of the national budget that he doesn't control somehow."

Tess shrugged. "Okay, so?"

"So, here's where it gets interesting," Derek said, getting into his subject matter. "Normally, when a hotel comps a room, it just writes it off as a business expense. When that suite was booked for 'Mr. X,' the room charge was billed back to Federated Enterprises."

"One of the shell companies that owns the ranch," Oliver said slowly.

"One of the shell companies that owns the shell company that owns the ranch, yeah," Derek said with a grin. "That made me even more curious. Since Sam's laptop has evidence that Federated Enterprises might be the source of his payment for the hit on you, Tess, I wondered what else Fed Ent paid for. From the bank routing numbers, I found that Fed Ent has been making monthly deposits into a bank account in McLean, Virginia, under the name of Felicity Llewellyn."

"This is way too complicated," Tess said. "Can we skip to the part where you tell us who Sam is and why the hell he tried to kill me?"

"That's what I'm trying to do, babe. Cut me a little slack. I worked hard on this. I'm not your everyday hacker, you know."

"Fine. Who's Felicity Whatshername?"

"She's dead, is what she is. As for who, she *was* Latham's mother."

"Wait," Oliver said. "You mean that a sitting U.S. senator paid for a hit on a high school student?"

"Hey!" Tess said. "Not just any high school student. *Me!*"

"I don't know," Derek said. "That's what it *looks* like. But it's more complicated than that."

"Oh, no," Tess said. "Here we go again."

"Sam got two payments upfront. The other bank routing number that deposited money in Sam's account belongs to a bank here," Derek said.

"In Seattle?" Tess sat wide-eyed.

"Yeah, and this transaction wasn't as sophisticated as the other one. It was pretty easy to trace the money back to a specific account at the bank. The account belongs to MondoHard."

"What?" Now Tess trembled, shock on her face more evident.

"I told you you weren't going to like it," Derek said.

"But that could have been anyone," Oliver said. "At least anyone with authorization on the account."

"True," Derek said, looking around uneasily. "I can try to find out, but I'm guessing Travis is at least one of those people."

Tess shook her head violently, her mouth a grim line. "No. I can't believe it. I won't. Travis? After all that's happened? And why pay to have me killed when he could just do it in person?"

"To keep his hands clean? Or maybe so he can show you how invaluable he is at keeping you alive. I mean you did survive the attack, thanks to his security team."

"I survived because I defended myself!" Tess shouted.

"Calm down, babe," Derek said. "Look, I'm not even saying it was Travis. I'm just telling you the facts, and the fact is at least some of the money paid to Sam came from MondoHard."

She shook her head. "I don't believe this. What the fuck is going on?"

"I'm not happy about it either, babe. I work there. Why do you think I asked about a bug?"

"I don't get it," Oliver said. "I admit I don't know much about it, but isn't digital currency a better way to hide a transaction like this? Why use bank accounts? Even offshore shell company accounts?"

"If I gave you some Bitcoin or a handful of NFTs would you know what to do with it?" Derek said.

Oliver scratched his head.

"Right," Derek nodded. "That's what I thought. Most people like currency they're familiar with, money they can use to buy stuff."

"Stop it!" Tess cried. Her mouth trembled, and she was on the verge of tears.

"What's wrong, babe?" Derek said.

"You two are missing the fucking point!" she yelled. "It's not about the money. Someone is trying to kill me! Why? Why do they want me dead? What did *I* do?"

33

Sensing Travis's gaze, Robyn quickly relaxed her face into a neutral expression, fear still twisting her in knots. She had to think. She offered a wan smile.

"Was there anything else?" she said.

"I guess not," he said, chin tipping down. He hesitated then turned and slipped back into his office.

As she watched his broad shoulders slump, she realized his retreat was more like slinking away with his tail between his legs, something she'd never seen him do. He approached everything with the ramrod straight determination of a soldier. *He couldn't have feelings for her, could he? Did he feel rejected?* She felt bad, but her fear overpowered any instinct she might have had to assuage his male ego.

As soon as the door to his office shut, she pulled up the text on her phone again.

Go to your car and wait for instructions.

Trembling, Robyn glanced around, sure that the executives in the suite could feel her discomfort. But no one took any notice. Most doors, like Travis's, were closed, some offices empty, their usual occupants traveling or out at a meeting somewhere. Gathering herself, she stood and straightened her skirt, picked up her phone and keys, and walked purposefully down the corridor to the elevators. Janine barely looked up, busy at her desk.

Heartbeat drumming in her ears, she shifted her weight from one foot to the other until the elevator car arrived with a soft *ding*. Her thoughts raced as she got on and the elevator descended. *Why her car? What instructions? Did they want her to go somewhere? What could they possibly want from her?* She was convinced "they" were behind this, not "he" or "she," and the thought chilled her. One person was a personal vendetta, a wrong that could somehow be righted, or an individual who could be caught and brought to justice. *They* meant a conspiracy, a faceless entity without a soul.

The elevator stopped with a gentle bump, the doors sliding open to the chill air in the underground garage. Nervously, she stepped out and headed for her car, footsteps on the concrete echoing loudly in the cavernous space. A press of the key fob in her hand provided a reassuring chirp and flash of lights from her car. She climbed in, shivering, and shut the door quickly, locking it just to be safe.

How would they get instructions to her in her car?

Robyn twisted her head wildly, nervously scanning for signs of anyone approaching the car.

Were they watching her?

The hands in her lap curled and twined, her fingers cold and nearly numb. She started at the ring of the phone she'd dropped in a cupholder.

Who would try to use cell phones in a parking garage?

Cell phone reception was notoriously bad in underground concrete structures. Which was why MondoHard had installed mini cell towers and Wi-Fi repeaters on every floor of the garage. A fact "they" would know only if very familiar with the company's headquarters.

She stared at it, frowning as it rang a second time. Only it wasn't her phone ringing. Following the sound, she reached down and felt under the seat. Her fingers touched something hard and smooth, and she drew out a small smart phone as it rang again.

How had that gotten there? Had someone broken into her car? If they'd gotten into her car without setting off the alarm or breaking a window, they were more sophisticated than the average extortionist. A chill ran through her.

Slowly bringing the phone up to her ear, she connected the call but didn't dare breathe lest it come out in a scream.

"Listen carefully," said a scratchy, metallic voice. "Do exactly as we say and no one will get hurt. Defy us, and you will pay."

"What?" she whispered, unable to keep a tremor out of her voice. "What do you want?"

"There is a document we want."

For the second time in the past twenty minutes she'd been asked about a document.

"What kind of document?" she asked.

"You know the answer to that. Stop stalling."

"I don't know where it is." She fought back tears.

"Find it!"

"Why me?"

"Because you knew him! Better than anyone. You know where to look. You have seventy-two hours."

"But I can't—"

"Three days! Starting now. We'll be watching."

The connection broke. Robyn dropped the phone into her lap and shuddered. She buried her face in her hands and wailed in frustration and fear. Her thoughts hurtled down a one-way track toward disaster, seeing nothing ahead but a cliff and a sign reading, "Bridge Out Ahead." There had to be a way, a side spur that would save both her brother and her. When push came to shove, she realized, she didn't care about herself. She would do anything to protect her brother.

Anything.

34

After a long moment of silence, Oliver's the first to speak.

"If Latham really is involved, we need to find out what's so important to him that he'd pay to have someone killed."

"Me!" I say. "Not 'someone.' *Me*. How could I possibly be a threat to a person like that? I don't know anyone in Washington, D.C. I never heard of Latham."

"Look, I'm good at what I do, man" Derek says. "I learned this much without anyone knowing I hacked into their systems...I *think*. But if we're up against a guy like Latham, not to mention the company I get my paycheck from, we are way out of our league. We can't take any more chances or they'll crush us like bugs."

"So what are you saying?" My voice sounds shrill. "We just sit here and let them send someone else to kill me?"

I don't hear any bright ideas from either of them. My brain has turned to shit, thoughts buzzing around it like flies. I'm better than this. I'm a 4.0 Honors student, a once and future royal. And as bad as the past eighteen months have been, as grueling and painful as rehab was, and as crappy as my reception at school is, I don't want to die. I don't want to be a target for shadowy conspirators in some evil plot to take over the world or whatever this crap is about. I just want to be normal, to get through the rest of my senior year so I can get out of this fucking place. Which reminds me that I haven't written my college application essays. *Fuck*. What else can go wrong?

You know there's no way we can take this guy down, right?" Oliver says in a low voice. "Even if we have proof, and I mean indisputable, airtight, proof, we'll never convince anyone. If they don't kill us before we try, that is."

"Don't you think I know that?" Derek says. "Why do you think I'm telling you this? We've got to get out in front of this. Figure out an insurance policy."

"Stop!" I say. "Just stop. I don't know anything! Why are they trying to kill me?"

"If they thought you knew something, babe, they wouldn't be trying to kill you. They'd be trying to snatch you."

"I think Derek's right," Oliver says. "It's more likely they perceive you as a threat."

"What kind of a threat?" I feel like I'm losing my mind. "How am I threat to anyone?"

Oliver groans as if I'm being a pain. "Not this again."

I'm about to really lay into him when I sense he's not talking about me. The ambient noise in the house is suddenly missing.

"What's wrong," I say, my heart thumping faster. "What's going on?"

35

Hearing the soft knock on his office door, Travis looked up expectantly from the work on his desk. When the door opened and Robyn poked her head in, he blinked in surprise.

"Robyn." As if she didn't know who she was. He could have kicked himself.

He didn't know why he was surprised. She was his assistant; there were any number of reasons she might knock on his door. He couldn't figure out why she had this effect on him after all this time. He wasn't able to think straight when in her presence. Hell, even when she was somewhere else he seemed to think about her every five minutes like a love-struck eighth grader.

Then he saw the expression on her face, not quite unsettled, but not normal either. As if a storm raged beneath a placid surface.

"What is it?" he said.

Robyn stepped all the way inside and closed the door behind her, but didn't venture any closer. She moistened her lips and tucked a stray strand of hair behind her ear.

"Um, I've changed my mind," she said. "If you don't mind, I would like to come. To dinner, that is."

"Dinner?" Why couldn't he think?

"If that's all right," she said hurriedly, twisting her fingers together. "I don't want to put anyone out."

"No, no, of course it's all right. It's no imposition at all."

She looked relieved. "Oh, good. There's just one thing."

"Anything. Name it."

"I'll have to bring Benjamin."

"Benjamin?" Travis felt his brows knit. He pasted a smile on his face and tried to keep his voice light. "You don't need a chaperone. Really, Robyn, I'll be completely honorable."

Her smile in return was wan, a low-wattage version of her usual good cheer.

Puzzled, he tried again, amping up the charm. "Seriously, Alice will be there. I don't try to get away with anything around her."

Robyn looked at her feet and said nothing. Raising her gaze, she seemed about to speak when the light finally dawned on Travis that she wasn't talking about bringing a "friend.".

"Oh, your *brother*, Benjamin." He wanted to punch himself. He'd faced off against some of the most dangerous fighters in the world, had braved overwhelming odds and come out on top, had cheated Death more times than he could count, and this diminutive pixie had enchanted and transformed him into a mass of quivering jelly. "Of course, Benjamin."

She nodded. "You don't mind, do you?"

He shook his head and swiped the air. "No, no, of course not. He's welcome to come. Why haven't I ever met him, by the way?"

She tucked her head in her shoulder shyly. "You were always off somewhere defending our freedom. And after James…well, after…"

She startled as the lights flickered. Travis hesitated, but once they steadied, she focused on him again.

He nodded, feeling even worse now. "I know. Nothing's the same. I'm so sorry. I know how close you were."

"Well, now you'll have a chance," she said brightly, suddenly blushing. "To meet Benjamin, that is. So, see you around six?"

36

The tall narrow windows on either side of the massive stone fireplace let in the only light in the library, the gray day outside keeping it to a minimum.

"Power's out, babe," Derek said.

"Just like the other night," I said. "It's not windy, not even raining, really."

"Big whoop," Tess said. "What's the big deal. If it doesn't come back on, the generators will kick in. Wait, what do you mean, the other night? When?"

"At the dance. Before all hell broke loose. The lights flickered, then went out for five or ten seconds."

Tess shrugged. "It happens. Good thing is we have generators that keep everything running."

"Yeah, well, it's kind of weird. Creepy, too, when the lights go out."

"I don't know about you two, but I can find my way around just fine in the dark," she said.

"With a little help," I muttered.

"Excuse me? What did you say?"

From her tone, I knew perfectly well that she heard every word and I was in serious trouble. Fortunately, the power came back on just then.

"Whoa, lights are on," Derek said. "I guess my work here is done."

"Wait, what about Latham?" I said.

"What about *me*?" Tess cried.

"Hey, I dig you," Derek said to her, "but no way we're going on a date until you lose the Seeing Eye dog. And—"

"Hey!" I said. "Watch it."

"And," he went on, ignoring me, "like you said, Latham is a powerful guy. We don't stand a chance against someone connected like that."

Tess folded her arms. "So, what you're saying is you're full of shit."

"Yeah." Derek looked at me smugly then did a double-take, his smile disappearing fast. "Wait, no! What do you mean?"

"I mean," Tess said, "that you've been going on about how you're the best hacker there is, bragging that my dad hired you because you're such an amazing coder, and it's all bullshit."

"Oh, it's no bullshit, babe."

"Then why are you afraid to go after this guy? Criminy sakes, Derek, he hired a military assassin to kill me!"

"That's exactly why I'm exercising caution. Prudence. I'm not afraid of Latham. Not exactly. I'm just very wary of the power he holds, his reach."

"Bullshit," Tess muttered again. "And, news flash, I wouldn't date you if you were the last man on Earth."

Derek threw up his hands. "What do you want from me?"

Tess looked mad enough to spit nails. I thought it might be a good time to interject and break up the clinch.

"Look," I said, "the only way we get Latham is with proof. Proof he can't deny. I think what Tess is saying—"

"What I'm saying," Tess blurted, "is that if you're as good as you say you are, then you should be able to get dirt on the senator without him even knowing it. Hack into his damn computer, his email server, his whatever, and find out why he's doing this to me. How hard can it be? Since you're so good and all."

Derek silently turned bright vermillion. Tess couldn't see it, but I took an almost perverse pleasure in his discomfort.

"Yeah, okay, fine," he mumbled. "I'll see what I can do. Shouldn't be that tough. I'll start with email and go from there. It'd be good to have some insurance. Anything else, princess?"

"Just find out why they want to kill me. Okay?"

"I said I got it." He grabbed the laptop. "On my way."

Quiet blanketed the library as he headed out the door. Tess seemed lost in thought, a worried look on her face. I didn't know what to say, and the one thing I'd learned with her—as recently as a few minutes ago—was that saying nothing was better than saying the wrong thing. Her silence, though, started making me nervous. I was about to suggest she start on homework to take her mind off her crappy day when her phone buzzed. She shook her head as if trying to clear it, and reached for the phone.

Holding it in both hands, she said, "Read text."

I stared at the screen over her shoulder.

"One text," the phone said, "from Unknown: hey bitch ur lighting up s.m. mayb u should just off yourself now."

"Damn it!"'" she cried. She turned her head wildly as if looking for something. "Is he gone?"

I frowned, momentarily confused. "Derek?"

The low rumble of a powerful engine rising in pitch, audible even through the insulated glass windows as it grew more distant answered her question.

"He said he could trace who's sending these," she said, her voice rising. "Ohmigod! It's never going to end. They'll never stop!"

"Calm down." I put my hand on her shoulder. "It'll be okay."

She shrugged me off angrily. "It's not okay. It's fucking messed up! I want my life back! My reputation is ruined. My *life* is ruined."

"No, it's not," I said, hearing how stupid it sounded. "You don't know that. You don't even know what they're saying. This is just one asshole trying to make your life miserable."

"So what are you telling me? You want proof, Oliver? Is that it? You want me to show you how utterly humiliated I feel? You want to see me disgraced? What? Put in my place? You think because I live in this big, fancy house, with people like Yoshi and Alice at my beck and call, you think because I have money that my life is *easy*?"

She stared at me, tears brimming in her eyes, and I squirmed under the onslaught of words and emotions.

"I... I don't..."

"No," she said fiercely, "you don't. You don't know shit about me or what I've been through. You don't know squat about what it's like to be a girl, to be in high school, to be a royal whose life has been ripped out from under her! You want to know what they're saying! Fine!" She waved the air. "Go on! Go online and see what they're saying. Do it!"

I slowly pulled her laptop from her backpack and opened the lid. It blinked awake. The social media site she used was already loaded in her browser. I clicked on it.

"What's your screen name?" I asked quietly.

"Valkyrie."

"Really?" I stared at her, astonished. "I thought—"

"Why do you think they played that stupid opera," she snapped, swiping her eye. "I hated it."

Chastened, I entered the name in the search bar, and the first item to pop up was the porno video. I scrolled to the comments under it, and one came in even as I started reading.

"Oh, man," I muttered.

"What? Read them out loud. I want to know how bad it is."

"If you're sure. Okay, here goes.

"**Bender3939:** i wish the bitch'd suck me off like that

"**JollyRoger:** OMG, Bender, that's gross. no one's going to touch your ding-a-lingy-ding-dong

"**MadH8r:** once a diamond and an ace, witness now her fall from grace

"**Addled2:** TGINMBF

"**GeorgeousGorge:** can't believe she 8 the whole thing

"**4tunehunter:** who's the doggyknobber? lucky guy

"**MadH8r:** Chon. Such a chon. A chunky chon-ky

"**Paigeinator:** WC? Does any1 have Prescott's homework assignment?

"**MadH8r:** Srsly? With a face like that who'd stoop low enuf to stuf it?

"**Bender3939:** I wud!!!

"**JollyRoger:** STBY Bender. in ur dreams

"**4rcUvN8r:** .02 she can kiss Harvard goodbye

"**MadH8r:** boo-hoo TMOT no1 deserves it more

"**Paigeinator:** B3. Can someone puhleeez txt me the assignment. It's not posted

"**Addled2:** shut up Paige. at least we know her true colors a real hoe"

Tess threw up her hands. "Stop! That's enough."

She flopped forward on the table, face buried in her arms, and stayed there a moment, while I wondered what the hell I was supposed to do. Finally, she raised her head, screwed the heels of her hands into her eye sockets, and faced me.

"Now are you convinced?" she said. "They hate me."

"Nah," I said, trying to lighten the mood. "They're just jealous."

Her eyes widened, then she snorted and turned her head. "Ri-ight. 'Cause everyone wants to be a porn star in high school."

"Do you even know who these people are?"

She nodded. "Some. Addled2 is none other than my former bff Addie. Who just called me a whore, in case you didn't notice. GeorgeousGorge is George Klein, a gay guy in theater group. Hmm, let's see…oh, Bender is a jerkoff—a jock on the football team. He's a junior. Mad—did you say MadHater?"

"Yeah, it's Mad, H, the number eight, letter R."

Her hand flew to her mouth, and she paled as if she'd seen a ghost.

"MadHatter," she whispered.

"Yeah. No, mad-hater." I drew out the words slowly. "Who's MadHatter?"

"It's Madison. Maddie. Gotta be. The names, they're too close. And no, I don't believe in coincidences. Not when it comes to shit like this."

"Really? Are you sure you're not jumping the gun?"

"Oh, please. Every one of my so-called friends would like nothing better than to see me taken down several pegs and leave room at the top for them. It's what I'd do."

"I don't believe that. You'd do that to your friends?"

"For a chance to be a royal? Hell, yes."

"No, you're not that mean. Well, maybe... But why now? They've all had more than a year to fill the power vacuum. I mean, didn't Addie already steal your boyfriend."

"Thanks for reminding me."

I could've cut her sarcasm with a dull spoon. "Wait, you don't think Madison is behind the video, do you?"

"I don't know, but I wouldn't put it past her. I wouldn't put it past any of them."

"There's an easy way to tell," I said, letting a slide show of images flash quickly through my head, trying to find the right one.

"What? What is it? Well?"

"The tattoos," I said.

Ah, there! I glimpsed a fragment of an image in my memory. Well, the image of *what* I was looking for, but not *who* was wearing them. Something must have distracted me in the moment. So much for photographic memory. I knew that in time, I'd remember the context of where I'd seen the tattoo, and that would remind me of all those in the scene, including the tattooee. Which wasn't much help here.

37

My house is big. Big enough to get lost in. So big that three or four of those ratty-ass tents that homeless people live in would fit in my closet. Large enough for an entire tent city. I used to see those encampments alongside the freeway and wonder why those people didn't get jobs, why they would choose to live outdoors, with no water, no heat, no electricity, no place, even, to go to the bathroom. Now I know it's more complicated than that. A lot of them are druggies. A lot of them are cray-cray. They need a lot more help than just a job. But I still don't think homeless people should be allowed to pitch a tent anywhere they feel like it. And it pisses me off that cops won't get rid of the camps. They're just a bunch of trash on the side of the road. At least that's how I remember them.

I shudder at the thought of squatting in a ditch along the road to take a pee. That's to hide the fact that I'm really scared shitless of someone taking another shot at me. And I know these racing thoughts about stupid crap like homeless camps is my mind's diversionary tactic. I realize that I was about to ask Oliver, "What about the tattoos?" When I open my mouth to do just that, I flash on why my thoughts weirdly wandered to whack-a-doodle street people. Because my house is so big it's rare that sounds can be heard from one room to the next, I remember. But sounds drifting down the hall into the library from the front door are what jacked my thoughts from tattoos to tents.

I frown and stand up.

"What?" Oliver shifts in his chair.

"Someone's here."

I strain to listen to the voices—Alice's and one, no, two others' that I can't quite make out and don't recognize. Or maybe I do. I'm not sure. I drift toward the door, the voices pulling me.

"Hey, wait."

A caster squeaks as Oliver pushes his chair away from the table, and the soft tread of his footsteps follows me out into the hall.

I keep my voice low. "Who is it?"

"Besides Alice, a man and a woman."

I flash him a look.

"What? I don't know who they are. I've never seen them before."

"Oh, don't sound so hurt."

"Me? I'm not..."

I put my hands on my hips. "Well, what do they look like?"

"Older than me."

I shake my head in disgust. "Oh, that really tells me a lot. Give me another hint."

"Uh-oh."

"What?"

"They're looking this way, and the man—at least I think it's a guy; I mean a man, not a kid—is...is..."

A piercing yell comes from down the hall. "T...T...T...Tee-e-e!" And what sounds like a herd of elephants thunders toward me.

"Hey!" Oliver calls out. "Buddy, better slow down. I mean it!"

I sense Oliver step in front of me.

Suddenly he's gone, and his voice comes from behind me. "Hey, watch it!"

The reverberating footsteps halt, and strong arms wrap around me in a bear hug and lift me off the ground. My heart pounds in terror, and my mouth opens to scream.

"Tee, I missed you," the bear says, sounding almost as if he has a mouth full of food.

"Benjamin?" I know that voice, but I can scarcely believe it. "Benj, is that you?"

"Of course it is, silly."

Oliver's at my side again. "You know this guy?"

"Uh, yeah, this is—"

"I'm Benjamin." His declaration is louder than it needs to be given how close he is, but I swear I can see the smile on his face as he says it. "Who are you?"

"Oliver," Oliver mutters, then in an even lower voice he says, "You do know that he's, uh..."

I turn on him, a flash of anger coursing through me. "He's what? Don't say it, Oliver. Benjamin is perfect just the way he is."

"That's me," Ben says proudly. "I'm p-practically perfect in every way."

Oliver groans, then mumbles, "Oh, god, don't start singing. Sorry, Tess, it's just that, well, you being a royal and all..."

"I've known Ben a lot longer than I've been a royal," I say, my face hot. "Look, I don't have to explain myself to you."

190

"No, you don't. I'm just supposed to be looking out for you, that's all. And I thought you said nobody calls you 'Tee.'"

"I said I didn't want *you* calling me that. It's okay if Benjamin does." Ben always had a tough time saying my name, never getting past the "T," so I told him a long time ago it was okay to call me that. "Wait, you said there's a man and a woman at the door."

"I—"

"No, s-silly," Ben interrupts. "That's not a man; that's A-Alice. You really c-can't see, can you?"

"Nope." I try to keep my tone light. "Blind as a bat."

Ben laughs.

I take a not-so-wild guess. "You came with Robyn, right, Ben?"

"Yes. I got a d-dog!"

"You did?"

"For a little while, at least," a familiar voice calls. "Hello, Tess."

"Robyn." I swallow the queasiness I feel at the sound of her voice. "It's been a long time."

"Too long," she says softly. "I'm sorry about that. I should have been here."

I shrug and paste a smile I don't feel on my face. "That's okay. You had more important things to do. So, what's this about a dog?"

"I found it," Ben says, "but I didn't get to keep it. We had to give it back to Mrs. Jackson."

"Long story," Robyn says. "I'll tell you later. You must be Oliver. Alice mentioned you. I'm Robyn Alia."

"Oliver Moncrief. I hope Alice's report wasn't all bad."

Oliver's voice has a coat of polish I've only heard when he's trying to impress someone or talk his way out of trouble. I'm still thinking up a dig when Alice joins us, too.

"I'll be revising that report if you haven't helped Tess finish her homework," she says. "Robyn and Benjamin are joining us for dinner. We're eating in half an hour."

"Half an hour!" Ben says. "Gotta find Yoshi."

"Ben, wait!" I say. I know better than to disturb Yoshi in his work, whether in the garden, one of the sheds, or now, I remember, the old darkroom.

But Ben has already bolted down the hall from the sound of his heavy footsteps.

"Oliver, a little help, please" I say as I touch my fingertips to a wall and take off after Ben.

I'm familiar enough with the house to find my way around most of it—slowly—without help. But I think I know where Ben is going, and I haven't been in that part of the house in years. I'm relieved when Oliver gently clasps my arm and falls into step as I slow to an impatient walk.

"Whoa," he says. "Where is he going? He disappeared."

"I think he's headed for Yoshi's apartment. I don't want him bugging Yoshi. Ben can be a little too…"

"In your face?"

I'm about to take offense when I hear the amusement in Oliver's voice.

"Who are they, anyway?" he says. "What's the deal with you two?"

"There's no '*deal*' with us."

"Okay, so how do you know them?"

He slows and pulls me to a stop.

"Why? Is that so important? Come on!"

"Which way?"

I blink. "Oh. Um, there are stairs in the mud room."

"Up to Alice's apartment?"

I'm surprised he knows the layout of the house that well. "Alice lives over the kitchen and offices. Turn the other way at the top of the stairs. Yoshi lives over the garage."

"Okay," he says, giving my elbow a nudge. "Stairs in three, two, one."

"I know how many there are," I tell him as we start up. I figure I might as well answer his question. "Robyn is—was—my dad's executive assistant. I assume she works for Travis now. Benjamin's her brother. He's…"

"Mentally challenged?"

I shake my head. "Don't say that. He's just different. He has Down syndrome. But he's not stupid."

He stops. "We're here."

Yoshi's door is open a crack, judging from the whoops of excitement and Ben's braying laughter floating onto the landing.

"I'll tell you the rest later," I say.

I reach out and push the door open, then step through. Memories rush at me like bats leaving a cave at dusk as I'm assaulted by a hundred scents, some familiar, some foreign, some pleasant, some acrid. A breath of air caresses my face as something whirs past. I hear giggles close by as I wave my hand to swat at it, but it darts away.

"Benjamin, if you're in here, you better stop bugging Yoshi and come with me right now," I say. The voice that comes out of me sounds startlingly like my mother's.

Ben stops snickering. "Aw, d-do I have to?"

"Ah, so, time to put toys away," Yoshi says from the far side of the room.

"Sorry, Yoshi, about the interruption," I say. "Benjamin took off before I could stop him."

"Always happy to see him. And you. Been long time since you visit me here."

"What is this place?" Oliver murmurs next to me.

I envision the long, open space with the arched ceiling, bright lights bathing the tables in the center of the room and the work benches along the walls, all littered with tools, meters and motors, wires and widgets. The greenhouse is where he experimented with plants, grafting trees and cross-pollinating flowers.

"Yoshi's lab," I whisper. This is where he fixed things.

"I thought he was your gardener."

"Is true," Yoshi says loudly. His hearing must be better than mine to catch what we said from across the room. "I like grow things, but I am scientist."

Mad scientist, more like. I've never known Yoshi not to tinker. His words suddenly register—*scientist*, not *like a scientist*—reminding me of how little I know of his life before coming to work for us. I file it away for later.

"Analysis complete," a woman says in soothing tones. I know better. It's the synthetic voice assistant on Yoshi's computer. "Two bi-pedal hominids, one male, one female. Primary female scent based on chemical make-up likely a floral Oriental perfume with top notes of orange, heart of jasmine and rose, and base notes of patchouli and vetiver. Primary male scent very complex and subtle but seems to be a woody floral musk with notes of black tea, cardamom, and cedar. Also detecting hints of sodium chloride and nitryl chloride. Scents are a ninety-eight-point-three percent match to Tess and Oliver. Facial recognition confirms one hundred percent match."

"When did we buy a scent analyzer?" I say. Yoshi told me about scent analyzers during my rehab, when he brought me things to smell, but I never thought we'd buy one. Most are limited to specific odors, and the few that detect a wide range of smells are expensive.

"Not buy, missy. Build."

"You built one from scratch?"

"*Hai.* Scent analyzer very accurate."

His scent analyzer may have figured out the perfume I'm wearing and whatever it is Oliver showers with. What it can't do, I bet, is tell what effect those scents have on other people, like the tingle all over and warmth flushing from my chest up my neck into my face that I feel sometimes when Oliver's close enough to get a good whiff. Or the bigger tingle lately that Derek's scent gives me. And if I don't stop thinking about both of them, my thoughts will be evident to everyone else, too.

Ben giggles again from somewhere in the middle of the room, and Oliver mutters behind me, "What the hell is a scent analyzer? What's going on here?"

I shush him with a hand gesture. "Was that what you waved near my face a second ago?"

Before Yoshi can answer, Ben bounds across the floor, and I cringe, hoping he'll stop in time. He snatches my wrist and pulls my arm out in front of me.

"It flies!" He places something on my palm.

I'm about to touch it with my other hand when its slight weight is replaced with a puff of air that quickly diminishes and disappears.

"It's a tiny drone," Oliver murmurs, "but it's not like any drone I've ever seen."

"*That's* what got in my face? That can't possibly be an e-nose. It's too small." I pause. "I don't understand."

I'm confused. I don't know why Yoshi would need an artificial nose, or why he has experiments hidden all over the house. I realize the room is very quiet.

"Ben," Yoshi says softly, "you show Oliver gym and teach him basketball, *hai*?"

"N-Now?" Ben whines. "But—"

"I come find you in a few minutes," Yoshi interrupts firmly, "and you teach *me*, okay? Show me your moves."

"All right! Let's go." Footsteps tromp past me. "S-see you later, T-Tee."

I whirl left and right, darkness in either direction. "What's going on? Yoshi?"

Footsteps approach, his soft tread ominous in the quiet.

"We need talk, missy."

38

Ben tugged me along by the hand without the least bit of self-consciousness. Unlike me, whose masculinity inexplicably felt threatened by this man-child. Or perhaps whose sexuality was called into question. I shook my head, hard. There was nothing wrong with holding hands, and I should have felt more secure in my own skin. I wasn't homophobic, nor did I play for the opposing team. Lord knows, more than platonic thoughts of Tess had kept me awake a few nights, and I typically felt flattered, not alarmed, when my gay friends flirted or hit on me.

Ben's complete trust and lack of inhibition, I realized, put me off initially, but when I recalled the behavioral characteristics of people born with Down syndrome, I relaxed. Truthfully, his enthusiasm was infectious, and I felt my excitement grow as he pulled me through the house. Besides, I hadn't seen the gym yet, wasn't even sure I knew there was a gym. I envisioned a large exercise room with a hoop on one side for practicing shots, maybe one of those basketball arcade games with the ramp that return the balls. I started to think a little shoot-out with Ben might be fun. I'd let him win, of course.

When he led me through a wide set of double doors on the lower level, I blinked in surprise, certain there was some mistake. I didn't even notice that Ben let go of my hand and moved off to one side until the dim emergency lighting paled. The varnished wood floor of a full-sized basketball court gleamed under the bright ceiling lights snapping on far overhead as Ben cheerfully flipped switches in a big control box on the wall. I gazed in wonder, trying to take it all in.

High above the court hung what looked like volleyball nets, soccer goals, tennis and pickleball nets, and half-court basketball backboards, waiting to be dropped into place with electric winches. Low-rise retractable bleachers flanked the sides of the court. A running track hung overhead around the perimeter of the cavernous space.

Behind a towering glass wall past the far end of the basketball court I could see a rock climbing wall, climbing ropes, a trampoline and harness, rings, a balance beam, a couple of ladder-like stall bar exercise stations bolted to the wall, and uneven bars. Though maybe not as large or complete as that in a large high school, the gym was state of the art with top-of-the-line fixtures and finishes. I'd seen the fitness room on the same level and knew a lot of high-end houses had similar set-ups, but I couldn't have imagined this being part of anyone's house.

"Come on!" Benjamin called.

I shook myself and glanced over to see him open a door along one wall and step inside. I started toward the opening, but he emerged with a basketball balanced in one hand. I finally noticed what he'd been clutching in his other hand ever since he'd arrived—some sort of e-reader device. He carefully placed it on the bottom tread of the bleachers, then bounced as excitedly onto the court as the ball. Curious about the device, I moved closer to take a look.

"Don't touch it!" He stepped in front of me, his lower jaw thrust forward. "It's mine."

I took a step back and held my hands out. "I wasn't going to touch it. Just look at it."

His face softened. "Okay."

"So, what should I call you, 'Ben' or 'Benjamin?'"

"You can call me B-Ben, if you want. Let's play."

He dribbled out onto the floor and took a shot. The ball hit the backboard, bounced on the rim and went in. Benjamin's face lit up like a Christmas tree.

"Two points!" he yelled.

I hustled onto the court and scooped up the ball. Basketball, and sports in general, hadn't been my thing in school. I wasn't much of a team player, and the whole sweaty exertion thing seemed more effort than it was worth. That's not to say I wasn't athletic in the sense that I was reasonably fit, wasn't overweight, understood the basics of the three sports most people cared about, and could throw, pass, kick, catch, dribble or shoot any of the three balls in question. But after five minutes, even though Ben couldn't dribble worth beans, he was up double digits on me in scoring. He rarely missed, and when he did he would swoop in under the basket, knocking me aside, and take the rebound. Finally, bent over laughing at one improbable no-look, over-the-shoulder swish, I held up an arm in surrender.

"You win," I said, breathing heavily. "I give up."

His smile grew even wider, if that was possible, and he followed me over to the bleachers. I collapsed and sprawled across two tiers.

I pointed at the e-reader. "So what is that, anyway? I've never seen anything like it."

Ben put the ball down and picked up the device gently. "It's my b-book. Uncle James made it for me."

"He made it?"

"Yeah, see?" He slid toward me, and held the reader out in the air in front of us.

It opened like a book, revealing the pages inside. Thin and flexible, but some sort of film, not paper, they were covered with illustrations. I leaned forward and peered at it.

"That's me," Ben said, poking a pudgy finger at one of the figures. "I'm a superhero."

The face in the drawing did resemble him, but the character, muscles bulging under a tight-fitting suit of Spandex with a stylized "B" on the chest looked little like the Ben on the bleachers. A comic book. Or graphic novel. Something else I hadn't spent any time with as a kid.

"So, what are your powers?"

"I'm soop-a-fast," he said, slashing his hand in the air. He curled the hand up and flexed his bicep. "And super strong."

"Cool. So, what's the story?"

His expression turned serious, and he shifted the book toward me. "I fight bad guys. See? And some bad guys I don't know keep bothering my friend, Tee. See? She's sad. It makes me mad I'm not there to get the bad guys."

He turned the pages as he spoke. Too quickly for me to read all the panels, so I focused on the illustrations instead. They were good, professionally drawn, and the likenesses to real people was startling. Tess's dad had thought enough of Ben for some reason that he'd spent a lot of money on what seemed to be a one-off custom book. The illustrations had been transferred somehow to these e-ink pages.

"But I get an idea," Ben goes on. "See? Tee is a superhero, too. Now we both fight bad guys."

"Wait. How did she get super powers?"

"I showed her," he said. "P-pay attention. I showed her how to charge up her p-power. That was my idea. I told you."

I peered at the illustrations, trying to track what he was telling me. "Turn back a page."

He flipped a page over. I scanned the panels. Bad guys remotely set off a charge that topples a tree as "Tee" walks by in the rain; Super Ben races to the scene, catches the tree before it falls on Tee and lets it rest on the power lines; Super Ben turns to get Tee out of the way, but the tree snaps the power line; Super Ben races to get Tee out of the way before the tree falls on her; just as he snatches her, the live power line falls on the wet street and the current hits them both; Super Ben is so strong he barely feels it, but Tee vibrates from the jolt; Tee levitates out of Super Ben's arms and realizes she can fly; Tee is in a caped costume with a short skirt reminiscent of a cheerleader's outfit, calculating where the bad guys have gone using her new heightened super smarts.

I had to hand it to whoever had come up with the concept and story. Impossible and implausible, it was imaginative and clever, too, and affirming for someone like Ben who probably got teased and bullied more in a day than I had been during my two short years in high school.

"Ah, I get it," I said with a smile. "That was pretty smart of Super Ben."

"Like, duh."

It was the perfect rejoinder to what had probably sounded patronizing, even to Ben. I snorted, then laughed. And when Ben joined in, I laughed even harder.

39

"Yoshi, what's going on?" A steel band of worry tightens around my chest, making it hard to breathe. I think I might get sick.

He approaches on nearly silent feet and stands in front of me. I smell his earthy scent—loam and compost from the garden, and fallen leaves—mixed with the clean smell of soap.

"You not come here for long time," he says again, softly.

There's no reproach in his tone, but I feel guilty anyway. Yoshi is the one who never treated me with anything but kindness and patience during my rehab, who never flinched at the furious flurries of ugly words I spat at him—and Alice—whenever the pain grew too unbearable, or fists when the words didn't drive them away. Alice punished my tirades by simply walking away from my rage and giving me the silent treatment for hours or even days. Yoshi punished me by absorbing all that blackness, soaking up all my hate and pain until I used it up and fell back spent and exhausted. He never reflected any of it back on me, instead tucking it away somewhere so that all I felt and heard from him was gentleness, compassion, caring and concern.

He takes my hand now, and I feel all of that all over again, rushing through the warm roughness of his calloused hands. I feel like crying, but I don't. He's been hiding something. I need to know what.

"Come," he says with a little tug. "Sit down." He leads me to one of the stools in front of the workbench and lets me lean on him while I find my seat. It feels so familiar, yet so strange. This is where I'd sit for hours when I was younger and watch his experiments. The stool seems shorter, the room smaller, its sounds—humming, buzzing, bubbling, beeping—closer.

"What's this all about?" I murmur. "Why are you building a drone?"

He sits next to me and takes my hand again, clasping it between his two. "I must talk to you about your father."

I pull away from him. "What does my dad have to do with this?"

"Your father do lot of work for government. Top secret work."

"Well, yeah, I know that the company has a bunch of government contracts."

"Not just company. Your *father*."

"My father," I say firmly, "developed video games. He was good at it. No, brilliant."

"*Hai*. Very smart. Never know person so smart." He pauses. "Why you think government come to company? For video games?"

He lets me think about it, but I can't see my dad actually working with some mindless, gray-suited bureaucratic pencil-pushers in the "other' Washington.

"He could hire anybody he wanted," I say. "People who could work on those projects."

"Government come to MondoHard not for games but game theory," he says, more insistently. "Your father know many things, but one thing he very good at is predicting what people do when given choices—if this, then that; if the other, then something else."

I nodded slowly, wrapping my head around what he was telling me. "Yeah, okay, which I'm guessing is why the company's made so many advances in AI." Like that game app, *Never Bitten*, that Derek had developed, the one that had almost gotten Vice President Dunn—well, all of us, really—killed. "And I can see why the government would want that. But what's that got to do with drones?"

"In beginning, nothing. Is long story."

That's the signal for my attention to wander. I flash on our surprise guests. Ben and I used to play together as kids, even though he's a lot older than me chronologically. I wonder where he and Robyn were when the shit hit the fan, and why they've suddenly reappeared like a joker and queen of spades in a card trick. I don't have time for this.

"Give me the Cliff Notes version," I snap. As usual, he doesn't deserve it, but I don't care right now.

"James build tiny drone for fun," Yoshi says, unperturbed. "Like hobby. But he dream big, see how it might be part of video game. Then he dream bigger, imagine how it help people."

I make a face. It was so like my father to dream and ignore reality around him. "How?"

"Find people trapped in earthquake rubble maybe," he says. "Drone get into even smaller spaces than dog, or places too dangerous for dog."

My mind can still conjure up images, so I "see" where he's going, and whisper, "Like a bomb threat. That's why you're working on the scent analyzer."

"*Hai*, missy. But some peoples James work with hear about drone and want him to build for army to do same thing."

It makes sense. The army has lots of bombs. Which can produce the same effect as an earthquake. I know my father wouldn't have wanted to work with the military if he had a choice, but I'm not sure what Yoshi's getting at.

"Why are you still working on it? You're not building it for the army, are you?"

"No, no. I want to honor your father's wish to help people, so I try to make even better."

"Like adding the electronic nose," I murmur. "How'd you even do that?"

"By changing whole design." His voice is filled with pride. "Instead of rotor, like helicopter, I use turbo fan like jet plane."

"An electric jet?" I wish I could see it.

"Hai. Yes, is canard. You know this?"

My mind instantly trips to Madame Beauvoir's French class. *Canard* means duck in French. I frown. Then I remember it's also an odd-shaped airplane with two wings near the nose. I nod.

"Each wing have many fan jets. Each lined with different sensing material to sniff air passing through. Data sent to computer for analysis."

Clever. I flash back to the last time he pulled me aside to talk about my father. "And your experiment in the darkroom?"

"One way to charge battery. Entire surface area also covered with thin-film solar cells. Body made of special ceramic fiber resin, so super strong. Also act as one big solid state battery. Light weight. No fires."

I don't understand half of what he's telling me despite my 4.0 grade—at least for now—in AP Chemistry. "How do you know all this? I thought you said this was my father's project."

"I was your father's teacher. Soon, he smart enough to teach me. But I still know thing or two. Just read his notes and go from there."

I nearly fall off the stool in shock. Why did I never know this? I knew my parents befriended Yoshi when they were in college, but I always thought he was a groundskeeper or gardener, not a teacher. It makes me wonder how many other secrets he and Alice have been keeping from me. And how many things my parents never mentioned. Or why.

"You were a professor at a university? Why didn't you tell me?"

"It make no difference. I was teacher. Now I'm gardener. Is same thing. Both try to make things grow."

I'm angry at him, but I don't know why. He's right; what he did before he came to work for us doesn't really matter. And I have only myself to blame for being so self-centered all these years that I never even thought of asking Yoshi about himself.

I shake my head. "I don't understand. Why would you give up being a professor for this?"

"Why not? I believe in your father and his dreams."

Again, he challenges my assumptions.

Then he says, "What army really want is new weapon."

I think of the little piece of fluff that sat on my hand a few minutes ago. "What? That little thing? Don't they have big drones that carry bombs and stuff?"

"Little drone not so easy to notice. Can get very close to people."

I think of the nearly silent breath of air that brushed past my face when I walked in. "He wouldn't do that. There's no way my father would give the government something that could be turned into a weapon." I pause, thinking.

Something else occurs to me. "Why are you telling me all this?"

"Is time. You need to know." Again, he takes one of my hands between his. "I try to keep you safe. Alice, too. But this now bigger than all of us."

"'This?'" I frown. He's not talking about the little drone. "This what? What are you talking about?"

He sighs, but says nothing.

My thoughts race. "Wait. You think someone's trying to kill me because of some stupid toy my father built? Why? I don't know anything about it."

I want to scream. I have bigger problems, like finding out who wants the world to think I made a porno. Or like finishing the essays for my college applications. Or trying to get my rep as a royal back. None of that, of course, means diddly if I'm dead.

"I tell you this so you better prepared. Same way I teach you jiu-jitsu."

I am freaking out inside. Because I don't know what any of it means. Or who I can trust anymore.

"Prepared for what?"

"Anything," he says. "Everything."

40

Robyn didn't know how long she stood unmoving in the foyer after Alice excused herself to go see about having dinner catered in. She felt terrible, and had apologized profusely to Alice for the imposition. She should have known better than to trust that Travis would have the situation in hand. Instead, Alice had been completely surprised by her arrival with Ben in tow. Though Alice had been gracious, as always, she had managed to let slip the fact that she had taken over for the household cook only a week or two before and hadn't yet had a chance to find a replacement. Robyn finally conceded that Alice would quickly and efficiently resolve the problem. Alice probably had a half-dozen caterers on speed dial, and if all else failed would resort to delivery from one of the city's finer restaurants.

She shivered from a sudden chill, and glanced over her shoulder, half-expecting to see the front door open, bringing Travis in on a cold breeze. But the door was shut tight, the foyer as quiet as a tomb. Ghosts, she thought, then shivered again as she realized it could be all too true. She hadn't set foot in this house since before the accident. There'd been no funeral, no reason to come...except for Tess. Squaring her shoulders, she forced the thoughts and fear from her mind and set off down the hall. This was the perfect time to start what she came here to do.

The slightly musty scent of leather, old books, wood polish and smoke as she entered the library nearly stopped her dead in her tracks. Again, ghosts threatened to invade her consciousness and trigger old memories and emotions. She shut them out, focusing on a section of bookshelves on one side of room. Wondering if she remembered the right location and the proper sequence, she moved some books aside, and let out her breath when she saw the keypad and scanner. Still, she worried that the security codes had been changed or her profile had been locked out.

She keyed in her six-digit passcode, and again let out the breath she didn't know she'd been holding when a little LED glowed green. Placing her hand on the glass next to the keypad, she leaned forward, opening her eyes wide. While the laser scanner read her palm print, a video camera photographed her iris, and within two seconds, a faint click and whir signaled the door unlocking and the bolts withdrawing.

Relief released the tension in her shoulders. With a light touch, the two-ton door swung open silently, and Robyn slipped inside. She'd only had occasion to visit this room a few times before, but she knew exactly where everything was. She crossed directly to the credenza, opened the bottom drawer, and thumbed through the file folders. The contents all looked straightforward—bills, contractor proposals and estimates, insurance records, tax receipts... The upper drawer yielded more of the same, mundane information— project notes, correspondence, vehicle maintenance records and receipts...

Mildly disappointed, Robyn turned to the laptop on the desk with a sigh. Finding the codicil couldn't have been *that* easy, as much as she wished it was. Mentally crossing her fingers, she typed in the last password she had for James and hit Enter. James's home screen came to life, and Robyn scanned the Desktop folders with a sense of satisfaction. James would have been more likely to have a digital copy of a document than a physical copy. But the more folders she opened, the more discouraged she became.

Most of the files were more personal—photos, music, notes and letters—which made sense, but she would have expected to see more project files from work. Most of the files pertaining to the household, Robyn knew, were on the computer in Alice's office, though she found some here on the laptop. She found nothing that even looked like it pertained to his final wishes, no legal documents, no correspondence with an attorney or law office, nothing. She searched the hard drive using every pertinent word she could think of—will, codicil, last wishes, final testament, addendum... Still nothing.

She leaned back and stared into space, mind churning. A presence slowly crept into her consciousness until she couldn't ignore it any longer. She turned her head and startled at the sight of Tess standing inside the door, staring at her. Robyn's heart hammered against the cage around her heart.

"Tess," she said. "I didn't hear you come in."

"What are you doing here?" Tess said quietly.

Robyn pinked, squirming under Tess's gaze, despite the fact that Robyn knew Tess was blind. She turned back to the screen, silently urging the search function to move faster.

"I told you, Travis invited Ben and me to dinner. I didn't think you'd mind."

"No, what are you doing here?" Tess said, more sharply this time. "This is my father's office. You shouldn't be in here."

Guilt plucked at the edges of Robyn's conscience, but she shrugged it off and sighed. Nothing had come up in the search window. She wracked her brain to think of where else James might have hidden a copy of the document. She was sure Travis must have checked the fireproof safe hidden in the floor under the carpet. She could ask him later. She glanced up.

"I worked with him, Tess. You know that."

"Worked. Past tense." Tess folded her arms across her chest. "This is his private office, not his work office. You need to leave."

Robyn rose as another idea struck her. She needed to find that document before Travis did.

"Tess, be reasonable. I knew your father longer than you've been alive." Robyn crossed to the built-in bar, paneled in a rich, red alder wood. She opened a cupboard above the counter, and let her fingers guide her to the hidden latch that opened a secret panel.

"He trusted me," she said as she worked. "How do you think I got in here? Besides, I thought you and I were friends."

"Friends?" Tess snorted, again facing her as if she really could see. "We were never friends. If we were friends, why didn't you ever visit after the accident? Or call? Something! I'm not stupid. I know why you were always over here, and it didn't have anything to do with work."

Robyn shivered as if Tess had stabbed her with an icicle. Fleeting snippets of memories flashed in her mind like broken pieces of film in a home movie projector. So many happy memories of days here with James and Sally—picnics on the boat on the lake; Ben and Tess, when she was little, exploring the shallow water along the shore; late-night dinners and conversation by the fire until dawn about their dreams, their visions for their futures. She and Ben had been regular fixtures here then. Family. Ben and Tess had been best of friends. Despite their difference in chronological age, they'd been close in emotional and intellectual age.

But Robyn had noticed Tess's growing awareness as she'd gotten older, her attention to what the adults did and said. Like all kids, Tess had found most of it boring, especially if it didn't involve her. Every so often, though, Robyn would catch Tess listening, a thoughtful expression on her face, processing some insight into the adult world around her. Robyn had been afraid that Tess would notice too much, so Robyn had gradually pulled away, making excuses first not to stay, then not to come at all when Sally or James asked. Each time she'd refused an invitation had felt as painful as a bandage being ripped from her soul. Now, Tess treated her like a stranger. Maybe she was.

She summoned up all the indignation she could muster. "I'm not sure what you think you know, Tess, but if I wasn't here to work, I was here because your parents wanted me here. Both of them. I was their friend long before you came along. And maybe I haven't been here for you since the accident, but did you ever stop to think that I might be hurting, too? Or Ben? Did you ever consider that we might miss them as much as you do? Stop being a little princess, and think about someone else for a change."

Robyn peered into the space behind the secret panel without waiting for a reply. *Empty.* Her heart fell. She slid the panel shut.

"I want you out," Tess said. "How dare you? This is *my* house. My father's office. Get. Out!"

"Whoa!" a deep voice called from the opening to the library.

Robyn whirled around as Travis stepped into the room.

"What's going on here?" he said, eyes narrowing.

Tess faced him and tossed her head. "I found *her* in here, going through stuff that's not hers. I want her to leave."

"That's not going to happen," Travis said.

"What the hell? You're defending her now?"

"That's enough! Robyn is here because I invited her."

"She has no right to go through my father's personal things!"

"She's doing what *I* asked her to, looking for an important document."

Horrified, Robyn's head swiveled as she watched the two of them. Anger boiled off them in waves. She couldn't believe how stubborn they both were, couldn't believe they were related to the two people Robyn had once loved more than anyone in the world.

"I don't care!" Tess shouted. "I want her to leave!"

Travis took a step toward Tess, his face as dark and ominous as a thundercloud. "Tess, I'm warning you..."

"What are you going to do?" she taunted. "Kill me? There's nothing you can do to me that someone else hasn't already tried."

"Don't push me, Tess," he growled. "I'm still your guardian. Legally, I can put you in a cell where you'll never see light of day again."

"Hey!" called another voice.

Startled, Robyn looked up. Oliver came through the door and quickly moved to Tess's side.

"Don't threaten her," Oliver said. "She's been through enough."

"She's *my* niece. I'll deal with her the way I see fit."

"You'll treat her with respect and a little empathy."

"Don't forget who you work for, Oliver," he said.

"I work for her," Oliver said hotly. "And even if I didn't, I'd protect her with my life."

"Stop it!" Robyn cried, putting her hands over her ears. "Stop fighting!"

All three of them turned to stare at her, mouths hanging open.

"Can we please all just try to get along?" She bit back tears.

In the sudden silence, Robyn heard a clock ticking somewhere. Then through the opening came the muffled but firm tread of sensible shoes, and Alice appeared in the doorway.

"Dinner's ready, *children*," Alice said. "Benjamin is already waiting. My goodness, all that caterwauling sounded as if someone was torturing a small animal. Well? Get a move-on before the food's cold. And don't forget to wash your hands, all of you."

41

I hadn't seen so many dour faces in one place since my profligate grandparents took me to their private club for lunch when I was nine or ten. Donald and Edith were miserable excuses for human beings who squandered their lives trying to spend their way into a ritzier, snobbier class of people, never recognizing the fact that to billionaires that sort of largesse was pocket change. For my grandparents, that sort of capital outlay, year after year, quickly depleted the family fortune that my great-to-the-nth grandfather had amassed, leaving them destitute and the trust fund for my (continuing) education drained.

Their club, in one of the tonier neighborhoods near Palm Beach, was sustained by a membership list that included scions of polite society (along with the impolite, such as my forebears), with a sprinkling of senators, a few former governors, a handful of retired four-star generals and rear admirals, at least one Secretary of State, and a former VPOTUS among them. Edith had been quick to point out an aging movie star who hadn't made a film in twenty years, and Donald had casually dropped the names of the CEOs of a couple of Fortune 500 companies, two major league ball players, the president of the Miami Federal Reserve Bank branch, a U.S. District Attorney and a Russian oligarch. No one in that club had looked like they were having fun, me included, and all the conversations had been about making money, spending it, or decrying the fact that the Grand Old Party had slid steadily downhill since the Reagan presidency.

No one soul in *this* dining room appeared to be enjoying themselves, either. Yoshi seemed worried, his forehead creased. Robyn fidgeted, eyes downcast most of the time, looking so miserable I figured this was the last place she wanted to be. At the head of the table, Travis seemed to vacillate between irritation and helplessness, depending on whether his gaze fell on Tess or Robyn, or both. Alice exhibited her usual brisk efficiency, but her lips were set as she sat at the other end of the table. And smoke still drifted in wisps from Tess's ears. She looked as mad as a wet cat. I was nearly sweating from the heat of her anger. She glared, alternating between Robyn and Travis—at least it appeared that way. I reminded myself that she couldn't actually stare, just scowl.

Even Ben's chatter sounded a little less cheerful than it had earlier, maybe because we'd all kept him waiting. I appreciated the running commentary, though. Otherwise, the silence would have been painful. Ben was in the middle of a surprisingly detailed historical oration on why Gary Payton had been a better point guard than Isaiah Thomas when Marcus showed up. He, too, looked as if he'd been sucking a lemon. Tess's face swung in his direction, her nose turning up.

Alice wiped the corners of her mouth with a napkin as she swallowed whatever she'd been chewing. "Ah, Marcus, I'm glad you could join us. Dinner for your team is laid out in the kitchen. Would you let them know before you sit down?"

"Of course." He pulled out his phone and tapped on the screen, then took the empty seat between Alice and Yoshi.

"All set," he said. "Thanks." He reached across the table and helped himself to a platter of flat iron steak with *chimichurri* sauce.

"May I please be excused?" Tess said, pushing away from the table. "I'm not hungry, and I have homework to do."

"We have guests," Travis said.

"A heads-up would have been nice," Tess snapped.

Travis opened his mouth, but Alice raised a warning hand. "Yes, Tess, you may be excused."

"I better go help her," I mumbled. I forked in another bite of food, wiped my mouth and shoved my chair back.

Tess was already in the hall when I caught up. "You want to tell me what's going on?"

"No, I don't want to fucking tell you what's going on."

"Jeez, keep your voice down, will you?" I muttered.

I put my hand on her shoulder to guide her. She shrugged me off angrily and touched the wall, lightly trailing her fingertips along the surface as she walked.

"Look, I might not have a job tomorrow because I jumped to your defense. The least you can do is tell me what I defended you from."

She turned into the library. "I didn't ask you to come to my fucking rescue, Oliver. I'm perfectly capable of defending myself."

"I'm well aware that you can stop bullets, fight off mercenaries and hold your own against cyberbullies. But Travis? If he's your guardian, he's doing a piss poor job of guarding you."

She stopped dead and burst into tears, hiding her face in her hands.

I stood there, helpless. "Oh, God, I'm sorry. I didn't mean to make you cry. Honest."

Tentatively, I wrapped an arm around her shoulders. She let it rest there this time as she sobbed. I put my other arm around her and pulled her into my chest. For once, I didn't think about it, I just did it. If for no other reason than to stop her from crying. She threw her arms around my waist and wept against my chest until her breathing slowed and her wailing quieted to a murmur then stopped. I had to admit that it felt good to hold her, but I held my breath, too, not daring to move. She sniffed a couple of times, then slowly seemed to grow aware of where she was. Suddenly, she brought her hands up between us and pushed against my chest. I let go.

"What are you doing?" she said.

"Nothing! You just looked like you could use a hug. It's no big deal."

"Yeah, well..." She swiped her eyes with the back of her hand. "As long as that's all it was."

"That's all it was. What, you don't trust me?"

"I don't *know* you. Beside, you're...you're..."

"Too old for you?"

"No, you're not my type."

"And what type is that? I'm not Derek, you mean. Or Toby."

"I told you, Toby and I are finished. He's with Addie. And who said I was interested in Derek?"

"I suppose it's just his Ducati you're interested in."

"I like Derek. He's a friend. He's *your* friend, too."

"Yeah, but you don't *know* Derek, either. Neither do I. We met him, what, three weeks ago? And it's not like he and I are hang-out drinking buddies. Whatever. Look, I was just trying to be nice. God knows you don't make it easy, but I care about you. I keep telling you, you're not just a paycheck."

"Well, *that's* reassuring." Her tone was caustic, but her mouth turned down in disappointment. "Just help me get set up at the table, okay?"

I took her elbow and steered her to the long table under the green glass-shaded library lamp. I got her settled in her usual spot and pulled books and assignments from her backpack. Before she started, though, I decided to press her one more time.

"Are you sure you don't want to tell me what's up with you and Travis?"

She frowned. "Travis is Travis."

"Well, yeah, but what does that mean?"

The frown turned into a grimace. She opened her mouth, hesitated, then said, "He and I don't agree on much, but he's not the problem."

"Then what were you arguing about?"

"Her."

I blinked. "Robyn? I thought she seemed nice."

"She shouldn't *be* here." She pouted. "I caught her in there, looking for something. That's my father's private office."

"And a safe room for the whole house, right? Besides, you're in there all the time."

"That's different. She's not a member of the family. I saw what she was trying to do before the accident. Sucking up to my mom so Mom wouldn't suspect what was going on."

"What do you mean? Your dad must have trusted her. She's been with the company since the beginning, hasn't she? She must have been as close to your parents as Alice or Yoshi."

"You don't get it." Her voice rose. "I saw the way she looked at him! It was pretty fucking obvious what she wanted."

I didn't respond, letting her cool down while I thought it through. After a moment I said, "Your dad, you mean. How did your dad look at her?"

Her lip curled as she folded her arms, then her brow wrinkled and her unseeing gaze dropped to the table.

"If he never encouraged her," I said gently, "I doubt anything ever happened between them."

"I can't believe he was that clueless," she murmured, as if she was talking to herself. "It's like he never saw it."

I didn't have personal experience, but I was a romantic. The trait was in the crazy Moncrief genes.

"Maybe what he saw was your mom," I said. "Some guys, believe it or not, don't ogle everything in a skirt. As the song says, they only have eyes for the person they love."

She didn't respond. It took me a moment to remember that wasn't the only thing bugging her.

"What was Robyn looking for?"

"I don't know," she said. "Travis said it was some sort of document."

An image of Travis talking to a short, balding man popped into my head. "Codicil to a will," I murmured.

"What? What are you talking about?'

"Your dad's will. They're looking for a codicil. You know, a—"

Her mouth turned down. "I know what a codicil is. I don't care about fucking legal documents. I don't care about this stupid homework, either." She shoved the books on the table away from her. "I *care* about not having to listen to some assholes whistling at me at school tomorrow, and asking when it's their turn. Or some bitches yelling at me because their boyfriends are mad that they don't put out like the girl in the video."

"So, what do you want me to do? Derek already said he'd try to find out who posted it."

"I want to find the bitch in the video and whoever put her up to this."

"F…Find the bitch! F…Find the bitch!" Ben's voice brought my head up sharply. He stood inside the library door and laughed with delight.

"Benjamin!" Tess said. "You shouldn't swear."

"You shouldn't use bad words, either, T…Tee."

"I won't as long as you're around."

Ben shrugged. "Okay."

After spending time with Tess, I wondered how anyone could be so guileless and cheerful.

"S…SuperTee! I have to go now."

"Really? You just got here." Tess looked surprised and a little guilty.

He shuffled his feet and looked down. "Robyn says it's time to go home."

"You'd just be bored if you stayed," Tess said. "I really have to finish this homework."

"That's okay. I need to go to bed soon."

"Why?" I said. "It's still early."

"I have to go to work in the m…morning."

"Well," Tess said, "Maybe you can come over again sometime."

"Really?" For a moment he looked like he might cry. Then a big smile spread across his face. "If you get charged up, you'll be SuperTee! And I can be SuperB!"

"Sure, whatever." Tess offered up a smile with the wattage of a nightlight.

"I'll be back soon. I missed you." Ben waved and turned away.

"Yeah, I missed you, too," she said, then muttered, "sort of."

"Think you ought to curb your enthusiasm?" I said when Ben slipped out the door.

"What? I was being nice."

"If you call that being nice... He's a sweet guy."

"Yeah, well..." She shrugged. "What was all that about SuperTee and SuperB?"

"He has a comic book. Showed it to me when we were playing basketball. In the story, he was SuperBenjamin, and you were, well, Tee. SuperBen saves you from a falling telephone pole in a storm, but the wires on the wet street give you a power jolt and turn you into SuperTee."

"You're kidding. Where the hell did he get it?"

"From your dad."

"My father?"

"That's what he said. It was slick, too. Custom. Great artwork—really looked like you two. Done in some sort of electronic ink."

Eyes glistening, she bit her lower lip. "Bastard. He did that for Benji, and left me with nothing but problems."

Her bitterness left a tang in the air I could taste. I didn't know what to say.

"I'm sick of this shit," she said. "Time to make somebody pay."

42

Fingering the key hanging on the delicate white gold chain necklace I'm wearing, I mull over the plan again in the car on the way to school. I spent the whole night thinking about it, and now I catch myself nibbling at the edge of what was a perfectly manicured nail. I quickly drop my hand into my lap.

"You remember what you're supposed to do?" I say.

Next to me, Oliver sighs. "Eidetic memory here. Yeah, I got it."

For a moment, I hear only the muffled thrum of the car's engine and whispered wind rush through the acoustic glass. I tap my thigh with my fingers, then feel for the window switch and lower it a crack. It's too warm in the car's close confines, and the air feels good on my flushed skin. I'm not sure I believe him. I'm about to quiz him when he breaks the silence.

"Are you sure about this? You seem awfully nervous."

"I'm positive," I snap. "It's the only way I can salvage what's left of my reputation at this stupid school. And I'm not nervous; I'm pissed off."

I'm not sure at all, but I can't tell him that. This isn't who I am, but I'm not above taking matters into my own hands.

"Okay." He sighs again.

We finish the ride in silence. The car stops. I put the window up. I hear him get out, and the door closes with a solid thunk that squeezes the air, putting pressure on my ear drums. He's at my door before I can open it, and he gives me his hand to steady me as I climb out.

"You know," he says as we start walking, "she's not going to cave that easily just because you think it's her."

"Don't worry, I'll convince her. I know one of her secrets."

After a moment, he says, "How do you know she'll even be there?"

"Trust me, I know. I've been there."

Sophomore year, when I was co-captain of the cheer squad. Trina Reynolds, a senior, was captain then. To be picked as co-captain over other seniors on the squad, or even juniors, was an honor, but one I deserved. Of course, what no cheerleader knew, and no co-captain ever revealed, was that the responsibilities of the position included all the scut work—scheduling practices, maintaining all the team's gear, wiping down the sweaty, stinky tumbling mats we used during practice and assemblies before rolling them up and putting them away, repainting the outdoor cheer stands before football season, and making sure all the booster boards, trampolines, megaphones, training aids and conditioning equipment were in good condition.

All of that is tucked neatly into a storeroom built into the wall behind the retracting bleachers in the gym. The key I never returned now hangs around my neck. We sit at a table in the commons close to the gym doors and wait as the commotion before first period dies down. We have to time this right. I nudge Oliver.

"Yeah, I think we're good," he says. "Let's go."

I stand and find Oliver's shoulder, following his lead as he walks us into the gym and up to the locked door. I pull the chain over my head and hold the key out. Oliver takes it out of my hand and unlocks the door. As he puts the key back in my fingers, he guides my hand to the door frame. I step through.

"Hang on," he says. "I'll get the light."

"Uh, I don't need it." A light isn't going to illuminate my world.

"I do," he says, "unless you want me to trip and fall on my ass."

The thought makes me laugh, releasing some of the tension in my shoulders.

"What do you see?" I know what's in here, but it would help to get my bearings.

He describes the narrow aisle between mats and equipment that runs down the center of the room. To the left of the door are rolling racks of basketballs, carts of volleyballs and tall, heavy-based stanchions draped with volleyball nets, To the right, mats are stacked along the far wall, and on the other side of the narrow aisle, flyer stands are stacked on one end, booster boards and trampolines at the other. Beyond all the cheer gear are more rolling carts with badminton and lacrosse gear, net bags of soccer balls and stacks of plastic cones. I ignore that crap in my mental map. He tells me how far away things are—a few feet in one direction, a yard or two in another.

"Is there a place to sit facing the door?"

His feet shuffle on the floor, then his hand is on my shoulder, gently turning me. "Three steps," he says, and turns me back around after I count them off. "There's a stack of mats to sit on right behind you."

"Okay, you better get out of here before she comes. You know what to do?"

"I've got it, Tess."

I nod and listen to his receding steps and the sound of the door closing. And then there's just my heart beating too fast and my thoughts shouting too loudly in the tight, enclosed space. I think of the fact that I'm skipping Prescott's class to confront the bitch who caused my complete humiliation. I think of all the shit I've left undone—homework assignments, college essays, and God knows what else. I think of what my life's become, a bruising exercise in bouncing off walls and furniture and tangles of mixed up emotions as I try to navigate being blind in a sighted world.

April, the other girl Maddie destroyed on social media, pops into my head. Slight, quiet, shy to the point of phobia. The kind of girl who sat by herself in the lunchroom, whose body language screamed, "Don't sit with me!" Not unattractive, but someone who had gone out of her way to hide whatever assets she had, dressing in baggy coveralls, or jeans with oversized cardigan sweaters, wearing her long brown hair in pigtails or down to cover her face. No makeup. No style.

Last year of middle school, we'd catch her staring at us, the table of royals, during lunch. Only I figured out that it wasn't just us she checked out, but Maddie in particular. When I pointed it out, Maddie denied it at first, then got this look, this smirk, on her face. Two weeks went by before Maddie got up from the table and sauntered over. April looked like she wanted to crawl into a hole and die, but she let herself get talked into joining us. Poor girl didn't know what hit her.

It wasn't long before it was obvious that April was in love with Maddie—obvious to everyone but April, that is. And Maddie strung her along. Teased her, made her think that April had a chance. As if. April wasn't Maddie's type, gender- or personality-wise. While a lot of girls I know have fooled around with each other, Maddie was so grossed out by anything lesbian that she didn't even want to hear about it. Turned out April was pretty conflicted about her sexuality. Though maybe that's the wrong word. She knew she liked girls; she just wasn't one, yet. To our surprise, April was trans, and had been getting hormone injections since the onset of puberty. But "she" still had male equipment. When Maddie found out, she was furious.

Now, I try not to think of any of it. I stand and gingerly feel my way around the claustrophobic space. The smell alone is enough to

217

put me off cheerleading forever, not that I have a choice. As I move, I picture what Oliver described, mentally checking it off. I want to know how much room I have in case I need to move suddenly. When I've mapped everything in my head that I feel with my hands, I go back to my spot and sit on the mat. I wonder where she is. I know she has this period free—I checked.

After waiting for what seems like an eternity, I finally hear the scratch of a key in the lock. That's followed by a little rush of air as the door swings open, and I sense more than feel the warmth radiating from the light overhead when she switches it on. The scent of that cheap, sugary, candy-like perfume the rest of us gave up in middle school confirms who it is.

"Hello, Madison," I say.

She shrieks. "Holy shit, Tess! I almost peed my pants. You scared me. WTF? Why are you sitting here in the dark? What are you doing here?"

"Waiting for you, bitch."

'Me? Why?"

"Oh, don't play coy. You fucking know why, 'MadH8tr.'"

"So? I SnapChatted a few insults. Big whoop. Ever occur to you I wanted you to know?"

"Why would you say that shit about me?"

"You don't think you deserve it, slut?"

I blink. "Me? You know that's not me in that porno. You set me up! That's *you*!"

"You're out of your mind," she says. "I wouldn't be caught dead in one of those."

"You're not leaving until you admit it," I tell her.

"Oh, fuck off, Tess. I'm not admitting anything because I haven't done anything. You want everyone to feel sorry for you because you can't see. Well, boo-hoo. You were so five minutes ago even before the accident."

"You bitch! I can't believe you said that. You're forgetting one thing—I know what you did to April."

"You wouldn't dare," she whispered.

I nod. "Yes, I would, 'GngrVitus.' You're not the only one who knows how to use Clamor."

"How...?"

"Oh, please, like no one could figure out you're a redhead who likes to dance. You were merciless, relentlessly posting suggestive remarks. Oh, you were smart. Nothing overt, but clear enough to anyone who knew April—comments about her clothes, her hair, her mannerisms... You didn't give a rat's ass. I begged you to stop. You wouldn't listen to me."

My thoughts time-travel back to middle school again. To the school art fair. April was one of the exhibitors. She was good, too. She managed to make colored pencil portraits luminous, full of light, life and emotion. In the middle of the evening, when the gym was crawling with parents, grandparents, little kids and all our schoolmates, someone wearing a mask, dressed in black jeans and hoodie, ran into the gym and exposed April to the world. April was so shocked that before he/she could move, a dozen phones turned her way, capturing the moment and immortalizing it on the web.

"You can't prove a thing," Maddie says now.

"I've got you on video, Maddie." I had my phone out that night, too, but I focused it on April's mysterious assailant, not on April. I knew who the mystery person was. "I caught your hood slipping off as you flew out the door. You may have fooled people into thinking it was me on that porno, but no one's going to mistake your red hair in my video."

"You'd snitch now, after all this time?" Her voice quakes with rage. "It was a prank! I pantsed April. Big fucking deal!"

"The girl is catatonic! No one's been able to reach her for years!"

"Girl." She snorts. "Franken-It, you mean. She's better off being a veg."

"Take it back!"

"You're not a royal," Maddie sneers. "I can't believe I ever wanted to be like you. Who are you? Gawd, that accident did more than blind you, it scrambled your brains."

I smell her, sense her, and I'm so pissed I step forward and grab at her. I get a fistful of sweatshirt and pull her toward me as I step to the side. She flails at me, but I throw my arm around her neck and pull her into a chokehold.

"You put her in that state," I growl. "Take it back."

"Fuck you!"

I tighten my grip. "Take. It. Back."

I don't know why I'm defending a girl I didn't know very well and didn't like all that much. It's not in my nature to care about other people, especially those who don't run in my circle. But I don't run in my circle anymore. And maybe I'm just angry because Maddie set me up. Maybe I empathize a little. *She's just something to hold over Maddie's head*, I tell myself.

Maddie flails some more and smacks my forearm several times.

"All right, all right," she gargles.

I ease off, but don't let go. "Okay. Now fess up."

"What? The porno?" Her head shakes in my loosened grasp. She gasps for air. "Nuh-uh. That's all on you. I had nothing to do with it."

"I don't believe you!" I tighten my grip, but she struggles, throwing me off balance.

The door bursts open behind me. "Hey, hey!" Oliver says in a loud whisper. "What the hell are you doing? Any more noise in here and school security is going to bust us."

"Us?" Maddie says. "You're in on this crap with her? Why am I asking? Of course you are. Let me go, bitch!" She struggles even more, and I can barely hang on.

"No! Oliver, help me!"

"Uh, let her go, Tess," he says quietly.

I can hardly believe my ears. "What? No. Why?"

"It wasn't her," he says.

"I told you so!" Maddie says, jerking herself away from me.

I stand rooted in shock. "I don't understand."

"The tattoos," Oliver says. "She doesn't have them. Well, she does, just not the right ones."

"What the hell does that mean?" Maddie says, even angrier now.

"Are you sure?" I say, ignoring her.

"What's wrong with my tattoos?" Maddie says.

Oliver sighs. "Yeah, I'm sure. We better get out of here and get you to class."

He takes my hand and leads me through the open door.

"Hey, assholes!" Maddie calls behind us. "I'm not done with you. I want an answer to my question. And who's MadHater, anyway? It isn't me!"

Oliver and I walk away without a word. I'm too busy worrying. If it wasn't Maddie on the porn video, who was it?

43

"Senator Latham!" a voice called.

Latham glanced over his shoulder. Some ways behind him in the tunnel between the Capitol and the Russell Building, a young Senate intern waved his hand. Latham searched his memory for the young man's name. Murphy, that was it. Latham looked back again and saw Murphy break into a trot to catch up, dodging a gaggle of freshmen representatives. Latham didn't bother slowing down. He didn't have much time before his subcommittee meeting resumed after lunch. Just as he'd stepped out of the morning session, he'd received an alert on his phone. One that alarmed him.

The intern chugged past and circled around in front of Latham as if to stop him. The kid nearly got knocked on his ass as the senator bulled his way ahead. Startled, the intern stumbled out of the way and fell in step.

"Senator," Murphy said breathlessly, "the Speaker wants to know if he can count on your vote for the energy tax credit."

"Tell Speaker Ormsby that the day an Army MRAP runs on rechargeable batteries is the day I'll get behind the energy tax credit."

"He'll be disappointed to hear that," Murphy said.

"Oh, I don't know," Latham said with a small smile. "We'll have EV Humvees before you know it. Now, if you'll excuse me, I have to get back to my office for an appointment."

The intern slowed and turned back the way he'd come. Latham just increased his pace.

On his way into his office, Latham told his assistant to hold all his calls. Inside, he locked the door behind him and quickly crossed to his desk, unlocked the top drawer and took out a burner phone. He dialed a number from memory, and the call connected after three rings.

"I received an alert," Latham said, sitting down at his desk.

"I'm on it," a man said.

Latham knew him only as "Ray." What little else he knew was that Ray was supposed to be one of the best hackers in the world, and that his barely detectable accent suggested he was Russian. The FBI had used him as a consultant in some investigations, and

Latham had gotten Ray's contact information with one short call to Robert Gregory, the bureau's director.

"What do you know?" Latham said.

"Not much, at this point."

Latham felt ready to explode. "What do I pay you for?"

"Here's what I do know." The man's voice was cold. "This could be nothing more than a random ping or your worst nightmare. From what I've seen—in the four minutes since the alarm was tripped—someone knocked on the door, but didn't get past the threshold. What I'm running as we speak is a full diagnostic on your network, your server, your files, everything. If I find any footprints, anything at all to indicate you've been breached, I will find it and track it to its source. Now, if you'll let me get back to it, I'll have some answers in twenty minutes or so. Maybe less."

"Fine." Latham still wasn't happy, but a short wait was better than nothing. "Can I check email in the meantime?"

"I don't care what you do."

The line went silent. Latham tossed the phone back into the drawer and closed it, then picked up the phone and punched in his secretary's extension.

"Karen, I have to be back in the subcommittee meeting in forty-five minutes. Bring in whatever needs to be done before then."

He cradled the phone and sighed. Lord knew, he loved his job. But some days he wondered if any of it was worth the cost. So far it had cost him two wives, a son to a roadside bomb in Afghanistan, a daughter to marriage, and two-thirds of his life. But the people of his state kept sending him back to Washington, so he had to be doing something right. What none of them knew, not his constituents nor his family, was that his greatest source of pride was the work he couldn't reveal to them, the sacrifices he'd made in the name of patriotism.

The patriotism of the eight others he worked with could not be questioned. And though most hailed from different countries, they weren't at cross-purposes. While their nationalities made them competitors, rivals, they also shared common goals. One of which was to maintain the global status quo while enriching their own pockets. Latham liked to think of it as stabilization through destabilization. Foment a little divisiveness in the Baltics, or the Mideast, or along religious and ethnic lines in India, China, Pakistan, Afghanistan or dozens of other countries around the globe, and pride would force some countries or groups to mobilize troops and weaponry, which any of the nine through their fronts would gladly supply.

Karen interrupted his thoughts bearing a stack of pink phone message slips like a jury verdict. Handing them to him, she said, "There are more. I only gave you what I thought you'd manage in the time you have."

"Thanks." He sighed.

She hovered. "Problems?"

He looked up from the messages in his hand. She tucked a strand of hair behind her ear, and he noticed that the chestnut color was shot through with gray. She'd always been an attractive woman, but now he'd have to say pleasing. She'd matured, her face now etched by time and sun, her figure in the tailored suit fuller, heavier. He wondered when she'd grown old. He wondered when he had. He gave her a small smile, dim wattage compared to the one he used to win elections.

"Nothing I can't handle, but thanks." It occurred to him that she seemed overly concerned. The last thing he wanted was to draw more attention to himself. He amped up the smile a smidge to put her at ease. "How're the boys? Did I hear that Jason made junior partner?"

She nodded and flushed, dropping her gaze for a moment. "Yes, he did. Quite excited about it, too."

"And Rand's almost finished with med school? That must be a relief."

"It is, but now he's stressed out about where to go. He has four job offers already."

"Tough to have choices," Latham said.

Karen laughed, more relaxed now, and turned for the door. Latham watched her all the way out. He'd have to keep an eye on her now. And himself. He couldn't afford to slip up. He thought again about how attractive she was, and wondered why he'd never noticed before. Miriam, his wife, was too, of course, but he hadn't shared a bed—hell, a house, even—with her for years. They not only had no shared interests any more, they'd lost interest in each other.

And Miriam had never forgiven him for the family tragedy that had probably done more to win him re-elections than all the pork he'd brought into the state in his thirty-plus years in office. Their son Edward had been killed in Afghanistan just as the last of U.S. troops were being pulled out. Edward, the "happy" one... Latham still couldn't say "gay." Maybe that governor in Florida had the right idea—don't let anyone say it in schools and kids would never learn about it. Latham shook his head in disgust just thinking about it. Miriam had called their son "sensitive" and "creative," but Edward still had managed to flunk out of art school. For Latham, that was the last straw, and he'd frog-marched Edward into the nearest recruiting office to sign him up in the army. Maybe make a man out of him.

Andi—Andrea, Miriam insisted; their daughter hadn't gone by the name 'Andi' since fourth grade—wouldn't even acknowledge him at Edward's funeral, and hadn't spoken to him since. That one stung. She was the smart one in the family, and Latham had hope she'd go into politics, too. Not to follow in his footsteps. God, no. Just because she could make a difference, could change the tone, the direction the country was headed. Which, as far as Latham could see, was straight into the dumper. It was one of the reasons he'd formed his shadow council. *Someone* had to turn things around. Unfortunately, Andi—Andrea—had decided to work in the private sector as COO of some tech start-up that promised to earn her billions when it went public.

He dragged his thoughts back to the slim sheaf of pink phone messages, shuffled through them quickly, and pulled one out. With another sigh, he put on his game face and dialed the phone.

He'd just finished returning the last of the calls when his burner phone buzzed inside the desk drawer. He yanked the drawer open and snatched it up.

"Speak."

"I have good news and bad," Ray said. "The good news is I don't think the intruder made it past the security into your files."

"You don't *think*...? That's good news? What the hell is the bad news?" Latham felt heat rise up his throat into his face, and he strained to keep his voice down, his tone even-keeled. He sucked in a breath and let it out slowly, willing his pulse to slow.

"Bad news," Ray said, "is that the arrogant s.o.b. didn't do much to hide his tracks. I followed them back to Seattle. I couldn't pin down an exact location, but I'd bet money your hacker can be found somewhere inside MondoHard's headquarters."

Latham said nothing this time, even though he felt something cold run up his spine, something very unfamiliar that he presumed must be fear. He knew better than to show weakness, especially considering that Ray could use it against him. Ray had access to everything on his private server, all his secrets, all his plans. And unlike his relationship with those sitting on the council, Latham had no mutually assured destruction policy with Ray.

What he did have, however, was money and power. And he'd spent far too many years amassing both to be put off by some minor swipe at his flank.

"Find him," Latham growled. "I'll double your fee."

44

I've never felt so helpless. Not even when a gunman stood in front of Tess and I couldn't see him. This is far worse than a bullet. It's torture. It must be.

We slipped into Prescott's block class five minutes late, and I steered Tess to seats in the back of the room. Uncharacteristically, Prescott didn't miss a beat to harangue us for being late. I know he saw us, but he kept speaking with only a glance at us as we settled in. Not long after, he strolled down the aisle between the desks straight toward us, talking as he came.

"So, the question, people, is whether Daisy Buchanan is like a Kardashian..."

He stopped next to Tess and turned to face the front. Half the kids craned their necks around to look at him; the others bent over their desks, pens and pencils poised to write down his pearls of wisdom. With a smarmy smirk, Prescott put his hand on Tess's shoulder and gently rubbed it. She cringed and groped under the table for my hand. I took it and gave it a reassuring squeeze.

"...Or is she a product of her time, the daughter of a tiger mother who drilled into her that the only chance of success she had in life lay in marriage not only to money but to someone from the right sort of people?"

The class remained mute, mulling it over. I stared at Prescott, burning a hole through his skull, but he kept his gaze on the class. His focus, though, was clearly on Tess, and while there was no way to prove it, the mere fact that he was physically touching her made his unwanted attention a sexual assault. I wanted to knock his hand off Tess's shoulder, then punch his lights out. I should have just taken out my phone, snapped a picture and showed it to Principal Jenkins.

"I don't think either of your analogies is even appropriate, let alone presents a good case," I said.

He finally turned to look at me. "Oliver, is it? You're not a student here, are you Oliver?"

"I assist one, and I think a master's degree in literature qualifies me."

"Ah, but I have a master's degree in education. Are you qualified to teach, Oliver?"

"I simply answered your question." I waved at the class. "It didn't seem like anyone else wanted to."

"I suppose that's fair," he finally relented. Taking his hand off Tess's shoulder, he walked back to the front of the room. "Okay, people, why aren't my analogies appropriate? Or, why don't they make a case for Daisy's behavior?"

Tess let go of my hand, and I instantly missed it, to my surprise.

"Amy Chua," she nearly growled, "wasn't making class distinctions in *Battle Hymn of the Tiger Mother*. She was describing ethnic differences in parenting."

"So," Prescott said softly, "she has a voice. Good, Miss Barrett. Who else?" He stretched out his hand and sweeps across the room.

Pompous prick.

"Um," another girl said, "the Kardashians are more like Gatsby. Looking good is their business. Daisy is all about old money and privilege."

"Excellent," Prescott said. "Who else?"

The discussion grew more lively, and I silently breathed a sigh of relief that the spotlight was off Tess.

When class ended and we made our way out into the hall, though, the crap hit the fan again. All the way to Tess's next class, all I heard were catcalls and whistles from pimply-faced nerds and dumb jocks, and shouts of "slut," "bitch," and "ho" from girls. Tess had her mouth set in a grim line, but walked with her head held high. The barrage of insults must have hurt, but it probably didn't hurt as much as it would have if she'd been able to see her tormentors. Even if Tess hadn't had enough, I had.

We passed an empty classroom, and I pulled up short. Quickly turning Tess around, I led her inside, and the decibel level decreased dramatically.

"What are you doing?" she said, clearly peeved.

"Taking a break. I can't stand what they're doing to you."

"I don't want to be late."

"One minute," I assured her. "Just sixty seconds to let it quiet down a bit and I'll get you to class. It'll be faster anyway with fewer people in the hallway."

"Yeah, yeah, yeah. You know I'm not some delicate figurine you have to protect. I won't break just because some idiots call me a few names."

I still hadn't come up with a reply when a giggle of girls swarmed through the door, and none of them were giggling. Instead, they whistled and jeered, with taunts like, "If it isn't the rich chon-key and her boy toy," "Hey, slut, why don't you have that dog on a leash?" and "Hey, bitch, glad to *see* us?"

I didn't know the first few. Two of them headed straight for us, latched onto my arms and pulled me away from Tess. I tried to shrug them off in a gentlemanly manner, but they literally had their claws in me. Others followed them and surrounded me.

"Hey, handsome," one said. "Bet you wish you were in that video."

"Maybe he is in that video," said another.

"What's going on, Oliver?" Tess said.

"I don't know," I said. But I figured it out when I saw Addie enter in the middle of the group.

"Barrett!" she barked.

"Addie! I should have known. What do you and the 'jeer' squad want now?"

"A little chat," Addie said.

Two girls grabbed Tess's arms and spun her around. A group of four or five surrounded her in a circle and started pushing her back and forth inside the circle. She stumbled, almost fell, and was shoved again.

"What the hell, assholes?" she yelled.

I took a step toward her to help, but the two holding my arms pulled me back and the others pressed in, hands on my chest.

"Leave her alone!" I snarled.

Addie turned her head. "Or what? You gonna punch us out?" She faced Tess, while two of her girls gripped Tess's arms tightly, stepped in close and poked her hard in the sternum with her finger, then punctuated each word with another poke "Leave. My. Boyfriend. Alone."

Addie whirled on her heel and stomped out, airily waving her hand. The squad peeled away from us and followed.

"Yeah, bitch!" said one of the girls holding Tess. She took a parting shot, punching Tess in the stomach. Tess doubled over and groaned.

"Hey!" I yelled.

I pushed through the girls around me and bounded toward the door, but Tess's assailant was already down the hall.

I turned back and kneeled down next to Tess. "Are you okay?"

She groaned again. "No, I'm not fucking okay! Who hit me?"

"I think it was Brittney. I don't know them all. But they looked like cheerleaders."

"Why didn't you help me?"

"Because they were holding me back."

"You're a guy! You let some cheerleaders hold you back?"

"*Five* cheerleaders. And I thought..."

She grimaced at me. "You thought what?"

I took her hand and helped her to her feet. "Well, you're not broken."

She punched me. "Asshole."

"Hey!" I bent down and picked up her book bag and sighed. "Come on. Now we are late."

Hurrying, we finally ducked into the relative calm of Madame Villeneuve's French class thirty seconds after the bell. The warmth and friendliness Villeneuve had shown Tess the first week or so after she came back to school were gone, replaced by a cool demeanor and more demanding style. I sensed Tess's frustration, saw her jaw clench when Villeneuve called her out on her use of the wrong tense, or poor choice of word. I think I was as happy to get out of there when class ended as Tess was.

I led Tess into the little alcove outside the door and stopped before diving into the stream of students in the hallway. As it thinned, I braced myself and gripped Tess's arm. Just when I saw a break in the flow, Toby stepped right in front of us, blocking our path. He barely glanced at me, as if I was no threat.

"Tess, we need to talk," he said.

Tess wrapped her hands around my arm and pressed her cheek against my shoulder.

"Oliver, did you hear something?"

Toby reddened. "Aww, Tess, come on. You know we belong together."

"I wonder what Addie might have to say about that."

"Addie..." He shifted his weight and looked at a spot on the wall above my head, frowning.

"Addie's not me," Tess said. "We're pretty much complete opposites. You're just figuring this out?"

"You guys used to be such good friends. I thought..." He leaves the thought unfinished.

"Yeah, well, you're with *her* now. And you two so deserve each other. The bitch and her entire squad just cornered me in a classroom and harassed me."

"Tess, I'm sorry. I didn't know. She can be vindictive. It's why we...it's why I think I made a mistake. You know you and I were meant for each other."

"Really? You didn't even *visit* me when I was in rehab, and we're meant for each other?"

"We talked about it, remember? 'You and me, at USC.'"

"Oh, Toby, poor Toby. You're delusional. *We* didn't talk about it; *you* did. I'm not going to USC. I'm not even applying there."

"Wait. What? Where are you applying?"

"Oh, I don't know. Maybe M.I.T. Or Princeton. Carnegie Mellon. Harvard."

Toby's face turned red, and he spluttered in confusion. "But those are all East Coast schools."

"Wow, he knows his geography. The only West Coast schools I'd even consider are Stanford and Cal Poly, and that's only because my parents went there. Why do you even care, Toby?"

He shrugged. "What can I say? I want you back. I even forgive you for the video."

"The...? The porno? You actually think that's me? Oh, I get it now. You want to get back with me so we can be fuck buddies?"

"No. Of course not."

"And you forgive *me*? What about *you*? You're the one who let that goon squad in the back door a couple of weeks ago. They almost killed me! Am I supposed to forgive you for that?"

As much as I enjoyed the former lovebirds' bitchy banter, I was more intrigued by a girl standing in the alcove of a classroom door across the hall. Or slouching, maybe, almost as if she didn't want to be seen, her long, black hair hanging down so it half-hid her face. The image startled me because it seemed so familiar. The long black hair, the Asian features... It was Tess, but not Tess. Then the girl raised her head and looked at us, at Tess. And a photo image flashed in my head—the same girl with the crowd at lunch the day before. Not Tess, Emily.

She said something I couldn't hear because of all the noise in the hallway. The same thing, over and over. And then I realized that she wasn't actually speaking, just mouthing the words. I focused, trying to read her lips.

I'm sorry. I'm so sorry. Over and over.

Her gaze shifted slightly, and she caught me staring and jerked up in surprise. I started to point her out to Tess—duh moment again; Tess couldn't see—and when I looked back across the hall, Emily had slipped into the stream of students and disappeared.

"Come on," Toby was saying. "Ditch this dog. Get back with me. I can lead you around just as good as this Bozo. Better."

"Hey, watch who you're calling a clown, Clown." I mustered a titch of indignation. Hard to feel insulted by someone like Toby.

"In your dreams, Toby," Tess said. "Let's go, Oliver. I don't want to be late for class."

"Jeez, Tess," Toby said, "don't be such a PIT."

"Listen up, Toby," she said in a low voice. "I'm more ace than you'll ever be. Not a queen, or a princess, an ace. And the only thing I'm in training for is a black belt so I can kick your sorry ass. Now move."

I stared at Toby. "That's where you take a hint and step aside."

After a moment's hesitation, he shifted just far enough for us to get by. As we passed him, I said, "Oh, I wouldn't bother Tess anymore, if I were you. No means no. Got it?"

We hadn't taken more than about ten steps when Tess said, "God, I hate him! I can't believe I ever dated him."

She craned her neck as if looking behind us, then leaned into me. "He's gone, right?"

"Yeah, and good riddance." I thought about what I'd seen while she and Toby were arguing. "Say, how well do you know Emily?"

"Not that well. She came up on the squad the year behind me. We were all supposed to be one big, happy family. You just saw how that turned out. The truth is we didn't really hang out with girls who weren't in our class. And then...well...the accident. Why?"

I told her about Emily staring at her and mouthing an apology over and over. "Something's going on," I said. "I think we need to talk to her."

"Are you sure, Oliver? Why would she apologize to me? Was she there with Addie's jeer squad?"

I thought about it. "No. I only recognized a few girls, like Brittney and Jordan. Maddie wasn't even there. I don't know. Maybe Emily just feels bad for you."

She shrugged. "Maybe."

"What could it hurt to find out?"

If I'd only known.

45

"It's Nikolayovich," Andropov said when the call on his secure, encrypted phone connected.

"Yuri. Something has happened?"

"I apologize for the lateness of the hour." Andropov's country had eleven times zones. The country he called, despite its vastness had only one, but it was three hours ahead of his.

"That doesn't concern me. I was already up. A byproduct of getting older." The man chuckled. "So?"

"It's not what has happened. It's what hasn't happened. We've seen nothing of what our friend in D.C. promised. Our own plan to use Sled-Dog to help things along failed. I think it's time to send a message."

"What did you have in mind?"

Andropov tapped his finger on the top of the antique walnut desk in his home office, the one in the dacha on the shore of the Black Sea. He'd given the idea a lot of thought, weighing the pros and cons, and at this point he thought they had little to lose. Feeling confident, he continued.

"It's time to take down the grid."

"You have the resources in place to do that?"

"Of course. Nothing against your 'software engineers,' but the team at my disposal is considered by hacker groups to be more elite than 'Fancy Bear.'"

Liu Zhi was silent for a moment. "It's dangerous. They'll think your government instigated it. Or mine."

"Yes, which will confuse the issue. Further shielding us." Yuri could see Zhi's nod.

"And Latham?"

"We both agree that perhaps he is becoming a toothless lion. And a problem that we may need to deal with sooner than later." Yuri thought about the call he'd received less than an hour earlier to tell him that Latham's private server had been breached by an unknown hacker. It didn't appear that anything had been stolen or compromised, but Latham was quickly outliving his usefulness. Yuri didn't tell Zhi, though. Now was not the time to confess that the breach may have compromised them all. Yuri didn't know what Latham kept on the server, but he certainly didn't trust Latham.

"He'll come around," Zhi said. "He'll see the benefit to his agenda as well as ours."

"If he doesn't, then we'll know it's time for a change in the council's leadership."

Andropov again heard nothing but silence, but he knew better than to press the matter. Zhi would either agree in his own time, or not. As Yuri tapped his fingers, ash from the cigar he held tight in the V between them fell to the desktop. He brushed it onto the Persian rug, and wrinkled his nose. The room smelled of stale cigar smoke and alcohol. He set the cigar down in an expensive and, to his taste, unattractive crystal ashtray.

Yuri Nikolayovich Andropov was Russia's wealthiest man, though no one but he knew it. The world knew he had money, yes, but Andropov had carefully cultivated the persona, the avatar, that the public—and nosy intelligence, law enforcement and other government organizations around the world—saw in the media. Unlike his country's other oligarchs, Andropov didn't flaunt his wealth. His dacha, while comfortable and tastefully appointed with enough expensive art and trappings to signal his social status, was small compared to those of others. He didn't own a megayacht or even a superyacht, but he did have a pleasure cruiser moored in Antibes, in the Mediterranean, that he used to conduct business. He also owned several other large and expensive houses around the world—Barbuda in the Caribbean; Whistler on Canada's west coast; French Polynesia—but none were in his name. And if he had to do business somewhere else—say, Los Angeles, or London—he could easily rent an estate or townhouse.

What Andropov had was the ability to make things happen. Power. Between his wealth and his contacts, his reach was far and deep, and by staying under the radar, he effected change—from greasing the palms of local customs officials to facilitate a shipment of goods that were not exactly aboveboard like weapons or drugs, to assassination when other methods of persuasion had failed. He had the ear of others in positions of power, too, like the Russian president. And power was nothing, if not used.

"You want to force his hand." Zhi said at last.

"Yes. But not just that. I don't want to wait for Latham to get his hands on the technology."

"But our assets have turned Barrett's company inside out looking for it. I thought it died with Barrett, that the only chance was letting the brother try to recreate it."

"Latham's a fool if he thinks Travis Barrett and the people he has inside MondoHard can recreate what James Barrett invented. He doesn't even know what it was. He thinks it's a toy that can be used to spy on people. I know the project's true purpose—develop technology to eliminate reliance on fossil fuels. I'm sure of it."

"It doesn't help us if it doesn't exist."

Yuri smiled to himself. Latham had his network of eyes and ears, but Yuri relied on his own spies. And he offered lucrative incentives for success, and more dire consequences for failure.

"Oh, it exists, all right," he said. "We've just been looking in the wrong place."

46

Robyn sat down with her tea, finally able to take a breath. She'd dropped Ben off at the school, walking in with him and asking Marni to keep an eye on him to make sure he didn't go out by himself. And since arriving at work, she'd been busy prepping Travis's meeting materials for the day and getting the usual batch of correspondence out.

As she softly blew across the surface of the hot tea, she wondered if the previous evening could have gone any worse. Tess had been furious with her. Travis had seemed disappointed. Ben had definitely acted crestfallen, though he never stayed down for long. And she herself felt disheartened, and not because nothing had gone according to plan. Not even because she'd failed to find the codicil to James's will. No, she just felt like she'd made a mess of everything, even though she knew none of what had transpired had been her fault. Not really.

What really confused her was why Travis had invited her in the first place. He couldn't recreate what had been some of the happiest days of her life in that house. He couldn't turn back the clock. James and Sally were gone, and Travis wasn't James. So why did she have this fluttering in her stomach, this itchiness under her skin as if she couldn't sit still, couldn't feel satisfied until...? Until what? Until Tess turned back into her sweet pre-teen self? Until Robyn herself stopped pining for James?

She never should have allowed herself to feel anything but friendship for James in the first place. He'd never given her a reason to think he was anything but in love with Sally, and happy with his life, his career, his family.

And who was she fooling? She knew exactly why Travis had invited her. It hadn't been hard to miss. When he wasn't barking orders at people, then catching himself and backpedaling, trying to act like a normal person, not a drill sergeant, he mooned around his office like a lovesick puppy. Had she acted that way around James? She shivered. If so, it was no wonder that Tess had suspected something. No, what confused her, really, was why she might be having feelings for Travis. Was she? Hard to explain the case of butterflies any other way. But why?

Travis and James were nothing alike. Other than their adorable habit of inspecting their shoes whenever either of them received a compliment. But James had been so loose, relaxed, such a free thinker. Travis was so straight-laced, so rigid in his habits. James was kind and gentle; Travis was hard and brusque. That wasn't to say that James hadn't had discipline—he never would have built MondoHard into a multi-billion-dollar company otherwise. And Travis did have his lighter moments...

Maybe she should give him a chance, she thought. But she couldn't. Travis was her boss, and... She snorted, realizing she was rationalizing now. After all, that hadn't seemed to matter when James had been her boss. She set her mug down, feeling queasy all of a sudden, disgusted with herself. Thinking back on it, she was amazed that Sally hadn't banished her, prohibited her from ever setting foot in the house, or even insisted that James fire her. Instead, Sally had been nothing but kind to her, warm and loving, and the memory made Robyn fight back tears.

As she reached for a tissue to wipe her nose, Robyn's cell phone buzzed faintly. She dug in her purse and pulled it out. The screen showed she'd received a text from an unknown number. Her already queasy stomach felt like it dropped to the floor of a falling elevator as she read.

Be outside in 5 min. Bring the burner. We're watching.

Nearly frantic with worry, Robyn jumped to her feet, snatched her purse off the floor, and headed for the elevators. She didn't bother with a coat. Seeing quizzical glances on her way, she slowed her pace and tried to wipe the concern off her face. She knew it was impossible. After stabbing the call button, she dialed the school, then looked around nervously. *They were watching? Who? From where?*

Her call connected as she stepped into an elevator.

"Hill School. Marni Reynolds."

"Marni, it's Robyn." She could barely breathe.

"Robyn, you've got to stop checking in like this."

"Just stop, Marni. Is Ben all right? Is he there?"

"Yes, yes, he's fine. Really, Robyn, we have more than our share of helicopter parents here, but—"

"How do you know he's fine? Where is he? Do you even know if he's there?"

"Calm down, calm down. He's right here in the office with me. He came in to photocopy a project for Sylvia to hand out to the kids in her class. I'm serious, Robyn. Get ahold of yourself."

Robyn's heart pounded, but she could finally breathe. "I'm sorry, Marni. I just... After the other day..."

"Look, I know Ben is special. I know you worry. But he's safe here. What's this all about, anyway? What's going on?"

Robyn swallowed hard as the elevator came to a gentle stop and the doors opened. She stepped out and walked toward the front entrance of the building.

"Nothing, Marni. I'm sorry I lost it."

"Maybe you should see someone. You know, talk about it."

Robyn ignored the advice. "Tell Ben I'll pick him up at the usual time. I have to go."

She disconnected and pushed through one of the glass doors out to the street, slipping the phone into her purse as she went, fingers searching for the burner phone she'd found under the front seat of her car. It buzzed in her hand as she pulled it out, startling her. Certain that it hadn't been five minutes since she left her desk, she scanned the parking lot and street beyond as she brought the phone to her ear. Sweat slicked her palms, and in her nervousness, she nearly dropped it. She quickly grasped it with both hands.

"Hello?"

The same metallic voice she'd heard before squawked through the speaker. "We have another task for you."

"But I—"

"We know! We haven't forgotten. And we'll only be patient for so long. This is *in addition* to our other demand. Listen carefully. I don't want to have to repeat myself."

A siren sounded nearby, and an irate driver honked his car horn. Robyn pressed the phone to her ear and covered her other ear with her hand so she could hear better. The voice spoke for a minute, then asked if she understood.

Robyn's thoughts raced, her mind unable to accept what was being asked of her.

"They'll know it was me," she whispered. "I could go to prison."

"You could. Or we could kill your brother. Your choice." The voice paused. "You're a clever woman, Ms. Alia. You'll figure something out. We'll be in touch."

47

Derek stood and stretched, his joints popping, with a yawn that threatened to unhinge his jaw. He walked to the window and lifted the blackout shade an inch or two to look outside, blinking at the sudden flood of light despite the usual gray overcast. He liked having the privacy of an office since his promotion. The constant presence of fellow coders in the bullpen had gotten old.

Sure, he missed the camaraderie and the brainstorming and bullshit sessions over pizza and energy drinks. But he didn't miss the petty arguments over who was the best pro video GOAT (gamer of all time), or whose turn it was to buy pizza. Nor did he miss the purposeful procrastination that caused them to stay until ungodly hours of the morning when they were on deadline—which was most of the time. Or the fart jokes, and worse, the farts themselves, along with the smell of B.O., sweaty socks, and bad breath.

And even though the gang—his gang, at least—was mere steps away, camaraderie had flown out the window with his promotion because now he was their supervisor. Paul resented him because Paul thought he should have gotten the rung up ahead of Derek, even though Derek had done almost all the concept development and basic game play coding for the company's most recent hit, *Never Bitten.* Jeremy seemed scared half the time, as if certain that Derek was going to fire him, and pissed the other half that the deck was stacked against him. Arlo didn't seem to care, but it was always the quiet ones who went postal and shot up their workplaces with assault rifles and semiautomatic pistols they just happened to have lying around at home.

Derek mostly left them alone to do their thing, and he did his thing. He knew this made him a lousy manager or supervisor, but his job, his primary job, was producing brilliant code. What he had learned was how to challenge his small team—a relative term since there were dozens of folks on it—to match his level of output and creativity. They were decent guys—and girls—and the promotion was new, so things might work out. Derek was willing to keep an open mind.

In the meantime, he was glad he could work away from prying eyes. The first time he'd probed Latham's server, he knew he'd have to be extremely careful. This time was even more nerve-wracking, like performing brain surgery—the tiniest slip and the patient is a vegetable. Or dead. They carted people off to jail for less. The trick was to get in, look around and get out without anyone knowing. He'd found nothing on Latham's server that suggested Latham had ordered or paid for the assassination attempt on Tess. By itself, that didn't mean anything. Latham could have used an intermediary. It seemed likely, since they'd traced a payment to Sam back to MondoHard.

So, Derek had come up with a new plan that required even more skill. He'd hacked into Latham's server, searched it, and backed out, all undetected. He was sure of that because he'd done it after leaving Tess's house the day before. He'd seen the trip wires that would have announced his attempts to get inside the server, and he'd found a way around them.

This morning, he left breadcrumbs to suggest that he'd knocked on the door, so to speak, and had retreated when he'd found the door locked. Then he carefully scattered breadcrumbs across four continents. Not enough to make it obvious, but enough that someone who knew what he or she was doing could track him, but not without some effort. He sat down again and checked his laptop. For this part of the plan, he employed the most stringent security protocols possible, using a VPN and piggybacking on an outside Wi-Fi network so his computer was virtually undetectable, and linking first to a server in Kosovo. *Bingo!* Someone had taken the bait.

Derek's fingers flew over the keyboard. Each time someone found one of his breadcrumbs, Derek tracked the hit backward, trying to lock in on the person's location. Whoever had taken the bait was almost as good as Derek, but they hadn't expected the hunted to become the hunter. Most of the trails were dead ends— his adversary used the same strategy Derek had of bouncing to proxy servers all over the world to hide his identity. But Derek knew it was only a matter of time.

His thoughts raced as furiously as his fingers. Whoever this person was, Derek knew it couldn't be Latham. Probably someone Latham had hired to secure the server. And he or she was getting closer. Derek typed even faster, the adrenaline rush elevating his heart rate into triple digits and focusing his attention on the moving dots on the screen, one marking his location, the other homing in on a neighborhood just outside Washington, D.C. And at almost the same instant the tracker's dot landed on MondoHard, an IP address flashed on Derek's screen.

"Gotcha," he murmured.

He could find that person later. Now, he had to see who took the bait on this end. Quickly, he closed the laptop's lid, stood, and tucked the computer under his arm. As he hustled out the door, he almost ran into Paul.

"Whoa!" Paul's eyes widened as he back-stepped into the hall. "Can I talk to you?"

"Not now, man. Catch me after lunch, okay?"

"What's the hurry?"

"Got a meeting with Darya in QA. Sorry, man. I'm late."

Derek brushed past as Paul opened his mouth.

"Really?" Paul sounded peeved.

"Hey, man," Derek said over his shoulder, "this new gig isn't *all* fun and games." Paul would just have to get over it, Derek figured as he hurried to the elevator.

One floor down, Derek found his way to the area where the QA team working on his games lived. His counterpart, Darya, stood about as high as his armpit, and Derek had wondered if she was a big "little person," affected by Dwarfism, or if she was just short. He'd never asked because she was as fierce as a honey badger, and very good at what she did. If he pissed her off she could rip him a new one, or refuse to work on his games. Either way, he went out of his way to stay on her good side.

She and her team made sure that whatever Derek and his team created looked, sounded and worked the way it was intended. In game apps as big and complex as *Never Bitten*, or the sequel Derek was working on now, the team of software developers, coders, graphic designers, sound engineers, producers and so forth, was huge. Despite the constant communication and endless meetings, mistakes were bound to happen. Quality assurance specialists like Darya were essential to the process.

Dressed in black jeans and a white tank top that showed off her colorful sleeve of tats, she looked up at Derek from under a sheaf of thick hair—blue today—and held him with the laser gaze of her intense blue eyes.

"Ah, the boy wonder," she said in a thick Slavic accent, her voice seemingly too deep to be coming from such a petite body. "You are late."

"Yeah, only twenty-seven seconds, and I have a good excuse."

"What? Dog ate your homeworks?" Darya laughed.

"Nah. I was chasing a black hat through cyberspace."

She raised an eyebrow, but Derek didn't volunteer any more than that.

"We work, yes?" she said.

Derek nodded, set his laptop on her desk and pulled up a chair. She plopped into her office chair, swiveled around to face the pair of monitors on her desk and grabbed her wireless mouse. She started walking Derek through the issues she'd found with the most recent sections of *Second Bite*, Derek's latest creation. Derek typed notes on his laptop, but he paid only half his attention to what she was saying.

Darya's department, like Derek's, was seriously short-handed. MondoHard's gaming division still accounted for nearly half the company's annual revenue and profits, despite the rapid growth in government contracts and cloud services. That meant a lot of positions—and empty offices—waiting to be filled. Derek had picked the IP address of a computer on a desk not far from Darya's for precisely this moment. The person outside D.C. tracking his breadcrumbs would likely call someone here at MondoHard to check out who was using the computer on that desk. No one in Darya's department could point a finger at Derek because he'd done everything remotely, sending commands to that computer from his laptop. Now, all he had to do was see who showed up.

"...see, here." Darya pointed to one of her monitors. "Game is stop playing."

"Mm-hmm.'

"Hey, lover boy. Is me talking here."

Derek pulled his gaze back to the screen. "Right. Oh, wait. So, what, it's like a nanosecond delay?"

She shrugged. "Fix it, leave it in, is nothing to me. But legions of, how you say, fan boys will be in for blood—"

"Out for blood."

She glared at him. "Yes, 'out' for *your* blood. All because you don't fix nanosecond delay."

Derek frowned and stared at the monitor, then pulled the keyboard away from Darya and started typing.

"It's probably just AInsley thinking too hard," he muttered.

"Ainsley? Who is this Ainsley?" Darya's nostrils flared. "You get new person on team? And I get scraps for dog?"

"*Chikai.* Calm down. AInsley is the name we gave the artificial intelligence engine. Sometimes she has a mind of her own."

"Ha!" Darya's smile slowly disappeared. "That was joke, yes?"

"Yes, Darya, that was a joke."

The smile magically reappeared, and she punched Derek on the arm. "Good one."

Derek winced, then frowned. "I don't know what it is. I'll take a look when I get back to my office."

He hoped it wasn't AInsley. The last time the AI program had gone off the rails, the vice president's son had almost killed his own father. But that had been a clever bit of sabotage by—

Motion in his field of vision made Derek look up suddenly. *Speak of the devil...*

Dave Bradley walked up to the empty work station, his gaze taking it in—no personal belongings or photos, dark computer monitor, nothing on the desk top... Despite the fact that Dave Bradley—one of the "ancients"—was a senior veep and a company board member, he didn't belong on this floor. Bradley directed software development for the non-gaming side of the company. While that business was important to the bottom line, it wasn't what had established the MondoHard name, brand or considerable fortune.

Derek already knew that Bradley was dirty. Pretty sure, anyway. He'd found a copy of the infected beta version of *Never Bitten*—the one that had brainwashed the Dunn kid—on Bradley's computer. It wasn't proof that Bradley was up to no good—guys like Bradley were Teflon, and powerful, making it almost impossible to bring them down—but it was evidence. Derek wasn't surprised to see him scoping out the source of the "attempted" hack of Latham's server, but he couldn't help feeling nervous. The palms of his hands were damp, and his heart rate accelerated like it did when he goosed the throttle on his bike. He didn't think Bradley would recognize him, but he couldn't be sure. Keeping his gaze on Darya's monitors, he tracked Bradley's movements peripherally.

Darya stopped keyboarding and turned her head to watch Bradley, her curiosity piqued. Apparently, Bradley noticed.

"You know who sits at this desk?" Bradley called.

"Uh, no one," Darya said with a sarcastic tone as thick as peanut butter.

"Is anyone *supposed* to be at this desk?"

"Yes," Darya said simply.

Bradley grimaced and rolled his eyes. "Who?"

"I do not know."

"Well, who would know?"

"No one."

Bradley's face turned red. "Why the hell not?"

Darya shrugged. "Because we have not hired this person yet. We need bigger staff."

Bradley marched over, filling the entrance to Darya's cubicle, a thundercloud eclipsing his face. In a low, menacing voice he said, "Do *not* fuck with me. Do you know who I am?"

Darya tilted her head, gaze flicking across his features. She shook her head. "No. Do you know who *I* am?"

"Unemployed, that's who," he growled. Bradley swung his face toward Derek and peered at him. "What about you? Have you seen anyone using that desk?"

Derek shook his head. "No, sir. But I don't work here. I work up on the next floor."

Bradley threw up his hands. "Christ! I swear you're all stoners over here in Gaming."

He took out his cell phone, turned on his heel and dialed as he walked back to the empty desk. He conversed in low tones with someone on the other end for less than half a minute and hung up. Then he sat at the desk and pulled out the keyboard tray. Derek watched the monitor come to life as Bradley woke the computer.

"Who is this?" Darya murmured, her gaze still on Bradley.

Derek told her, and said, "He's pretty high up in the company. He's even on the board of directors."

She grunted. "He is big asshole, I am thinking."

Derek nearly choked trying to stifle a laugh.

When another man showed up a few minutes later, Derek abruptly couldn't find anything to smile about. On the face of it, Bradley calling this guy down made sense. But if Bradley had taken Derek's bait, then the man who'd just arrived could well be in league with Bradley—and Latham, by extension.

That would be bad. Very bad.

48

My life is about to end. Capping yet another day from hell, my humiliation is nearly complete. A question from Mrs. Jessup hangs in the air like a cloud of hydrogen sulfide, appropriate for AP Chem class. In the sea of silence that follows, my stomach ties itself in knots, my heart pounds, and I'm actually sweating—ugh, gross. Moisture tickles my ribs and beads under my hairline, threatening to drip down my face. Just as panic starts to overwhelm me, the bell rings, and the classroom erupts in noise—chairs scrape and squeak, shoes shuffle, voices babble, laughter bursts out. Next to me is rustle of paper and soft thud of books as Oliver packs up. A set of footsteps approaches, and scents of lilac and vanilla announce Mrs. Jessup's presence.

"Tess," she says, "I'm really worried about your performance. Frankly, I don't think you're ready for the mid-term tomorrow, and you can't afford not to do well."

"I'm fine, Ms. J. I'll be ready."

"I told you when you came back to school a few weeks ago that I was concerned you'd be able to keep up with your, uh, disability, and now it seems you may have other distractions to deal with."

"I can handle it," I say with a conviction I'm not sure I feel. "I've got this. Really."

She doesn't respond for a moment. "Well, I guess we'll see how you do tomorrow."

I'm about to breathe again when her scent grows stronger and she murmurs next to my ear, "I still expect you to answer the question."

I don't let out my breath until her footsteps recede to the front of the class.

"Get me out of here," I mutter.

I stand up. Oliver takes my hand and guides me around the desks. Once clear, I pull my hand away and put it on his shoulder. It's been a long day, and I don't want him to get the wrong idea. I'm too tired to deflect misinterpreted gestures or salve bruised egos. Mercifully, Oliver doesn't utter a peep on the way to the car. Once settled inside, though, he takes a breath.

"Don't say a word," I warn him. "Just in case you weren't paying attention, it's been a shitty day, and I'm not in the mood."

"I wasn't going to say anything," he replies in a quiet voice. "I was just going to ask if you want to go anywhere on the way back to the house. You know, to run errands, or get coffee."

I sigh. "Thanks, but no. We have coffee at home, and I don't want to go anywhere I might be recognized and ridiculed even more." Actually, I want to go lie on a secluded beach someplace where no one can see my pudge, where I don't have to think about AP Chemistry, AP English, college applications, or anything else for that matter. But I can't tell Oliver that.

"Okay. Got it."

He goes silent again. I don't care if I hurt his feelings. I have enough on my mind. Still...

"Look, I'm sorry I'm so bitchy," I say. "I don't mean to take it out on you."

"No, I get it. Really. It's no big deal."

The rest of the ride home is silent, which gives me time to think. Too much time, it turns out. I can't focus, and my thoughts ping-pong from one dilemma to another. I don't know how to extricate myself from several of them, and can't even begin to prioritize them in terms of importance. Life is ultimately important, but Sam is dead thanks to me, the threat to my life lessened if not minimized. Maybe finding out who put a contract out on me isn't as important right now as getting into college. Which means writing those college application essays.

But I'm not going to get into college if I can't even answer questions like how many elements on the Periodic Table are paramagnetic. Maybe I should focus on making sure I don't flunk courses like AP Chem. But I'm so angry at how Addie and Maddie and everyone else at school are treating me that I'm having trouble focusing on anything except finding out who made that porn video and salvaging what's left of my reputation. On the other hand, I'm definitely not getting into college if someone manages to kill me.

I don't even want to think about my other problems—getting Toby out of my life, dealing with Uncle Travis, figuring out why Robyn suddenly showed up again... My father—or whoever had me jumping through hoops a couple of weeks ago pretending to be him—told me I needed to save the world, "prevent the wings of the apocalypse" or some bullshit. I can't even tell if I have the right color of lip gloss on. How am I supposed to fix everything else?

It all rushes in so fast that I can't catch my breath. My face feels hot, and my heart flutters against my ribs like a bird in a cage. Panic wells up in my chest, my legs shake, my fingers and toes tingle and start to go numb. I feel weak, dizzy, as if it would take every ounce of strength I have to push myself out of the seat. At the same time, I feel a desperate need to open the door, jump out, and run before this monstrous ball of problems, responsibilities, overtakes me. Suddenly, my head is filled with the vision of that wall of white snow bearing down on our SUV and the fear in my mother's voice as she uttered one word, "James," my father's terse response, "No brakes," and the feeling of rolling, rolling, my body crashing into things each time the vehicle landed on its side, the roof, the other side, hearing the crack of bones breaking, my own cries of pain—

"Tess. Tess! Tess, look at me!"

I can't look, of course, but instinctively, my eyes snap open and I turn toward the sound of the voice calling me. My father's, I think. A hand grasps mine and squeezes gently.

"Breathe, Tess! You're okay." Oliver's voice, not my father's. "Come on, deep breath. In and out. Another. Slowly."

I do as he says, and my heartbeat slows, the shaking stops, and I melt into the seat. My hand feels good in his, so I leave it there and focus on breathing.

"You okay?" he says.

I nod, unable to speak just yet.

"You had me worried. I thought you were having a heart attack."

"It felt like it," I croak.

For a moment, everything else disappears, homework, jeering classmates, disapproving teachers, overbearing uncle, mysterious assassins, shadowy conspirators all gone, banished from consciousness. I feel safe, warm and content, a feeling I could get used. But is it because I'm with Oliver?

I don't know what I'm saying. I can't let this happen. I've been over this in my head a dozen times. Oliver's too old for me, and he works for me. And there's this other guy I like. Derek. I think he likes me, too, but I haven't really had the chance to find out. I'm confused. I pull my hand away and drop it in my lap. If Oliver objects, he doesn't say so. Disappointment washes over me, and I don't know why. I turn so my face won't give me away.

Back at the house, I make Oliver start with chemistry homework while my humiliation at the hands of Mrs. Jessup is still a fresh wound. I'm better than what I showed her today. To prove it to myself, the first thing I do is rattle off the names of the 32 elements that exhibit paramagnetic behavior. I know that given a different set of circumstances, all of them may exhibit other magnetic properties. And I might just throw that back on Ms. J. if she gives me a hard time. With the mid-term imminent, it's grueling work, especially since Oliver is clueless when it comes to chemistry. At least the kind learned from books. Maybe the other kind, too.

The house is quiet, perfect for getting work done. Whoever was on bodyguard duty had seen us safely home from school and inside the house, then left us alone. I don't know where Alice is. Probably in her office doing paperwork or making phone calls, negotiating with contractors and vendors. I never thought much about what it takes to run a household, manage a property, as large as this. We still don't have a new cook after the disaster of our last one—Rosa, the psycho bitch who tried to kill us all with a kitchen knife. But Alice, who still hasn't told us what happened to Rosa, stepped in to help. It occurs to me that she does a lot more behind the scenes to make us all comfortable than I give her credit for. I push aside the distracting thoughts and focus.

We take our senses, and how we learn, for granted. Oliver is as challenged helping me as I am learning what I need to know for the midterm. So much of AP Chemistry, like other STEM courses, is dependent on sight to learn. With history or literature, anything but visual arts, I can learn by listening. But chemical formulas, like math equations, are more readily learned visually. Fortunately, even though I can't physically see, I can still visualize from memory. Since I took basic chemistry freshman year, a lot of what I need to know is stored in my memory.

But it takes time for Oliver to recite electron configurations and atomic orbitals, or describe the data on a spectrometer graph. It's even harder for him to describe molecular chains, so he takes my hands and gently moves them on the surface of the table as he talks, telling me what element is represented at each position of my hands and the bonds between them. But I have to do all the math in my head, and it's painstakingly difficult without the reference of sight. I wonder if maybe Ms. J. is right that I should drop this course.

But I grit my teeth and keep going. I'll know after this mid-term exam if I can get a decent enough grade to make it worth staying in the class. I'll never get into any college, let alone MIT, if I don't get to those college application essays. One more thing to stress about.

I sit back and take a deep breath. "I need a break."

Oliver has walked me through about twenty percent of the two hundred fifty questions on the practice test. But we've been at it for more than an hour. I'm beginning to think my fall from royalty will be nearly complete when I have to get a waitress job because I can't get into college. Nothing against waitresses. Good ones anyone.

"Want me to get you something?" he says. "A snack? Coffee?"

I sigh. "Some water, maybe? That bottled ionic mineral alkaline water in the fridge?"

"Sure. Be right back."

The soft tread of his footsteps recedes toward the door, then silence washes over me. The stillness unnerves me at first, then centers me as I relax into it. The familiar scents of the library help—paper and leather with a little bit of mustiness; wood and lemon oil and trace of smoke and ash from a long-ago blaze in the fireplace; traces of green tea and dirt left in the air from the last time Yoshi was here; the faint lilac and wool that are Alice's trademarks. More pronounced are the clean scents of Oliver's soap and shampoo that are so similar they must be from the same brand. Something else lingers in the air, too, but I can't put my finger on it.

It's not unnaturally quiet—in the distance a leaf blower whines, and a light plane flies overhead. Somewhere closer, a clock ticks. Distantly, I hear Oliver in the kitchen, opening the fridge and a cupboard. Dull almost imperceptible thuds come from somewhere deeper in the house, more vibration than sound. The low rumble of an engine outside grows closer. Someone's coming. Moments later, the room pressure changes as the front door opens, and a heavy tread hurriedly thumps down the runner in the hallway.

I sit up, my peaceful break apparently over. My pulse quickens. It isn't Travis's walk, nor anyone's on the security team, at least that I recognize. But if it isn't someone in the house, that means the front door was open, which doesn't inspire much confidence in my security team's ability to guarantee my personal safety. I wish Oliver would get back. I wonder why it's taking him so long to get a bottle of water. I'm a little scared.

"Babe?" a voice calls. "Are you here?"

Derek.

"Ah, there you are," he says as he clomps across the room in what must be motorcycle boots.

"What are you doing here? And how did you get in?"

"Babe, really?" He sounds disappointed. "It's me, remember? I could hack your security in ten seconds flat. I didn't need to. You gave me the guest code for the gate last time I was here. I figured the same code would work on the front door. I was right. You ought to do something about that."

"Something about what?" Oliver says.

"Derek was just telling me our security here sucks."

"Nice." Oliver's sarcasm suggests he isn't happy to see Derek. He confirms it. "What are you doing here?" He puts a bottle of water in my hand. "What's he doing here?"

"I just asked him that."

"But you didn't give me a chance to answer," Derek says. "I've got news, and it isn't good."

"Just what I need. What the hell, might as well have the perfect ending to a perfect day." I sigh. "Don't keep us in suspense."

I hear him pull out a chair and sit across the table. "Okay, so you challenged me to find out if Senator Latham hired Sam to take you out. So, I hacked into his private server. As I suspected, it's heavily guarded. More secure than a lot of corporate IT systems I've gotten into. I guarantee you that Latham didn't devise the security measures by himself."

"Is there a point to this?" Oliver says.

"I'm getting there. Anyway, I got in without setting off any alarms, took a look around, and got out without leaving any tracks. Not easy to do, but not too terribly difficult for someone with my skill set. Oh, there's nothing to indicate Latham was involved, BTW, at least not directly."

"Okay." I'm confused. "So, what's the bad news?"

"Look, we tracked the money in Sam's account to MondoHard, right? So I thought maybe I could find out if Latham *was* behind the attack and is using the company somehow. Maybe he has an inside man. Or he intended to put the blame on MondoHard. Whatever. So, I deliberately set off an alarm in the server. Just to let them know I was there, not that I'd broken in, you know? And then I left breadcrumbs for someone to follow so they could find me. Well, not me, but a decoy."

"A trap, you mean?" I say.

"Yeah. An empty work station. And guess who took the bait?"

I freeze. I'm sure I look like I've seen a ghost. "Not Travis. Please don't tell me it's him."

He snorts. "No, babe. Not even close. First guy on scene was Dave Bradley."

"Wait," Oliver says. "Isn't he—?"

"Yeah, on the board, senior veep, yada, yada… That's the guy. But it gets better. While I'm watching him fume because he can't figure out how an empty work station is the source of a hack on Latham's server, someone else shows up—Cyrus Cooper."

I stifle a gasp.

"Chief of security," Oliver says.

"And Todd's dad," I say.

"Well, of course Bradley would call security," Oliver says.

"I wouldn't," Derek says. "Not if I was one of the bad guys. Unless, of course, the guy I called was in on it."

Oliver is silent. I can only imagine what's going through his head. I don't like it. Any of it. But I can't wrap my head around what it means because I'm distracted by the feeling that something isn't quite right.

"Something's going on," I say.

"You bet your damn skippy," Derek says.

I shake my head and sniff the air. "No, I mean now. Here. In the house."

"What do you mean?" Oliver says.

I hold my hand up for quiet.

49

I'm not sure what Tess was up to but she was a bird dog on point, head cocked, ears listening, nose up, sniffing, hand raised, finger pointing.

"What's—?"

"Shush!" She got up and stepped around the table, orienting herself so she had a straight shot for the door.

"Oliver," she murmured, "did you see Alice when you were in the kitchen? Or Yoshi?"

"No. What's going on, Tess?"

"No sign of them?"

"No. Though I heard some thumps that sounded like they came from the garage."

"That didn't seem strange to you?"

"Why should they? There are people around here all the time. I figured it was Yoshi or one of the security guys in the garage."

"What's the big whoop?" Derek said.

Tess headed for the door. "Something's not right. I'm going to find out what."

Derek and I looked at each other.

"Well?" he said.

"Yeah, I know, it's my job." I pushed up from the table and followed Tess out into the hall. I heard Derek on my heels.

Tess had already gotten as far as the kitchen and was moving fast. I still marveled at her ability to find her way around the house with little trouble and amazing speed. She was far less sure of herself in the outside world, though she moved with confidence when she had a hand on my shoulder or an arm wrapped in mine.

I liked the feel of her touch. I felt warm inside when she was close to me, more confident and self-assured, too, when she was with me, as if we somehow gave each other strength from somewhere the other didn't have it. We made a good team. I found it strange how much I'd grown to like her in a few short weeks despite her sense of entitlement, her princess-y ways. She was blossoming from a self-centered girly girl into a strong, caring woman. I wondered if I was falling for her.

I caught myself then, glad that Derek was still behind me so he couldn't see my face flushing. I couldn't be falling for her. She was too young. I was there to protect her, to guide and assist her, nothing more. The achy, empty feeling in my gut was probably nothing more than hunger, and my antagonism toward Derek simple vigilance for Tess's emotional safety. He was obviously the wrong guy for her. He would only break her heart. And he was only a few years younger than I, so still too old for Tess.

I lengthened and sped up my stride. Tess had turned the corner in the mudroom beyond the kitchen and mounted the stairs leading up to the two apartments on the second floor, Alice's above the kitchen and office, and Yoshi's above the garage. I had barely crossed the expansive kitchen when a loud, high-pitched argument broke out upstairs, and closed in on us quickly.

"You can't do that!" Tess shouted.

"You don't understand."

The voice was familiar. My memory put a name on it just as Robyn's face rounded the corner at the bottom of the stairs. She wore an expression of desperation, and a carried large handbag over her shoulder. She jerked up in surprise when she saw Derek and me in the kitchen, and the look on her face quickly turned fearful. Setting her mouth in a determined line, she hurried past.

"You can't just take things!" Tess yelled, clattering down the stairs and around the corner behind her. "What did you take anyway? Give it back."

"I can't," Robyn called over her shoulder. "You wouldn't understand."

"Robyn, stop! Oliver, where are you? Stop her."

"Right here," I said, startling her. "What's going on?"

"That's what I'm trying to find out! She was snooping last night, and she's back at it again today. I knew something was wrong. I could smell it. Well, don't just stand there. Stop her!"

"Are you sure about this? Doesn't she work for Travis?"

"I don't care! She just stole something from Yoshi's lab. You have to stop her! She'll get away."

"No she won't," Derek said. He grabbed Tess's hand. "C'mon, babe. We'll catch her on the bike."

They jogged down the hall, leaving me wondering if they'd all gone crazy. Alice seemed to have left the building, so I wouldn't get any advice there. But I'd promised Alice I wouldn't let anything happen to Tess. Shaking my head, I ran after them.

The blatting rumble and smoke from the exhaust on Derek's bike greeted me as I came through the front door. Tess pulled a helmet on as she swung her leg over the saddle behind Derek, and he goosed the throttle as soon as she put an arm around his waist. The pang that knifed me in the heart was jealousy, pure and simple. Glad that I'd left the car in the circle instead of the garage, I popped the locks with the remote as I ran over, and climbed in. As soon as I had it in gear and the nose pointed up the drive, I thumbed the hands-free button.

"Call Red," I said. He was the only guy on the security team I trusted. I didn't know if I trusted him all that much, but he was the only one who'd actually been cordial to me. Nice, even.

"Speak," he said when the call connected.

"If you're not busy, follow me," I said. "Tess is on Derek's bike. I'm going to try to keep them in sight, so you're going to have to haul ass."

"On my way. Keep the line open. What's going on?"

The car fairly leapt up the hill, but almost wasn't fast enough for me to see which way Derek turned out of the gate.

"You know Robyn?"

"We've met."

"Tess thinks Robyn stole something from Yoshi's apartment."

"Did she?"

"Looks like it. She's running."

"Okay, I'm moving. Which way?"

"North out of the gate. I think she's headed for the freeway."

"Not good. I'll let you know when I have a visual on you. Is Robyn still driving that beat up little SUV?"

I recalled the silver-gray compact SUV parked not in the circle, but along the side of the house. "I think so."

"So, kid, is this something I need to let Travis know about?"

The twisty road made it difficult to focus on driving and talking at the same time. I caught only glimpses of Derek's bike ahead. "I don't know," I said. "From what I saw last night, Travis may have a thing for Robyn. And Tess sure doesn't need any more aggravation from him. I mean I know she's his responsibility and all, but when it gets right down to it, he's not really involved in her life except to step in and bark at her when he thinks she's out of line. Doesn't seem fair. Alice and Yoshi are the ones who've been there for her."

"You, too, kid, these past couple of weeks."

His assessment took me by surprise.

"Yeah, well, that's what I thought, too," he went on when I didn't reply. 'Okay. We'll see how this plays out before we tell him. And kid? Thanks for calling me. Smart choice."

I concentrated on driving, powering the big sedan through the curves until I could see the gray SUV ahead of Derek's bike. Headlights blinked in and out of the rearview mirror, letting me know someone was back there. I hoped it was Red, so I turned my eyes back to the road ahead. Sweat dripped down my sides, and my grip on the steering wheel whitened my knuckles. I came up on Derek's tail fast, and quickly braked, realizing that Robyn couldn't push the SUV as fast as those of us trailing her. But as the road descended a long, gradual slope, we all picked up speed again, and after a curve at the bottom, a straightaway gave Robyn the confidence to step on the gas.

An intersection with a four-way stop was fast approaching, and after that the ramp to the freeway. If we didn't figure out a way to keep Robyn from getting on the freeway, we'd have a tough time of following her in traffic. My pulse pounded faster as we came up on the intersection. Robyn didn't even slow down for it, blowing right through the stop sign. As Derek and Tess followed, a car started to pull into the intersection from the right. Derek laid on the Ducati's puny horn and swerved, nearly throwing Tess off the bike. The car stopped with a short shriek of its tires. I saw the driver flip Derek the bird, then start to move forward. My heart leapt into my throat. I sounded my horn long and loudly as I yanked the wheel and swerved around the nose of the car, too, tires squealing.

Ahead of me, the motorcycle put on a burst of speed. Derek neatly pulled around and ahead of Robyn's car, and tapped his brakes, forcing her to slow. I zoomed up behind her SUV and boxed her in. And before I knew what was happening, the big SUV Red was driving roared up beside me and squealed to a stop next to Robyn's car, giving her no place to go. She opened her door as far as it would go with Red's vehicle in the way, squirmed out and slammed the door.

By the time I got out and ran up on shaky legs to prevent her from going anywhere, Derek had guided Tess back to the front of Robyn's car, trapping her. The knife blade of jealousy in my chest twisted, resentment pouring from the wound, filling me up, making me shake even more with all the adrenaline in my system from the car chase. Robyn looked at them, then swung her head back toward me, tears of frustration in her eyes, desperation still contorting her features. Her pain, so visceral and palpable, swatted away my feelings, at least temporarily. I could examine the green-eyed monster later. Now I needed to focus on what was going on.

"What did you do?" Tess shouted. Indignation rose from her like waves.

Robyn covered her face with her hands and sobbed. "I *had* to. You don't understand."

Red climbed out of the SUV next to us, folded his arms on the roof and watched us quietly.

On a hunch, I stepped closer to Robyn, and said in a low voice, "You're looking for the codicil to Tess's dad's will."

"Oliver," Tess said shrilly, "she—"

"Hang on, Tess. She'll tell us." I returned my attention to Robyn. "Travis already knows about the codicil, though, so you went looking for something else, too."

Robyn looked up balefully. "They said they'd hurt Ben."

Tess looked startled. "Ben? What, like threatened him?"

Robyn stifled a wail and nodded. "They said they'd kill him."

"Who's 'they?'" Red said softly in his deep voice.

She whirled toward him. "I don't *know*! Just some voice on the phone. Now they'll kill him for sure." She sniffed.

"Hold on," I said gently. "You don't know that."

"He's right," Red said. "Ben's your brother, right? If they kill him, they lose their leverage."

"I can't take that chance," she cried. "Don't you see?"

"What did they want this time?" Tess said, surprising me.

A battle played out on her face, fusillades fired on the right countered with blasts from the left and a bombing run overhead, forces tugging and pushing her from shell-blasted emotional ground to scorched earth, torn between what she felt and what she thought she ought to feel. She visibly softened, and her anger drained away. The change shocked as much as puzzled me, and something clicked into place as if waiting for this moment. I didn't know what it meant, only that I felt more complete.

"One of Yoshi's experiments." Robyn dug in the handbag that hung on her shoulder, and held out the little drone we'd seen the night before. "Here."

"What is it?" Tess said.

"The drone," I told her.

Tess blanched, making me wonder what she knew that we didn't.

50

My talk with Yoshi last night comes back to me. If it's true, what he said about the army wanting to weaponize the little "toy" in Robyn's hand, then other governments would be happy to steal it—or even kill for it. But for the chairman of the U.S. Senate Appropriations Committee to try to steal it makes no sense. Unless Latham is a traitor, and intends to sell the drone on the black market out of pure greed. My mind reels. This is all so Hollywood, so farfetched that no one will believe me if I give the idea voice. Oliver and Derek, maybe, and only because they've been through some weird shit with me in the past couple of weeks.

I'm not programmed to think this way. I'm programmed to think about what lipstick to wear, what fashion brand to buy this week, what names to drop, what social media influencers to follow, which boys to tease and which ones to dismiss or diss. Up until now, all I've thought about is how to be a royal, and when the accident took that away, I thought about how to get it back or navigate the rest of high school as if it didn't matter. Sure, there are nerdy girls who join the debate team, get jobs as summer interns in Olympia, and knock on doors after school passing out leaflets for the latest progressive to run for office, any office, from town council to U.S. Senate. But I'm not even old enough to vote. None of that has mattered in my world, or even made an impression.

All of a sudden, I have to consider conspiracies to undermine my father's company, and maybe the country itself. We *think* Senator Latham is behind it all, but to what end? When I think about all the technology Yoshi has managed to cram into the tiny device, I wonder if there's even more to what's happening than what meets the eye. Not mine, of course, since I can't fucking see. But I can hear just fine.

"Are you crying?" I say.

The sound triggers a memory, startling me. Benji and I play down by the water. It's a warm summer day, and the two of us are giggling as we run in circles on the shore. Benji tosses a beach ball to me. It's not very large, one of those inflatable multi-colored things, but to my six-year-old self it seems enormous, and as I stretch out my arms it bounces toward the shallow water. I lean, take a step, slip and fall in, banging a knee and an elbow on the rocky bottom. My wail brings Robyn at a run, and she pulls me from the cold water, wraps me in her arms, and carries me up the bank to a grassy spot to tend to my wounds—a bump on the elbow, and the tiniest of abrasions on my knee that I'm sure will cost me my leg as a trace of pink seeps from it. A bandage, magically produced from Robyn's bag, and kisses on the boo-boo from both Robyn and Ben make everything all right.

I smell the water, the fecund odor of moss, algae, seaweed and rotting vegetation along the shore, the scent of soap Robyn used, the freshly mown grass in the sun. I feel the warmth of the day, the gentle touch of Robyn's fingers, the dampness of my clothes. I hear the tiny waves lapping on the shore of the lake, the boats, motors at different pitches, an airplane in the distance. I see everything with crystal clarity, and now I'm sad and angry at the unfairness of my mind's ability to see the past when my eyes are unable to see the present. But right now I can hear Robyn trying hard not to sob.

"I'm the only one who's allowed to cry around here," I say. Maybe it's my sardonic tone, or my wry expression, but the sounds coming from her stop. I suddenly feel sorry for her because I know just what she's going through. Only in her case, someone she loves is being threatened, not Robyn herself. I try to imagine loving someone so much I'd steal, even kill, to save that person. If I didn't see another way, I guess I might.

"Why didn't you tell us, Robyn?" I say.

"I'm sorry. I'm so sorry. I just... They sent me a video of him at the school where he works. They watch me at work somehow. They could be watching now. I didn't know what else to do."

I sense she's close to tears again. I can hear it in her voice.

"You could have come to us. Alice or Travis would know what to do. They could help."

"You don't understand. None of you do. I don't care what you say, they'll kill Ben if I don't give them what they want. I know it!"

I think for a moment. "What do they want you to do now?"

"They said they'd let me know what to do once I have what they're looking for.

"Do they know what it is?"

"I'm not sure," she says slowly. "They just told me to steal a miniature drone and any papers I could find that look related."

"What are you thinking, Tess?" Oliver says.

"They can't hurt Benji and Robyn if they can't get to them," I say. "Robyn, you two can stay in the beach house. We already have security in place. Red, is that your voice I heard?"

"Yes, Ms. Barrett, it is."

"You didn't bring anyone else along, did you?" I feel momentary panic that Marcus, or worse, Travis, has been here the whole time listening.

"No, it's just me."

I breathe an inward sigh of relief. "You wouldn't have any trouble adding the beach house to your patrols, would you?"

"I'd have to take it up with Marcus or your uncle, but I don't see why not?" Red says. "We already patrol the shore on our rounds."

"What's the beach house?" Oliver says.

"Oh, you must have seen it," I say. "It's that little two-bedroom bungalow down on the waterfront."

"Not the boathouse?" Oliver says.

"No," I say impatiently. "Farther down the shoreline. And really well protected by a bluff behind it. No way anyone can get to it except past the main house. And it's easy enough to spot anyone approaching by water."

"It's a good idea, Miss," Red says.

"But we can't hide forever," Robyn says. "They'll still be out there, and even more determined to get what they want."

"Not if they already have it."

"You mean just give it to them?" Robyn says.

"Exactly." A plan starts coming together in my head.

"Oh, my god, no. I'd lose my job, go to jail. Travis would kill me for sure."

"I doubt it," I say. "But he can definitely be a pain the ass."

"You're not serious, are y—?"

"Who's a pain in the ass?" a voice calls out.

My stomach drops, and then I feel blood suffuse my face, and I wish I was as invisible to everyone else as they are to me.

51

Travis.

Tess blanched, then vermilion crept up her neck into her face until her scar stood out like a lightning bolt.

She bit her lip and stammered. "Um, I, uh..."

Nervously, I shifted my gaze to Travis as he walked past Red to peer at Tess over the hood of the SUV. The shit, I figured, was about to hit the fan.

"Aren't you grounded for life?" he said.

Tess looked confused, and I had trouble keeping my jaw from dropping. His tone was measured, not angry, almost light, as if he was asking about the weather.

"She was talking about me," I said hurriedly. "I'm the pain in the ass."

Travis threw me a glance that suggested he knew better, but didn't say anything, turning instead to Robyn. "Are you all right?" he said, with genuine concern in his voice.

She nodded, not trusting herself to speak.

"You're not hurt, are you?" he said.

She shook her head this time, but found her voice. "No, I'm fine, Travis. Really."

He let out a breath. "Thank god for that," he murmured. "I thought maybe you'd been in an accident."

"How'd you know to come?" Red said.

"Barney. Said a parade took off from the house like greyhounds after a rabbit. Which is more than I heard from you."

"Got it under control," Red said simply.

"You've got what under control?"

"Well, this." Red gestured at the group of us.

Everyone began talking at once until Travis held up his hand, and silence fell.

"Yes, I want to know what the hell is going on," he said, "but first we need to take the conversation out of the street. We're blocking traffic. We don't need cops poking their noses into whatever 'this' is, And Tess, I'd really rather you didn't stand out in the open making a big target out of yourself."

He pointed toward a parking lot next to the large park overlooking the lake, backdropped by the city skyline. "It'd be a good idea to move this conversation over there."

We all got in, or on, our respective vehicles and trooped down the street, parked, and assembled on the pavement behind them while we waited for Travis to retrieve his Range Rover and join us. A sprinkling of rain dampened our faces and hair. No one seemed to meet anyone else's gaze except Red, who kept a watchful eye on us, in case someone decided to bolt, and on our surroundings, looking for potential threats. Robyn looked miserable, eyes downcast, shoulders sagging, as if defeat was inevitable despite Tess's sudden change of heart. Derek had lost some of his swag, and shifted his weight nervously from one foot to the other. Tess had set her mouth in a grim line, as if anticipating another lecture or shouting match with Travis. I had to hand it to her, defiance must have been her middle name.

I tried to make sense of everything that had just transpired— why someone had blackmailed Robyn into stealing the little drone from Yoshi's lab; what had caused Tess's sudden shift in attitude about Robyn despite her being caught red-handed; Travis's change of tactics in dealing with Tess... It all made my head spin, and I couldn't focus on any of the changes long enough to come to any conclusions. We'd soon see if Travis's startling transformation— and Tess's—was short-lived or not as he pulled into the lot and swung his SUV in the slot next to Derek's Ducati. Robyn glanced up as he faced us.

"Tess," he said evenly, "since everything seems to revolve around you these days, you want to tell me what happened?"

She rankled at first, then tipped her head with a thoughtful expression when she didn't hear anything threatening in his tone. She launched into an explanation that pretty much summarized what had taken place, at least from my perspective. When she finished, Travis looked at Robyn, and even I could tell from his expression that he'd fallen hard for her.

"Why didn't you tell me?" he said gently. "You could have come to me."

She raised her head and held his gaze. "And said what? That someone was blackmailing me, but I couldn't say who? That I wanted to steal something from your home, from Yoshi of all people, who's trusted me as long as I've known him?" She gave a derisive snort. "You would have called me crazy and laughed me out of your office."

He shook his head. "No. Never. We'll figure this out. I'm not letting anything happen to you or to Benjamin."

"Um, I have an idea," Tess said. "We were just talking about it before you showed up."

"I don't think this is something you can help with, Tess," he said abruptly. "This sounds more like a security issue, something the team and I should handle."

Tess looked chastened, then angry. I started to object, but Red beat me to it.

"I think you should hear her out, Travis," he said. "Girl's got some moxie and a whole lot of smarts."

A cloud darkened Travis's face, and for a moment it looked like he was going to blow. But he apparently thought better of it, and gave a slow nod.

"All right. Tess, I apologize. Let's hear what you have in mind."

She told him about offering Robyn the beach house, which the security team could easily add to its rounds.

Travis mulled it over, and gave a nod. "Okay, but that doesn't solve the problem of who's blackmailing her."

Tess smiled. "That's simple. We give them what they want."

Travis frowned. "And what is it they want again?"

Robyn dug in the bag over her shoulder again, pulled out the drone and held it out. Travis stepped closer and stared at it.

"What the hell is that? Where did you get it?"

"It's a tiny drone," Tess said.

"I took it from Yoshi's lab like Tess said." Robyn burst into tears, and sobbed, "I'm sorry, Travis. I'm so ashamed. I just... I just couldn't bear the thought of anything happening to Ben. Please, please forgive me."

Travis practically squirmed under the onslaught, and I knew just how he felt—Kryptonite. Red, though, must have had immunity, and even was well enough prepared to nudge Travis and hand him a tissue. Travis looked at it as if he'd never seen one, then gave a little shake and passed it to Robyn. She traded the drone for the tissue and dabbed her eyes while Travis turned the drone over in his hands, peering at it.

Tess went on as if Robyn's outburst hadn't happened. "I'm guessing this isn't the only drone Yoshi has in his lab. He probably has several prototypes, knowing him."

"This design is amazing," Travis said. He looked skeptical. "Are you sure it works?"

"Of course we're sure," Tess said, offended. "We saw it. Well, Oliver and Ben saw it, but I felt it hover around my head. Yoshi says it has a scent analyzer, and he's...working on some other stuff."

She'd been about to say something, but changed her mind. I could tell Travis thought so, too, but he didn't pursue it.

"So, what you're suggesting is we give the blackmailers an older prototype," Travis said, still examining the device.

"Well, yeah. They won't know it's not the real one, and it'll get them off Robyn's case."

He shook his head. "I can't let Robyn take that chance. If they suspect anything, they could kill her. And Ben."

"I'll do it," Robyn said quietly.

"No, it's too dangerous," Travis said.

"I want to do it," Robyn insisted. "It's the only way to put a stop to these people, and the only way I can make up for what I've done."

"Robyn, please. I can't let you risk it."

"It could work, Travis," Red said quietly. "This could be our chance to go on offense instead of sitting around waiting for someone to take potshots at Tess or anyone else."

"What do you mean?" Travis said.

"Look, these people, whoever they are, have been after this thing for a while now, right? Wouldn't you like to find out who's behind it?" Red took his silence as assent. "Okay, so as soon as these people tell Ms. Alia where she's to hand off the device, we set up there around the perimeter. And we follow whoever shows up, see where they go, who they deliver the drone to."

Travis stared into the darkening sky for a moment, thinking about it. "Yeah, it might work." He turned to Robyn. "When are they letting you know where the drop is supposed to take place?"

"I don't know. They said I should text them when I have the device. Some time after that."

"Okay, first things first. We need to get Ben first. We can go from there. Ben's at work? Call them and let them know someone else will be picking him up today. Red can send Luis. Ben will like him. Make sure they know to have Ben ready by the back door, in case anyone's watching the place. Once the two of you are safely settled in the beach house we can send someone to your house to pack up clothes and things for you. We can go over the rest of it back at the house. That sound okay?"

With murmurs and nods, Robyn and Red got on their phones, and we made as if to leave.

Travis took two steps, stopped and looked at Derek. "By the way, aren't you supposed to be at work? And don't give me some bullshit about needing to work on Tess's laptop."

"I, uh... I'm doing some research for *Second Bite*?" Derek fidgeted. "I mean, between the Dunn kid and this stuff, I'm getting some great material."

"You want to try again?" Travis said.

"He's helping me find out who hired Sam," Tess said.

"Palmer?" Travis said. "I told you, Tess, I've got our best people on it."

"Yeah, well I don't trust your best people, and you haven't delivered on your promise yet."

"What? And Derek has?"

"He's working on it," she said, refusing to say more.

"It's not a game, Tess."

"I *know* that," she said, making an effort not to raise her voice or push his buttons. "Look, I can't go into detail, but I'm sure Sam and this drone business are tied together somehow."

"That's crazy, Tess."

"No, it's not," she insisted calmly. "Not if you think about it. So, if you want to find out who's blackmailing Robyn, here's how it's going to work. And Red, I'm taking it on faith—and Oliver's judgment—that you won't breathe a word of this."

Red held his phone away. "My lips are sealed, Miss Barrett."

Travis threw him a dirty look. "Go on, Tess."

"I get to be part of the surveillance team for this hand-off. And Oliver, too, of course. Sorry, Derek, but I need you to keep using your expertise on what we talked about earlier."

Derek shrugged. "That's cool, babe."

"No," Travis said, his jaw working. "Absolutely not."

"If not for me," she shot back, standing her ground, "you wouldn't know this even happened. And Robyn would have delivered Yoshi's best work into the hands of our enemies. *Our* enemies, Travis. Like it or not, you might run MondoHard, and even own a piece of it, but it's our family's company. *My* company, someday. I deserve to be part of this, to know what's going on. We do it my way, or Robyn doesn't send the text, and you can deal with the fallout."

Travis was silent for a minute. "I'll consider it. What else?"

"You can't say a word to Marcus about this. I don't want him anywhere near this."

"Tess, I know you don't—"

"Not a word! I don't care what you have to tell him, he's not part of this. Swear!"

I was sure that Travis would refuse, but the longer he thought about it, the less sure I became.

"Okay," he said finally. "But I have conditions of my own."

"I don't think I'm going to like this." She sighed. "What are they?"

"One, you do exactly what you're told." He turned to me. "That means you, too, Oliver. I'm trusting you to keep her safe."

"Like he did the other night?" Tess muttered. I started to object, but she said, "What else?"

"No more secrets. I'm not your enemy, Tess. We have to start trusting each other, or this is never going to work."

"Are you kidding me?" she said.

"I mean it." He glared at her as if that would have an effect.

"Okay, fine," she sulked.

"Good. Then since it's getting dark, I suggest we meet back at the house."

52

Travis was glad he'd thought to call Alice first. Efficient as always, she'd set up the dining room like a conference room, with coffee, water, juice and light snacks. She'd also alerted Yoshi, who wasn't happy that Travis now had him cornered.

"Look," Travis said quietly so the others wouldn't overhear, "I know where your allegiance lies, and I wish I could say we're not working at cross-purposes here, but we need your help. Putting aside what you've been hiding from the company—"

"I not work for company," Yoshi interrupted. "I work for family."

Travis gritted his teeth and stayed calm. "Putting that aside for now, I need to protect the family. Which means I need to find a way to remove the threats to Tess and to Robyn. They may be related, they may not be, but we can start by taking steps to find out who wanted Robyn to steal your work."

Travis opened his hand and held it out. "This is yours, I believe. It's an amazing piece of work, and I can only imagine what it's capable of."

Yoshi hesitated, then plucked the little drone from Travis's palm. "Maybe I show you sometime."

"I'd appreciate that. In the meantime, I don't want you to take any chances with that. Lord knows, if you gave it to me, I'd only blow it up."

Yoshi grinned broadly. "Like the one James give you, *hai*?"

"Yes, that one."

James had offered it to Travis for field testing in Afghanistan, not realizing that Travis intended to test it by sniffing out a terrorist cell in hidden mountain caves. Travis hadn't known at the time that it was the only prototype of its kind in existence, and when he'd ordered an airstrike on the terrorists the drone had been destroyed. The R&D teams at MondoHard had been trying to recreate it ever since.

"I know you remember it well, Yoshi. And I'm guessing that you've built several prototypes based on that original design."

"Perhaps."

"If you'd be willing to sacrifice one that was an improvement on the original, but not *too* improved, we might be able to fool people long enough to track them down before they realize their mistake."

"Ah, so," Yoshi said, the light dawning. "Yes, I think I can find just what you need. All my work based on ideas James develop, you know. So, I have what you call 'version two-point-two.' I go bring it to you."

"Thank you. I can't tell you how much this means."

Yoshi bowed and retreated quickly. Travis thought he detected a trace of embarrassment in Yoshi's face before he turned and hurried away, and he wondered if Yoshi was embarrassed for himself or for Travis. He also wondered how Yoshi, tinkering in a workshop over the garage, seemed to have managed to create something that the R&D team, with a lab and hundreds of millions of dollars at its disposal had not.

Red and Luis came through the door from the kitchen laden with comms gear and went around the table putting a set in front of each chair. Fred and Barney, aka Flintstone and Rubble, followed them in and took seats on either side of Derek, Tess, and Oliver, hemming them in. When Red finished spreading his gear out, he walked over to Travis.

"Any problems?" Travis said.

"Nah. Scott is asleep, Sergei and DeWayne are on patrol, and Dom is in the comms room monitoring the video feeds. Marcus is supposed to relieve Dom at the end of his shift, and Fred and Barney are spelling Sergei and DeWayne when we get back."

"Marcus?"

Red shrugged.

Alice materialized at Travis's side, startling him. Her sensible shoes generally gave away her approach, but he'd learned that she could operate in some sort of stealth mode.

"Marcus is up at the high school," she said, "dealing with some personnel issues on the security staff there. Apparently, some staff members misstated their experience and capabilities, so Marcus is shifting people around and setting up a new schedule."

"Thanks for the update."

"Of course," she said. "Is there anything else you need here?"

"Uh, yes, actually," Travis said as he surveyed the table. "Would you mind helping Tess and Robyn with their comms gear? I'm not sure they'd welcome male pairs of hands putting it on for them. You know how—?"

"I know what to do," she interrupted with a withering look. "Don't look so surprised, Travis. I knew Jack Turnbull before your parents ever met him, and as you well know, you're bound to learn something from the man sooner or later."

She walked away leaving Travis open-mouthed and with a furrowed brow. Of course Alice knew General Turnbull. In addition to being Travis's commanding officer at SICC, Jack had been a family friend since Travis and James were kids, and, in fact, was their godfather. Plus, he was a director on MondoHard's board. But how had Alice known him longer than his parents?

He watched as she leaned in to say something to Tess, then she beckoned Oliver to get up and follow her to the far corner of the room. Whatever she said to him, it got his attention and made him nod with a serious expression. Travis couldn't worry about it now.

"Okay, people, listen up," he said as he stepped to the head of the table. He grasped the back of the chair with both hands and leaned forward. "We need to be clear on how this is going to work before Robyn gets her phone call."

All eyes were on him now except Alice's as she concentrated on fastening and adjusting Tess's throat mic. He glanced down at the comms gear on the table in front of him and frowned. He didn't know how he was going to make sure this crazy idea of Tess's actually worked without anyone getting hurt.

He glanced around the table. "We don't know who's calling the shots here, so we have no idea how many people might be watching Robyn. Which means we'll need to have as many of us as possible keeping tabs on her. I expect whoever this is to throw her some curveballs to keep anyone—meaning us—from tailing her to the rendezvous point. So, we'll all take separate vehicles. Tess and Oliver in one together, of course. Derek, you take your bike."

"Wait!" Tess said. "He's supposed to be helping me."

"Tess, I don't like involving any of you three. You don't have the training or skill set. But if this is going to work, I need as many bodies and vehicles as possible to make sure we don't lose Robyn somehow."

"I can handle that other thing when we get back, babe," Derek said. "Shouldn't take me long, and I planned on an all-nighter anyway."

Tess looked distinctly unhappy, and while I didn't like to think of myself as petty, her displeasure with Derek sent a secret thrill through me.

Fred spoke up while Tess was still digesting Derek's comment. "Not so good if the four of us are in the SUVs, Travis. They all look alike. Anyone watching might suspect a tail on Robyn even if we switch off."

Travis rubbed the stubble on his face. "Good point."

He turned to Alice and saw she'd already met his gaze.

"I'll get the keys to my car, Yoshi's truck, and the family car," she said quietly. "With one of the security team's vehicles, that should take care of it."

Travis nodded as she passed by on her way out to the kitchen. "Okay, so we put two cars ahead of her at all times, ready to fall back and switch with cars behind her. I'll direct traffic."

"How do we know who's who?" Oliver said.

"To make it easy, we'll use our first initials. I'm Tango. Red, you're Romeo; you'll take the family car. Fred, you're Foxtrot, and you get Alice's car. Barney is Bravo; you can take Yoshi's pick-up truck. Luis, you're Lima; take one of the SUVs. Derek, you're Delta, and Oliver and Tess are Oscar. Robyn, since the R is taken, you can be Juliet."

"Oscar? Seriously?" Tess said. "Don't I get one of my own?"

Travis frowned. "Fine. You can be Tango. I'll be Papa. Alice is Alpha, and Yoshi is Yankee in case we need either one of them for anything."

"What if we lose Robyn in traffic or something?" Derek said.

"We won't, but Robyn can let us know, since she'll have a comms unit, too." Travis looked at her. "How have these people been communicating? Voice? Text?"

"Both," Robyn said.

Travis thought for a moment. "It'll still work. If they text you with instructions, you can tell us on the comms. If they call you, put the phone on speaker, and we'll hear what's going on, as long as you keep your comms unit open. But only if they're speaking. Otherwise, none of us will be able to talk as long as you keep pushing your talk button. Are you okay with that?"

She nodded nervously.

"We can't get too close or they'll get spooked," Red said. "You know they'll want her to come in alone."

"I'm hoping we'll find out where they want her to go with enough time to get a few of us in place before she gets there. We'll have to be careful going in because they're sure to have people watching." Travis faced Robyn again. "Robyn are you still sure you want to do this? I can't say you won't be in any danger, but with

274

these precautions it should be minimal. I just don't know who or what we're dealing with."

"If you can find out who these people are and stop them from threatening us, I'll do whatever I have to."

She'd already proved that, and suddenly Travis wondered if they—if he—should trust her. Tess had done a complete about-face from screaming at Robyn the day before, too. And Travis wasn't sure how much he trusted Tess, either. He took a breath, let it out. Robyn had just been under duress, he decided.

He nodded at Robyn. "Okay, send them a text."

53

I'm nervous, and I don't know why. It's not like I'm going to be in any danger. Travis is making sure of that. I don't even think they'll let me near any of the action, and part of me thinks I'm wasting my time, that I'd be better off studying for Jessup's AP Chem mid-term, or working on the Common App, at least for the colleges on my list that accept it. But another part of me wants to know if I'm right about Robyn, or if I let her sob story get to me. I don't want to think I'm losing my touch.

I realize I'm biting a nail, and yank my hand away from my mouth. I wipe it dry on my jeans, hoping Oliver has his eyes on the road, and casually rest my arm on the center console. Oliver places his hand over mine and squeezes gently. I'm mortified, but I can't just pull my hand away.

"Are you okay?" he says.

"Yeah, fine."

"You don't have to do this, you know."

"I don't *have* to do anything." Like let you hold my hand, I think. "Of *course* I have to do this. What's wrong with you?" I snatch my hand away.

"Wait." He hesitates. "I'm confused. You *have* to? Or you *don't* have to?"

I fume, unable to put thoughts and emotions into words. I try to find a way to explain what it's like to be a target, of someone's camera, of someone's gun. He may have been the victim of bullies, but he's never been threatened the way I have.

Finally, I say, "Don't you get it by now?"

The silence lasts so long I don't know if he's still thinking about it or just wants me to drop the subject.

"You want your life back," he says quietly. "Look, I won't pretend I know what you're going through, but I do know what it's like to feel you have no control over your life, to feel like you'd do anything to prove to yourself you can affect what happens to you, challenge Fate."

I grudgingly admit that he has a point, but I don't tell him that. The walkie-talkie or comms device, or whatever the hell it is, crackles in my ear, and I hear Travis's voice.

"Juliet is southbound on Rainier. Foxtrot, fall back. Delta, take lead position. Lima, move up and take my spot. Oscar and Romeo, hold."

One by one, everyone checks in. I remember the code names, but I focus on the voices and pay close attention. Oliver is the last to answer, and almost as soon as he's off the air, "Lima" comes back on.

"Juliet just turned onto 23rd Avenue South," Luis says.

"Okay, folks," Travis says in my earpiece, "shift over accordingly."

"Do you still see her?" I ask Oliver.

"Heck no," he says. "We're pretty far back. I could still see Luis's taillights a few cars ahead until he moved up. Now I don't know how far back we are. No, wait... That must be Fred."

"How can you tell in the dark?"

"Smell?"

"That's so not funny, Oliver."

"Sorry. One of the cars up ahead slowed down, so cars behind it have been shifting lanes to go around. It looks like Alice's car, so it must be Fred. That means we're good."

I didn't need the encyclopedic explanation, but I guess I asked for it.

"Are you scared?" he says.

Am I? A flash of anger courses through me, and I have to bite back a quick retort questioning his intelligence. Maybe he's just being sensitive, or empathetic.

"Nervous mostly," I venture. "I want this to work. I want these people found and dealt with. But yeah, I'm scared. Every damn day. I literally can't see what's coming at me, and that's frightening." I turn away and swipe at an eye that threatens to leak.

He puts a hand on my shoulder. I don't shrug it off, and in a moment his fingers gently massage my tense muscles. I sigh, wanting to lean into his touch, but I'm afraid to send the wrong signal.

My earpiece crackles again. "Juliet's on Lander heading west," Luis says.

"Copy that," Travis says.

Oliver takes his hand away, and a few moments later, I feel the car turn a corner. We continue on in silence for a minute or so.

"Why isn't Robyn telling us what's going on?" I wonder aloud.

"Maybe she's focused on driving. Or maybe they said something that scared her."

I wish I knew. Robyn can certainly hear us when we're on the radio, so she knows we're here, close by. Something doesn't seem right, but I can't put my finger on it.

"This could be it," Luis says. "Juliet just turned into a supermarket parking lot. I'm getting set to make the turn. Yep, Juliet pulled into a slot close to the street and parked."

"Everyone," Travis barks, "take the next turn and pull over! Hold until we know more."

Oliver turns on the blinker, and I feel the car ease around a corner, slow, and finally stop.

"Shit!" Luis says. "Juliet's out of the car, and headed across the street. I know where she's going! I'm following on foot."

"Lima, what's your situation?" Travis says.

"Light rail station," Luis says, his breathing faster and mixed with sounds of traffic. "Don't worry, I won't lose her."

"What light rail station?" I ask Oliver. I don't really know where we are.

"Beacon Hill," he says.

In the earpiece, I hear static, then nothing.

54

Travis keyed the mic on his comms unit. "Lima, come in." He waited ten seconds and tried again. No answer. He'd been afraid of that.

Staring out the windshield of his Range Rover, his thoughts raced, and his pulse quickened. A tendril of fear snaked through his subconscious looking for a toehold, a place to put down roots and spread. He quashed it. They were waiting for him. His troops. About as ragtag a bunch as he'd ever led. Maybe more so, even, than the farmers and villagers in Afghanistan he'd recruited to fight the terrorist ideals of the Taliban and groups like al Qaeda and ISIS. These troops, here, he knew, would fight as fiercely—if they only knew who the enemy was. Perhaps his niece more fiercely than all of them.

She had more to lose than anyone, yet here she was willing to put herself on the line for a woman she'd wanted thrown out of the house a day earlier. And not, as she'd said, because it might lead to the people trying to kill her. But because Tess, he realized, would ultimately do what was right. Travis hadn't given her enough credit, and she was proving him wrong in so many ways. He should have known. After all, she was James's daughter.

His troops were waiting now. Waiting for him to do what he'd done all his life—lead. He didn't know why he hesitated. Because it was Robyn? All the more reason. He keyed the mic.

"Listen up," he said. "I was afraid of this. Whoever's running Juliet is throwing one of those curveballs, one that unfortunately I didn't anticipate. If these people made Juliet go into the station, it was to get her underground where her comms unit is no good. So, we're just going to have to sit tight and wait."

"We gotta do something," Red's voice came back. "She might be handing over the drone even as we speak."

"She might," Travis said. "But I don't think so. I think our merry chase has a way to go."

"You just want us to sit here?" It was Barney's voice this time.

"Lima said he's on it," Travis said with more confidence than he felt. "He'll find a way to clue us in. We just have to give him some time."

"I trust the kid," Red said, "but how much time?"

The fear was back, hanging out like something in his peripheral vision, there but not there. He'd told Robyn he didn't think she was in any danger, but would they kill her to keep her quiet once they had the drone? No. he couldn't even think it. She was safe as long as she was in a public place.

"I don't know," he said. "Who's closest to the station?"

"I am," Fred said. "I'm sitting in the supermarket parking lot. I can see both vehicles and the station from here."

"Okay, we'll give it five minutes. If we don't hear anything by then, Foxtrot goes into the station to check."

"Copy that," Fred said. "Five minutes."

The radio went silent, and Travis sat in the dark trying hard not to check his watch every ten seconds. As the minutes dragged on, he cursed himself for not thinking this through. Civilian life had made him rusty. He felt like all he'd been doing at MondoHard for eighteen months was putting out fires, not planning an operation or a campaign. And while he'd been used to improvising on the fly in the field during his time in the military, planning for contingencies was important. He was losing his edge.

"Papa?" a voice said in his ear. "What do you want to do?"

Travis glanced at his watch. "Give it another minute." He crossed his fingers and held his breath.

He watched the second hand on the heavy watch face make its way around the dial. When it arrowed up to the top again, he reluctantly raised his hand to key the throat mic. Before he could, his phone buzzed, letting him know he had an incoming text. He wanted to ignore it, but it might be Alice or a client from work. He fumbled for the phone and held it up, the screen lighting up the interior of his SUV. His eyes widened in surprise.

On a train heading north. Juliet still clear.

Travis quickly typed in a reply. How?

Trains have Wi-Fi. Can use comms again when we're out of the tunnel.

Excited now, Travis keyed his mic. "Lima made contact. Juliet's on a train headed into the city. He's keeping watch. Everyone, head downtown. He'll update us when the train clears the tunnel. You all got that?"

One by one, his troops checked in. Breathing a little easier, Travis put the big SUV in gear and pulled away from the curb.

Five minutes later, his cell phone rang. He answered using the SUV's hands-free system.

"Barrett, here."

"Hey, Trav," Luis said. "Thought this would be better, actually. You know..."

Travis picked up on his lead right away. "You mean so it looks like you're having an actual conversation, and not like a Secret Service agent."

"You got it."

Travis heard the relief in Luis's voice. "So, you have our girl in sight, and no sign of a tail?"

"Not that I can see, but better safe than sorry."

"Got that right. Okay, so let me know when she gets off the train. Or if someone gets on and approaches her."

"Will do. Wish I could let her know everything's cool."

"She hasn't seen you?"

"I don't think so. I've seen her fiddle with the comms unit a couple of times, but I've hung back a little so as not to tip our hand."

"Wish I'd had more like you with me in the 'Stans, Luis."

"Aww, you're gonna give me a swelled head, boss. Won't be able to wear a hat no more."

"Remind me to pay you more."

"Count on it."

Travis broke the connection with a smile. He thought for a moment about the assets he had in play, then asked a digital assistant to find a route map of the light rail system and put it up on the heads-up display in the windshield. He studied the map as he drove, and keyed his comms unit.

"Okay, folks, Lima is running point on this, and will let us know when and where we need to step in and help out. To cover all the bases, we're going to have to play leapfrog. So, listen up. Foxtrot and Oscar head for the SODO light rail station and hang there until we hear from Lima. Bravo and I will cover the the Stadium station. Romeo and Delta, you take International District station. Got it so far?"

He listened as they all checked in. "Great. We're on the same page. If Juliet stays on the train at SODO, Foxtrot and Oscar hustle to Pioneer Square and wait there. If Juliet doesn't get off at the Stadium, Bravo and I will shift to University Street, and if Juliet stays on at the Chinatown station, Romeo and Delta move up to Westlake. Everybody clear?"

Again, they checked in one at a time, in the affirmative. But after everyone had sounded off, one more voice sounded in his earpiece.

"Um, Tango here." As if anyone couldn't tell. "What happens if Juliet doesn't get off at any of those stops? What next?"

55

Travis's little game of hopscotch or leapfrog, or whatever, gets old really fast. It's hard for me to be an enthusiastic participant when we go to the first spot, sit, and wait. And wait. And then go to the second spot and wait some more. Oliver isn't the greatest conversationalist when he isn't showing off his Jedi mind tricks of remembering minutia from before I was born. And I start obsessing over all the stuff I have to do, and thinking that this outing is a total time suck I don't need right now. Plus, I can't see shit.

Yawn.

One good thing is that Luis has added all of us to his texts, so we don't have to wait for Travis to tell us what's going on. Like, group chat. Oh, goodie. And then I start to wonder if Robyn has been playing us, that maybe her sob story was just that, a story. Which makes me feel like a first-class chump for believing her, except that why wouldn't I since Robyn has been nothing but nice to me my whole life? Of course, there is the way she used to look at my father, though that could be the overactive imagination of a middle school girl. And Robyn says he never would have stepped out on my mom anyway. So I don't know what to believe. I'm driving myself crazy.

I'm about to yell at Oliver to do something when our phones chime at the same time.

"Play text," I snarl, not giving Oliver a chance to read it first.

She's not moving. Maybe next stop.

I don't have time to react before Travis's voice is in my ear.

"You know the drill. Foxtrot, Oscar, Tango, to Capitol Hill. The rest of us hold until we see what she does at the next stop."

Oliver starts the car, and I feel it pull away from the parking spot. I shiver, glad that the heat is on again.

After a few moments, Oliver says, "Did you ever get in touch with Emily? You know, to see what was up with her silent apology?"

"Uh, no? When was I supposed to fit that in? Before chem homework? Or after homework and before college app essays?"

"Yeah, sorry. Dumb question. But now might be a good time. You've been bored to tears just sitting here."

"Sure. Why not?" I get out my phone and push the button that pulls up the digital assistant. "Text Emily."

"What do you want to say to Emily?" my phone asks.

"Maybe we should talk."

"Your text to Emily says, 'Maybe we should talk.' Ready to send?"

"Yes."

"Sending text."

A whooshing sound indicates the text launching itself into the ether.

"Happy?" I say.

"You didn't have anything better to do," Oliver says.

My phone chimes, surprising me, and announces, "Text from Emily: 'Yeah, we should. Meet me. Midnight. Gymnastics room. Outside door will be open.'"

"Well, that's mysterious," I say. "I didn't expect to hear from her that fast."

Oliver groans. "Looks like it's going to be a long night."

I do my best to mimic his voice. "You didn't have anything better to do."

He laughs. "Hey, I need my beauty sleep."

"I'll bet. You'd probably do anything to look better."

This gets another laugh, and I smile, realizing I like the sound of it.

"Maybe we ought to get a jump on things," he says. "How about I quiz you on your chemistry homework."

I hesitate. I really don't want to do homework here, or at home, but he has a point. If I do some now, I'll have less to do when we get home. "Sure. Let's go."

For the next several minutes, he quizzes me. I feel the car come to a stop, but he keeps on shooting questions at me until I get one wrong. As he's about to explain the right answer, our phones chime at the same time again. Another group text from Luis. Robyn still has made no move to get off the train. Travis redirects everyone except us. We have to stay put until Luis lets us know what Robyn does at the station we're watching.

"Come on," Oliver says. "Let's walk a little. I need to stretch my legs."

"Okay."

He gets out, comes around, and opens my door. I swing my legs out, and he takes my elbow and steadies me as I stand.

"Curb," he murmurs.

I step up with a half-smile. The boy is learning. He closes the car door behind me, and locks it with a chirp. The air is damp and chilly, and I shiver. He throws an arm around my shoulders and pulls me close.

I tip my head up. "Excuse me?"

"We're spies, remember? I'm just trying to make us look natural. Like other couples. Why, there's one now."

"Yeah, well, don't get any ideas." I snake an arm around his waist, and let my head fall on his chest. My sigh doesn't require great acting skills.

"Hey, kids," a quiet voice says beside us.

I nearly jump with fright as Oliver brings us to a stop.

Unperturbed, Oliver says, "Oh, hey, Fred."

"Have you got a light?" Fred says.

Oliver takes his arm back from around my waist and pats his coat and pants. "No, we don't smoke."

"Oh, for fuck's sake, Oliver," I say. "Speak for yourself."

It's been a while, but Addie and I used to share a joint after school occasionally, and giggle all through cheer practice. I dig in my coat pocket, find a lighter and hold it out.

"Thanks," Fred says, taking it out of my hand. I hear the flick, and smell burning tobacco. He takes a drag, blows it out and keeps talking in a low voice. "If this is where Juliet gets off the train, I think the park here across the street is a good place for them to set up a meeting. Lots of ways in and out, and easy to disappear in the city. I think you should be somewhere near the middle, here on the west side of the park. But don't stray too far from your car until we know for sure this is the right stop. I'm going back to hang near the station entrance on Broadway just in case they send her a different direction."

"Okay," Oliver says. "Got it."

"Thanks for the light." Fred takes my hand and presses the lighter into my palm.

I hear him drop the cigarette on the sidewalk and grind it out with his shoe. Then his footsteps recede until I can't distinguish them from the sounds of traffic.

Oliver drapes his arm over my shoulder again, lightly this time, as if he's wary of me.

"What? You think I'm just a good girl who never does anything bad?"

"I... I guess I never thought about it. I mean I've never seen you smoke."

"Yeah, well, there are a lot of things you've never seen me do." I pause and let him chew on that for a moment. "So, where are we, anyway?"

"Cal Anderson Park."

"Where they had all those protests?" During the pandemic, people all over the country protested racially motivated killings. In Seattle, they took over the area around Cal Anderson Park for more than a month after the murder of George Floyd in Minneapolis, even forcing police to abandon a precinct headquarters building. When two kids a year or two younger than I got shot, killing one of them, the police finally moved back in and removed the protestors.

"You were part of that?"

"God, no. I mean not that I don't believe in social justice. It's just not my thing."

He's quiet for a moment, then, "So, a bad girl, huh?"

"Bad enough." I don't know what made me say that, and I backpedal. "But not so bad that I'd be caught *dead* doing a porno, so don't go getting the wrong idea."

"Noted."

I shiver again as fine mist dampens my face and hair. I move in a little closer under the shelter of his arm. The muffled chime of our phones sounds in unison.

"Got it," he says, reaching into his pocket with his free hand. "She's getting off the train. This is it. We should probably turn our phones to silent."

I nod and feel for the switch on my phone. My earpiece crackles to life.

"Bravo, Delta, Romeo, head to the meeting place, pronto," Travis says. "Oscar, Tango, Foxtrot, stay alert until we get there. No matter what, nobody move to intercept the hand-off. I repeat, stay clear. I don't want to compromise Juliet or put her in any danger. Do you copy? Lima, are you getting any of this?"

"Yeah, boss," Luis says, his voice so soft I can barely hear him. "We're above ground. Juliet is heading south on Broadway. I'm hanging back."

"Got you covered," Fred says. "I have our girl in sight."

I tip my head up. "What should we do?"

"Wait until they need us," Oliver says. "Come on."

"Where are we going?" I say as he leads me along.

"I think Fred was right, so we're going to find ourselves a good vantage point."

"In the park?"

"Yep. Eight steps coming up in three, two, one…"

"Tell me what you see," I say as he leads me up and onto a path that crunches under my shoes—gravel, or cinder, I guess.

"It's busy," he says. "Busier than I would expect in this weather. Singles…hmm, walking quickly, like they're going somewhere, couples moving more slowly like we are. The path is lit by old-time lamp posts topped with white glass globes. It's brighter farther down, though. I see people running on a soccer field, and I know there are basketball courts and a skate park that are probably busy. It's not that wet.

"There's a gray stone building angled off to our left—the Gate House, which was the pump house for the Lincoln Reservoir the city completed in 1901. The new pump house is smaller and fifty yards in front of us. The reservoir was covered in 2005, expanding the park by a few acres."

"How do you know all this stuff?"

"Read it. Can't forget it."

My earpiece comes alive again. "Juliet is ducking between a couple of buildings," Luis says. "Looks like she's headed down some stairs toward a park. Across the street from the entrance to the community college."

"That's practically right in front of us," Oliver says to me.

"I'm still five minutes out," Travis says.

"Bravo, here. Me, too."

"Count Romeo out," Red says. "I don't know about Delta."

"I'm working on it," Derek says, voice garbled by wind rush. A horn honks in the background. "Out of my way, asshole!"

"We're on it," Oliver says, his voice coming in stereo from beside me and in my earpiece.

"I'm at the top of the stairs," Luis says. "Juliet is in the park, passing a small building. Crap. She turned and I lost her."

"I see her," Oliver says. "She stopped next to the small pump house. Wait, a guy just got up off a bench next to the wading pool. He's walking toward her. Jeans, black hoodie. His back's to us. I can't see what he looks like."

Travis cuts in. "Do not engage, Oscar. Got it?"

"Got it," Oliver says. I can hear him rolling his eyes. "Okay, he's standing in front of her. Looks like this is it."

"Shit!" Luis says. "Oscar stay on him. I've got a homeless guy all up in my face and can't get around him."

"Foxtrot?" Travis says. "Where are you?"

"I've got the same problem," Fred says. "We've been made."

"Take them out," Travis growls. "Do whatever you have to."

"The guy's walking away," Oliver says. "He's got the bag Juliet was carrying. What do you want us to do?"

"Keep him in sight," Travis says, "until Lima and Foxtrot get free. But don't get too close!"

"Come on," Oliver murmurs.

He takes my hand, and I match his pace as he pulls me forward.

"We can't let this guy get away," I say, worried now. We apparently have no backup.

"I know," he says, picking up speed. "We won't."

I stumble and almost fall trying to keep up. His grip on my hand tightens.

"What the hell?" he says, coming to a sudden stop.

Shouting erupts from all around us.

"What is it?" I say. "What's happening?"

"The power's out. All the lights just went out. It's pitch black out here."

I tug at his hand. "No, it's not. Come on! We can't let that guy go. There's enough light. Your eyes will adjust."

"I'm telling you, Tess, it's totally dark."

Over the din of voices around the park, I hear cars honking, probably at intersections if the traffic lights are out. I think furiously, trying not to panic.

"There must be headlights from cars. I know you can see something."

"Cars over on Broadway, maybe," he mutters.

"Just follow me, then." I can barely keep the desperation out of my voice. I can feel our opportunity fading quickly. He reluctantly lets me pull him along.

"Yeah, okay, I can just make out the path. And a bunch of people have flashlights."

"Duh! Get your phone out and use the flashlight! Let's go!"

"I'm so stupid. All right, got it. I'm with you."

I feel him take the lead again, confident now that he can see. Maybe he finally knows how I feel. But we don't go more than five or six steps when someone snakes an arm around my waist, clamps a large hand over my mouth, and yanks me backward. My scar burns under the fingers covering my cheek, and I reach up and grab his forearm, looking for enough leverage to throw him over my shoulder or hip, anything.

I take a deep breath through my nose and smell coconut.

56

The power outage freaked me out a little—I'd never seen an entire city go dark. But as generators in the surrounding buildings kicked in and more people in the park got out phones or flashlights, I felt more secure about the almost-blind leading the blind. But we hadn't taken more than a few steps when Tess yanked her hand out of mine. I whirled around, and the flashlight's glare caught her in the grip of something black, darker than the night. It enveloped half her face. Eyes blinked in the negative space above her head, and I nearly jumped out of my skin.

Tess thrashed and wriggled in the thing's grip, but it was too strong. Frozen, I watched her position her hands and attempt one of her jiu-jitsu moves, but she suddenly levitated, feet kicking inches above the ground.

"Put that light out," a familiar voice snarled softly.

I shoved the phone in my pocket, recognition dawning.

"Don't scream, Miss Barrett," the voice said quietly. "I'm going to put you down and take my hand away."

"It's okay, Tess," I said, still amazed at the strength it must have taken to hold her off the ground with one hand as he set her down. "It's Marcus."

"I know who the fuck it is," she spat. "I want to know what the hell you're doing here. How did you find us?"

"Keep your voice down," Marcus said. "Don't look, kid, but there's a man with a gun just over your left shoulder, about forty yards away."

Suddenly, the power came back on, and the lighted globes dotting the park traced the network of paths. Out of the corner of my eye, I spotted a man in the unlit open area lifting a hand and tucking something into the waistband of his pants. I couldn't swear to it, but the object briefly silhouetted in the dim light looked an awful lot like a pistol.

"I told you not to look," Marcus growled.

I swallowed hard. "Who is he?"

"Hell if I know, but sure looks to me like he's guarding the rear flank of the guy you're after. If I hadn't stopped you, he would have killed you both."

"How do you know who we're after?" Tess demanded. "You still haven't told us what you're doing here."

"I'm doing my job," he said coolly.

"You're supposed to be at the high school taking care of some security issues." Her voice dripped with the sort of condescension that comes with being rich and entitled.

"I'm *supposed* to keep your pretty little keister from getting shot off."

Tess fumed. "Yeah, well, you managed to screw up our only chance of finding out who's so set on shooting it off."

"Don't be melodramatic."

Travis's voice crackled in my ear. "Somebody want to tell me what's going on? Report in!"

Marcus thrust his chin at me. "Travis?"

I nodded.

He took two steps toward me, pulled the earpiece from my ear, put it in his, and keyed my throat mic. Leaning in, he said, "Travis, it's Marcus. The kids are with me. Your operation's a bust. I'm sending them home. You can debrief me back at the house."

Marcus handed the earpiece back to me. "You two, go home." As he turned and strode up the grassy lawn toward the park's north entrance, I saw him reach over one shoulder and grab something dangling from his jacket collar. He brushed the side of his head before letting his arm swing down at his side. I couldn't swear to it, but it looked as if he had a comms set like the ones we used. So why had he used mine?

Luis jogged up to us. "Where did he come from?"

"Marcus?" Tess said. "That's what we want to know."

"What happened?"

I told him, leaving out the part where Tess had to remind me my phone had a flashlight.

"And you saw this guy?" Luis said when I finished.

"I saw *a* guy," I hedged. "And it looked like he had a gun. Hard to tell."

"Hey, is Robyn okay?" Tess said.

"She's fine," Luis said. "A little shook up by the whole thing. Fred's with her."

Care and concern for someone other than herself sounded foreign coming from Tess's mouth. "I thought you didn't like her."

"I've always liked Robyn," she protested. "I just didn't trust her. At least not until all this happened."

"Well, I should get back," Luis said. "Ms. Alia and I need to hitch a ride with Fred to pick up our cars. I'm glad you're okay, Miss Barrett. Sorry we weren't able to track these guys down."

"Thanks, Luis. I know you tried." Tess sounded depressed.

"Come on." I took her hand. "I'll drive you home."

57

I don't say anything on the way, either on the walk back to the car or the drive home. I'm glad Oliver keeps his mouth shut, rather than offer some lame consolation. Rain is coming down steadily by the time we get back. Oliver parks in the garage.

Inside, he pauses to lead me through the mud room into the hallway outside the kitchen, but I push past him. I know where I'm going. Loud voices float down the hall from the den that Travis took over as his office.

"You put a tracker on her car?" Travis almost yells it.

"Hell, yes. I put one the kid's bike, too," Marcus says.

"You can't do that!"

"Sure I can. You hired me to protect her. I can't do that if I don't know where she is. Your permission to tag the vehicles you own is implicit in my job description."

Oliver puts a hand firmly on my arm, and grabs my wrist when I veer toward the open door the voices come from. Reluctantly, I let him tug me away, and in several more steps we enter the hush of the library. Oliver quickly shuts the door, just in time.

"That asshole!" I fume. "Can you believe it?"

"I don't like it either," Oliver says, "but he's just doing his job."

"He doesn't have to spy on me. I wondered how he knew where we were. Now I *really* don't trust him."

"I wonder what he thought when he realized his security team was doing something he didn't know about," Oliver muses.

"Like I care."

"Maybe you should," he murmurs.

"You know what I mean," I snap. "Wait, why? Did you see something?"

He answers my question with a question. "He may have used the tracker to follow us, but how did he know what we were doing?"

The door opens and I whirl toward the sound, already aware of who it is. "Alice, how did Marcus find out about our plans?"

"The man's no fool," Alice replies, "though he may feel a little foolish after what happened. I didn't tell him, if that's what you're asking. When I said I didn't know where any of you were—which was the truth, mind you—he went to the guest house. I imagine he figured it out, because I saw him come out a few minutes later with a set of comms gear, get in his SUV and leave."

"He ruined everything," I moan.

"I heard he may have saved your life," she says primly.

"I highly doubt it. And by interfering, he let them get away. With Yoshi's drone."

"Don't you think Yoshi is too smart for that?" she says quietly.

"What?" I'm confused. "Yoshi wasn't there."

"Yoshi plans for contingencies." She said it as if she thought someone else hadn't. Like Travis, maybe.

"What plan? What contingencies?"

"Oh," Oliver says softly. "I get it. You can't fly the drone unless you can communicate with it, and you can't do that unless you know where it is. It has a geolocator, right?"

"Yes. Yoshi will track it to see where it goes," Alice says.

"Why can't Travis send people to stop those men?" I say. I sound like a princess—not the sort of royal I hope to be again, and I wish I could take it back.

"If he did, we might never find who's ultimately responsible. Better to wait and see where Yoshi's device ends up."

I think about it, and nod. I don't have much choice. Something else occurs to me. "Alice, did the power go out here? Oliver says the whole city appeared to have lost power."

"It did, but not for long."

"Do they know what caused it?"

"No, not yet. But there are rumors that it was a targeted attack on the grid. The news media are saying that the entire west coast was affected."

"Will we be okay?"

She hesitates. "I don't know. Of course we have generators, so we'll have power. But it depends on the nature of the outage, and how long it might last."

I have more immediate issues to focus on. This seems more important somehow, but no sense worrying about things I can't control. I sigh and nod.

"Anyway," Alice says, "the reason I came in here in the first place was to see if you two would like something to eat. You must be starved."

"Yes, please. Do we have any of that chopped salad left?"

"I'm sure we do. Oliver?"

"Can I help you in the kitchen?" Oliver says.

"No, I think Tess needs you here."

"Then whatever's easy is fine," he says. "Any leftovers will do."

"All right. I'll be back in a few minutes."

"Let's get started,"" I say when I hear the door shut. "We don't have a lot of time."

"Yeah, about that," he says. "Don't you think it's weird that Emily wants to meet that late?"

"Midnight? Most kids I know are still up at that hour. Why?"

"I don't know. Most parents don't want their kids out that late. Do Travis or Alice let you stay out until midnight?"

"Oh, hell no."

"Well, how do you plan to get out of here?"

I grin. "What they don't know won't hurt them."

58

The few hours we had flew by faster than I would have believed possible. Both of us were preoccupied, and several interruptions made study difficult. Alice checked on us one more time before turning in for the night, though I had a sneaking suspicion that Alice didn't sleep, or if she did, she slept upside down hanging from the rafters. Robyn stopped in to thank Tess for offering the beach house, and told her that Ben remembered it and absolutely loved being able to stay. And Travis came by to tell Tess that Yoshi did, indeed, have a way to track the drone, but it would only be activated if someone figured out how to power the drone up. He spoke quietly, and seemed chastened somehow. I'd always been uncomfortable around girls, but to see a buttoned-up military man like Travis confounded and laid low by the two women in his life whom he couldn't tell what to do was a shock.

I prepped Tess as well as I could for her AP Chem mid-term, and better for her AP English Lit/Comp block exam. But Jessup was being especially tough on Tess in an attempt to convince her that she wasn't cut out for STEM courses, at least not with her disability. And Prescott was a prick, plain and simple. So, I wasn't about to put odds on the outcome of either test.

At 11:30, Tess pushed back from the table and yawned fiercely, stretching her arms over her head. I fought off the urge to copy her, and then fought other urges at the sight of her taut midriff as her blouse rode up and her breasts straining the fabric.

"Are you sure you don't want to just crash for the night?" I said.

"I'm fine. But I think I need to change into something a little more comfy. And, no, I don't need your help getting upstairs, thank you. Should I meet you back here?"

"Uh, I think I want to check the car for that tracker. How about I meet you in the kitchen in ten?"

She nodded. "Okay."

We parted ways at the library door. As I headed down the hallway, motion detectors switched on soft cove up-lighting to guide the way, the effect both comforting and menacing at the same time. I felt as if someone watched me. A dim blue glow emanated from the LED control panels on all the equipment in the empty kitchen. The hallway darkened behind me as I entered the laundry and mud room, the way now lit by motion-activated nightlights on the electrical outlet plates that cast their glow downward on the floor. The house was eerily quiet, reminding me how late it was. I squelched a yawn and let myself into the garage.

The BMW was in the second of the six bays, where I'd parked earlier. Here, too, sensors alerted to my presence, turning on the lights on the garage door opener directly over the car. I started at the front on the driver's side, crouching next to the car and running my fingers along the inside of the fender over the wheel. They finally touched a protrusion in the third wheel well I tried, and I pried it loose. The small black plastic box was about the size of a matchbook. I stared at it. Anyone tracking it would know if it moved. A light bulb was on over my head, I realized. Reaching up, I put the tracker on top of the garage door opener. The magnet pulled it tight with a soft clunk.

Tess was feeling her way down the hall to the kitchen when I stepped back into the mud room. I hurried to meet her. She'd changed into faded jeans that hugged her hips, fleece-lined boots, and a gray hoodie. I'd heard her complain about her chunk on several occasions, but I didn't see an extra ounce on her.

"Are you positive you want to do this?"

Her short laugh was nervous. "You're the one who doesn't seem too keen on going."

"I'm not crazy about the idea. Especially the trouble we'll be in if Travis or Alice finds out."

"Chicken. You found the thing-y, right?"

"The tracker? Yeah, it'll say the car's in the garage. But it's not like someone won't see us leaving on the surveillance cameras."

"As long as they don't know where we're going. I'm so sick of everyone knowing exactly what I'm doing every minute." She paled. "Ohmigod, you don't think they put cameras in my room, do you? I'd die if I knew those pervs could see my muffin top."

"Uh, I don't think you have to worry about either one."

"That's sweet of you to say, but you're not the one who has to get into these jeans."

Just the one who wants to get you out of them. I slapped the notion out of my head.

"What was that?" she said.

"Um, just me trying to wake myself up."

"Well, let's go, then. You're not the only one who needs beauty sleep around here. I have mid-terms tomorrow, remember?"

We made it off the grounds without raising any alarms, and pulled up behind the high school less than ten minutes later. Tess got out and stood next to the door while I came around the car. The buildings were dark and shrouded in mist, the campus spookily quiet. I had to admit, it creeped me out a little. I shivered, found Tess's hand and put it on my shoulder. She fell into step behind me, then slid her hand down my arm until her fingers twined with mine. My heart skipped a beat or two, and I wondered again what was happening to me, why I even allowed a hormonal physical and emotional response to her touch to hold sway over my intellect.

We weren't the last two people on the planet. We didn't need to repopulate the human species. There was no reason for me to think about her as anything but an employer, a job, a responsibility. And there were too many reasons not to consider any other sort of relationship with her, not least of which was the fact that she wasn't interested in me, especially not romantically. But her hand in mine was sending a different message entirely, and made my head spin in circles, my heart pound, and my face, neck and more southerly body parts flush with heat.

"Do you know which door it is?" I whisper. "I don't even know if we're in the right place."

"Why are you whispering?"

"Because I don't want to get caught?"

"Why? Is somebody here?"

"I don't think so. Why would anyone be here at this time of night?"

"That's my point. F-F-S, Oliver. Grow a pair. And how am *I* supposed to know if we're in the right place. I can't *see*, remember? If we're behind the school, there should be double doors on the left that lead to the locker rooms, and a single door in the corner on the right. That's the door to the gymnastics room."

"Okay, okay. Don't get your undies in a bunch."

"Don't get my...? How quaint. That's so cute, Oliver."

"Ha, ha. Very funny."

Streetlights, and a floodlight over the double doors provided the only illumination, which wasn't enough to dispel the murk the weather had brought on. But the door was easy enough to find, and I pulled on the handle, expecting it to be locked. To my surprise, it opened easily, with a faint squeak of a hinge that needed oil.

"Here we go," I murmured. I stepped through the opening and held the door for Tess.

The door closed with the same creaking sound, leaving us in even dimmer light than outside. The cavernous space was as large as the gymnasium. Only a few of the dozens of pendant lights hanging from the ceiling glowed feebly, illuminating a huge cubist sculpture. Monolithic blocks of vinyl-covered foam hulked in the gloom, creating an obstacle course of varied levels and shapes, stretching twenty or thirty feet, rings dangling or high bars and uneven bars arching over them. To the right, four-foot-wide tracks ran nearly a hundred feet toward the far end of the facility, some ending in in a vault, others covered with a trampoline mat and ending in a pit of foam blocks. And deep pits of the foam blocks were scattered in other areas. Toward the far end stood rows of balance beams and pommel horses, most set up over crash mats, others surrounded by spotting blocks as big as king size mattresses standing four feet tall.

"Emily?" Tess called. We wandered farther inside when no one replied, and Tess tried again. "Emily? Are you in here?"

"She's not going to show," I said. "Let's go."

"Wait. Do you hear that?"

I strained, and picked up on what she heard—hushed weeping. Tess made her way forward without me, hands waving in front of her face. I caught up and took her arm. As we passed an eight-foot tower of spotting blocks, I spotted a figure slumped on a crash mat not far away, long dark hair hiding her face. She looked up as we approached, eyes darting in all directions like a frightened doe looking for avenues of escape. She swiped a sleeve across her face.

"Tess?" she said timidly. "I thought you'd be alone."

"Jeez, Emily. Yeah, sure, and I'd drive myself here, too."

The girl gave a nervous laugh. "Sorry. Shit, that's about all I can say these days."

"What's this about, Em? I've got mid-terms to study for."

Emily started rocking back and forth, keening coming from her throat, soft at first and building to an eerie wail.

"Oh god, oh god, oh god," she cried. "I never thought they'd do this to you, Tess. I swear it."

"What're you talking about? The video?" Tess *tsked*. "Welcome to high school. People don't have anything better to do than tear other people down."

"But it wasn't sup...supposed to be you!" Emily cried. "*I* was the one he wanted to humiliate."

"He, who? Wait..."

I stepped in front of Tess, put my hands on her shoulders, and walked her back two steps.

"What are you doing?" she said, putting her hands on my chest and pushing back.

"Sit. This could take a while."

She stopped resisting, reached behind her and found the crash mat, then lowered herself slowly. "What's going on, Em?"

Emily sobbed and hiccupped. "I didn't know," she groaned. "I really didn't."

"Didn't know what?" Tess said. "Emily! Get it together. Tell me what's going on."

"He... He caught me cheating," she sniffled. "On a test. He took pictures of the answer key in my desk. He said he'd turn me in if I didn't do what he wanted. My...my parents would kill me if they knew. I'd g...get suspended. And f...forget college. I *had* to, don't you see? You have—you *had* parents like mine."

"You had to what? Pretend to be me?" Tess said.

Emily swung her head up and stared at Tess. "No! That's the point. He said he'd forget about the answer key if I...if I...you know, gave him head. I didn't know he'd take a video! I swear!"

The video flashed through my mind.

"It makes sense," I murmured. "Emily looks enough like you that with some good editing, people thought it was you."

"And you didn't say anything?" Tess said, her ire mounting.

"I...I... It was just so humiliating that when everyone thought it was you in the video, I felt relieved. How could I admit to doing that? I know it was wrong. Why do you think I'm here? I...I just can't stand this. This mess is my fault. It stinks. I'm sorry, Tess. I'm so sorry."

Tess was silent for a moment. From somewhere in the yawning space I thought I heard the sound of a creaky hinge. But not from where we came in. My imagination playing tricks on me, maybe.

"Someone used you, Em," Tess said quietly. "Someone used you to get back at me. I want to know who and why. Who did this, Emily? Who put you up to this?"

"Nobody put me up to it." Emily's voice was shrill. "I'm telling you, I didn't have a choice!"

"Who was it?"

Motion in my peripheral vision dragged my attention to a figure stepping out from behind a tall stack of spotting blocks.

"Don't say another word, Chen!" a guy said. Adding to the menace in his voice, he raised an arm and pointed a pistol at Emily. It had an unusually long barrel that I realized had a silencer. The sight chilled me to the bone.

"Who's that?" Tess said, startled.

Emily let out a wail. "Oh god, oh god, oh god... Go away!"

"I'm warning you, Chen," the guy said. "One more word and you're dead!"

His face was shadowed, but the voice was familiar.

"Tad?" Tess said. "Is that you?"

"Shut up, Tess!" Tad said. I recognized the voice as belonging to the dickwad who'd attacked me in the commons a couple weeks earlier, the kids whose friend Carl had been shot driving Tess's car, which he basically carjacked from me.

"That's him!" Emily yelled. "That's him!"

Tad swung back to Emily. "I warned you, bitch."

The gun jerked in Tad's hand with a loud snap, like one of those Pop-Its fireworks we used to throw on the ground as kids, and Emily pitched over onto her side. With certain dread, I knew we were next, and as the long barrel of the gun swung toward us in slow motion, I wanted to piss my pants. Instead, I turned, shoveled my hands under Tess's pretty ass and shoved her as hard as I could, launching her off the crash mat into a pit of foam blocks. She disappeared with a shriek. And just as I scrabbled after her, everything went black. Pitch black.

The gun snapped again, once, twice, three times as I tried to tunnel down into the foam blocks. I bumped into something harder than foam, and came up beside Tess.

"What the hell?" she whispered. "What's going on?"

"He's shooting at us. He shot Emily! I think he killed her."

"With what? A cap gun?"

"He's got a sound suppressor on a very large pistol," I hissed.

"Can you see him?"

"The power went out. Another blackout. I can't see shit."

"Join the club," she muttered.

"Come out, come out, wherever you are," Tad said in a sing-song voice.

"If we keep talking, he'll know where we are," I whispered.

"I can't hear you," Tad sing-songed again.

"Fuck this shit," Tess said, and pawed through the blocks away from me.

"What are you doing?" I croaked.

"That's better," Tad called, squeezing off another shot.

A foam block in front of my face jumped with a soft *pffft*. I dove to the side and furiously tried to figure a way out of this. How were the two of us going to get away from a madman with a gun? Tess, it seemed, had decided that she could sneak away in the dark. Maybe I could do the same.

"You can't hide forever," Tad called. "I *will* find you. Tess, you first, since it was *your* car that Carl was driving when he got shot. I paid good money to see you put in an early grave. But no, I have to do everything myself. It's okay. It'll be more satisfying this way."

He paused, as if waiting for a response to his goading.

"And you're next, Ollie," he went on, his voice moving closer. "Good doggie, leading that bitch around by the nose. You just gave Carl the keys, like you *wanted* to see him get killed. Asshole! I think I'll save a couple of bullets for you, not just one. You know, make it hurt a little first before I put one in your brain."

As silently as I could, I pulled some blocks over me, trying to bury myself in the pit. Suddenly, a light popped on, like a flashlight or phone, the beam sweeping the big dark room, searching for Tess and me. I followed the beam, and for a brief moment, I saw Tess's silhouette heading behind the spotting block tower where Tad had first appeared. She wasn't trying to get away. She was trying to circle around him behind him in the dark! But she didn't know he had a flashlight now, and if I yelled to warn her, Tad would know right where to find me—and her.

I lay there, paralyzed with indecision, the beam of light slowly sweeping over me again. I had to find a way to distract him. I couldn't let him know what Tess was trying to do, couldn't let him find her. He'd kill her for sure. And no matter what might happen between Tess and me, or even if nothing ever happened, I realized that I couldn't live with myself if she got hurt, and I didn't want to live without her.

Light. That was it! I dug in my pocket for my phone and pressed my hands and face down under another layer of the foam blocks to prevent light from the screen leaking out. As quickly as I could, I activated the phone's camera, making sure it was set to manual flash. Then I felt for the edge of the pit and pulled myself out into a belly crawl away from it as silently as I could.

Tad turned slowly to his right, his phone's flashlight revealing Emily's crumpled body, then a panorama of gymnastics equipment until he'd turned far enough for the light to once again silhouette a figure almost directly behind him. I bit my lip to keep from gasping.

And just when I was sure he'd gone far enough to see the threat Tess posed, the cone of light stopped and panned back toward me.

I drew my knees up under me and crouched, watching the beam slowly come my way, focused now on its source. As the bright wedge came closer, his face turning toward me, I charged him with a roar, holding my phone out and pressing the camera button over and over, the flash popping off again and again...

59

Sleep eluded Travis as events of the day whirled in his head. He was disappointed but not surprised that Yoshi hadn't trusted him enough to tell him the drone had a tracker. Travis had suspected as much, but he'd put a lot of people in play—and in danger—to see who would show up to get the drone from Robyn, and where it would end up. He worried about Tess, of course. And now that Robyn had agreed to stay in the beach house, Travis worried that she'd think he'd suggested the idea to Tess. Which meant he'd have to watch himself around Robyn and be completely above board. Circumspect, even. If he had any chance at more than just a professional relationship with her, he didn't want to blow it.

After tossing and turning for hours, unable to turn off his brain, he got up, pulled on some jeans and a T-shirt, and padded down to the kitchen. Blue LED lights on the microwave and oven blared the time, close to midnight. The double doors of the fridge spilled light on the kitchen floor when he opened them. For a few moments, he stared blankly at the contents without seeing them, his thoughts still racing. With a shake of his head, he forced his eyes to focus and picked out ingredients for a sandwich—bread, cheese, sliced turkey breast, lettuce, mayo...

His thoughts strayed back to Robyn, He felt terrible that she'd thought she couldn't trust him. He wasn't sure what that said about him. He'd tried to be relaxed and open with her, to give her no reason *not* to trust him. Then again, he didn't know what he would have done in her situation. He didn't know what these people had threatened to do to Ben. After seeing their level of organization and planning to get their hands on the drone, he imagined it must have been pretty bad. And it hadn't even started with the drone. They'd blackmailed her into looking for the codicil to James's will, too.

That thought sent his mind down a whole new rabbit hole. No one seemed to know why James had written a codicil, or what was in it, but it had to be important if Robyn was pressured into stealing it. Either someone knew what was in it and wanted to use it somehow, or they simply wanted to keep it from finding the light of day. And why had Blair Wallace been so intent on finding it? Was it really the embarrassment of not having done his job properly, like he said, or was it something else? It would definitely help if Travis could get his hands on it. It would likely explain a lot.

Done assembling the sandwich, he wrapped up the fixings and put them back in the refrigerator. Setting his plate on the island, he sat on a stool and took a bite. He chewed contentedly, and was about to take a second bite when Yoshi shuffled in on old and well worn *uwabaki* slippers wearing a plain gray, cotton *yukata*, mouth yawning widely. He startled when he saw Travis. Quickly regaining his composure, he bowed.

"*Konbanwa*, Barrett-*san*."

Travis nodded. "Yoshi."

Yoshi grunted at the disrespect and turned to fill an electric kettle with water. While it was heating, he took a cast iron teapot from a cupboard and filled its infuser with loose tea from a sealed container. Then he took two earthenware mugs with no handles from another cupboard and set them next to the teapot.

Travis watched him curiously. "Couldn't sleep?"

Yoshi sighed. "Not even meditation will chase away worries."

The kettle boiled. Yoshi poured the hot water into the teapot, and carried it to the island. Then he retrieved the mugs and set one in front of Travis. Travis raised a hand to object, but Yoshi ignored him and filled Travis's mug and then his own with the steaming, pale green tea.

"You don't like me much, do you?" Travis said.

Yoshi shrugged and sat, cupping his mug in both hands. "Is not a matter of like or dislike. Like you fine. Is a matter of trust."

"Ah," Travis said, as if that explained it all.

"James trust you. And now he is gone. I not bound by blood. I can choose to trust or not."

"So, you don't trust me."

"I not *know* you. I have not made up my mind."

"That's why you haven't told me about your work on James's little toy."

Yoshi let one corner of his mouth rise. "Is just play, not work."

"The engineers at MondoHard have been trying to recreate that drone for more than a year, and you completely reinvented it."

"I am just one man. I cannot compete with James's company."

"Yet, you managed."

"I had good place to start."

Travis tipped his head, appraising Yoshi. "I'm beginning to think James wasn't as brilliant as we all gave him credit for. It looks like he had a lot of help."

Yoshi gazed into his mug before meeting Travis's eyes. "We help each other."

"You could have told me you put a tracker in the drone. I put a lot of people in danger tonight."

Yoshi blinked. "And what did you learn?"

"That maybe I shouldn't trust *you*."

"Perhaps more, *neh*? Women in your life not so helpless."

Travis felt his face flush and gave him a rueful smile. "That's an understatement."

"And Marcus?"

Travis stiffened. "Clever. Speaking of trust, I haven't made up my mind about him."

Yoshi nodded. "Besides, if you think, you already know drone has tracker built in. Is same as one you used in Afghanistan."

Travis knew he was right. He hadn't been thinking clearly lately, and if he didn't get it together, someone would get hurt. He had to do a better job of considering all the possibilities before organizing an operation like the one earlier in the evening.

"So," he said finally, "no signal yet from the drone?"

Yoshi gave his head a single shake. "Not yet."

Before Travis could ask anything else, Alice rushed into the kitchen.

60

I'm not sitting idly by and letting Thaddeus "The Tadpole" Cooper kill me, or ruin my life. And while my Seeing-Eye dog may not be able to see in the dark, I've had practice, and I put it to use. Oliver flipped me into a foam pit. I wasn't happy about it in the moment, but I am grateful, I suppose, for his quick thinking when I hear asshat Tad's gun go off again. From all those gymnastics and cheer squad practices I know how to get out of a foam pit quickly. I roll to an edge and pull myself out, then listen.

Fortunately for me, Tad's one of those villains who likes the sound of his own voice, droning on incessantly about his goals, motivations, and pretty soon, no doubt, the childhood insecurities resulting from screwed up relationships with his parents that had led him to a life of crime. I cut a wide circle around the voice, hands out and listening for changes in volume and pitch to find the cover of tall stacks of spotting blocks or crash mats. If I can come up behind him while keeping something between us as long as I can, I might get close enough to surprise him. And I'm pissed off enough to take him down and disarm him, maybe even shoot him with his own gun. Not kill him, of course. Just hurt him. Maybe shoot him in the ass.

So I listen, really listen, the way Yoshi is teaching me, to hear sound reflected off soft surfaces and hard, to hear it bend, echo and distort. And I know, when I come around the corner of some spotting blocks, that I'm behind him, only a few steps away, and Tad is still facing the crash pit where he thinks I am. I'm so scared, I'm sure Tad can hear my knees knocking, and if he doesn't shoot me I'll choke to death on the heart that's in my throat, the one that's thumping about a hundred miles an hour. Since I figure Oliver's pretty much useless in this fight, I suck it up and get ready to make my move.

Suddenly, Oliver yells like a banshee, and his timing couldn't be better. I move in quickly, getting close enough to Tad to sense him, to smell his sour, sweaty scent of fear and loathing, to feel his leather jacket under my fingers before I even touch him. It's almost too easy. He's tense, confused as Oliver approaches, and I don't understand why he doesn't just pull the trigger.

I use the opportunity to step in. I know from following Oliver that I have to reach up high with my right hand to find the right shoulder of his jacket. It's leather, smooth yet sticky at the same time, soft and supple. I grab it tight. Startled, he swings his right hand around. I thrust my left hand under his armpit as if I'm putting on a coat, and wrap it over his arm in a lock, holding on tight. I step across with my left foot, and turn so we're back to back. Hitching my hip, I use his momentum as his natural instinct makes him turn to look for what or who has him in his grasp, and flip him over my leg so he lands flat on his back at my feet.

It's like a dance I've practiced for so long that I can do it with my eyes closed. Or the flips I did in the air as a flyer on the cheer squad, the switch backside double cork 540 I could do on the slopes. I see it all in my head in slow motion, even though I know it happens in a blink, and for an instant I'm awestruck by what I've done. Tad's breath leaves him with an *oof!* that brings me back to my senses. I drop to one knee, landing on his arm, and pin it to the mat in case he hasn't yet let go of the gun. I think it's already gone flying, though.

"I got him!" I yell.

"Hang on," Oliver says. "I'm coming."

The thrill of excitement running through me is short-lived. Tad punches me in the head with his free hand. I yelp in pain as he squirms loose. He scrabbles away, and I hear a thud and another *oof* as he collides with Oliver. Then I hear running footsteps, and Tad screams in frustration, "Why can't you just die?" A door slams, and the only sounds left are those of heavy breathing, the beat of my heart in my chest, and blood singing in my ears.

"Are you okay?" Oliver asks.

It takes me a moment to find my voice. "Yeah, fine. You?"

"I'm okay."

I work it out in my head. "Tad hired Sam, didn't he?"

"It sure looks like it."

I feel a little deflated all of a sudden. I should have known better than to believe the grand conspiracy theories that Derek and Oliver espouse. Then again, I don't know anyone, royal or not, with a classmate who's pycho enough to try to kill her.

"Stay here," Oliver says. "I want to check on Emily."

I hear the squeak of his shoes on vinyl as he walks across the mats. I pat the floor around me, feeling for the gun.

After a moment, Oliver calls out, "She's still alive! But there's blood everywhere. I don't know if she's going to make it. What should I do?"

"Stop the bleeding, Oliver! Where is she hurt?"

"She's shot in the chest. Right side, up high."

"Put pressure on it."

"Right. I got it. What are you doing over there, anyway?"

"Looking for the gun," I say, just as my fingers brush cold metal. I latch onto it.

"Don't touch it!" he yells.

"Why not?"

"Fingerprints! Tad wore gloves. You're not. The cops will think you did it."

"Ri-ight. Blind girl shoots classmate dead."

"I'm just saying we're the only two people here. Your prints are the only ones on the gun. It might be tough convincing the cops that someone else did it."

I clutch the gun to my chest, panic setting in. "So we won't call the cops."

"We have to call 9-1-1. Emily needs help or she's not going to make it."

"Call Alice," I say quietly. "She'll know what to do. And she likes you." I sense his hesitation. "Please, Oliver, just do it. If she decides to call the cops or an ambulance, or whatever, I'll live with it. But we know now that bastard Tad is the one who paid Sam to try to kill me."

"And we'll figure out a way to get him. But we have to get help. So, Alice it is."

A moment later, he murmurs into his phone.

And then, we wait.

61

"Ah, there you are," Alice said.

Travis gawked at her. She'd plaited her graying hair in a single braid that fell down her back instead of pinning it up. Instead of her usual conservative skirt and blouse, like him, she had dressed in jeans and a sweater, clothes he'd never seen her wear. They made her look younger.

"Couldn't sleep either?" he said when he found his tongue.

"I need your help," she said. "Come with me."

From her serious expression, Travis knew better than to even ask. He followed her out to the garage, stepping into some boots and grabbing a jacket from a locker in the mudroom on his way. Alice quickly strode to her car, an electric crossover that Fred had thoughtfully plugged into its charger when he'd returned it earlier. Travis climbed in the passenger door and buckled up.

"I got a call from Oliver," she said as she backed out. "He and Tess are in a bit of trouble."

"Wait," Travis said, anger starting to bubble up inside. "They're not home?"

She shook her head and accelerated up the driveway. "It seems they had to meet someone tonight, someone who had important information to give them."

"Does this have to do with Tess's theory about who's been trying to kill her?" Travis couldn't keep irritation out of his voice.

"Don't dismiss her, Travis," Alice said sharply. "She's a smart girl, and you'd do well to give her credit now and then. She and Oliver met a young woman regarding a problem Tess has been having, heard her out, and just when she was about to reveal a name, she was shot."

"Shot?" Travis blinked. "Tess was shot? Is she alive?"

"Tess is fine, Travis. The other girl was shot, not Tess."

"Oh. Is she okay?"

Alice shrugged, keeping her eyes on the road. "Apparently the girl is in rough shape. Tess and Oliver weren't sure what to do. Tess forced the assailant to drop his gun."

"Tess...? Wait, where was Oliver?"

"Charging the shooter, apparently. And yelling loudly enough to distract him. I don't know all the details yet, Travis. But Tess made the mistake of picking up the gun—"

"And now her prints are on it," Travis said grimly. "Did they at least get a good look at the shooter?"

Alice nodded. "You're not going to like this. It's Cyrus Cooper's son, Tad."

"What the hell...? What is going on?"

"That's what we need to find out. I told Oliver to call 9-1-1 immediately—the girl could bleed out—but only to ask for medical assistance. I felt we ought to assess the situation before involving law enforcement, but we have to get there before the EMTs see that the girl was shot and call the police."

"God, yes. Thank you, Alice."

Travis suddenly took notice of his surroundings as they drove. The road was pitch black, with no street lights or house lights evident anywhere. He frowned.

"Power's out again?"

"Yes, and it's not just local," Alice said quietly. "This outage is very widespread. From what I've been able to glean from news reports, this has affected the entire west coast."

"Good lord! When did it happen?"

"Shortly after midnight, apparently."

"Somebody shoot up a substation again?"

"No. Authorities are afraid it's a cyber attack on the grid."

"That's not good. I didn't even notice back at the house."

"Our generators kicked in automatically, and they're so well insulated, they're practically silent."

"Wow, what a mess this night has been."

"It's not over yet," Alice said.

62

For once, I'm glad to see Alice. Well, not *see* her, but grateful she's here. And even stranger, I'm comforted by Travis's presence. It's not that I need a parent—Oliver smothers me enough as it is—but it's nice to have an *adult* in the room. Someone who knows what to do here. Though I'm proud of myself for getting through this without freaking out so far. And, yeah, part of me is proud of Oliver for distracting Tad long enough for me to take him down.

The EMTs stabilized Emily and rushed her to the big trauma hospital downtown where they take most gunshot victims. After we told Travis and Alice what happened, Travis let me know that while he couldn't make this go away, he would do everything possible to help me. He started by calling Dan Steingart, our family attorney, waking him up.

Dan showed up less than ten minutes after the call, and had Oliver and me quickly recap the situation one more time. When he was satisfied he understood what had happened, he called the police and asked the duty sergeant to send Pete Erickson up to the high school. Detective Erickson's been here for twenty minutes so far, and he asks us to walk him through the sequence of events for the second time. Oliver does the walking, and I do the talking. When I finish, the detective is silent for a moment.

"Tell me again," he says, "why your friend Tad was so upset."

"He's not *my* friend," I say.

"Mine, either," Oliver interjects.

"Oh, right, right," Erickson says. "Oliver, you and Cooper got into a fight when Cooper accused you of getting Carl Gant killed. In your car, as I recall, Miss Barrett."

"What's your point, Pete?" Dan says.

"No point," Erickson says. "Just sorting through the facts. I'll talk to the Cooper kid and get his side of this. But I don't hold out much hope. If he's involved, you can bet he's lawyered up, too, by now. No offense."

"Tess and Oliver have cooperated fully, Pete," Dan says. "I'm here for the same reason you are—just getting the facts."

"You don't believe us," I say, not disguising the anger I feel.

"I'm keeping an open mind, but you say your fingerprints are on the gun, and you were angry with Emily for letting people think she was you in this video that's going around school."

"Newsflash, Detective," I snark, "I'm blind."

"We counted five shell casings. One out of five, maybe you hit your target. I'm still trying to figure out what the Cooper kid has to do with this."

"We already told you; he blames us for Carl's death. But we didn't have anything to do with it." My voice is shrill in my ears.

Alice pats my arm and murmurs, "Calm down, Tess."

My stomach is churning, and I'm about to flip her off when a sudden thought makes me wonder how I could be so daft. I frantically pat my pockets.

"Wait! Oliver, where's my phone? Does anyone see my phone? It has to be here somewhere."

I hear scuffling everywhere as those around me, search.

"The foam pit," Oliver says, and his footsteps race away. "Can someone get some light over here?"

More footsteps head toward his voice. The wait is excruciating.

"Got it!" he yells. He runs up and breathlessly hands me the phone. "What's the deal?"

I fiddle with the phone, my fingers now all thumbs. "I couldn't figure out what Emily could possibly want to talk to me about, so I recorded her. I didn't turn it off. Maybe I recorded Tad, too."

"Here, let me help," Oliver says, gently pulling the phone from my grasp.

Feet shuffle closer as Oliver presses "play" and Emily's voice comes through the speaker, sounding small and far away—*Tess? I thought you'd be alone...*

Tad's voice is muffled even before the phone falls into the crash pit. His words are barely intelligible. But at least it indicates that someone else was here, and my voice asking "Tad, is that you?" is clear as a bell. The training room falls silent for a long time when Oliver stops the recording.

"Dan...?" says Uncle Travis.

"Well, Pete?" Dan says.

"I don't know," Erickson says. "Voices are pretty garbled, but I'd say this is probable cause. Enough for me to bring the Cooper boy in for questioning, and maybe arrest him. But you know that he'll be out in less than twelve hours."

"I know Cyrus Cooper well enough to agree with you," Travis says. "He won't let Tad go to jail without a fight. At least now you know that Tess was telling the truth."

"I do. I apologize, young lady, if it seemed otherwise. And if it's not too much trouble, I'd like you to come down to the station tomorrow and make a formal statement. It would really help the investigation."

I shrug. "I have mid-terms this week. I won't be there first thing, if that's okay."

"No problem. Come at your convenience."

I'm sure he's being nice now because he knows we have money. I could tell he wasn't happy that our attorney called him to the scene, not me or Oliver. I barely hear him leave, or hear Dan excuse himself, too. I just nod and smile politely, my thoughts roiling.

Finally, Travis steps up and says, "I'm not thrilled you snuck out tonight, Tess. You could've gotten yourself killed. But I'm incredibly proud of how you handled the situation."

"So, maybe you trust me a little more that I can take care of myself?"

"I realize I don't have much choice," he says. "That doesn't mean I'm going to stop worrying about you."

"It means," Alice interrupts, "that mutual respect and a little common courtesy can go a long way, you two. Come on, Travis. Oliver can bring Tess home when she's ready."

"I can take a hint," Travis says.

Their footsteps recede, and then it's just Oliver and me.

"You were amazing," he says.

"You weren't bad yourself," I admit. "That, or you're just plain crazy. What were you thinking, charging at a guy with a gun?"

"Me? What about you?"

I laugh, and with the release of all the tension and adrenaline, it's all I can do to keep the maniacal laugh from sounding like that of a movie villain, or from bursting into tears. Oliver laughs with me, making me feel less self-conscious.

"I've been wondering," he says when we calm down. "Do you think Tad came up with this on his own? He doesn't strike me as being that smart."

Tad isn't that smart, but the thought that he might have had help suddenly makes me want to hurl. I don't care that some people don't like me, but to hate me that much definitely stings.

"Why?" I say hesitantly. I'm not sure I want to know.

"I noticed Emily has the same tattoos as the girl in the video."

"Because she *is* the girl in the video," I say impatiently.

"Well, yeah, sure, but it reminded me of why it seemed familiar. I remembered where I'd seen them before." He pauses. "Adrienne has those tattoos."

My head spins, and the blood drains from my face. I sit down hard before I fall over, and clutch my stomach, trying to hold down the contents. Addie, my BFF and confidant, the girl I could tell all my secrets to, the yin to my yang all those years before the accident... Is it possible? Does she really hate me that much? What did I ever do to her?

Oliver's at my side in a flash, his arm around my shoulder. "Are you okay?"

My lower lip trembles, and my eyes fill with tears. Oliver pulls me close, and I press my cheek to his chest. Despite all the extra security Travis has arranged due to everything we've been through in the past few weeks, I feel safest with Oliver, I realize.

I heave a shuddery sigh. I will not cry. Certainly not over the loss of my friendship to that bitch. That obviously ended when my parents' car rolled down a mountainside in an avalanche. And I stopped mourning a long time ago. I think of revenge, and the craving vanishes almost as quickly as the thought arises. I still don't think of her as what she's become. Something has turned her into a mean girl, and while she might think it was something *I* did, I won't take credit for her problems. The best revenge, I decide, will be taking the high road.

I thumb my phone on. "Text Addie," I say.

"What do you want to say to Addie?" the phone replies.

"RUT?"

"Your text says, 'RUT?' Ready to send?"

"Yes."

"Okay. Sending text."

A few moments later, my phone pings and says, "Yeah, still studying. WUW?"

I tell the phone to text, "IKWYD. You might want to get out in front of this."

She texts back, "In front of what?"

I tell her, "Tad shot Emily. Tried to kill me 2. Do you hate me that much?"

Her text back says, "What? AYS? No! Ruin your life, yes. Kill U? No way."

"Thanks," I tell her. "That's what I thought. Whatever our differences, I don't think you should go to prison for attempted murder. Tell the cops what happened before Tad throws you under a bus. I'll vouch for you."

My phone doesn't ping, and I think I've lost her—she doesn't believe me.

"Come on, Oliver," I say. "Help me up. Let's go home."

He stands and takes my hand. Pulling me to my feet, he says, "That was brave. Probably braver than kicking Tad's ass."

I laugh. He's right. He hangs onto my hand, and it feels good.

On the way out, my phone pings again. Addie's text says, "You'd do that for me?"

I smile, and text back.

"OFC."

63

"I'll make a pot of coffee," Alice shrugged off her light jacket and draped it on the back of a chair.

Travis felt his brow crease. "It's pretty late."

"I have a feeling we're going to need it," she said as she busied herself at the counter.

He looked at his watch, and immediately wished he hadn't. "Late" was an understatement. Early was more like it. Too early. Maybe coffee wasn't such a bad idea, though the house was quiet. Yoshi had apparently gone back to bed. Tess and Oliver weren't home yet, but he didn't think they'd stay up much later. Then again, that depended on whether Tess still had homework or studying to do, he guessed.

"I'm worried," Alice said. "There's no news on the cause of this blackout."

"I'm just glad James had the foresight to install back-up generators when he built this place."

"That's part of what has me worried. If this goes on too long, we'll quickly be divided into the haves and have-nots."

Voices drifting in from the garage kept him from replying. Tess and Oliver walked in through the mudroom, Tess smiling at something Oliver said. For the first time he could remember, she looked happy. Travis's mouth opened, but nothing came out. Despite what she'd been through, especially in the past few days, she appeared unfazed, stronger.

"Is that coffee I smell?" Tess said.

"It will be ready in a moment," Alice said.

"Alice, you're still up?" Tess said.

"Travis, too," Alice said. "Are you sure you want coffee?"

"I still have studying to do," Tess said. "It could be an all-nighter. Well, I guess it already is."

"Would you like your coffee in the library?"

"Here is fine," Tess said. "I need to chill for a bit before I hit the books again."

More voices drifted in from down the hallway, sounding like the whispers of conspirators planning something nefarious.

"Who the hell is that this early?" Travis muttered.

"S...See, I told you!" Ben said as he bounded into the kitchen. "They're awake!"

Robyn shuffled in behind him in yoga pants and a hoodie—a far cry from her usual business attire—looking disheveled and half-asleep. She stopped and ran fingers through her hair. "Oh, my, I wasn't expecting anyone to be up. I'm sorry to intrude, but Ben couldn't sleep after the power went out. You know, sleeping in a strange bed, all the excitement..."

A flush crept up her neck. Travis almost pinched himself to keep from staring, marveling at how amazing she looked in casual clothes and no makeup.

"You're not intruding. And we do have power."

"I know, but Ben sensed it, and then he heard the generator," Robyn said. "I guess he read for a while, but he couldn't get back to sleep, and, well, here we are." She plunked down on a stool and sighed. "Mmm, that coffee smells good."

"It's a p...party!" Ben said. "Super T, you're all ch...charged up! You got the bad guy!"

"How did he...?" Tess said, looking suddenly pale.

Travis threw a sharp glance at Alice, but she offered the merest shrug.

"How did he do what?" Robyn said, her dark eyebrows knitting together. "What did I miss?"

"Someone tried to kill Tess again," Travis said, his face grim.

"Oh, my god! Tess, what happened? Are you all right?"

Tess sighed. "I'm fine. No biggie."

"No biggie?" Oliver snorted. "She took down a guy with a gun. Crazy, but amazing."

"I had help," Tess said, her face flushing.

"Who was he?" Robyn said, the words rushing from her mouth. "Why did he try to kill you?"

Tess related what happened as briefly as she could, making the incident sound like the most normal thing in the world. Travis silently applauded her composure. He'd faced a lot of firepower in his assignments overseas, and had to admit, though he'd never say it out loud, that on most of those occasions he'd been almost scared enough to piss his pants.

"I told you she's all ch...charged up," Ben said, waving the book James had given him. "She's S...Super T! Here, I'll show you."

Travis let the tension ease from his shoulders. Ben set the book on the counter, and Oliver moved to stand next to him, expressing interest. Travis gave him a mental nod. He liked Ben, but wondered where Robyn found the patience to deal with him every day.

"Uh, Travis," Oliver said quietly. "I think you should see this."

Travis stood and walked around the island. Ben had connected a cable to the book and had plugged it into an outlet.

"When he first showed me the book," Oliver explained, "I didn't see any way to plug it in, but figured it doesn't need to be charged anyway. The electronic ink doesn't need power. But when Ben plugged it in just now, the pages changed completely. I guess the electric charge stimulated a hidden layer of e-ink."

"Well, that's pretty cool, Ben," Travis said, trying to be nice.

"You might want to take a closer look," Oliver said.

Travis frowned, but humored him by leaning in over Ben's shoulder. "What the hell is this?"

"H-E-double-hockey-sticks," Ben said with a huge smile as he pointed a finger at Travis.

Travis couldn't believe his eyes. "Uh, Robyn? I think I found the document we've been looking for."

Robyn jerked upright and blinked. "The codicil?"

"Well?" Alice said, "Enough suspense. What does it say?"

"'I, James Finlay Barrett, being of sound mind,' *yada, yada, yada...* More legalese... Okay, here it is...'do hereby assign all...'" Travis fell silent for a moment while he read, trying to wrap his head around what James was trying to do. "He put all the corporate assets into a blind trust, and names Tess as trustee."

"I thought everything already was in a trust," Tess said.

"It is," Travis said. "Or it was."

"What's the difference?"

Alice answered this time. "Your parents' estate—this house, their investments, your father's shares in MondoHard—are held in trust until you turn eighteen, and a trustee makes decisions on how the estate is handled for you until then. Even after that—until you're twenty-one, I believe—you'll have to ask the trustee for permission to do certain things.

"This blind trust, if I understand Travis correctly, affects the company's assets only. Essentially, as trustee, you've been given complete control of the company. Well, the forty-seven percent your parents' estate owns."

"Wait. I thought my father owned the company," Tess said.

"Most of it," Alice agreed.

"But that's not even half," Tess said. "Who owns the rest?"

"Institutional stockholders, mostly," Alice replied. "Large investment banks and a number of individual shareholders. Your godfather, Jack Turnbull, owns about one percent, as does Travis. Yoshi and I also each own the same percentage. And Robyn, though she might not be aware of it, owns about half a percent, with half in her name and half in Ben's."

Robyn sat up straight again, eyes wide and mouth open. The silence was deafening. Travis hadn't realized he owned that much stock in the company James founded. He'd never cared all that much, and had left the investing to James. The company paid him a generous salary for what he did, but he would have done the job for nothing. He felt he owed it to James. Apparently, James had gifted him with a lot of shares.

"Just so you know," Alice went on, "Yoshi and I have already stipulated that our shares will always be voted the same way as the family's shares."

"So, that makes forty-nine percent," Tess said slowly.

"I'm sure Travis and Jack will side with you on most issues," Alice said. 'But it wouldn't make any difference. A lot of that stock is in the form of preferred shares, which gives each share more voting power than a share of common stock."

"I still can't believe James did this," Robyn said, shaking her head, "but you can count on our vote, Tess."

"Thanks," she murmured. "But I don't know anything about running a company."

"This ought to be fun," Oliver said under his breath.

Tess laughed. Travis joined in.

Even Alice cracked a smile. "Yes, actually, I think it will."

Suddenly, Travis heard a sound from the front of the house as if someone had just come through the front door.

"Alice," he said, "remind me to talk with you about security around here. It sucks."

64

I hear Travis get up and walk past me out of the kitchen, his footsteps quickly fading, muffled by the runner in the hallway. Then voices, Travis's loud and accusatory, the other low and indistinct, growing louder as they approach, falling silent before I can make out more than a word or two. A scent tickles my nose though, even before they're close, and it occurs to me that I've become like a dog, honing in on smell and sound before sight, since I don't have that, of course.

I catch hints of leather, cedar and citrus, overtones of sweat—produced in this case by a couple of acids and a couple of hexanols, I learned from Yoshi—and, I swear to god, notes of pizza, yeasty, cheesy and meaty. In the space of a few seconds, thoughts and emotions are spinning and tumbling through me so fast they register as streaks of light or feeling barely formed. The chemical bases for the scents reminds me of my AP Chem mid-term and the influence Yoshi had on why I chose the course in the first place. The scent markers—unmistakably Derek's—sow confusion, both in my head and heart.

I don't know what I want. For most of the night I've felt a connection to Oliver that wasn't there before, and yet the smells I detect make my pulse pound and my stomach flutter. Do I feel something for Oliver because of the way he's protected me, because he's willing to die for me? Do I want Derek because I think we'd be good together? Because I think he's probably smoking hot and the perfect kind of guy for my first time? Or because he's *not* Toby—or Oliver? Why do I even think about this shit when my life is a disaster? I have more important things to focus on.

"Derek," I say when footsteps reach the kitchen. "What are you doing here?"

"Sorry to barge in like this," he says, sounding at least a little apologetic. "Like I said, I know the guest security code here, so I let myself in figuring if everyone was asleep I'd just go work in the library. Because it's a zoo out there with the power outage and all, though it's calmed down a little. But it's made it too tough to work at the office because the generator power there is all routed to the servers to keep them online, so there's no bandwidth for anything else, and you all have a T1 line that's faster than anything we have at work. Sorry, Travis, but it's true. And, yeah, I've consumed way too many energy drinks. I should probably shut up now, but I came, you know, because of that project you wanted me to work on? I mean I know who sent you those IMs. And who posted the video. It was—"

"Adrienne Moss," I say, nodding. "We know."

"Wh...? How?"

"Oliver did a little sleuthing of his own. We'll tell you later. But thanks for confirming it."

"Tess?" Travis says. "Something you want to tell *us* about?"

"No, that's okay," I say sweetly. "It's all good. We've got it under control."

Someone takes my hand and puts a steaming mug of coffee in it. The aroma alone gives me a jolt of energy and wakefulness.

"One drop of sweetener," Oliver says, "the way you like it."

"Thanks."

I hear more soft footsteps quickly approach, and catch hints of fresh, grassy matcha and woody, herbaceous tea tree oil carried in, too, and know that Yoshi has joined us.

"Good morning, Yoshi," Alice says.

"Yoshi!" Ben says brightly.

Grunts and a murmured "Morning" emanate from the guys.

"Ah, so," he says, "*Kon'nichwa.* Barrett-san, I thought this cannot wait for you to get up, but I see you are all awake. I have waited all night for this; the drone was powered on. Transmitted location."

"Where is it?" Travis says.

"Russia."

"Russia? There must be some mistake."

A shiver runs up my spine, and Oliver squeezes my hand.

"No mistake," Yoshi says. "Is on coast of Black Sea near Sochi."

"Impossible," I say. "How could it get from here to Russia that quickly?"

Derek jumps in. "A fast private jet, on a polar route with a good tail wind could get there in nine or ten hours."

I do the math in my head and groan. "Is it really five in the morning? I still have to study."

"Good work, Yoshi," Travis says. "If you can zero in on the location, we might learn who wanted it so badly."

"*Hai.* I know *where.* Do not know *who* yet."

Someone's phone rings, and after the second ring, Travis says, "Hello," pauses, then says, "Good morning, Jack. Let me put you on speaker."

"Sorry to bother you this early," the general's voice booms, filling the kitchen.

"Good morning, Jack," Alice says.

"Alice, is that you?" General Turnbull says.

Travis interjects before she can reply. "You just happened to catch the entire contingent, sir." He rattles off our names.

"Well," Jack says, "good morning, everyone. Travis, I, uh...could I have a word?"

"What's this about, sir?"

"The blackout there."

"After the week we've had, I think I'd rather have the whole team here listen in."

The general hesitates, but only briefly. "Very well. Any word on what may have caused it?"

"Not that I know of. Just rumors."

"Well, we think we *do* know. Some IT systems people at a power generating station—in your neck of the woods, in fact—found some code in their control software that didn't belong. One of them thought it looked familiar to a virus developed by a Russian hacker group that we believe is sponsored by Russia's military intelligence ministry. That's not what's important here, though. What we need is your best minds on the problem. If these people take down the rest of the grid... well, you know how disastrous that would be."

"Everything grinds to a halt."

"Without power, it all falls into chaos," Jack says.

"The Russia connection might be more important than you think, sir," Travis says. "As for bright minds, I think I can come up with a few, but they're not mine to give you anymore. It seems that James put Tess in charge."

"What? How...?" General Turnbull seems to be experiencing an uncharacteristic loss of words, but he doesn't wait for an answer. "Never mind. You can tell me later. Tess, any problems with my request?"

"No, sir," I say. "In fact, I already know someone who might be able to help. He seems to think he's hot shit, anyway." I can't resist a dig at Derek, since he was a little late figuring out Addie was the one who instigated the porno.

"Good. Thank you, young lady. If your performance at the board meeting a few weeks ago is any indication, the company is in good hands. Now, Travis, why is Russia important?"

"Yoshi?" Travis says. "You want to explain it to him?"

"*Hai*, Barrett-*san*." Yoshi briefly tells the general about sacrificing the prototype of the drone he's been working on, and how he's tracked it to some location in Russia.

"Which version did you give them?" Jack says.

"Is like one Travis test in Afghanistan. But not even have artificial nose."

Jack chuckles. "I should have known. Send me the coordinates on that location, Yoshi. I know some folks at NSA who can find out who the property owner is. Travis, I'll send you the infected software program. Call me back when you get free and bring me up to speed. Sounds like it's been busy there."

"Will do, sir." The connection is broken, and Travis says, ""Everyone know what you're supposed to do?"

I moan. "Homework."

Suddenly I smell coconut, and footsteps approach the kitchen. I didn't hear the door from the garage open or close, though. My nose wrinkles.

"Everything okay here?" Marcus says. "Oh, wow, a party. I saw the lights on and thought it was early for people to be up. Especially with the power out. Guess I was wrong."

"I just made fresh coffee, Marcus," Alice says. "Help yourself."

"We're all good," Travis says, "but I'm glad you stopped by. I want to chat with you about staffing, and beefing up patrols now that Robyn and Ben are staying in the beach house. Grab your coffee, and we can talk in my office."

"Uh, Travis?" Derek says. "Can you get me a copy of the power company's software?"

"I'll send it to you as soon as I get it," Travis says.

"Great. I'll be in the library with Tess and Oliver, if that's okay."

"Gee," I grumble, "they'll let me run a multi-billion-dollar tech company, but won't let me decide if I want a guest or not."

I don't hear anyone laughing.

65

Another week or so and the colors of the foliage outside the window would be at their peak. Fall was Senator Latham's favorite time of year. The sauna that was summertime in Washington had dissipated, the temperature dialed back to a far more tolerable 69 or 70 degrees, the evenings cool enough for sleeping but not so chill that a walk in his neighborhood was uncomfortable. He'd been at his desk since 5:30, the result of an ingrained habit of getting to work early and the sleeplessness he'd heard comes with aging, something he'd not considered until recently.

He smiled ruefully. The notion that one will never age, or at least never grow old, was the folly of youth. With age comes wisdom, but unfortunately the most important lesson he'd learned from having lived so long is that time is fleeting, and virtually everyone wastes it until it's too late. So he felt entitled to stand behind his desk and take in the view of the Capitol through the autumnal ochre and crimson, gold and umber. The street was full of morning traffic, the sidewalks bustling with pedestrians on their way to work, girded for battle in the armor of designer power suits and armed with attaché cases and *venti* cups of coffee.

The noises from the outer office increased in variety and volume, and he knew he could not hold off the business of the advancing day much longer. He'd already had an early breakfast meeting with the House Speaker to press for support on a bill, after which he'd put in an hour of work at his desk. He knew that Karen had been in for close to an hour, too, getting a jump on the day, like him. And from the sounds, he could tell that most, if not all, of his staff had arrived. But Latham planned to fiercely guard his private time for as long as he could. It lasted another ten seconds, as it turned out, when the burner phone in his desk drawer buzzed insistently. He sighed and turned away from the scene outside.

He retrieved the phone and said, "Speak."

"You're aware of the attack on the grid?" said the voice on the other end.

"Who isn't?" Latham replied. He glanced up at the television monitors on the wall, all tuned to different news broadcasts. It worried him, of course. Something that massive shouldn't have occurred on his watch. He'd already conferred with colleagues on the Senate Committee on Energy and Natural Resources, as well as Sheldon Meyers, the chair of the Select Committee on Intelligence.

"There's been a development that may or may not be related."

Latham's mind kicked into overdrive, contemplating what it might be. "Go on."

"A prototype of the hardware you've been after seems to have found its way to the Caucasus."

Latham blinked. "Are you sure?" His heart rate was jolted into dangerous territory.

"A data burst from the transceiver sent its GPS coordinates— it's about ten kilometers southeast of Sochi."

His panic subsided. Latham even managed to let a small smile cross his lips. He was disappointed, of course. Not in the turn of events so much as the person, or persons, behind it. But he could use this to his advantage.

"Anything else?" Latham said.

"The girl is now in charge."

"What?" Latham's eyebrows rose. "What do you mean?"

"Barrett found a way to transfer the company assets to a blind trust and named her trustee."

"Travis...?" Latham was incredulous. The man was a soldier, an order-taker, not nearly smart enough to devise such a strategy.

"No, James. A codicil to the will surfaced."

"Jesus, Mary, mother of God," Latham muttered. He thought for a moment. He'd have to come up with a new strategy of his own. "All right. Keep me posted."

"One other thing," the voice said. "Cooper's kid tried to kill the girl last night."

"His son? What on earth for?"

"Personal bone to pick, apparently. There's more."

Latham braced himself.

"The kid might have ordered the contract hit a couple of days ago. The money came from one of the corporate accounts Cooper has access to."

"Find out," Latham said. "I want to know for certain who the shooter was, how much he was paid, and who was behind it. The girl's about to become too public and too valuable to let anything happen to her. I'm counting on you to make sure no one can get to her."

"I understand."

Latham disconnected and put the phone back in the drawer, running the details of the call over in his mind. He went to the safe he'd had installed behind a cupboard door under the wet bar when he first moved into the office years before. Quickly spinning the dial, he unlocked the safe and took out a satellite phone. Only eight numbers were programmed into the phone. He chose the second one on the list and dialed.

"Yuri, my friend," he murmured as he heard it ring, "what have you done?"

66

I'm exhausted, drained of all emotion, my mind numbed by the procession of letters and numbers running through it as Oliver quizzes me over and over on chemical reactions.

"The name of a chemical compound ends in 'ide,'" he says. "The compound is A) acidic; B) basic; C) binary; D) an oxide; or E) a solid."

I try to hide a yawn, but my arm feels so heavy I barely cover my mouth with my hand before I'm halfway done. My eyes feel scratchy, though I can't blame it on overuse or staring at small print for a long time. I slump in the chair, my queasy stomach and heartburn letting me know I should have added creamer to the coffee. I feel irritable and impatient, and my hair feels greasy. I must look like a hag.

Two people have tried to kill me in the past three days. My former BFF tried to ruin my life by making it look like I was the star in a porno film. And I'm about to fail my mid-terms. One of my classmates was shot and is in intensive care. I haven't started writing essays for my college applications, and I can't decide which of the two guys in my life I really like. I wonder if my life can go any further in the dumpster.

Then I look on the bright side. One of my would-be killers is dead, the other is definitely going to jail. Knowing how fast gossip spreads at school, the fact that I'm *not* a porn star and the girl who was shot *is* will give everyone something new to talk about besides me. Even if I fail my course load this semester, I'm now the head of one of the biggest tech companies in the country, so I'll be too busy to go to college anyway. And both guys are annoying me right now, Oliver with his relentless pursuit of my excellence, and Derek's mumbling from across the table as he does whatever it is genius coders do when confronted with a problem.

"Tess?" Oliver says. "Got an answer, or are you still thinking?"

I sigh. "Can we take a break? I need five minutes, okay?"

"Yeah, sure. You want more coffee or anything?"

"No. And Derek, would you stop with the mumbling? You're driving me nuts."

"Sorry, babe. It's just every time I think I have this software bug beat it rears its ugly head somewhere else. It's like playing whack-a-mole."

"Well, if you can't shut up and let me concentrate, you can whack off somewhere else."

"Babe," he says sorrowfully. "Ouch."

The library door opens and I raise my head expectantly.

"Everything all right in here?" Alice says. "More coffee? Something to eat? Tess, you should have some protein or something to keep you going."

"I don't think my stomach could handle it right now, Alice. Maybe a banana."

"Oliver? Derek? Coffee?"

"Please," they say in unison.

"Alice, have you heard whether they've arrested Tad yet?" I say. I don't like the thought of him coming to school.

"No one has been able to find him. Travis thinks his father is protecting him, and I have to agree. I can't say I wouldn't do the same thing if I were in Cyrus Cooper's shoes."

"But he tried to kill me!"

"And didn't do a very good job of it, at that," Alice says briskly.

Derek snickers. Oliver, at least, has the decency to keep his snickers to himself.

"Well, if there's nothing else, I'll go get you coffee and fruit," she says. "One of these days I really must replace Rosa. I haven't prepared this many meals since you were little."

I feel my face flush. "Alice, please."

"Right. Well, then..." Her footsteps retreat.

When she's gone, Derek says, "Why didn't you tell her and Travis about Latham?"

For a moment I'm not sure what he means. "Why would I do that?"

"He's the guy who's really behind the attempts on your life, not this Tad kid, whoever he is."

"He's got a point, Tess," Oliver says.

"Are you crazy?" I fume. "I'd say Tad shooting at me counts as an attempt to kill me. And you found the link between Tad and the money that Sam was paid to kill me."

"No, I traced half of the money back to Latham, and half to MondoHard, remember?" Derek said. "It's more likely Tad's father arranged to pay Sam that money, not Tad."

"It makes sense," Oliver says. "In any case, though, Latham *is* involved, and we need to find a way to take him down."

"Well, I'm not talking about it now," I say. "We have to leave for school in less than an hour, and we haven't even finished the practice test."

They both fall silent, but I know they're right. And I made a promise to Sam. Oliver quietly starts quizzing me again, but my thoughts keep drifting away from chemistry to snippets of the events of the past few days, the sounds and scents, trying to visually imagine the scenes, the settings, frustrated almost to tears that I can't see. And even my wandering mind is distracted by yet another set of footsteps entering the library. Maybe Alice returning with more coffee, but the tread, pace, and shoes tell me it's Travis.

"Hey, how's it going?" he says softly.

Oliver says "Good" at the same time Derek says "Okay," but my response, chiming in with theirs, is, "Excrementitious."

"That craptacular, Tess?" he says, a twinkle in his voice.

I roll my sightless eyes, but can't keep a corner of my mouth from turning up. I know he's trying to make nice, but Travis might be a little more deece than I give him credit for.

"She's actually doing really well," Oliver says.

I stomp on his foot under the table to shut him up.

"So, Derek," Travis says, all business now. "Any luck?"

The abrupt change in tone sparks my antennae. "Why?" I interject. "What's going on out there?"

"Nothing good." Now Travis sounds grim. "There's been a lot of looting in parts of the city, people starting fires, turning over cars. Roads and streets are a mess, gridlock everywhere because none of the traffic signals are working. Cell service is getting spotty. Towers were so jammed with the increased call load, they've been using their backup power too quickly. A lot of people without heat. Lines a half-mile long outside gas stations with people trying to fill both their tanks and cans for generators. Grocery stores are giving away food rather than let it spoil, or worse, seeing mobs break in and steal everything off the shelves. It's pretty bad."

"Ohmigod," I say. "It's really serious."

"I'm trying, man," Derek says. "It's like I told these guys—"

"Whack-off," I say. "Yeah, yeah, we know. That's not helping."

"That's 'whack-a-mole,'" Derek says indignantly. "Wait a sec. That's it! Of course. Why didn't I think of it sooner?"

"Babbling again, Derek," I say.

"Sorry, I just got this crazy idea."

"All your ideas are crazy," Oliver mutters, echoing my thoughts.

"Yeah, well, the thing is, I just realized that if I tweak it, I can probably use AInsley to fix this."

"Who is Ainsley?" I feel a pang of jealousy. "A girlfriend?"

"No, AInsley is the AI engine that messed up *Never Bitten*. We've been using her—it—to make the sequel even better. I might be able to get it to search out malicious code in the power station's operations software."

"That's good, Derek," Travis says. "Get on that and let me know how it goes."

"Congratulations," I say. "Now, would either of you like to take my chemistry test?"

Travis chuckles. "Got it, Tess. I'll check in later. Good luck with your exams, but I have a feeling you'll get a reprieve."

My face squinches. "What do you mean?"

"I doubt school will be open unless the power comes back on. You'll know soon, I'm sure."

My stomach clenches and my mouth opens but nothing comes out. I want to throw something, hit someone. I pulled an all-nighter for nothing. I grit my teeth and stew as Travis leaves.

"Great," I mumble. "Just great."

I suddenly feel like I would if I'd eaten salad an hour ago—totally unsatisfied. I'm uneasy. Sam is dead and Tad's on the run; I'm safe for the moment. By lunchtime the porn video will be yesterday's news, and Addie's on notice; she won't mess with me. Better yet, now she owes me. I *will* pass my mid-terms, even if my GPA suffers. And I'll finish my college essays before application deadlines. After the past few weeks, I have no shortage of subject matter. But I have too many unanswered questions nibbling at the edges of my consciousness to ignore.

As if that's not enough, my phone chimes with an incoming text. I pick up the phone and say, "Play text."

"You have one new text from Dad," the phone says.

I screech, and my heart hammers my ribcage.

"Oh, boy," Oliver says. "Not this again."

The text begins to play, and all I can hear is silence at first. Then there's a crackling sound and voices.

The package is down.

For good?

Wait for it. A pause. *Boots are on the ground! It's a go.*

Roger that. Go, go, go!

"That's Travis," Oliver says. "And Fred. What the...?"

Travis again, sounding pissed: *Marcus, I don't see you. Are you in position?*

Marcus: *Coming up on my mark now. Setting up took longer than I thought.*

There's a long pause, and then echoing as if from a distance the sound of squealing tires, a large *thump,* and several seconds of screeching like the sound of metal on concrete or asphalt.

More silence, then a loud blast like a cannon going off startles me out of my chair, followed seconds later by the dull whomp of a distant explosion. The sequence is repeated, and then all I hear is the growing hiss of a giant wave. Cold washes over me like an icy shower and my hands shake uncontrollably. With growing horror, I understand exactly what I'm listening to.

"Hey, are you okay?" Oliver says. "What is it? What's wrong?"

For a moment I can't speak, and when I do, it comes out a whisper.

"The avalanche..."

It's too awful. I can't even say it. All I can do is lift my hand to my face and feel my scar under my fingertips.

# # # #

Acknowledgements

We all know it takes a village. I could thank everyone from the software coders who developed the word processing program I use to the truck drivers who deliver books to stores and libraries. But the village I want to acknowledge here is the one populated with readers. Without you, dear reader, there's little point to this exercise. Yes, a tree that falls in a forest makes a sound, but with no one to hear it, the sound is moot as well as mute. I need only a laptop and my imagination to research, write, produce and publish a book. Writing truly is a solitary and often lonely endeavor. And it's all for naught if there are no readers to appreciate what I've created.

The best thing you can do for any author is read his or her work. The next best thing you can do is tell others in your village about it. Write a review. Post a comment on the village bulletin board. One star or five stars doesn't matter. What matters is that you let others know a book exists. If you don't, the sound it makes with the words herein might as well have been a falling tree in an empty forest.

Writing this chapter in the life of Tess Barrett took three long years. I was sidelined, flummoxed, flabbergasted by the events taking place in real life—a worldwide pandemic that so far has claimed nearly seven million lives; four years of a demagogue in the nation's highest office; an increasing number of mass shootings every year; social justice protests across the country; an autocrat's invasion of a small country that did nothing to antagonize a war... Nothing in my imagination, nothing that I could possibly dream up could rival the daily news headlines.

I persisted, if only to find a way to make sense of the ridiculous. Mystery and thriller writers try to create order out of chaos, a place where the good guys win and justice, of a sort, is done. I found, not surprisingly, that even fiction, like life, has messy endings, or no endings. Which gives authors a chance to tell another story.

For a preview of *Blind Spot*, the continuation of Tess Barrett's story, turn the page...

Michael W. Sherer

BLIND SPOT

1

This is a nightmare I'll never escape, a bad dream from which I'll never wake. The scar under my fingers throbs with pain as the sound coming from my phone yanks me back in time to that awful day—the fights with my parents, the disappointment of being told what I couldn't do, the meanness I felt, the trip down from the pass that ended almost as soon as it began when the snow on the mountain gave way and roared down the steep slope, engulfing our SUV and rolling it over and over... Waking in a hospital later to the physical pain of being broken in a dozen places, and the emotional pain of losing my parents, feeling wracked with guilt because it was my fault.

I relive it all in the space of an instant as the audio message "from Dad" plays. When the sounds emanating from the phone stop, I'm filled with growing dread, a different kind of horror. The voices in the sound clip are those of the men who are supposed to be protecting me, guarding me from forces we don't yet understand, but which might reach some of the highest pinnacles of the U.S. government.

"The avalanche...?" Oliver says. "The one that...?"

"Blinded me?" I say, my tone sharp. "You can say it, Oliver. I've lived with it long enough to know it's not a temporary condition."

"But that's not possible. The voices... It has to be something else. What would the security team—Travis, especially—have to do with *causing* the accident?"

I wrap my fingers in my hair and pull hard, as if the pain will wake me. "I don't know! But I *do* know what an avalanche sounds like. I've seen how avalanche control teams trigger a slide. And I definitely know the sound of my uncle's voice."

"It could be something totally unrelated, babe," Derek says, his voice maddeningly calm and assured.

"Like what? April Fool's?"

He ignores my sarcastic tone. "Something they did in the army. Or maybe they're really part of an avalanche control team."

"Or maybe the clip is a fake," Oliver says.

"Sure," Derek says. "Something I could check out at work. We've got audio engineers who could probably tell if it's real or not with one pass. Though AI is getting really good at this shit."

"You don't get it, do you?" I say, keeping my voice barely above a whisper now. I don't know who might be listening in, and I can't seem to get enough oxygen all of a sudden. Sweat tickles my ribs and dampens my hairline, something that never happens to me unless Yoshi is really pushing me during jiu-jitsu practice.

"Why would my father send me this clip unless it was about the accident?" I go on.

Oliver groans.

"Listen to yourself, babe," Derek says. "Your dad's dead. How can he keep sending you email and texts from the great beyond? It's just as likely this is a scam."

I grit my teeth to keep from screaming. "Whoever this is, he seems to know a lot about me and everything my dad was working on. Oliver, you know it's true. Derek, you do, too. You met him."

They both fall silent, then Oliver says, "Whether your father sent the clip or not, what do you want to do here? Do you really think Travis killed your parents? Why would he do that?"

"To get his hands on my father's company, for one. That's about fifty billion reasons right there. Maybe more."

"Yeah, but that just changed. The blind trust your father set up puts you in charge."

"All the more reason," I say. "In case you forgot, people have been trying to kill me. Maybe Travis is behind it all." I turn my palms up and lift my shoulders.

"So, what do you want to do, babe?" Derek says. "You can't confront Travis with this. He'll just deny it."

I shiver, and almost can't stop I'm so scared. "Damn it! Just when I was actually beginning to trust him..."

I pull at a strand of hair again, hoping to tease a coherent thought out of my head. My mind whirls, launching me on a carnival ride of emotions, and I chew on my lower lip as if it's a remedy for motion sickness.

"I can't stay here," I blurt. "I have to find someplace safe until we can figure out what this means."

"We?" Derek says.

"Well, I can't do this alone. Oliver has to get me where I need to go, and you, *stud*, have to help."

"Uh, if you haven't noticed, I have my hands full trying to stop this power outage and save the world from a dark, post-apocalyptic dystopian future in which you, a blind girl, would be queen."

"Oh, shut up! This is serious."

"So is getting the power turned back on."

"Okay, kids," Oliver says, "we're not going to solve the problem by fighting. Tess, what do you have in mind?"

I think furiously. "We're going to need cash, lots of it, because we won't be able to use cards. Burner phones. A laptop that can't be traced. A car, too, that isn't instantly recognizable."

"A place to go, maybe?" Oliver says, a little too flippantly.

"I'm working on it," I say. "Derek, can you get us a spare laptop from your office? And set up some email accounts for us?"

"Sure, I guess. I'll make up some excuse about needing to go back to the office to work."

"Matt," I say.

"Tsang?" Oliver sounds surprised. "I thought he was in jail or a mental ward or something."

"House arrest," I say, "with one of those ankle bracelets. And psychotherapy. Hey, we know it wasn't *his* fault."

"Don't look at me," Derek says. "*Never Bitten* didn't make him shoot up your school cafeteria; AInsley did, and that's only because some bad people convinced her to go rogue."

"Thank you, Derek." The words slide off my tongue and clink like ice cubes in a glass. "We *know* that. And I wish you'd stop referring to my father's AI program as 'her.' You're giving girls—excuse me, women—a bad rep. The point is, Matt's got a hideout. Well, his family does. He told me about it when we were in middle school. A fishing camp up in the mountains. I think it belongs to his uncle. Anyway, off the grid. Perfect for our needs."

"You think he can convince his uncle to let us stay there?"

I hike my shoulders. "I'm not safe here. I have to try."

"Give me your phone," Derek says. "I'll set up a VPN so you can text or call him without anyone eavesdropping."

"Okay, people," Oliver says, rubbing his hands together, "let's make a plan."

"Hang on a sec," Derek says, his voice so crestfallen, I stiffen. "You can't leave."

"Why not?"

"The minute you walk out, you're a dead girl walking."

I want to scream...

About the Author

Michael W. Sherer is the author of the Tess Barrett new/young adult thriller series, including *Blind Rage* and *Blind Instinct*, as well as the adult thrillers *Mistaken Identity*, *Stolen Identity*, and four books in the Seattle-based Blake Sanders series, including *Night Strike* and *Night Blind*, which was nominated for an ITW Thriller Award in 2013. His other books include the award-winning Emerson Ward mystery series, and the stand-alone suspense novel, *Island Life*. He and his family live in the Seattle area.

Please visit him at michaelwsherer.com, or follow him on Facebook at www.facebook.com/thrillerauthor, @thrillerauthor on Instagram and TikTok, or @MysteryNovelist on Twitter.

Photo: Valarie Kaye-Sherer